GR886
LOT 1332

23232-W. 12/6

£8

THE FACE BESIDE THE FIRE

By the same Author

★

IN A PROVINCE
VENTURE TO THE INTERIOR

The Face Beside the Fire

A Novel by

LAURENS VAN DER POST

1953

The Hogarth Press

LONDON

PUBLISHED BY
The Hogarth Press Ltd.
LONDON

★

Clarke, Irwin & Co. Ltd.
TORONTO

Printed in Great Britain by
Ebenezer Baylis and Son, Ltd., The
Trinity Press, Worcester, and London
All rights reserved

To my wife Ingaret Giffard
for having accompanied me on
the most difficult journey of all.

*"Donna è gentil nel ciel, che si compiange di
questo impedimento, ov' io timando, sì che duro
giudizio lassù range."*
DANTE'S INFERNO

("Heaven hath a noble Lady, who doth take
Ruth of this man thou goest to disensnare
Such that high doom is cancelled for her sake.")

CONTENTS

PART I

In the Beginning

have called it, between David and his father and mother

CHAPTER 1

W HEN "the crisis", as he always called it afterwards,
occurred in the life of David Alexander Michaeljohn, I
believe I was the only person who might have been of help
to him—and I was far away in Africa. There was not a
moment in our lives in which we had not been friends. Our
homes were next door to each other, in a village in the remote
interior of Africa, and because our parents, too, were close
friends and because I was born only three days after David,
they decided to christen him David Alexander and me
Alexander David.

The decision to do so was not reached in his family without
considerable argument between his father and mother. Apparently there had never been an Alexander in the Michaeljohn family, and old Albert Michaeljohn, who was a man of
tremendous character and the most violent and obscure pre-
judices, disliked the name intensely and would have preferred to keep it as far out of his life as possible. I have never
forgotten how one afternoon, some years later, the old man,
half-drunk as he often was towards his end, sent me home
crying for an explanation to my mother by referring to me in
a tone which I could not mistake even if I did not fully
understand the meaning of the words, as the "young man
with the lowland appellation".

In my own family on the contrary, there had hardly ever
been a generation of Frasers without an Alexander. My
grandfather too had been christened Alexander and there
was never any doubt as to what I was to be called. Fortunately
Mary Michaeljohn succeeded in concealing from her friends
the differences of opinion she and her husband had on the
issue, and as she, besides being a woman of great beauty and
charm, could also be a person of character and determination,

the christening took place on the same day in the Michael-johns' large dining-room, according to her and my mother's plan. But it always struck me as significant in after years that there should have been "this thing" as we children would have called it, between David and his father and mother, almost from the moment he was born.

I was an only child. David was the sixth of seven, all born at intervals of eighteen months of one another. Of the seven, only two are important to David's story: the one daughter, Anna Maria, born just before David, and the youngest child, Edward George, born just after him. The four elder brothers had no specific influence on his life beyond adding in general to the burden of people with whom, according to the custom and beliefs of our community, he should have been on the most intimate and affectionate terms but from whom, in sober fact, he felt himself inevitably and inexplicably estranged. Anna Maria matters most to him, as she certainly did to the rest of the family. Her father, I always suspected, loved her more than the rest of his family put together. It was astonish-ing what a delicate and lively light came into his eye when this little girl was near him, how attentive and almost lover-like was his treatment of her. Not a morning passed, when he was at home, that he did not go into her room to call her himself with a posy of flowers that he had just picked in his very lovely garden. Often I would see him stare at her with a strange lover-like look in his eyes, the sort of look I always imagine Lewis Carroll gave the little girls, the little Alices with long yellow hair, as he prepared to dress them up for his curious photography. It was as if time had been made to stand still for the old man in these moments and he had been permitted to look beyond the change and decay that set such inexorable limits to our days, at some unchanging wonder-land on whose shining threshold his daughter stood, as a winged messenger, to fetch him in. There is a strange thing about children: what has impressed me most since those far-off days is not their youngness but their oldness. No little girl

4

of five has ever looked so young to me as the girl who has just become a woman. Adolescence really is their painful, their private and personal birth. But before that they belong to time and the past. The spirit of an incalculable antiquity burns with a clear flame in them, and whoever touches their being touches a myth rather than a human entity; touches, perhaps, the original and abiding dream of life itself. I am sure, anyway, that for Albert Michaeljohn, Anna Maria trailed clouds of glory from some far primordial home.

Their father's attitude to his daughter occasioned no surprise among the boys in the family who were, all in their several ways, under the spell of the same instinct. But I am sure that Mary Michaeljohn, deep in her heart, did not like it altogether. Often in the evenings after dinner when the old man took the little girl on his knee and sat there in his easy chair, wordless and rather apart from the rest, stroking her hair until, as Anna told us afterwards, her head ached as if it would burst, I would see Mary give her daughter a cool, detached, technical scrutiny, which, as it communicated its mysterious conclusions to her, transformed itself into such a look of resentment, of fairy-tale rage, that I was filled with discomfort, and found warm refuge in the thought that I was an only child.

David started off in life, as his father and brothers did, by loving Anna Maria in a manner we shall never wholly understand. There was not a moment in his young life in which he did not love her and in some ways she was even more important to him than his mother was, because she was so much nearer him, so much more texture and substance of the same vivid dream. I can still hear him announce at tea, one afternoon very near our conscious beginning: "Mother! when I grow up I am going to marry Anna Maria!"

"Well, I won't marry you, see," Anna replied with a severe little voice and a quick, impatient tap of her spoon on her empty glass, which sent forth a precise peal of alarm.

"I am going to marry a member of Parliament, like my father."

"I'll be a member of Parliament too, so you'll have to marry me," David answered undismayed, giving Anna his most adoring and obliging look.

Anna to everyone's surprise, but not altogether to her mother's dissatisfaction, beat the table furiously with her spoon, crying almost in tears, "I won't, I won't, I won't. I'd much rather marry Edward George."

This reference to Edward George took all the heart out of David's proposals: his wide, grey eyes clouded. He looked for a second as if he would cry but catching sight of me, cheered up and said bravely and defiantly, "Well, I'll marry Alex then." Whereupon David's eldest brother and a pimply school-friend of his, to our amazement, started sniggering so hysterically that they had to leave the room.

The Michaeljohns were all a remarkably good-looking family, even if the looks of most of them did tend to favour the flesh rather than the spirit. The exceptions were the mother, Anna Maria and David. Mary Michaeljohn was an extremely beautiful woman with a most shapely figure and head and an indescribably moving face, and somehow all that was lovely and fine in her seems to have been passed on to Anna Maria and David. Like their brothers, they had inherited a full share of their father's vitality and physique without the whole weight of his bone and muscle. The family design, in their case, was more finely drawn, determined by a more meticulous and fastidious art. Anna Maria to this day is one of the most beautiful women in the country. She has had her girlhood wish, if one could use such a free word in connection with such an innately-compelled person. She has married a member of Parliament who has also become a Cabinet Minister, and who may one day well achieve the Premiership, provided he can control his craving for drink. For this is the strange thing about the man of Anna Maria's choice: after years of a conventionally virtuous life, spent largely with what society regards as unselfishness in the public cause, he who had neither smoked nor drunk before, began suddenly at the age of forty-one to smoke and drink excessively, just as old Albert Michaeljohn had done before him. Or is it perhaps not strange at all? Perhaps after all, the logical consequence of transgression of some natural law we do not understand, but whose existence among the many other mysterious forces that determine our destiny, draws attention to itself furtively and obliquely, in the remark of a little girl uttered thirty years before. "I am going to marry a member of Parliament, just like my father!" Is it too far fetched to suggest that in the writing on the wall of life—the "just like my father" may well have been written in italics? I find no comfort in this, for if it is true, it means that Anna Maria has been a prisoner to something beyond herself, something which has prevented her from being what life intended her to be. Her looks, beautiful as she still is, alas confirm the impression. Her face has hardened a good deal; the clear light in her eyes has darkened and her features look as if they might belong to someone else. But she wore no mask when David and I first knew her. Her face fitted her frame and spirit like a flower and there was for David and me something almost miraculous about it.

I can never forget the first time I became aware of Anna Maria as a separate and individual being with a face, character and behaviour all her own.

Every year in the spring, my father and mother and I went camping "in the blue" as we called it, with the Michaeljohns. We travelled in three or four ox-wagons, with tents, beds, guns, fishing nets, rods, wonderful supplies of food and scores of black and brown and yellow servants, like a cavalcade of oriental royalty. The daily round of schools and books fell magically away from us, and we entered a natural world which was very close to our instincts. We had camped on this occasion on the banks of a very deep and wide river that ran for about nine miles through one of the Michaeljohn farms.

We had arrived late because the way down to the river proved to be much more difficult than we had expected; and because there was so much to do before night-fall, we boys were all sent out to help the servants collect firewood. David and I were together and had gone some distance from the camp when it suddenly got quite dark. But not for long, for almost within a second or so, it seemed to us, the light of a full moon, rising beyond the hills at our back, caught the top of the steep cliffs of the mountains on the far side of the river. A lovely streak of phosphorescent light shot along the dark crest and as it spread, silvery and vibrant into the sombre recesses and deep angry gashes in the mountain side, the baboons, first one by one, and then soon in a continuous chorus, with deep, booming voices began to bark longingly at the moon.

We spent about twenty minutes collecting our bundles of dry wood in this weird atmosphere of spreading, subtle, quicksilver moonlight and mounting and indescribable animal nostalgia far beyond the powers of the bark of any baboon to express, and then started back for camp. We were within fifty yards of the camp, still in darkness except for an old hurricane lamp flitting about like a firefly, when hardly a hundred yards behind us, a male lion let out a long, impassioned and full-throated roar. It was so loud and so close that the wood on my back and the hair on my head seemed to vibrate with the sound of it. The baboons instantly stopped barking, the human voices in the distance ceased, the whole river valley went so silent that I heard the light, evening breeze far above us in the full silver of the moonlight casually fingering the mountain tops. Then the lion roared again; easily, passionately, without fear or inhibition of any kind, as if it were emperor of all the world.

David and I, hesitating no more, bolted towards the camp as fast as our loads would let us go. As we broke out of the bush, the first of the camp fires burst into wild, leaping flames that threw a most reassuring circle of light far round the camp, and there, near the fire, was Anna Maria sitting in a camp chair, together with old Klara the Michaeljohns' Hottentot nurse who was brushing her hair.

David and I stopped dead in our tracks and stared at this serene little scene in utter amazement. At one moment it had been dark, and night, under the spell and command of the lion's roar, both air and mountain tops hushed with a sense of ancient dread; and the next there was this surge of flames, and, framed in their Hindu shape, this delicate, beautiful, antique little face.

We dropped our bundles and walked slowly forward. As Klara brushed Anna Maria's hair it seemed, in that light, to twist and curl like a kind of moon-mist round her brown fingers. I have never seen hair of so fine, so light a quality as Anna Maria's. I have never seen it so beautiful as it was that night. As we came near her she looked up at us from under that wide, serene forehead she had inherited from her mother, her blue-grey eyes shining with a light so deep that it seemed to belong to a world before our world, and she said in a voice alive with excitement but bright and clear as a silver bell: "I say, outjies,* did you hear him roar! Wasn't it wonderful! Klara says he's not dangerous. He's just calling for his mate."

I did not realise at the time what an impression that vision of Anna Maria made on me, but it has stayed with me and constantly surprises and amazes me with its power and vitality. It seems to lead a life of its own inside me, independent of my normal volition and desires and at all sorts of odd moments it will present itself to me with the freshness of a flower cut with the dew still on it. In a flash there is the sudden leap of flame in the dark, a fire standing up before me like a Hindu temple at the dawn of our history, and beside it the face of Anna Maria, shining like a star in the darkest and remotest recesses of my mind, and it leaves me with a sense of unbearable tragedy that this face beside the far-off fire-

*Outjies: A South African term of endearment: literally meaning Little Old Ones.

light in our initial darkness has to wear the worldly-wise mask of to-day.

I have said that David loved Anna Maria: I wish I could say that she loved him. They were so close in years, so alike in looks and temperament that one would have thought it inevitable. But for some reason that I do not pretend to understand, Anna Maria, from as far back as I can remember, seemed deeply irritated by David, and the irritation increased as they got older. I am sure it was beyond anyone's personal blame. Not even Anna Maria could really be blamed. I have so often seen her puzzled and dismayed by it, trying hard to be different ; but over and over again this strange, inexplicable hostility would evade her defences and reveal itself in a quite unprovoked fit of irritability with David. Afterwards she would be so miserable with remorse that we all forgave her instantly, for do we not all know, in our aboriginal hearts, that the tragedy of the individual is not so much not being loved as being unable to love, as if some dark impediment cut us off from the full rhythm of life? It certainly was no fault of David's. The whole thing had the deep irrational cause, was typical of the obscurely compelled issues that so often arose in the Michaeljohn family. Yet if I were forced to blame some-one, I might be unable altogether to absolve Mary Michaeljohn, who moved through our world with such astonishing beauty and grace and such obvious goodness. No one could say that she was not, by all the standards we professed, a really good woman, a dutiful wife, a devoted mother and a most public-spirited member of the community. She and her husband never failed every year to give one-tenth of their income—which was enormous—to the Church. There was not a charity which ever appealed to her purse, her time, and her great organising ability in vain. But, as an inexperienced child without even the knowledge to look for such things in people, I could not help feeling that part of her was not displeased when Anna Maria, who got the best out of all the rest of the family, failed so conspicuously with the most outstanding of her children.

In some ways David understood Anna Maria's hostility towards him better than anybody else. He hardly ever appeared surprised by her sudden and apparently causeless outbursts; was very patient and long-suffering under them, and until that final Sunday never resentful of anything Anna Maria ever did to him. The reason, I suspect, was that he felt very much the same irritability towards the youngest child, Edward George. It is significant that the first really bad beating David ever got from his father was because of Edward George.

It was on the day of the baby's christening. Albert Michaeljohn took a much greater interest in the baptism of his youngest child than he had in those of the others. The name had been entirely his own choice. Mary, perhaps as a result of her battle over David's, had taken no part in it beyond instantly accepting her husband's wish when it was communicated to her. About two years previously her husband had been decorated by King Edward for his work on behalf of a United South Africa. Shortly afterwards the King had died but now out of gratitude to him and in deference to his successor, Albert Michaeljohn decided to call his last born Edward George. A tremendous show was made of the christening. The Governor agreed to act as Godfather and for days beforehand the occasion had been the source of much excitement in the family and the village. On the morning of the christening, Edward George, fully dressed in the most expensive robes, was put in a sunny corner of the Michaeljohn veranda which gave on to the garden where the other children were playing. He was asleep and Klara, in whose charge he was, had just left him for a few minutes to do something in the nursery when suddenly she heard the child crying. Albert, who was having a last look round the domestic organisation, also heard it. He and Klara arrived at the same moment to find that David, who could only just walk, had emptied a dark succession of mud-pies on Edward George's voluminous and immaculate finery. David was instantly whisked off into his father's study and so badly beaten that his mother had to intervene. Many of his subsequent beatings also were entirely on Edward George's account, and his mother, who could be so neutral where David and her daughter were concerned, on these occasions was actively and decisively not on his side.

As David grew older he became more and more distressed by the effect his youngest brother had on him. He tried hard but he could not change and yet he knew how unreasonable and unfair his behaviour was. For no normal person could help liking Edward George. He had the happiest and most imperturbably cheerful disposition of any child I have ever known. Anna Maria instantly took him to her heart against David's irritability. Poor David's defences against irrational behaviour were thus doubly turned. He lived in an increasing state of rebellion and dissatisfaction with himself and his surroundings. How deeply the problem exercised his young mind soon became obvious.

Every Sunday morning after church Mary Michaeljohn assembled all the youngest children in her large, sunny bedroom. She sat us all on cushions round her easy chair and for one hour read fairy-stories to us. She read beautifully in a wonderfully plastic voice that allowed full and delightful play to an unsuspected gift of drama in her nature. We had some of the happiest moments of our childhood round her chair in that room. One Sunday as she put down her book with the stock phrase that denoted the end of that particular session: "and then came an elephant with a large trunk and blew my story right out", she noticed David sitting with a clouded forehead and an unhappy far-away look in his eyes.

"What is the matter, David Alexander," she said, rather on her mettle. "Don't you like my story?"

"I like it all right, mother, except for the ending," David replied reluctantly, but truthfully.

"What is the matter with the end? Surely it was happy enough?"

David had to be pressed again before he answered, rather dejectedly.

"Yes, mother, but why should it always be the youngest son who gets everything?"

"Why not?" said Anna Maria, rounding on him instantly.

"What do you mean?" asked his mother at the same time.

"Well," David said guardedly to his mother, ignoring his sister. "In all the stories you tell us it's always the youngest child who defeats the giant and gets the princess and the treasure. Why can't it ever be one of the other children for a change?"

"Oh! he's just jealous, mum," said Anna Maria scornfully, dismissing the issue at once.

"I'm not," David said in that slow way of his, looking pleadingly at her. "But I don't think it's fair, that's all: not giving others a chance."

"I don't think 'youngest' in these stories means what we mean by 'youngest'," Mary began with immense tact. "It's just a manner of speaking, of describing a young person and not necessarily the youngest one. It is meant rather to remind us as the Bible does, that the first shall not necessarily be first and that often what we think is last and least in the end can become first and most."

But a chorus of subsidiary arguments among the children and a savage, "Oh, Little Mr. Jealous!" from Anna Maria, showed that her explanation had gone by us and that David, for once, had scored a point on almost everyone's behalf.

As time went on David looked more and more to my home for his joy and delight. The Michaeljohns found it increasingly convenient not to discourage it.

What so attracted David to my home was first and foremost that we were in the most profound sense of the word a truly simple family. I cannot imagine any other home more free of complications and less prone to quarrel with its own

13

shadows. My father and mother were so well matched and so happily married that one never thought about their relationship at all but accepted it as one of the great and abiding factors of life, just as one takes it for granted that the sun will rise each day, no matter how dark the night. They had the same background and the same interests. Even their great-grandparents had been friends and had come out to Africa as young people together from Scotland with the 1820 settlers. In fact, my father's great-grandfather had been the master printer who helped the poet and great-grand-uncle of my mother, Pringle, to print his poems and independent newspaper in an epic struggle for freedom and expression. I could give scores of other instances of how close the associations were between the forefathers of my parents but it is sufficient for this story to say their lives seemed to have merged as naturally as two streams at the foot of a hill and to have flowed on steadily and confidently as one broad river. I cannot recall a single case of real discord between my parents and I grew up so naturally and firmly rooted in my home that I have never wanted to change or to leave it. In fact except for the war, I have never left it to this day for more than a month or two at a time. I have found everything I wanted in that small world; it has been sufficient for my deepest desires and needs and all that I have of imagination has reached out to consolidating and enforcing its basic features, to beautifying the house, farm, and gardens, to preserving in our community the best from the past while combining it with what is good and living in the present. In whatever I have ever done, and wherever I have ever been, no matter how far back I go in time, I have felt this undisputed one-ness of my father and mother round me like a warm blanket on a winter's night.

David could not claim the same for his home. Yet most people if asked for a comparison of the two homes standing there side by side in the immense, metallic sunlight of Africa, pressing a deep, wide fringe of the greenest trees against their blanched gables like eye-shades on a forehead shielding face and eyes against the blinding glare of summer, would not have hesitated to declare the Michaeljohns' home by far the more interesting. For the world in which we move and live is fundamentally not interested in happiness. I respect happiness as I respect nothing else and though I detest the popular concept "duty" if I had to allocate one duty to humanity I would allocate, with the highest possible priority, the duty of the individual to achieve happiness. But few people will agree with me. They not only no longer know what happiness is but also have no faith in its being a practicable possibility. In as far as they are aware of it they confuse happiness with some of its lesser parts like pleasure and gratification and would not begin to understand, for instance, that happiness which loves the great necessities of life like a bride. Happiness does not exclude unhappiness but merely discovers and preserves its meaning. The foolless Lear who could say at the moment when he and Cordelia were about to be thrust back into prison: "We shall be God's spies and take upon us the mystery of things," was happier, in the true sense, than Lear the King on his throne giving kingdoms away with a right royal hand. Happiness for me is health in its most complete state just as a sense of beauty is its awareness and love its fulfilment.

I do not want to digress or exaggerate but the fact remains that most people without hesitation would have dismissed the truly happy life of my father and mother as humdrum, while they would have declared the Michaeljohns' as "remarkable", "sympathetic", "fascinating", or "absorbingly entertaining", whatever the fashionable phrase for approval happens to be.

Undoubtedly at first most of the credit for this, if credit it is, went to Albert Michaeljohn. There was always a mystery about him which, even to this day, is not fully explained, and nothing excites general interest more than a suggestion of a mystery. He was not born in Africa and no one really knew anything about his origin and background except what he himself chose to tell. Though he talked freely about his past, one always felt that he was presenting only a selection of the facts which gave him pleasure, and that a portion, a vital portion perhaps, was being withheld even from his wife and children.

He had arrived in Africa, no one quite knew how or why, as a young man of nineteen. He had obviously not been without means for he had immediately gone to a university to study law. People who knew him there speak of him as a pleasant but rather silent, determined and unusually serious young man, with extraordinary application to his studies. He had graduated with honours, qualified brilliantly at the Bar and within a few years was one of the most successful and talked-of lawyers in Fort White. He did not appear in our remote country community until he was thirty-three, when he was suddenly presented to our fathers by the central organisation of the governing party as their candidate for Parliament. This arbitrary action in an independent and rather rugged community at first provoked much outspoken criticism but it quickly disappeared as one by one the critics got to know the brilliant young advocate. He was handsome, spoke well and amusingly, was particularly good with older people, had the civilised European gift of appearing a really good listener, was obviously and truly a person of immense culture, and brought into our land-locked community a flavour of the wider world, of the Europe which keeps at the back of the most firmly transplanted souls of white Africa a shimmer of nostalgia like a mirage on the horizon of one of our fathomless summer days. Then on top of it all he was a man of considerable means, successful and still a bachelor.

From the start he promised the electors that he had had enough of towns and that, if they chose him, he would make his home (as much as a person like himself could have a home) right in their midst. At the same time he conveyed the impression without ever saying so, that he was lonely, tired of bachelordom and anxious to marry and have a family of his own, if only the right woman would come along. With such an approach, with such advantages and such indisputably great personal qualities, his success was assured with all sections and both sexes of the community. He was returned to Parliament with a shattering majority and from then on represented our community until his death.

He for his part kept faith both with his spoken and implied promises to his electors. He made his home forthwith in their midst and within eighteen months had married Mary de Beauvilliers, the daughter of the largest landowner and most respected man in the district. The whole community, after quite a number of expectant maternal hearts had recovered from their disappointment, agreed that it could hardly have been a better match. Henceforth they accepted Albert Michaeljohn as if he had been born in their midst and had lived there all his life. No explanation of his past was ever sought or appeared necessary, though the sense of mystery remained.

But was it such a good match after all? My mother, who had known Mary de Beauvilliers all her life, never took the appearance of success this union presented to the world at its face value. Although she admired and, even in spite of some intuitive reservation she could not formulate, liked Albert Michaeljohn, she never thought the marriage was quite right for Mary, to whom she was devoted. She told me one day when I was much older what she knew of the courtship.

When Albert arrived in the district there were two de Beauvilliers children in the family, two girls, Margharieta and Mary: there had been an older brother but he had been killed in a native raid some years earlier. Margharieta, the elder, my mother says, was a charming, sweet girl, rather dreamy and introspective and an unusually accomplished pianist, but she had none of the character, the fire and quest-ing spirit and absolute beauty of Mary, the baby of the family.

"If I had been a young man," she told me, "I know which

17

one of the two would have made my heart turn a somersault: it would certainly not have been Margharieta."

Yet to my mother's amazement Albert from the start made a dead set at Margharieta and she believed he would have married her had she not died in the dreadful typhoid epidemic of that year.

"And this is the thing," she said very seriously, "which has worried me all my life: had Albert really cared for Margharieta, he would have been heartbroken at this sudden, this cruel bereavement, but not a bit of it. After a perfunctory show of sorrow, he made as dead a set for Mary."

My mother did not want to be unfair to him, he had never been engaged to Margharieta but his attentions had been unmistakable. She could only conclude, though she hated so unchristian a thought, that although Mary had captured his heart from the start, Albert had courted Margharieta because as the eldest she would have inherited the largest portion of her father's vast estate.

Mary, it appeared, was as puzzled as my mother by Albert's sudden and apparent change of heart, but "Poor Mary, from the moment he made up his mind to marry her, did not have a chance really." It was all the more heartrending because Mary had watched this rapidly growing intimacy between her sister and this dazzling young man from Fort White with unfeigned joy. She herself was emotionally quite unaffected by Albert's arrival on the scene. Ever since my mother could remember Mary had been deeply attached to Pierre le Roux, the son of a poor neighbour of theirs. They had been to school together, been on the same national picnics, in the same catechism and confirmation classes and would long since have been engaged had not old Mr. de Beauvilliers, who had much of the fanaticism and uncompromising rigidity of his Huguenot forebears, made it quite clear that he would never let Mary marry anyone so poor and feckless.

"It is," my mother said, "alas! a sin to be poor in our community; but if it were a sin it is the only one this boy,

Pierre le Roux had." He came of a good family with a most distinguished pioneering record, but unfortunately they could not abandon the taste for pioneering when pioneering ceased to be necessary. Instead of settling down on their farms and developing them properly they were always going off into the blue, into unknown country, for months on end, hunting and exploring useless land. They did not prosper but they were wonderful people for all that, good-looking, athletic, gay, amusing, rather reckless and oh, so independent. I should have seen Mary's young man, my mother exclaimed. No one could shoot or ride as he could, no one had such a figure, such broad shoulders and such black flashing eyes which were quite incapable of hiding a falsehood or disguising a feeling. Nature had loved him in a way which his world failed to understand. Pierre never had a chance, nor had Mary, my mother emphasised again. It was not that Mary lacked courage. She was capable of making a stand for both of them, but to whom could she turn for help or advice? I who know and love our community could see her terrible predicament so clearly. Marriage with us is not the consummation of inevitable individual relationships, but a rigid, ruthless and barbaric social institution. The whole community automatically and instinctively would have been against her making a free choice. Everyone thought, even if they did not say so, that it would be a form of insanity to reject Albert and accept Pierre, everyone, that is, except my mother, who suspected it might be madness not to do so. All the people Mary knew and respected in some odd way felt that their own marriages, their own choice of mates, were on trial in this issue. The immense, subtle and collective machine, so pitiless of individual wants when it feels its security threatened, made it its business to prevent her choosing Pierre.

And then there were her parents. She was now their only child and all that this child had of love and gratitude and pity for them became the most powerful weapon, attacking her not from outside but from deep within her most tender and loving self.

Finally, if the devil himself had wanted to add one of his choice refinements fatally to confuse the issue for Mary he could not have done better than produce Albert as his advocate. For Albert, with all his worst faults, was not a negligible and ignoble being. On the contrary, to anyone who knew his real story, there was something magnificent, even heroic, about the way he had made a life for himself in a strange land. His greatest fault was that he was not Pierre. When Albert touched Mary her whole being did not instantly and without hesitation leap into the fire of a single flame, as it did when Pierre came near her. I cannot imagine a cruel choice more forlornly put to a young and inexperienced girl, and I am not surprised that she knew not how to argue the electricity of love against the solid, serried and immovable matter of her world.

In her desperation apparently she did go to the priest who had baptised and confirmed her, but who had also baptised, confirmed and buried her brother and sister. She went to him one Sunday after church, with Bible and hymn book in hand, and with a simple, silk sunbonnet pulled well forward to shield her eyes and the face that had gone strangely pale and tired recently, against the noon-day sun. Though she knew him so well she had gone with a rapidly beating heart because he was the undisputed spiritual ruler of our community, and once she had asked him for guidance she knew his word would be final. She had told him with great diffidence, for though he was a priest he was also a man and she had never talked to any man of anything so close and intimate.

He had listened to her attentively, standing before her in his dimly lit library with its comfortable and expensive furnishings, while the smell of the rich luncheon that was being prepared for him drifted in through the shuttered but open windows and mingled with the smell of leather books and cigar smoke clinging to the curtains. He had listened carefully but he never asked a question. The issue in his mind, as he listened to this shy, unhappy, troubled and pure young girl, was never in doubt. In the end he spoke up, not for love, not as I chose to think for God, but for the community which gave him his comfortable living. He quoted the old Testament, the relevant text from the ten commandments about honouring one's father and mother, referred solemnly to the evils of the flesh, the old Adam and Eve within all of us, drew her attention to the example of sacrifice set by our Lord, and asked with professional gentleness who was she to set her mind and desires against the opinions and wishes of the wise and experienced people who loved her? He was sure it was God's will that she should be directed in this matter by her parents, and he would pray for her to have the strength to take up her cross "manfully" and with the "manfully" he sighed a smile of whimsical humour at her. The interview was over. He went into his lunch and she walked out into the wide-open afternoon of summer, dark and sombre with blueness. Obviously the person who could have helped her had not yet been born. And, of course, she rejected Pierre.

"I have never heard anyone weep," my mother, who was one of her flower-girls at the wedding, told me with some of the distress of that far-off moment still in her eyes: "as Mary wept the night before her wedding. I have never seen her cry, really, since." And I suspect the argument went on inside Mary consciously and bitterly for years, continued when she had forgotten it and was passed on into the spirit and lives of the more receptive and sensitive of her children. She, so well equipped by nature for the task of bearing children, bore Albert his first child only at the end of the seventh year of their marriage.

Only one thing saved Mary from being broken by her marriage: her implicit faith in doing her duty, in doing the right thing by her parents and her people. She has never, I think, done anything that she has believed to be wrong. Her whole life has been founded on the "right" principles and if she had thought for a moment that she had been wrong not to disobey her parents, she would have been lost. After her interview with the priest she never consciously doubted. She never forfeited honour with herself for her decision. She became a devoted, a dutiful wife and mother and above all a fair and just woman, even if she had lost a loving heart. To this day the sign of the conflict is visible in her features; it gives her beauty its moving quality. Unlike Anna Maria's face which resembles it so much, it has never become a mask. It has recorded and grown old close to its own bitter experience, and the austere faith which has kept it whole is clearly marked on it.

Hard as the decision was on Mary it could not have been easy for Albert. Consider the man and his nature for a moment. He was already carrying the burden and partial paralysis of a vital secret. I have hinted at this secret before and the moment has come to be more open about it. Albert was the illegitimate son of a distinguished English nobleman and an Irish servant-girl. All his life he had had to throw an elaborate fantasy as camouflage round the miseries of his childhood and the shame of his schooldays. With his blessed release, under a new name, into the unknown of Victorian Africa his whole life was inevitably directed to getting the recognition he had been denied in Britain. Born outside the law, a furious compulsion drove him to seek compensation in becoming both interpreter and maker of law. His love of culture, his genuine appreciation of music and painting, suggested that if he had been born a normal child he might well have become something quite different; but all his life he remained a stranger to his initial and special self.

He kept his secret, I have said, until he died, but the remark needs qualification. We fool ourselves in the most pathetic and dangerous manner when we think we can really have secrets from the people we love. All we can do is to deny them awareness of this thing which lames the free movement of our spirit: but we can have no secrets from our inner life. The submerged knowledge is passed on in the most indirect and destructive way by its influence on our actions, by the impediment it causes in our being, and by all the subtle withdrawals, abstentions and negations it produces in our living contacts. The secret is known as surely as an astronomer knows the position and nature of some black midnight star which, although beyond the range of his strongest telescope, is accurately charted from its effect on the visible constellations in its vicinity.

The Michaeljohn family, without being aware of it, shared their father's secret in the dark of their young lives and were influenced and moulded by it.

And now with his marriage to Mary, Albert Michaeljohn had added another heavy burden to his soul. He was tied for the rest of his life to a woman whose deepest nature would not allow their union to be complete. True, the marriage had its compensations and particularly in the social and worldly compensations that were so dear to his ambitious mind; but his own especial nature knew that it had been rejected by Mary just as it had been rejected by life; and it smouldered with a sense of injury and with sullen rebellion.

I find it significant in this connection that at forty-five Albert's life began to undergo a violent and revolutionary change. Always so sober, so conscientious, so controlled, so correct and sociable, he began to develop disorderly and licentious habits. He began to drink heavily and smoke incessantly. He lost interest in his work, resigned from the Cabinet, would hardly ever accept a brief and could barely be persuaded to hold his seat for our community. Had it not been for Mary, who never wavered and who indeed drew nearer to her husband as his powers over herself and others waned, he would have disappeared altogether from public life along a dim track into the unknown where none could have followed him. He had already started on this strange internal journey when David was born, and when I knew

23

him the second half of his life seemed set to cancel out what he had so laboriously built up in the first.

To the outside world, however, the Michaeljohn home must have appeared to function as well as ever. There was the same, steady flow of distinguished and unusual visitors to the house. In comparison with my home it crackled, like a radio mast, with activity and energy. I have never known such a house for letters and telegrams: the telegraph messenger seemed to be coming and going from it all day long. The large grounds were always full of Michaeljohn children and their friends playing wild and elaborate games of their own invention.

There was one whole year in which the large estate became the questing ground for Knights of the Round Table, armed with home-made shields and spears, and one could hardly pass a tree without being held-up by an aggressive Sir Bors, Sir Gawaine or some other of the belted members of the legendary gang, while somewhere in the background Anna Maria functioned effectively, as her fancy took her, as Guenevere, Lynette or Elaine of Shalott. It all looked healthy and normal and moved according to some well-founded and confident plan.

Even Albert Michaeljohn, faced with his guests and the inevitable overflow from his public past, rarely failed to rise to the occasion; but more and more he preferred to be left to himself, emerging only occasionally from his silence and self-imposed isolation to make an impulsive demonstration of affection to his wife or one of his children, or to perform some sudden and quite exaggerated act of generosity in the community. Conversely, though happily not so often, he flew into the wildest and most obscure rages.

Once, it happened only once, suddenly in the middle of family dinner he picked up his empty plate, as if no food in it could ever again be to his liking, and from his position at the head of the long table threw it against the far wall where it exploded into many fragments. Then, with tears in his eyes, and without a word, he rose and walked from the room to drink brandy silent and alone in his study. Once in his sleep (Mary and the children told it as a happy illustration of what an original character the head of the family was), he lashed out with his right fist with all his great strength, and smashed the lovely and delicate Italian carafe in which Mary kept water for the night at her bedside. I would give anything to know the details of the dream that accompanied that act, but all Albert said the next day was that he had been troubled by nightmares and he must have had too much meat the night before.

Most of the day he spent in the garden and orchards which he had made lovely and rare with years of unfailing care and attention. But there too his behaviour underwent some curious change. For instance, he developed more and more a passion for hiring convicts from our local gaol as gardeners. It was an odd thing to do for he had his own trained servants, but suddenly he insisted on finding work for the petty burglars, stock-thieves and chronic alcoholics of our community, who knew far more about picking locks than picking the right fruit or flower. And when they did turn up, escorted by a warder armed with a loaded rifle, his behaviour became even more odd. Sooner or later (David and I often saw him do it) he would entice the warder into the kitchen for refreshment and then slip furtively from cover to cover in the garden distributing forbidden things like tobacco, snuff and sugar to the convict labourers. I have even seen him on cold days giving them swigs of raw brandy out of a flask hurriedly brought from his pocket.

To supply alcohol to the black and coloured members of the community was an offence subject to the heaviest penalties, to give it to black and coloured criminals doubly so. But he appeared undeterred and unperturbed by the risks he ran. At the end of the day's work, with a look of fathomless compassion and understanding in his eyes, he was always there to say good-evening to them and to watch these uniformed outcasts of our community being marched off to their cells. I would give anything to know what he was thinking then. Did, for instance, the heavy oak door of his own home clang behind him too like a prison gate? Did he sometimes in the dark of night, alone, see himself as his own gaoler? But perhaps the matter had gone too deep either for his, or our, thinking. Perhaps the one thing that could have given his life meaning was as shattered as his dinner plate against the wall, or as empty and broken as Mary's delicate carafe on the bedroom floor.

I myself, as time went on, felt less and less comfortable in the Michaeljohn home. It was, I know, largely because of David for he felt the complications of his home, instinctively, more than any of the others. One night when he was having dinner with us he said to my mother, just as if a great light had suddenly illuminated a shadow that had long been puzzling his mind: "I do love your house so: everything's so easy in it."

By that time my home had become almost as much David's as mine. It was certainly his spiritual home, and I could well understand and share his discomfort about his real home. But it worried me also on my own account. Things that happened in the Michaeljohn family never seemed to be what they appeared. One sensed another content which belonged neither to the moment nor the place of the occurrence. For years, for instance, I had a fantasy about the cellar which ran the whole length and breadth of the immense Michaeljohn house. I was afraid to hide there during our games lest I should discover the concealed presence that really controlled and directed the people in the house. Every now and then something happened which was, to me, as frightening as it was inexplicable. There was, for instance, what to this day David and I call "Black Sunday".

CHAPTER 2

DAVID always took a most intense and unusual interest in his mother's clothes. All the family knew about it and teased him about it mercilessly as families do, calling him "little Mister-Miss Dressmaker" and saying things like "You should have been born a girl", or "You had better become a dress designer". But the teasing had no effect whatsoever on his interest, which, until this Sunday, continued unabated. He was really an amazingly acute judge of clothes for so small a boy and, though not surprisingly for one who became so good a painter, possessed a very sure and fine feeling for colour. Mary, who knew how real this interest of David's was, and who was to some extent more flattered and supported by it than she realised, humoured him in this as she would never allow herself to humour him in anything else.

On the Friday before "Black Sunday" she and her husband had just returned from Fort White, where she had bought a new church-dress made out of a very fine and expensive French material imported straight from Paris. Church-dresses for women in our community were more important than any other kind of clothes—not excluding evening dresses. Unfortunately it was impossible in these days for our women to show much originality in their church-dresses. They had to conform very much to a rigid and exacting tradition, which demanded that they, like their men, should dress on Sundays in black of some kind. So Mary had no option but to have a black dress and all she could do was to get a new effect by choosing a material as original as possible in texture and weave. On this occasion she had chosen, most skilfully, a heavy dull silk brocade woven in slender parallel lines of an alternating weave, with the result that the material always caught the same light from a different angle and so seemed to be alive with rapidly changing shades and tones, yet was never actually shining or shrill. I have never seen black more subtly used in a material. There were moments when, at a distance, it took on a deep purple hue, or became a dark twelfth-century Chinese green. The dress too had been beautifully moulded and cut. From Mary's slim waist upwards it was closely and simply gathered round her shoulders and breasts, which were always shapely and firm like a young woman's. At the neck it was drawn together—and it was this that was really the most daring and reckless innovation—by an absurdly young-looking collar of delicate lace of pale cream. The sleeves were long, puffed and gathered at the shoulders like a Tudor doublet, but tight from the elbows to the wrist with wide cuffs, bunching into a spray of the same fine lace. From the waist it flowed outwards in long easy folds and fell to the ground like the water of a dark woodland fountain. She wore only one ornament with it. Where the ends of her delicate lace collar met round her throat, as smooth as an altar candle, she pinned her favourite brooch, made out of a single unrefined nugget of virgin gold and shaped like a deep-sea shell.

When she had dressed and prepared herself to her satis-faction on this Sunday morning, she sent Klara, who had been helping her, to fetch David with the message that "his mother had a surprise for him".

While she waited and surveyed herself in the long mirror she smiled with a sad and gentle amusement at herself thinking, I have never dressed up for any particular man, not even my husband, as I have for this strange little boy. An emotion of pity for herself and of a warm and loving tender-ness for David, such as she had rarely felt for any small person, went like an acute physical pain through her heart and brought a fierce smart of unshed tears to her eyes. For a moment she looked intently and searchingly at herself in the mirror. The clear, nostalgic sun of an African winter was just beginning to clear the tree-tops, to come through the wide window, to shed along the edges of the carpet and round her tall graceful figure, a delicate, silvery glow, so subtle and intimate, that it seemed to emanate as much from within her as from without. She felt as if she was looking not at her reflection but at a portrait of herself, in which some great artist had portrayed a personal defeat so great and yet so heroically and gracefully borne that it had become almost a form of victory. She lifted a hand to her heart, or rather to the heart of the person she saw in the mirror, in a gesture of the most delicate and compassionate understanding, and at that moment the door of her bedroom flew open and David rushed in, almost breathless with excitement, crying "Oh, Mummy, Mummy! what's it? Klara says . . . ." and then he too saw her reflection in the mirror, stopped suddenly, stood silently gaping at his mother's graceful back and her luminous reflection beyond, and said "Golly!"

Mary had not turned for she could see quite clearly behind her own reflection the open door and David standing in it, his eager face first flushed and excited, and then dissolved in an instant trance of wonder.

Suddenly she felt loth to leave their reflection in the mirror and wished she could perpetuate the moment, for perhaps if they could but stand there long enough, some answer would be born to flush the meaningless inarticulate yesterdays with the meaning of this new to-day. She felt more real, more alive in that reflection of herself than she had done for years. Her son's unfeigned admiration, vivid and true with the healing integrity of the spontaneous, made her feel strangely fulfilled and reassured her that what she saw in the quick-silver frame was no illusion of her poignant mind. But, once she'd turned her back on this illumination of herself she knew she would be again in the familiar room and life she had known so well these thirty years and more. She longed to throw herself in the arms of the woman she saw in front of her, to weep and to weep long on that mediæval shoulder and ask forgiveness for some wrong she may have committed.

29

Then she raised her other hand and beckoned to the David in the mirror. He came up to her, she put her arm round him, and said in a young voice that rose up in her like a fountain from some deep well of the past: "David! Do you like it?"

"Oh! It's terribly beautiful, Mother," he answered instantly. "Where did you get it?"

She told him, while they continued to stare at the reflection in the mirror, their arms round each other.

"It's lovely, Mother," David said again, and added in a dreaming, far-away tone, "and I think you're the most beautiful woman in the world."

She sank down impulsively on her knee and, strangely moved, took her son in her arms and kissed him warmly, saying, "You are a very sweet and understanding fellow." She held him close to her there on the ground.

The door opened and Klara came in. The church bell began to toll with a violent, almost hysterical solemnity, until the delicate nerves of the sunbeams in the room themselves seemed to tingle with it.

Mary let David go and stood up. She felt as if a large stone had crashed from heaven into the waters of a deep, still pool in some sunlit forest of time where she had first discovered the magic of her own reflection, and shattered the bright image for ever.

"I'm afraid we must go or we shall be late for church. Just wait for me a moment, little fellow, I shan't be long," she said and left the room.

David remained standing there in a patch of sunlight in a dream of his own. He had never in his young life felt so happy and so close to his mother. All the other moments in which he had been happy and close to her were reborn and came alive before that cool and glistening mirror, and made music in his ears, and colour before his eyes. He thought of one moment, in particular, that had not only made him happy but had also delivered him from great dread. Once, about two years before, he had woken up in the night with a violent fear. He must have cried out aloud in his sleep for as he woke with this agony of fear stabbing in the quick of his being, the door of his room had opened and his mother, miraculously, had walked in, picked him up like a baby and taken him into her bed with her—her husband was away at the time. Pain and dread had suddenly vanished before an inrush of warmth and a sense of unshakable safety and he had gone to sleep again almost at once. He felt rather like that now. Her presence and the embrace of a moment ago was still round him like a warm and sunlit sea. He followed the beam of sunlight which lay like a lagoon of flame among the shadows round his feet, up to the window and there, lying on the wide sill, he saw a new black bag bought to match his mother's dress.

"She didn't show me that," he thought, and walked over to it, picked it up, opened it, rummaged inside it, closed it, put it down again and said to himself, "It's really all very lovely," and instantly was lost again in that sense of wonder that had come to him some moments before. He stood by the window, the sunlight wrapped like silk around him, looking far through the blue of the day, into a warm, still centre of himself. The church bells stopped ringing, a flock of pigeons came darting over the stripped tree-tops on wings as swift and sure as messengers of fate. They swished and swirled recklessly round the housetops and then landed in an explosion of wings on the lawn below the window, where they began pecking and cooing briskly in the sunlight.

Mary came back and in a voice still quivering with the moment's emotion said, "Oh! there you are, David, good little fellow. We can go now and join the others just as soon as I have found my bag. Do you know what I have done with it, Klara?"

"Here it is, Mum," David said, turning round and taking it to her. Klara was watching him intently with a look of apprehension in her ancient Hottentot eyes.

"Thank you, darling. I'll just see if I have got everything

I want, and we'll be off." Mary opened her bag, looked inside it, picked through the contents with quick, elegant fingers and then said in a puzzled tone: "But what has happened to my sovereign? Surely you saw me take it from the master and put in here, Klara?" Every time Mary went to a church service she put a sovereign in the collection. We had no paper money in our community in those days: we had gold sovereigns, gold guineas, gold ten-shilling pieces, and silver and copper coins, but no paper money of any kind. So every Sunday morning before church Mary drew one gold sovereign from her husband, and this morning had been no exception.

"Yes, my Nonnie, I saw you do it," old Klara answered at once, then hesitated, looking at David, as if to say, "Well, why don't you speak up?" and added, "Perhaps the little master can tell you."

David looked at her with unfeigned surprise and said: "Me! Why me?"

At the same time his mother asked: "Why, David, do you know anything about it?"

"No, Mum," David said unperturbed, glancing upwards in her eyes. "I did look at your bag just now. It's lovely, really lovely, I think, but I don't remember seeing a sovereign in it."

"Dear beloved lord! How can the little master be so naughty, when I saw him do it!" said old Klara, thoroughly roused. "I saw him take that gold coin out of that black bag as sure as I am a Hottentot. I saw him take it, and hold it in the sun, look at it with those great, big eyes of his and put it in that pocket of his Sunday-go-to-meeting suit."

"Why, Klara, you fibber," David cried outraged. "God will surely punish you for telling such fibs."

"Me a fibber," Klara was puffed out with righteous indignation now: "Me a fibber! Look here." She seized David impulsively by the hand, pulled him towards her, put her hand into his left pocket and pulled out the missing sovereign, and handed it to Mary with a scornful: "There, Nonna: me a fibber!"

"Oh, David, how could you, how could you do such a thing?" Mary said, her face exposed and naked with horror.

"But, Mummy, I didn't," David protested, almost in tears, quite overwhelmed and dazed by the disaster that now clearly hung over him. He could only moan: "I didn't do it, Mummy: I promise you I didn't."

"How did it get into your pocket then? Coins have no feet of their own," Mary said harshly, unbelief clearly marked on her features which had quickly travelled the brittle years between them and the face in the mirror and once more become those of a just and dutiful woman.

"Some one or something must have put it there, Mummy, I promise you I didn't," David pleaded, now in tears.

"Don't you look as if I did it to you," the embattled old Klara began, and then seeing his distress and the white set look on Mary's face, she relented and said earnestly, "Oh, come on, little master David: why don't you own up and tell your Mum it was just your little joke and it will all be over and we'll forgive you, won't we, Nonna?"

"But I didn't do it, I swear I didn't do it," was all the tearful David could say.

"My God! a son of mine a thief," Mary began, in great flint-like distress. She would have gone on to say more but the church bell started tolling again, more peremptorily than ever. A sudden decision came to her. "We have no time now. There's the last bell. We'll deal with this after church. Not a word to anyone, Klara. Come on, David. Wipe your eyes and stay next to me."

Mary, with David by her side, and the rest of the Michael-john family—with the exception of Albert who had given up going to church recently—emerged from the main gate of their grounds a little ahead of my parents and myself. We followed just behind them all the way to church, and I knew at once that something awful had happened to David. I could tell it from the way he held his slim upright body, the angle of his head and neck to his shoulders, and by all the great and invisible signals that fly from one person to the other he loves. I walked that wide dusty main street of our village with a cold fear in my heart and held tightly on to my mother. And the atmosphere in our main street just before church on a winter's morning does not help a heart in trouble.

There is the church at the top of our street standing like a seasoned sentry, presenting its spire like a rifle with bayonet fixed, at the menace of the immense, empty, infinitely demanding earth of Africa about it. There are the stony, barren hills of winter hemming in the earth and village, and a sky without fleck or blemish of cloud swollen with light of a melancholy clarity and blue with the longing to be redeemed from so bleak a season. In the village itself during those five minutes before church service begins, there is no sound to be heard except the mooing of a cow, the bleating of a sheep, and the spasmodic betrayal of silence by the hysteria of a distant cock-crow. The community does not talk on its way to church, unless in a whispered question: "Have you got your hymn book?" or "Daddy, did you give the children their collection money?" The street is just full of silent people dressed in black, silently moving on to the church in their own family groups.

It was so still that morning that I heard clearly through the sound of steps muffled in the dust, the continual "swish, swish" of the heavy black silks and satins of the women in the street. With their long skirts trailing out in the dust behind them and particularly with their men showing the white of their shirt fronts and Sunday bow-ties so flashily against their dark coats, the street looked as if it were full of large black crows converging on a kill. Wherever we walked by one of the white walls of the houses, the slanted sun of winter threw silhouettes of these midnight shapes on to them that were so exaggerated and imposing that they seemed far more real and important than the people who made them.

Throughout the gloomy service, I could not take my mind or eyes off David. Our pew was at right-angles to the Michaeljohns' and what I saw confirmed my worst fears. Something awful had happened to David. His face was as white as his Eton collar and at one moment when the parson read the ten commandments and came to the "Thou shalt not steal," and Mary put her hand on his shoulder, a tremor of despair and rebellion against the implications of his mother's gesture shook him so plainly that I feared he was going to cry.

When the church service ended, I went over as usual to join the Michaeljohns for our Sunday story. But David could hardly summon life enough to greet me and a spirit of gloom seemed to have banished the high-spirits with which release from church usually filled us. We walked back home almost the whole way in uncomfortable silence. When we reached the Michaeljohn gate Mary bent down and said to David in a low tone that I could only just hear: "Please, David! I have prayed so hard for you, please own up and we'll forget all about it."

For the first time I saw David quite beyond himself, push at his mother fiercely as if to get away from her, and say in a voice half-choked with feeling, "Can't you leave me alone? I told you I didn't do it."

Mary stood up and turned a sad and stern face to me, saying: "I am sorry, Alex, but there won't be any stories this morning."

"But David will come for lunch, won't he?" I pleaded, for he always had Sunday lunch with me.

"No, I am sorry, Alex," she said firmly.

I felt like going down on my knees to her then to allow David to come, for that something horrible awaited him inside the house was now quite plain. But one look at that stern and austerely beautiful face showed me how powerless I was to make her change her mind. I watched her take David in through the gate, saw it clang to like a prison, and then for the first time I could remember I was shut out from the Michael-john house.

I went home in despair. I could hardly eat a delicious Sunday lunch. The day had suddenly been darkened by an immense and legendary shadow. I felt as if battle between invisible and tremendous elemental forces had suddenly flared up in our midst. It seemed to me as if a giant had suddenly come up out of the river-valley nearby, strode over the hills and stood astride the Michaeljohn home with upraised club calling for David's blood. And I longed to be a giant-killer.

I prowled all afternoon round the Michaeljohn house and garden walls. It stood there like a calm and confident fortress but I was not deceived. In the late afternoon about four, I could bear it no longer. I slipped through the private gate that connected the grounds of our two homes and instinctively made my way to a large Japanese pine, in the centre of the grounds. David and I had years before found two secret perches for ourselves right in the top of this tree, where we often went to read or talk on our own. I stood silently and apprehensively at the foot of the tree for a minute or so looking about me, and then I heard an involuntarily dry sob coming from above. I went up the tree as fast as I could and there was David clinging to the top-most branch of the tree, his arms about it. I looked on a white young face, unforgettable in its misery. I noticed his Eton collar had gone soft and yellow with tears.

As Mary, with David beside her, came down the long tiled corridor of the Michaeljohn house, she found the rest of her children waiting by her bedroom door. Curtly she told them there would be no Sunday story, said they could do what they liked for an hour, and asked them to send Klara in to her. How our mood conditions the value of our material surroundings. Mary walked into her room like the judge of a supreme court going to his chair on the bench, David like a prisoner into the box, Klara, apprehensive and in revolt against herself for ever having mentioned the matter, followed hard on David.

Mary lost no time in re-examining them both at great length. Klara made what excuses she could for David, said she was sure it was only a game, why should he want to take money suddenly for himself when she who had nursed him all his life knew that he had never even stolen an apple, said that he was just a stubborn little boy. "Ach, Nonna, you know what men are like, particularly little men," she added with all the talent of the oppressed for appeasement. "They are all obstinate. The little master will tell you in a minute it was all a joke." She looked appealingly at David.

But Mary was not to be side-tracked and came again and again to this question.

"You have no doubt you saw him take it, Klara? Think carefully, it is terribly important."

Old Klara would hang her head and looking neither at her nor David would say sadly: "Aye! I saw him take it, Nonna," adding the last time the question was put to her, rather reproachfully and petulantly, with typical Hottentot realism: "Ach, why bother so, Nonna, you have got your money back."

David for his part could only repeat, until his head and heart reeled with it: "Please, please, Mummy, I didn't take your money. I promise, I didn't."

"Then how did it get in your pocket?" Over and over again she flung the question at David, until at last he said in despair, "Perhaps the devil put it there." And she regarded him steadily for a minute or two.

Just for the moment the shadow of Mary of the mirror clouded her clear and circumspect mind. The secret knowledge of where thirty years of high principled living had led her sounded its own submerged warning in her blood. She came as near as she had ever been to the realisation that flesh and blood need a loving and understanding heart far more

than a just and knowledgable mind. But in the world wherein
we lived, the eyes of faith and love were blindfold, while the
eyes that looked outward were wide open and in need of
sleep. With a note of desperation, as if she were plead-
ing with her son to save her from her own principles, she
added:

"Oh, Davie, David! Please be a man and own up and we'll
forget all about it."

"But I didn't do it, Mummy!" he said for the last time,
very quietly, looking at her with wide-open and utterly
defenceless eyes.

"Very well then," she said in a harsh, unnatural voice.
"You leave me no option but to hand you over to your
father."

She took him by the arm and marched him resolutely and
quickly, almost as if she feared her courage would fail her,
down the long corridor and out of the front door. There was
a brief moment in the winter sunlight, and then, rounding
the side of the house she came to her husband's study.

She did not seem to notice that there was the sickly, strong
smell of Cape brandy in the room, and that the atmosphere
was thick with cigar smoke, but David's eyes smarted with it.
Albert was in an easy chair, his feet up beside the hearth, a
French novel on his lap, a glass and decanter of brandy by
his side.

"Why, Mary, this is a pleasant surprise," he said, getting
up slowly. He was in a good mood and seemed genuinely
pleased to see her.

But as she quickly told him why she had come, a heavy
scowl possessed his handsome features. "Do you mean to tell
me I have a son who is a thief and a liar?" he said with a voice
tense with alcoholic melodrama. "Well there is only one way
to deal with thieves and liars. You had better leave him with
me, Mary."

For a moment she hesitated. Instinctively she kept her
head averted from David, who was looking at her with all

the appeal his nature could summon. Part of her urged her to see the punishment through to the end; part shrank from seeing physical pain inflicted on any living thing; so when her husband again urged her to go, she left without a backward glance.

As the door closed Albert went to the corner of his study and selected a long, quivering quince lathe from the bundle he had kept there for years for these rare occasions.

"Come here," he said.

David walked over slowly. His throat and lips had gone very dry as he came near. He said in a croaking little voice, "Oh! please, Papa, I didn't do it!"

Albert, who was by no means a hard-hearted person, but who could be harsh and cruel as he was gentle and kind only on impulse, really disliked the role that had been thrust on him for all the automatic readiness with which he had accepted it in front of Mary. As he looked at the shrinking, apprehensive boy a confused panic seized his emotions. He feared that if he did not beat David quickly he might not beat him at all, and so his authority as dispenser of judgment and justice would suffer a grave blow.

"Stop lying to me," he roared at David, as much to rouse the executioner in him as to silence David.

It did not fail him and one angry thought after another rushed into his head. How monstrous of the boy to put a father that wanted nothing but peace and quiet and affection into such an unfair situation! How wicked to force a decent, kind-hearted man to outrage his best self in this manner, and all this from a son who had been, from birth, a constant problem and source of irritation to him! How wicked he must have been if Mary, who had such a damnably subtle and delicate manner in her approach to the boy, should ask for him to be punished! What monsters, outsize monsters, little boys could be! They stood there and looked so small and helpless, so full of starlit innocence; but their appearance belied them. Their smallness was just a cunning disguise.

They were powerful bullies and despots; they were insatiable tyrants who sucked one's life-blood and energy dry, and even stole the affection of wives from their husbands. My God, not only stole their affection but plunged their dirty little hands deep into one's wife's bag and snatched one's own gold from it. It was too much. All the deeply resented frustration from the past rushed up in him and made of this a moral pretext with which to unlock the dungeon of his self-control. "Stop lying, you little thief," he roared again, and seized David by the collar in a rage such as he had never known before.

It was not the first time that David had been beaten by his father but every instinct he possessed warned him now that this beating would differ from the others in its deadly seriousness. He had lived spontaneously and naturally as a little boy and now the answer came to him as it had always done, like a flash of lightning from far down inside himself. Another boy as old and experienced as life itself seemed instantly to come alive in him, to take charge of him and to give him quick, deft, confident orders: "Not another word to him, get it over. Forget about the pain for the moment. . . . There is shock coming, a dull shock that's all. . . . We'll arrange things so that you only feel the pain of it afterwards when it can't interfere with what we have to do. . . . Watch his eyes. You saw that rush of red into them. Yes, he's going to beat you now. It's coming. . . . That's right, turn sideways as you did then, and give a little, just when the stick gets to you. Excellent! You are doing well! Smell his breath? Yes, he's been drinking, but he's not drunk. . . . Watch that. Don't panic. Keep your head and arms out of the way. He'll break them if you are not careful. That's much better. . . . Fifteen, sixteen, seventeen. I know it's a lot. But you can take it. Besides I think the cane is breaking. Don't speak! don't make a sound! you'll only provoke him. . . . Twenty-one twenty-two, not a sound. He will beat you for every year of his life if we're not careful. Good, it's broken! Get up and go quickly. Can't you hear him shouting at you?"

Albert Michaeljohn, breathless and shaking all over with exertion and emotion, was roaring at David.

"Get out of here. Get out. Don't let me see you again!"

David got up from the floor where he had fallen and groped towards the door.

"Don't cry just yet," the boy within said. "No one must see you. Slip down by the side wall, they'll be in the drawing-room nearby. Duck under this window. Make for the garden. See that bed of old cape gooseberry bushes! Crawl in there. No one'll see you. There's the pain for you now. I'm afraid it'll hurt a lot, so the moment to cry is now. It'll help."

David cried until he could cry no more. He lay there for some hours exhausted. Then he heard first Klara and after a while Mary calling him. His mother's voice suddenly broke into the silence of his pain with the most wonderful silver urgency; how it trembled with deep instinctive alarm. It was no longer the dead voice of a woman of Judgment pronouncing sentence of death, but the living cry of a fallible and anguished heart. Never had it sounded more lovely or more welcome.

David longed to shout out: "Oh! Mother, Mummy, here, come quick!"

But no, it was not possible. He had crossed a far frontier between himself and Mary in that short morning. He was in rough new country and something would not let him answer her. As she stopped calling the clock in the church struck three.

He thought, "I am too close to the house." Fearfully he crept out. Ducking from bush to bush he reached the Japanese pine, went up it as quick as his bruised legs would let him. Five minutes later I found him there and quickly took him home with me.

My mother looked tremendously relieved when she saw us come slowly into the drawing-room. Mary Michaeljohn had been there in my absence, had, in fact, just left a moment before, and had told them the whole story as much for her and Albert's justification as for our information. She had not seen David, they could not find him anywhere and that, together with her husband's distended emotionalism since the scene in his study, made her fear that the punishment had gone farther than she intended, although the "wicked little boy did ask for a thorough chastising." She said she had to go out almost at once to a most important church meeting, so would my mother please help to find David and please keep him for a day or two. Her husband was in a terrible state and swore he would never have the boy in the house again, and she feared what would happen did he see David again in his present mood. She would look in later in the evening.

So now, the moment my mother saw us she jumped up from her place by the fire, ignored me, took David in her arms and kissed him tenderly and said:

"David boy, I am so glad you have come. You are staying with us for a few days. I have arranged it all with your mother. Alex, just run over and tell Aunt Michaeljohn that David is all right and with us now."

I had never felt prouder or more grateful to my mother for having known so instantly what we two wanted. I shot out of the house to the Michaeljohns as fast as I could.

When I came back David was propped on cushions and covered with rugs between my parents on the floor by the fire. He was, as my mother had said, all right but only barely so. Mother had immediately given him a sedative while my father had examined his bruises. He was covered with dark, angry, red-blue weals that radiated from his behind, down his legs like the spokes of a wheel, but fortunately he had received most of the strokes where they could best be borne.

"Do you know, Davie," my father had said, "I don't think I've ever had a beating like that, and if I had had I would not have been able to take it as well as you've done."

This had so pleased David that he half turned over and tried to look at his behind over his shoulder, but his body smarted so that he quickly desisted and fell back on his tummy. My father then rubbed him gently with olive oil from head to foot, put him into a very old, thick and smooth flannel nightshirt, wrapped him in some cashmere shawls, and so I found him, royally anointed and installed by our fire-side, sipping a bowl of hot, sweet milk. Already he was much calmer and getting more reassured every minute. The relief in my own mind at having him there, safe with us, was indescribable.

We four who understood one another so well had the good sense not to talk. We sat quietly and silent for a long time sipping our milk and our tea, my mother replenishing the bowls and cups without our asking. I sat next to David on the floor. My father was in his favourite chair, smoking his pipe and reading the new *Countryman's Weekly*. My mother was knitting in the way that only she could knit, calmly and steadily without the neurotic urgency that possesses so many women when they feel the needles between their fingers. Every now and then she gave David and me a look that went far beyond the meaning of mere words. The fire flickered warmly round our feet, lapped like a golden tide of summer at the shadowy foreshore of the room. I felt not only warm but safe beside it. But I would not have left it willingly for I was not sure that all the danger had been dispelled.

As the darkness closed in on our home and the maids came in to bar the shutters and draw the curtains, I caught a glimpse of the gaping hole of the winter night outside and it looked the perfect ally for those great and legendary shadows which had stalked the village in the morning, the born friend to that invisible but real and gigantic presence which had taken up its position astride the Michaeljohn home at noon. We four, I felt, were still in a jungle where only a bright and sure flame could save us.

David broke the silence first. Sitting up stiffly and rather painfully he suddenly asked my father:

"Uncle Fraser! Have you ever stolen anything?"

My father took his pipe slowly out of his mouth, and

43

tapped it out on the side of the grate. We all knew the question was of transcendent importance and both my mother's heart and mine beat faster lest he should fail us.

That quick tap, tap of his on the solid grate was like the rap on the door of a postman with urgent news.

"If by that you mean taking someone else's property by mistake, Davie," my father began in that deep measured voice of his: "Why, yes, I have done it often."

My mother, who had dropped her work in her lap, picked it up and confidently resumed her knitting.

David, with a new light in his eyes, was looking with interest at my father. "You? Often? Really and truly, Uncle Fraser?" he said with some of the old brightness in his voice. "And were you punished for it, too?"

My father smiled and said: "Look, David. I know what you are thinking and I want to tell you at once that neither I nor anyone in this room think you stole that coin. You may have taken it or not. I do not know, but I am sure you did not steal it. If you did, then I am a thief too, and should have been in gaol many times. I am always finding things in my pockets that I didn't, or rather do not, remember putting there. Six months ago when we were up in Fort White, for instance, I spent one morning in a bookshop, ordering Christmas presents. When I got back to my hotel I found I had a book under my arm that I don't remember taking, and certainly did not pay for. And what is odder still, the book was in French and I can't read a word of French. I am sure if the owner of the shop had found me with the book outside his shop and on my way home, he would not have accepted my explanation and taken me for a thief."

"Oh, how wonderful!" David said, and sank back on his cushions, shut his eyes and relaxed.

And so the incident of the yellow sovereign was settled for ever between the four of us. But not so between David and his family. For them the issue was not settled, merely suspended and postponed.

We'd hardly finished talking when there came the first visitation from the house next door. Old Klara announced herself with a plate of David's favourite doughnuts that she had made herself. The old woman took him in her arms, wept over him and said over and over again that she had not meant to tell on him. "How could I know the Nonna would fuss so once she had the money back?" she asked us plaintively.

Hard on her heels came Anna Maria and Edward George. And with their coming the machinery of the fatal, sinister and submerged content seemed to whirr in my ears again. For what could have inspired Anna Maria with such colossal tactlessness as to present herself to David at such a moment, hand in hand with Edward George, and bearing such a gift? She looked as beautiful as ever, her clear brow and eyes darkened with some deep and confused concern as she held out a money-box to David and said with the searing voice of someone performing a calculated christian duty: "We're so sorry, David, for what has happened. We're terribly sorry and we've brought you this."

David, who had sat up and had immediately been assailed by all kinds of profound intangibilities as he always was when Anna Maria came near him, shrank back from the proffered gift.

"Please! It's for you!" she said again.

Then, as he still refused to take it, she stood up and put it on the dark surface of the table, where its pillar-box red, in the flickering firelight burned like the small, furtive fire in one of our native huts in the veld.

The room was intensely quiet. For the first time I became aware of the solemn ticking of the clock in the corner, ticking as if it were spreading out the last seconds before a fateful choice. The room seemed charged with ancient and abiding significances, as if all our childhood days were about to come to a final point in this moment. I felt that if I listened carefully I would hear the wings of a dragon beat the darkened air outside.

"You think, Anna Maria," David said, going straight to the point that mattered most to him, "that I stole the money . . . don't you?"

"Oh, David, can't you forget it. We all want to," she cried distressed, but not daring to meet his question. "We're so sorry about everything. Please take this."

David looked at her as one looks at someone to whom one is saying good-bye for ever, and with whose going a part of oneself also perishes.

"Auntie Fraser," he said at last, in a voice almost inaudible with misery, "please help me. I feel so sick." And with that he buried his head in the cushions.

When Mary came late that evening, David was asleep. We always slept outside in the winter and though my mother had wanted to put him to bed inside, David had begged to stay next to me on the veranda. We loved it there. The veranda had no roof but had an immense and very old vine trellised over it. In the summer the vine gave the veranda shade, but in the winter, with its leaves gone, it let in the sun by day and the stars and moon at night. Lying warm in our closely blanketed beds with the crisp clear air of the highveld winter around us, we had an incomparable view of the sky.

I know no land which matches so well the dark continent of the sky, with its fountains and pools and lakes and rivers of light and its deserts of darknesses, as does the vast and sombre earth of Africa. It takes the night to itself like a bride chosen from among equals. As the sun goes down it brushes the shy, virgin twilight impatiently aside, and then the two of them fly passionately into each other's arms to be close together in an untroubled oneness. I have watched the scene all my life and I have never got used to the majesty and fitness of their dark mating. It has been in a way I cannot hope to describe an unfailing source of reassurance to me. I can only say this: as I watched from childhood, night after night, the familiar lights go up in the sky, the glittering constellations move into their appointed places, the vast

46

Babylonian cavalcade of the sky start out for the dawn of renewal with such irresistible confidence that the far-off thunder of their advance set every star-beam a-tremble in our midst, and as I saw at that selfsame instant, Africa hurl its immense land swiftly at the distant horizon to salute one brave battalion after another as they passed, and send its great peaks soaring swiftly upwards and spread out its own rivers and lakes to hold the sky jewelled and alive in their deepest depths, at that instant something of oneness of being, longing, and destination of this cosmic occasion unfalteringly has been communicated to me. I have felt part of the same steadfast and unfailing rhythm and I have been without regret of the past or fear of the future.

But this night, with David lying asleep and restless next to me, was an exception. For suddenly, as we lay there in our large bed I saw Mary's graceful shape, brushing aside the stars, as she bent over us. I quickly shut my eyes and pretended too to be asleep. Scarcely daring to breathe I waited apprehensively for her to go. Then I heard her whispering to my mother in the doorway and as I half-opened my eyes I did so fearfully, as if I expected the order of the sky to be disarranged.

The stars were there as before, it is true, and brighter than ever. The tightening frost now had given them a precision and clarity greater than before. Their tears were frozen and their pointed and crystal rims held long lances bristling with an icy armament of Antarctic whiteness. In their movement across the sky their lances and spears seemed to pluck at the frozen strands of darkness and far off, a faint harp-like music fell with the pattern of their light towards the land. From end to end the earth responded as the coldest wind of Africa came swiftly down the hillside passes and over the shining veld to make it moan in unison with this orchestration of darkness and light. Yes, I looked and listened to the familiar order of wholeness and oneness in things, but for the first time in life I feared it might not always be so.

I have often thought back on this moment. Now that I am older I would put it differently. I would still affirm that the sense of oneness of longing, being and destination as I felt it then, is no illusion. I would go farther and say that finally it is the only reality, that it is so great a oneness that it is not troubled and confused but created and sustained by the apparent multiplicity and diversity of things. I would emphasise that it is of such transcendent importance that if life cannot achieve it by fair means, it is forced to do so by foul. And I would add that we, out of our individual and social arrogances, out of our blind, partial awareness of the basic design of our being, and out of our passion for elevating selected fractions of life above the whole, are continually forcing it to seek its wholeness by foul means. To-day I would be far more concerned with our effect on the stars in their courses, than on their effect on us. I would remember that a great astronomer has just told us that every time we lift a finger we affect the disposition of the stars, and that one day the amount of cosmic readjustment thus produced may well be capable of mathematical measurement. I would say to myself: on the morning that Albert Michaeljohn raised his stick twenty-three times to beat David, by so doing he lengthened the axis of the earth which runs through him as, indeed, it runs through all of us. And by lengthening the axis he slowed down the motion of the earth and so produced such a realignment of cosmic forces that the aboriginal darknesses had been encouraged dangerously to close in on the uttermost outpost of starlight.

THREE months later, in the spring, Albert Michaeljohn suddenly died. He was by no means an old man and to all appearances still healthy and strong, and he had, after all, not begun to drink excessively until well into middle-age. But now he complained, one day, of a pain underneath his heart and a week later was dead. The doctors and eminent specialists summoned from Fort White were never sure of the precise nature of his illness and at the end vaguely ascribed the cause of his death to heart failure.

I am not surprised that they were puzzled, for one of the main causes of his death, I suspect, was one of which medicine has no official cognisance. It was symptomatic of the man's whole problem with himself and life that he should have chosen to die in the spring. I say "chosen" deliberately because if Nature had ever intended by the force of its own example to encourage the sick and ailing to recover and the weary at heart to live again, she did so in this spring; and I am convinced Albert died only because he wished it.

This spring our world, down to the minutest and subtlest details, was aflame, and afire, and asparkle with the most irresistible and uncompromising renewal of life. But I can well imagine that Albert Michaeljohn, as he regarded its beauty with his drink-reddened eyes, was filled with a deadly sense of irony. I can imagine him then admitting to himself, as he had not dared to do before, that his spirit could never again take part in this renewal. His life was finally contained in a circle of steel from which he had failed to break free, and he could only go on repeating endlessly the enigmatic variations of himself of which he was already so tired. At best he could live some more winters in the spring, and in the summer, when the world about him was bowed down under another golden harvest he could watch the dead leaves of his yesterdays being whirled by their cold wind up and down the dim highway of his spirit. His being rejected such a prospect; and so, appropriately, with a pain underneath the heart, he died.

Death came to him very quietly. The doctor who was with him noticed the reaction in his pulse and quickly summoned Mary, who immediately fetched the children and a few intimate friends already staying in the house. They trooped in silently and stood round his bed, a hushed, wide-eyed and fearful little group in flannel dressing-gowns. The night was cool and tensely quiet. There were no comets flashing in the sky, no earth tremors or thunder and lightning. Outside the universe looked as ordered and calm and permanent and abiding as it could possibly be, as if this reckoning taking place between Albert and all his years, in that dimly lit room, was too small a matter for it to notice.

Yet one curious thing did happen. David says, as he stood there with the others in a silence so great that he could hear the quickened beat of his own heart and his blood like a far-off mid-day breeze singing in his ears, he felt as if the very earth began to tremble under his feet. Then they all heard a wind come tearing down the pass in the grey hills on the veld with such force that it was audible long before it reached them. This was most unusual in the spring, and the wind, as it reached the village, sent all the scores of windmills clanking furiously and their melancholy clank-clank in some odd way synchronised with the beating of David's heart, so that he too seemed to go clank-clank inside himself. Then the wind began to moan and sing round the tree and roof tops in the most heartrending fashion. For three-quarters of an hour while they stood there the wind wailed round the house; then suddenly it stopped. As it stopped David distinctly heard a night bird send a piercing call out across the veld and a jackal, a long way away, barked three times. At that moment, Albert died. As Mary put her face in her hands and

Anna Maria began sobbing bitterly, the clock in the hall struck one.

Albert's death caused a tremendous stir not only in our district but in the entire country. When it became known that he was dying, the Michaeljohn home, my own and the houses of all our friends and relations, had been filled to over-flowing with people who felt they owed it to him and his family to be close at hand when he died.

Death needs no outside assistance to make it dramatic. It is in itself, in its own dark night, so charged with drama that although we see it constantly around us we never get used to it, and although we know it makes no exceptions, we never fail to be shaken and surprised when it visits anyone close to us. Our community behaved as if it was about to encounter death for the first time. I would not be surprised if the bee-hive murmur of anxious and whispered inquiries at all hours of the day and night at the doors and in the muffled corridors of his house did not penetrate to Albert in his darkened room, and cheer him on his way. I know it sustained Mary. To her who had lived in the most complete sense for the community and by its values, this impressive demonstration of its rein-forced concern for her husband's fate was evidence that her initial sacrifice had not been in vain. But I am not sure it helped Anna Maria and David, for it reinforced the already formed impression in their minds that something both ab-normal and monstrous was happening to their father.

After Albert's death, of the two, Anna Maria was out-wardly by far the more shaken. She had wept all night and most of the day and her wide eyes were swollen and almost closed with grief. David did not cry. His eyes were dry and wide-open as if he would never sleep again and had a bright, brittle look in them. The afternoon of the funeral, as he and Anna Maria and I were in the garden picking great baskets full of sweet-smelling freesias to put in their father's coffin, I noticed he had over-night developed a new habit. He would stop picking flowers, look over his shoulder anxiously for no apparent reason at all, lick his lips with a quick, nervous tongue, and then, not without relief, return to his picking again. Even Anna Maria would gladly have turned to him that day but he seemed impervious and curiously apart from all of us.

While we were picking freesias the church bell began tolling. It was the final act before the funeral service and according to our custom the bell had to toll out solemnly and clearly once for every year lived by the dead person. We understood exactly what it meant; we had always made it a rule to stop whatever we were doing, even in the midst of our games, to count the strokes as it tolled out the life of someone unknown to us. Anna Maria started weeping again now as the great bronze notes fell on the tense afternoon calm of the garden and set the shadows trembling like darkened water under the trees. A flock of pigeons taking alarm rose up on a wild burst of blue and white and fawn feathers and darted on whistling wings through the sunlight towards the hills where the first faint shadows of night were beginning to form in their laps.

Anna Maria, sick with misery and alarm, clutched David by the arm and held him tightly, as tears bright like crystal in the clear sun, rolled down her face. But he hardly seemed to notice her. He had automatically stopped picking flowers, and now stood up straight, his head half-turned to count the strokes, saying half to himself, and half to the trees straining and bursting with blossom, "One-two-three—" until he came to "twenty-two" when he stopped abruptly. Looking at us like someone just released from a hypnotic trance, he said in a hushed dry little voice, so unusual for him, "We'd better take these in, or we shall be too late."

We found Mary looking for us and she took us and put us at the tail of the long procession of intimate friends and relations waiting to pay their last respects to the dead man. Our baskets of freesias in that dim corridor by Albert's bedroom door burned with a strange ecto-plasmic glow and threw the most poignant and living sweetness on that air already so charged with death. I cannot to this day get even the faintest whiff of their scent without instantly being carried back to that corridor, by that silent door, where I once stood holding David and Anna Maria's hands, and waiting fearfully to go in.

Yet finally, when we stood by the bier, it seemed strange that I should have been frightened by the prospect. Albert looked calmer, and more at peace. In retrospect I am tempted to say that he looked happier than I had ever seen him look alive. The dissatisfaction on his handsome features, the angry flush of the war within that suffused his living face had gone. He looked like a not ignoble monument of himself, as if in the moment of dying he had rediscovered his original innocence, as if every line and expression in his face had been determined to reaffirm for the last time before they dissolved the initial design from which Albert and the world had worked so industriously and intelligently to estrange them. Very appropriately he was white as only death and polar snow can be white. The coffin was lined with unsoiled white linen and round him lay masses of the whitest of flowers. The air was laden with the scent of flowers. The coffin smelt not of death and decay, but like a bridal bouquet, and if one had to judge the occasion by the scent alone one would have pre-supposed a wedding rather than a funeral. And, perhaps, this is not as fanciful as it sounds. Perhaps this was a wedding as well as a funeral. When I recall my last view of this great man of our district, this King of Anna Maria's and David's world, lying there coffin-small like the humblest of his electors, I see him not so much as dead and about to be buried, but as someone wedded to the inevitable, someone restored to necessity. I think that accounted for the composure on his brow and face. After a bitter winter of separation he was once more at one with the inevitabilities of life, even though the cost had been the inevitability of death.

We who now surrounded Albert's coffin were the ones

from whom composure and certainty had fled. As we piled our freesias round Albert, Anna Maria cried as if her heart would break. Mary had to come to us and led us on one side. When we passed by Albert's head, she made us bend down one by one and kiss his cold, marble brow. That kiss of death was as cold as the kiss of love is warm, and I wish I could forget it.

David was almost as white as his father's corpse when he stood up after imprinting a fierce abrupt kiss on Albert's brow. He came over to Anna Maria and me with bright unseeing eyes. As he joined us, four men stepped forward with the heavy lid of the coffin, put it in place, and began screwing it down with quick, business-like turns. A low moan broke from the people in the room, as if only now on hearing the harsh, hysterically purposeful turn of the screws, they accepted the finality of what had happened to Albert.

"Oh, Alex," David said in an awed tone. "How very angry those screws sound," and I confess I found "angry" even then a curious word to use.

That night after the funeral I had the first and most serious quarrel I ever had with David. It was not one of my making and before I knew what was happening I found myself in the midst of it.

We were standing, the three of us, disconsolate and aimless in the twilight at the Michaeljohn gate. The crowds who had packed the village for the funeral had dispersed and gone to their homes. A strange quiet and unusual lack of tension seemed to have descended on our street. We felt as children do when they suddenly walk out of a theatre where they have watched the most tense of dramas about Kings and Queens and great issues of life and death, and find themselves on a wet pavement with a long journey home before them and at the end of it the dreary task of doing their school homework.

"That was a terrific funeral," David said in that peculiarly preoccupied voice he had been using all day.

"It was tremendous!" we agreed.

"I think it is the biggest funeral the world has ever seen," he re-asserted with a certain aggressive emphasis.

"It is certainly the biggest we have ever seen," I said innocently.

"I tell you it is the biggest there has ever been," David insisted, determined to make his point. At this time both our homes were full of special numbers of the illustrated papers brought out at the time of King Edward's death and burial.

Before I had really thought it out, for I always said to David whatever came into my head, I remarked: "I don't think it was as big a funeral as the King's."

David instantly was possessed of a rage so uncharacteristic of him that I could only gape in amazement. With tears of anger streaming down his cheeks, he shrieked at me and the street in general:

"I tell you it is the biggest, the most important funeral the world has ever seen. How dare you be so insulting about my father's death. I won't speak to you again."

And with that he ran into the house.

CHAPTER 4

MMEDIATELY after Albert's death one became aware of a subtle sense of relief running through the Michaeljohns' impressive show of grief like a bright red silk thread in a skein of dark wool. The moment Albert was out of the house and in his grave, the atmosphere in David's home felt lighter. Mary's face, which long training had taught to assume so gracefully the expressions expected of it, perfectly fitted the part of the bereaved mother of seven, but we who knew her well noticed that she was more relaxed than we had ever seen her. The determined expression round her finely moulded mouth softened, the look of sensitive austerity was gentler, and the very tone she used when speaking to the children was warmed through with a new and living tenderness.

It was not that she felt no grief at all over Albert's death. A woman could not live with a man of Albert's quality for thirty years, bear him seven children and then not feel sad at his dying. But the grief she felt was human and general, rather than personal and particular. Her inmost self was hardly darkened by grief. On the contrary part of her deepest being experienced such a wild, barbaric upsurge of relief that it could find no frank and undisguised place in her conscious christian thinking, in the high-principled conception of herself by which she had lived and been upheld these thirty years. She could look the beautiful widow of a distinguished man, dignified and noble in grief for all the world to see and admire, and from which her daylight self too could take heart. But she was only technically a widow. She was in terms of the fundamental values of life and of her own special being, not a bereaved wife but the virgin mother of seven. Somewhere far down within her the drums had started to beat again.

The children, the servants, even the dogs and the cats in the household knew with instant intuition that some profound restraint had suddenly been abolished in Mary, and instinctively they readjusted themselves accordingly. With the inevitable exception of Anna Maria and David, they fell overnight into easier, more spontaneous relationships with their mother and with one another.

I was astonished on walking into the Michaeljohn household very early the day after the funeral to hear peals of laughter coming from the children's rooms. At first I thought they must have strange children staying with them because I had never heard Michaeljohn laughter like that before. It was real, undisguised laughter and to my amazement when I walked into the boys' room, there was Mary, lovely in a rich dressing-gown of royal purple, with a high, broad coachman's collar, upturned sleeves, and a belt of a fine cream wool, surveying a pillow-fight with the most benign and serene of countenances.

But David and Anna Maria reacted differently. I do not want to exaggerate, for after all they were children and young and impressionable and not immune to the prevailing spirit of the family. There were moments when it looked as if the current of the change flowed as smoothly through their lives as it did in those of the others; yet one was conscious of deep-seated reservations in both of them.

More sensitive than the others, they were more aware of the implications of the change in Mary. Anna Maria in her heart of hearts was terrified of what it could mean to her. I am sure she had no conscious image of her fear. How could a young girl of twelve, brought up in our community where mother love is taught as one of the infallible and sacred fundamentals of one's existence, think of Mary except in the highest and most flattering terms? Had anyone suggested to Anna Maria that she was afraid of her mother at this time, I am sure she would have laughed him to scorn. But the facts of our being are greater and more important than our conscious interpretations of them. They have a will and a way of their own which is more than a match for ours. One fact in this situation alone was of greater significance than all the graceful and dutiful preservation of the conscious decencies that went on ceaselessly in the Michaeljohn home.

Anna Maria had loved Albert in a way Mary never could, without qualification or reservation of any kind. She had got from him a delicate and imaginative response, such as her mother had never had. And Mary, at times, had deeply resented this. Anna Maria in every cell and nerve of her being felt her father's death as a personal bereavement of the bitterest kind. She not only failed to understand her mother's relief but also found it unforgivable. Anxiously she must have asked herself what it could mean. Hitherto she had taken her relationship with Mary very much for granted. Now it was as if the relationship had had its foundations removed and came toppling about her ears. And what was to take its place? Mary looked as if she had rediscovered within herself a real and living warmth for her daughter; she behaved as if she could be more generous and wished to draw her daughter closer into her own personal life as a fellow-sufferer and near-equal. Yet Anna Maria remained in spite of herself curiously on guard with her mother. The first sign of the final mask began to shadow that lovely, plastic, pliable and sensitive little face.

As for David, he continued to remain preoccupied. All that had been spontaneous and immediate in his relationship with Mary had already tended to disappear since that unforgettable Sunday. It became worse now. Yet when she was not with him, an unreasonable and almost unbearable anxiety about her seized his mind. If she went out and stayed away longer than expected he would hang round the front entrance of the house until he saw her approaching, and then, oddly, would go away without waiting to greet her. In her presence he seemed to cease from being a young boy and shrink into a kind of funny old man with the burden of the world and its guilt on his mind. At times his attitude to Mary would be one of a grave, resigned and melancholy responsibility. At others he was irritable and shrank under the most solicitous and affectionate touch of her hand on his shoulders. When he kissed her good-bye or good-night, he did so quickly and fearfully almost like someone committing a crime. That lovely, early morning quality, that bright and dewy innocence and up-fountain urgency of the David of our childhood had suddenly gone. It was as if a Paradise had been lost, and how was it to be regained? David was happy now only with me, or with my parents, and when Mary announced her decision to go away for a time David pleaded, and both mothers wisely agreed, for him to stay behind with me.

This sudden decision of Mary's to go away was characteristic of the change in her. No sooner had Albert's will been read than she announced with unpremeditated gaiety that she was going to give the whole family, servants and all, "a proper holiday" with part of the substantial fortune left her by Albert. I am sure that the phrase "proper holiday" reeks of its own underground cunning, that it was a diabolically contrived phrase to get past Mary's high-principled defences which otherwise would have rejected it. Nothing could sound more harmless and respectable than a "proper holiday".

Within a fortnight of Albert's death, a long cavalcade of Michaeljohns, their servants, and their pets set out on its ponderous journey to the far-distant coast. David and I stood at the gate in the twilight and waved them a glad good-bye while the large house behind us sagged suddenly under its own heavy emptiness.

Now David had always possessed one characteristic in common with Albert: a love of drawing, painting and all forms of visual art. Where so much was confused, wrong and obscure in the relationship of father and son, this interest ran true and straight and was a healing and living contact for both. The last present from Albert to his son, like the very first birthday present David could remember, was a magnificent box of paints. Not long after that dreadful Sunday Albert had come back from Fort White bearing this gift like a peace-offering to his son. He had been too shy and embarrassed to give it to David himself and had asked Mary to hand it over. After that he had not gone near David for some days but had watched him unobtrusively until one afternoon he saw him sketching alone on the veranda. He had then gone quickly, stood behind David and asked to see what he was doing. Father and son had a purely technical discussion on the subject of David's choice and after this tactful opening, diplomatic relationships were once more re-established.

One of my earliest memories is of David drawing and splashing paint on everything he could find. Most children, I know, go through a phase of this kind. But it was not a phase with David. It lasted and consolidated itself in his young life with every day he grew older. Very soon the outlines of an ordered and pre-determined design emerged from the chaos of scribbles and colours that stained the nursery paper and drawing books like a battle-field. At a very early age he astonished us all by beating the little negro boys at making clay models of animals. This achievement was so unusual that even the grown-ups in the village talked about it. It was a notorious fact that no white child could model in clay as well as the little black boys and girls. Every year after the rains groups of black and white children would gather on the edges of the pools in the vleis and dry-river beds and make toys out of clay. The black boys would quickly have clay wagons drawn by superb, long-horned oxen, beautifully-moulded and majestic in their stride and carriage; they would have whole hunting scenes in which great athletic figures armed with spears chased lion, eland, elephant, and gnu with flying tails. Besides this realistic and variegated achievement, the European children rarely produced more than a few lop-sided animals that toppled over when they put them in front of their wagons. As for wild animals, they rarely had any idea of how their limbs and heads fitted together. Even in modelling horses, which was the favourite subject of white children, the black boys excelled. But David stood out head and shoulders above them all. He used the clay with a tense but happy absorption as if it were a part of his own substance.

Albert, as I have indicated, took a real interest and delight in this unexpected talent of David's. His other children had interests conditioned entirely by their environment, but here was something which his European heart could understand and to which it could respond without reservation. He did everything he could to encourage David, in spite of Mary's disapproval, who wanted David to enter the Church and who in any case did not like him looking at all the paintings of nude females in the books in Albert's library.

It was a very fine library and Albert saw no harm in giving David a free run of its copiously illustrated books on the arts. Sometimes he would join us there and talk to us about art, well, intimately and with a rather moving nostalgic air, as if he were also addressing a receding image of himself. He knew the work and lives of the old Masters in great detail and always had an appropriate anecdote with which to adorn the illustrations before us. He would talk of the paintings he had seen in his youth in Europe. Above all he admired the Dutch Master, Rembrandt. He had an acute fellow-feeling for this painter, and as he neared his end his admiration increased until it became almost an obsession. He thought Rembrandt's self-portraits, and particularly the portraits of his old age, the greatest pictures ever painted. We found him several times with the large book of Rembrandt reproductions open on his knee, a glass of brandy by his side, staring with searching concentration at Rembrandt's last self-portrait, rather as I have since seen condemned people look at their own reflections before being taken out to their execution. One day, a little drunk, he exclaimed:

"See that! If ever you children want to know what a man who does 'what he would not' looks like, here is one! If you

want to know what it feels like to be old and to look and look
at yourself in a glass darkly and ask 'What the hell have I been
about?' and to get no answer, except to be told to go on and
on looking, here it is."

Many years later, talking of this occasion, David said to
me: "I could no more have put into words the feelings the
old man roused in me than fly. He was always filling me with
premonitions, forebodings and emotions far beyond my
experience and capacity for expression. But the odd thing is I
once tried to paint the effect he had on me. I painted an
immense dark green sea, with the sun just about to go down
into it. The sea was dead and still without the least vestige
of a movement. The rays of the sun shone on a foreshore dry
and bleached like the pearly white bones of an ancient skele-
ton. The foreshore was hemmed in by an immense cliff of
white chalk glowing like sulphur in the fading light. Beside
the sea, incongruous in a black frock-coat and a top-hat,
double normal size, walked my father slowly, deep in
thought. From his feet his shadow shot outwards with
terrific speed across the foreshore, up the cliff until it
dominated the scene like a giant many times Albert's size,
rampant, enraged, and about to crush him."

"Was that Albert?" I asked David, a light going up in my
mind.

"Of course it was Albert. Who else? But you don't mean to
say you remember it?" he asked amazed.

"Indeed I do!" I answered. "I used to call it 'Between the
devil and the deep green sea'. But I didn't know it was supposed to be Albert."

"So you did," said David meditatively. "So you did. A
very apt description it was too. Only I would remind you
the sea was dead."

He stopped, looked at me as if to make sure that the
significance of the deadness of the sea was as clear to me as to
him, and then added: "It would have been better really to
call it 'Between the devil and the deep dead sea'."

We make a great mistake when we think that people whose lives have been intimately woven into our own, cease to influence us when they die. While they are living they are to us, as Albert was to David, many things. But with death, change and colour are sealed off. The quintessential thing that they have been in our lives is fixed and stabilised for good. All the rest is discarded. The dead become part of the dynamics of our spirit, of the basic symbolism of our minds. They join the infinite ranks of the past, as vast as the hosts of the future, and so much greater than our own little huddle of people in the present. The dead become allied as it were to the gods themselves and walk in company with the favourites of gods, sail on the seas of our spirit from the beginning to the end of our time or else sit immobile and dark with frustrated love and hatred on some twilit and receding foreshore of our being.

No sooner was Albert buried and Mary and the children gone, than David began painting with a concentration and energy most unusual in one so young. Soon the nursery looked like a habitation of Africa's early rock-painting cave-dwellers. Its walls were a-flicker and aflame with the colour of game moving across it in our trembling sunlight. In this David was ostensibly continuing the natural, spontaneous interests of his childhood.

Yet I did not feel altogether comfortable about it. At the time I put it down to the fact that we suddenly neglected or dropped altogether so many other things we had loved doing before Albert died. For instance, it was most difficult now to get David to come out riding, to join me in our long excursions with fishing-lines and guns to the river, or to tramp the hills with our rifles and our expert and fond band of black boy hunters. He could hardly even be persuaded to come swimming. Of all his old interests, only his passion for painting and sketching really remained.

But looking back I would say it was more than that. What added to my depression was an instinctive warning that in a manner beyond understanding, David's young spirit had been invaded by something alien to it. He had been deprived of a vital part of his own special and personal freedom. However plausible and logical this air of naturalness appeared in the continuation of his old interest in painting, my instincts could not be deceived. An element of outside compulsion had entered it. It was almost as if painting had become a form of vital appeasement to him, as if he were hastening to avert some secret and sinister menace in his young life.

One painting that he did at this time stands in the forefront of my memory. I have it to this day. It is a picture of Albert's study empty except for its great tiers of books and heavy dark oak furniture. Yet the painting feels full of all sorts of presences. The room is painted a deep, brown darkness. David used it here for the first time but it ultimately presided like a permanent sort of back-cloth on the stage of his finest colour. The light against the one window shown suggests it is late afternoon of great, wide, golden richness; but the picture gives one the impression that the room resists the day, that it is content with its own, inward, subterranean glow. Only one shaft of light is allowed to enter the room and it falls on that small twilit world like a trumpet call, like the last post, on the silence at a graveside. It illuminates only three things; two chairs and the wide-open fire-place. In the honey-yellow stone of the fireplace is a pearl-grey pile of ashes. The two chairs near by are put side by side—as I have never seen them—and contemplate the ashes. They stand immediately in the centre of one's interest. One is a mediæval chair with a very long high back to it. It has a wide seat with high curved wooden arms. It is covered and cushioned with a dark red leather held in place by round bronze studs. The other chair is exactly the same except that its back is shorter and more rounded. The high-back chair was used only by Albert, the other was always given to Mary on the rare occasions when she visited him there. In that light the red of the leather is a deep, royal purple and the bronze studs are pure gold. The whole picture has a tense, concentrated quality of hidden and submerged drama. It was David's first picture and was an unusually mature revelation of the gift for which later he was to become so noted. He had a remarkable capacity for painting a subject as if it existed as much inside himself as without, as if its colour and light were part of the light and colour of his own urgent heart, as if he lived with his perceptions at a point in life where two inadequate and divorced halves become a rounded whole.

Yet the painting did not make me happy. The two empty chairs and the ashes on the hearth made me want to cry. To this day some of the sadness comes back to me when I look at the name that David gave it and printed underneath in his own hand, "The Throne Room". The letters are so meaningly fresh, innocent and inexperienced and the vision beside them looks as desperate, old and knowledgable as time itself. I wished then that David could have gone on painting the flame-flickering shapes of the prancing African antelope for ever.

CHAPTER 5

VERY soon, much too soon for us, spring changed into summer. Hot gusty winds came down from the hills and covered the gardens and sidewalks with the delicate petals and colours of fruit blossom. What might have been peaches with skins of yellow Chinese silk and cheeks of ruby, apricots like harvest moons and pears swinging in the shade like pearls at the ears of a Polynesian goddess, were trodden underfoot and blown away with the common dust. The whole look of the country hardened and everyone said that if the rain did not come soon, there would be precious little fruit, no harvest and even no meat.

Then one night lightning began to flicker along the horizon. It was most exciting to see the long electric flashes lashing and flickering like a serpent's tongue at the jagged, black line of the horizon. Every evening David and I climbed on to the roof of our house, as we had done every summer since I could remember, to see if the lightning was getting any nearer. But this year David seemed strangely reserved about this game which had hitherto been such a success.

One night we saw what we had so longed to see, not only lightning but also an immense, curled and plumed peak of thunder cloud sticking out in the brief gold illuminated sky, like Bartholomew Diaz's Cape of Storms in the blue Atlantic. I scrambled down a drain-pipe so fast that I tore the skin off my knees, and burst into the drawing-room with a glad shout: "It's coming! The rain's coming!"

I turned round and found that David had not followed me. I had to climb back on the roof to fetch him down. He was sitting there sombrely watching the lightning lashing out at the darkness. When I asked him what was the matter he answered me with an irritable: "Oh! Nothing! Nothing!"

and then instantly regretting it, stood up, took my arm, called me by the name he had recently given me and said in a gentler voice: "Nothing—Oh! Alexander the Great, why should there be anything? I was just thinking, I honestly don't know what."

We stood there for a moment, arm in arm, while a tremendous long flash of lightning, shot like the yellow cobra of Africa out of one black hole, wriggled in coils of fire along the horizon and darted down another dark hole of the night. David turned his back on it, and I thought a shiver went through him.

"You're not cold up here? You're not ill?" I asked him anxiously.

"Golly, no," he said, responding instantly to my concern. "Tell you what: shall we go out hunting to-morrow? Would you like it?"

"Can a duck swim?" I said, and with a happy heart went down to supper.

The morning broke bright but unbelievably sultry. As David and I and four of our chosen black companions climbed very early into the hills, the sweat burst quickly through our skins. By nine o'clock it felt as close and hot as it normally did at three. By ten o'clock we had not seen a buck, hare or beast of any kind except some rock-rabbits darting about like compact shadows in the shade of the rocks. But, so hot was it, that the snakes, lizards, scorpions, spiders, ants, and all the creeping and crawling things of the underworld were out in full force. Before the morning was over we had been forced to kill three jet black cobras with foam-white rings under their hooded and swaying heads, glistening like oil on sunlit water; one puff-adder, immobile and sparkling like a Maya necklace in the sun, and one twelve-foot mamba lashing the bushes as it came for us like a dark whirl of wind.

As we laid out the dead mamba to step-off its length, one of the black boys said to David: "We shall not see any buck to-day, Inkosan. It is too hot and they are all hiding in shel-

ter against the sun and the rain that is coming, big rain.
Look!"

He stood up and quickly flashed a long slender black arm,
with an ivory bangle round its wrist, from the north west-
wards to the south. I followed his arm round and as far as I
could see the clouds were astride the sky and riding the dark
horses of their shadows across the land with a desperate rein.

We there and then decided to make for home. But we had
been out since dawn and had a long way to go. Far away we
could just see the village huddled fearfully round the church.
It looked terribly exposed and small and defenceless against
the masses of twisting, turning cloud pouring down on it like
the last charge of the Valkyries. The scene excited the black
boys and me intensely. Rain now seemed a certainty. We
all shouted "Hurrah" when we heard the first roll of thunder.
But David did not join in the cheer. With a white and tense
look on his face, such as I had never seen before, he pressed
on silently beside me at such a pace that it was hard to keep
up with him. He seemed to be in the grip of some fierce but
nameless and incomprehensible agitation.

Soon it became obvious that we could not possibly reach
home before the storm broke. The sky in front of us was now
black from end to end. The sombre blue clouds had hidden
their flaming, spuming silver crests from us and merged into
one solid mass of darkness. Lightning flamed and flashed in
this deepening gloom incessantly and the sound of thunder
was now continuous. So we decided to make for the nearest
shelter, an abandoned cattle outpost. We had just tumbled
almost breathless on top of one another into the hut when
there was a vivid flash of lightning as if the sun itself had split
in two, and an immense whip-like crack of thunder followed
by a deep bass roll that seemed to rattle the rocks on the hills
like pebbles on a gale-pounded beach. At the same moment
the rain came down like machine-gun bullets in the dust
around the hut.

"Auck! Inkosan!" one of the black boys said to me, his

dark eyes wide and bright with excitement. "That one was close. I can still smell it." He sniffed significantly at the air, and added, "It struck that little hill at the back here. Afterwards we can go and find its stone and make great medicine."

But I hardly listened to him, although it was one of the dreams of our childhood to find this thunderstone of which the black people continually spoke and by whose magic properties they swore. As the roll of thunder died away and in the brief interval before another as vivid and vast took its place, I had heard a strange, strangled, sobbing sound behind me. There was David, on his knees, deathly white, his hands folding tightly in prayer, saying in a voice which was shaken with involuntary sobs and which did not seem to belong to him: "Dear Father in Heaven, please spare me to-day. Please save me, for Jesus Christ's sake. Please forgive me. Please spare me, for Jesus Christ's sake. Please forgive my sins. Please spare me."

I had been with David in many storms worse than this one. I had experienced nothing to prepare me for seeing David like this and I was amazed and distressed beyond words. For the hour and a half of the storm's duration he continued like this on his knees until his voice was quite hoarse and croaking. When a sudden gleam of faint, watery sunlight at the entrance of the hut at last convinced him that the storm was over, he turned a twisted face to me and said with profound conviction: "God has been good to spare us to-day."

Worrying and perplexing as this incident was to me, a fortnight later something happened which was even harder to understand. David and I and the same four black boys decided to repeat our hunting expedition to the hills. It was a lovely sunny day, fresh, unoppressive without wind or a cloud in the sky. We walked on happily and briskly for some miles, when a frightened gasp at my side made me look at David. He had stopped dead in his tracks, was white and trembling and asked in a tense voice: "Oh, God, Alex! Did you see that?"

"No! What, David?" I said, instantly catching the fear in his voice and nervously looking round at our feet for snakes.

"That flash of lightning," he said.

"What?" I asked, not believing my own ears.

"That flash of lightning," he repeated in a watchful, apprehensive tone.

"Nonsense, Davie," I answered with a laugh, feeling much relieved. "Look at the sky, little old one! There's not a cloud in it. How could there be such a thing?"

"I tell you I distinctly saw the most terrific flash of lightning," David said fiercely, trembling at the knees. "Have you never heard of a bolt from the blue?"

He was so obviously sincere, and his fear was so real, that a cold shiver of apprehension went through me. Just for a moment the hair on the back of my neck tingled as the light morning air touched it. But a look up at the sky reassured me. It was a deep, serene and empty blue. High above us hung an eagle, almost motionless, swaying lightly and confidently on some fine-spun silk of the air like a spider at the end of its own cord.

"Oh, don't be such a chump, Davie!" I began, but before I could finish, anger and confusion at his inability to account even to me or himself for the vivid vision he had just seen added so much to his agitation that he thrust his rifle with a harsh "Here!" into the hands of one black boy, turned round, and started running for home as if the devil were after him.

To this day I can see his slim, athletic figure, streaking for home, the dust exploding round his heels and that immense, calm, indifferent and uncommitted blue sky making a mockery of the fear that was driving him.

The memory too has reproach in it for me. I still feel a poignant reproach for the chagrin I then felt, for my own lack of understanding, and my helplessness in the face of this fear so irrationally inflicted on David. With all to-day's wisdom I can see so clearly how terrible it must have been for David to wake up one day and find that what had been to him, for

years, a welcome and blessed phenomenon of nature, overnight
had become a monstrous force bent on his own personal
destruction.

Yet what can we do about the irrational fears of others,
particularly the fears of those we love? Officially we can
refuse to recognise them in the hope that one day this refusal
together with the example of our own lack of fear will banish
them for ever. This I did intuitively. I never tried to talk
about the incident to David and he never seemed to feel the
need to mention it to me. This, indeed, was another curious
aspect of this strange, new fear of David's. Once the thunder
and lightning were gone from the sky, his fear fell from him
like a discarded old coat, seeming to leave no memory behind.

It was as if David's inner sovereignty did not extend to every
part of himself; as if part of him was ruled by some alien
power which made its own laws and governed itself without
reference to the laws and the rule of his general being. This
autonomy existed inside him in its own secret and powerful
right and there was nothing he could do against it.

David made a valiant stand against all this. He acquired
subconsciously, as some epileptics do, a technique for concealing his disability from the world, of manœuvring his life
so that when the storm broke, there was always some corner
into which he could go for shelter, creeping like a sick dog
into a dark corner, while the spasm lasted. Only I knew from
the way in which his eyes automatically scanned the sky, daily
appraising the portents of wind, clouds and rings round the
moon, that the rule of the dark invader persisted. This dark
invader waited only on thunder and lightning to leave his
shelter and sally forth to attack David's integrity.

CHAPTER 6

YET for all these dark and inexplicable shadows, David and I were very happy that summer. I don't think we have ever been closer to each other. Then almost before we knew summer had begun the last fruit had been gathered, the harvest was in, and the water-furrows filled with dead leaves. The nights closed in rapidly. Bats vanished from our twilight hour, the glow-worms were extinguished in the hedges and the fire-flies withdrew their quick, red stitches from the heavy folds of evening.

We were glad as one letter after another came from Mary postponing her return. "The holiday was doing them all so much good," she wrote, "that it would be wicked to cut it short. If my mother did not mind having David longer, she would extend the holiday for another month or three." Of course, my mother did not mind and I believe Mary might well have continued the holiday indefinitely, if an alarming communication from Albert's trustees finally had not brought her back in a hurry.

On paper Albert had left Mary and the children close on £200,000. He had always conducted his own affairs himself and had never discussed them with Mary, the children, or even his closest friends. Business in our community was exclusively a male concern and it would never even have occurred to Mary to ask Albert for information as to how both his and her own affairs were going. Like everybody else she assumed that all was well, and Albert had not the least difficulty in keeping his business affairs entirely to himself. But now his trustees, trying to establish the current value of his assets, were shocked first into a state of angry unbelief and then, reluctantly, into acceptance of the grim truth.

For the past twelve years, ever since his last will was made,

72

Albert had been living on capital. As they examined one bank account after the other, one stock exchange transaction after the other, it was only too easy to see how he had acquired his reputation as a public benefactor. On top of that he had been more than generous to his own family. He had never stinted them or grudged them either money or luxury. But by far the greatest portion of his fortune had been expended on the strangest and most prodigal bequests.

The picture of Albert's state of mind conjured up by this record of fantastic finances left the trustees so shaken that one of them said openly: "He must have been mad." Another, putting it differently, said: "It looks almost as if Albert set out deliberately to ruin himself, for if a man had ever intended to leave the world as naked as he entered it he could not have done it better than Albert." The truth, which this trustee so unwittingly uttered, is so great and conclusive that really it cannot be improved upon. I would only add that financially the last years of Albert's life were of a piece with his emotional and spiritual design. His submerged deliberation to be in the last half of his life the opposite of what he had been in the first, perhaps concealed such a powerful and precise purpose that only death, with a sinister logic, came when this purpose had been fulfilled down to the last material detail.

Fortunately for Mary and the children, her own vast inheritance from her father was intact. Albert had been unable to lay his hands on the immense lands of the de Beauvilliers family. For the time being however Mary had seven children to educate and was without ready money; though her trustees assured her that with proper management of her own property, the situation would gradually right itself. They emphasised, however, that not a day was to be lost, and so Mary came home to attend to urgent and exacting affairs for which she was untrained and unaccustomed.

They arrived late one afternoon in the winter. A cold wind blew dust and crackling dead leaves down the street. Although our hearts were beating fast with excitement, not untinged with a vague but painful anxiety, David and I shivered with cold as the sound of the urgent pounding of horses' hooves, and the noise of carriage wheels turning the corner at the top of the street, brought us running to the gate.

Mary stepped out first with inevitable almost incredible grace. She looked as fresh and beautiful as if she had been on a fashionable afternoon's outing instead of a week's journey. She had on a long, warmly-glowing black fur coat and a small, close-fitting black fur hat with a light, delicate veil which shielded half of her face. Her pearl brooch seemed to find a sheen of reflected glory on the glowing, dark surface of the fur. The cold had brought out the colour in her cheeks and, as she came towards us, she made the afternoon look spiteful and mean and our street dingy and small. Cold as it was, the face that bent down to kiss David and me was wonderfully warm and alive. We had not been mistaken. The change had been real and she had continued to mellow and to become a softer and gentler person.

David could not take his eyes off her. As she began to give directions to the servants and to the rest of the family still wrapped in rugs inside the coach, his eyes followed her round with a look of desperate and poignant concentration. He looked at her as one might look at a being from another world whose essential experience one could never share or understand; from whom, in fact, one was set apart by the shadow and fear of lightning and thunder in the sunlight, and the vision of two empty chairs by a burnt-out fire in an empty room.

As for Mary, I saw her just for a moment look disconcerted and robbed of her graceful defences. She was staring at the Michaeljohn home and a light of fatally wounded unbelief came into her eyes. She murmured to herself like someone who has just seen in concrete form for the first time something she had been dreaming of for years: "It is true then; this really is what it looks like."

The change in Anna Maria was even more striking. In her absence she had become a young woman. She had acquired

74

youngness, had been born at last into the uneasy youngness of
our existence in the world of to-day. She was dressed like a
younger edition of her mother, and the black of her clothes
in the bleak light brought out something set and severe in the
expression of her lovely face and its delicate and sensitive
features.

While an amiable, beaming and benignly enlarged Edward
George in the background looked on, she fell on David's neck,
gave a cry that was a little too spontaneous and said: "Oh,
David! It's been such an age! How absolutely marvellous to
see you!" And she kissed him with an appearance of warmth
such as she would never have allowed herself before.

It was too good to be true, and it was true in a way that was
not good. My heart was filled with dismay. For years I had
longed for Anna Maria to be able to feel for David all that
that embrace implied. But I would have preferred the old,
strange, inexplicable but honest hostility to this slick and deft
concealment. Anna Maria had crossed the frontiers of our
wood-fire and lantern-lit antiquity and passed into the grown-
up world of calculation and deliberation, of graceful and
infinitely intelligent pretence. She had learnt to hide her feelings, to dissimulate and to pretend. The shadow of the
Michaeljohn secrecy was welling up slowly from far back in
the light of her eyes. And in that moment of welcome in the
cold wind and the dust by the gate David and I too seemed to
be dragged across the ancient frontier after Anna Maria. Our
childhood died round us like the light of a long white candle
whose swaying tree of flame is suddenly cut down by a clumsy
hand. We were left at the mercy of a panther of shadow.

That night my mother looked sadly at David's empty place
at our table.

As I lay outside, alone in my bed, on the stoep and watched
battalion after battalion of armed and pointed stars go by,
just as I had watched them a year before with David at my
side, I cried bitterly out of loneliness and growing apprehension.

PART II

The Flight

CHAPTER 7

MARY MICHAELJOHN, as I might have known from her remark on the afternoon of her return and from the look she gave her old home, did not stay in it long. One quick glance and David's home stood condemned as surely and irrevocably as if sentence had been passed on it by an implacable and disillusioned old judge in a criminal court of appeal.

Mary did, however, produce the best and most intelligent of reasons for abandoning it. Three sons, she pointed out, were already at universities, a fourth was about to go, and very soon even Anna Maria would have gone as far as the village school could take her. She was too poor now, Mary said, to afford to pay for all their school and university fees as well as their board and lodging. The sensible thing would be to set up home for them all in Fort White where every conceivable educational facility was available.

All this sounded plausible enough, though a critic bent on quarrelling with her reasoning might well have pointed out that her financial difficulties were only temporary and that properly managed the broad de Beauvilliers lands would soon give her an ample income for all her needs. But to most people in our community her argument made good sense and was regarded as yet another justification of the esteem in which Mary was publicly held.

The real opposition to Mary's decision, much to her apparent surprise, came from within the family itself. For once Anna Maria, David and Edward George joined forces to oppose their mother. The elder children appeared indifferent but these three fought their mother with every weapon that children can use against their parents; they argued, pleaded, wept, sulked and even went off their food. For days they would deliberately suppress the laughter which rose so naturally and constantly to the surface of young and resilient spirits.

Anna Maria in particular took it badly. It was as if, instinc-

79

tively, she felt the decision to be a decisive personal defeat. She had not realised since Albert's death how much she had looked forward to her departure for boarding school. She wanted to get away from Mary, though she had no desire to change her home. She looked on boarding school as an unavoidable necessity, a form of escape in exile to be redeemed by moments of delicious return at the holidays. Now, in one swoop of Mary's, both escape and return were dead; and years of close, vigilant domination and rule by her mother stretched out cheerlessly before her. There were bitter and violent scenes between mother and daughter. Anna Maria conducted her opposition to her mother's plans so thoroughly that Mary, at moments, was very nearly in tears, and moved to complain of the ingratitude and lack of understanding of her selfish children.

Then there was one terrible scene when Mary came home late one night from a meeting with the church council, apologised sweetly for having kept them from their dinner and added, almost casually: "But it was rather important. I've persuaded the church to buy this property. They are going to turn it into an orphanage, and pay us a good price for it."

There was no pretence about the shock this news, so lightly imparted, gave her family. The question of selling the house had hitherto not been mentioned nor, for that matter, even suspected. Everybody had assumed that Mary would let the house until her duty by her children's education was accomplished, and that ultimately she would once more re-establish it as a permanent home and base for children and grand-children.

Anna Maria, without hesitation believing the worst of Mary, was up-in-arms at once. Caught off her careful guard, her eyes flashed fire and tears simultaneously. In a voice bright and true as the blade of a sword, she called out with indignant conviction: "What a damnable and wicked thing to do!"

Mary, like most people who live by principle and a clear conception of their public and collective duties, could stand almost anything except having her goodness questioned and she promptly ordered Anna Maria to her room. But before leaving, the young woman, standing there in the half-light of her new and desperate youngness with tears falling down her cheeks, took courage from her despair, stamped her foot at her mother and cried repeatedly: "I wish I was dead! I wish I was dead!" The nature of her cry was unmistakable. The technique is as old as life itself. Wherever there is powerlessness, oppression and deep-rooted fear, human beings make themselves the subjects of wishes they dare not inflict openly on those who cause their fear and impotence. Since the wish is too urgent and too powerful to be repressed its involuntary begetters are forced to parade themselves also as its victims. Mary's noble and dignified mind saw in Anna Maria's behaviour only the most reprehensible lack of respect to a conscientious mother doing a difficult and painful duty. But her instincts could not be deceived. "She means, of course, that she wishes *you* were dead," they drummed in Mary's blood.

I saw her look at Anna Maria as she had not done since those evenings when in the soft light of an old lamp by the fire Albert took his daughter on his knees and, with a tender and inapprehensible longing, stroked her hair until her head ached under his hand. Then she said tightly: "I wish I were, *were* dead, Anna Maria! Now go to your room!"

The rest of the family, however, were prepared to give Mary the benefit of the doubt with regard to the selling of the house, and said, simultaneously, in voices that were both questions and denials: "You're joking, Mother? You don't really mean it?"

But Mary, her composure and sweetness quickly returning now that she was alone with her sons, explained her reasons patiently and at length, with many an expression of the heart-ache and anguish that the cruel necessity for such a step caused her. Too wise to spoil her case with tears, they yet welled close enough to the surface and gave her deep, finely rounded grey eyes a most moving and eloquent brightness.

She had no difficulty in convincing the children she was in earnest. The fact of what she had done was plainer even than her words and clearly revealed the depth of her determination in the matter. The agitation of utter despair seized the younger ones. For the first time I saw Edward George cry as if his heart would break. But the elder ones had already rallied to their mother's side, the placid eldest son saying: "It's a drastic thing to do but I'm sure Mother has extremely good reasons for it. She'd never do what is not right."

David, once the uselessness of rebellion had become clear to him, took the decision very quietly. His problem differed so much from that of the others. They, after all, were losing only one home: whereas he was losing two. His own personal panic over the step Mary was about to take was due almost entirely to the realisation that it meant separation from me and my mother and father. Technically his home was with Mary, but his real home had always been with us. Indeed, if it had been only a question of giving up his Michaeljohn home I do not think he would have shed a tear. Provided he could have stayed either with me or near to me, he would have been content. Part of him, the real, living, warm, creative essence of him so deeply and darkly circumscribed in the obscurities and icy circumspections of the Michaeljohn home, had long since started to strain away as the first instinctive step in a struggle for survival. That large house now sombre with a valedictory and condemned air, had long since lost a true and living meaning for him. What meaning it possessed in the past was dark and obscure and what little of it emerged into the daylight of his and my understanding was not much to our liking. It stood always behind one, trying to hold one at the edge of a black and pooled moment in time where one waited, inarticulate and powerless, for the dark waters to give up some criminal secret. For how could David give up a secret that was not his, and confess to a crime he had not done? How could he provide the key to a knowledge that he did not know he possessed?

But, young as he was he knew, because of the life at stake within him, that he had really come to an end, not only with his home and its associations, but also with the individual members of his family. Young as I was, I knew it too because I loved him.

If there is one telling image inherited from the past that causes much fatal, cynical and ironical misunderstanding it is the image of the blindness of love. If there is one thing love is not, it is blind. If it possesses a blindness at all, it is a blindness to the man and the mind-made blindnesses of life; to the dead-ends, the cul-de-sacs and hopelessnesses of our being. In all else it is clear and far-sighted as the sun. When the world and judgment say: "This is the end," love alone can see the way out. It is the aboriginal tracker, the African bushman on the faded desert spoor within us, and its unfailing quarry is always the light.

Because I loved David I knew things on his behalf that I did not know nearly so well for myself. I knew that whatever contribution fate had intended Mary, Albert, Anna Maria, and the rest of them to make to one another's lives, whatever courses and permanent influences it had wanted established, these had now been made. Little that was new and creative could come out now from that family relationship. It could add to its own massive quantity but its creative qualities were exhausted. Like actors who had learnt their parts its members could now only continue to repeat their lines endlessly whilst getting relentlessly older. Their audiences alone could be renewed and refreshed, unless, of course, someone in the family could break free.

But breaking free is not just a matter of walking out of one's home and slamming the door behind one. One does not walk out so easily from the house, the solid and cunningly fortified building, the labyrinthine court-yard that the family has built in the mind, spirit and emotions, in the very sinews, nerves and reflexes of its members. It may not even always be desirable that one should do so.

In my own case, I have never been tempted to try. My home was as pure a structure of love as simple, unpretentious flesh and blood could make it. But there are so many houses of the mind which are not homes and fortresses, but cages and prisons of the living spirit. These prisons have long, winding corridors and deep cells and dungeons from which one must escape unless, like Albert, one is to become one's own gaoler. Indeed, this breaking down of prison doors, this riding forth to build one more warming fire against the storm and greater darknesses, is perhaps one of the more truly heroic tasks of life, for which the enduring spirit is allied to our frail and impermanent flesh and blood. For without it, life might so easily stand still and fail itself. It might fail because by standing still it forfeits the great, blessed, uncomfortable but heroic privilege of life which is to create beyond our immediate natures.

I do not pretend that David and I were conscious of all these considerations at the time. I am writing of a period nearly thirty years ago and I obviously have a knowledge and an experience to-day which I did not then possess. Yet the past itself still lives inside me. I have only to look at something David painted at that time, or to find myself in my garden on an afternoon with the nostalgic prattle of the wind in dry and barren tree-tops and the clanking twang of windmills beating a lugubrious rhythm to the contracting moment, and the original emotion assails me with the old freshness and violence.

Within three months of Mary's return, the Michaeljohn home was turned into an orphanage, and the whole family packed off to Fort White in such a hurry that Albert's grave was abandoned in the churchyard just as the grave-diggers had left it on the day of the funeral, heaped up with the dark-red earth of Africa which was so foreign to his initial self, and with the same withered and leafless wreaths covering it. It stayed like that until my father, to forestall a scandal, had it put in conventional order.

Henceforth I only saw David in the longer vacations from school which he was allowed to spend with me. We never had any difficulty in resuming our relationship where we had last left off. In fact these separations seemed to add meaning, intensity and a growing precision to the feelings which united us. Our moments together were all the more precious to me because I knew instinctively with each return of David's that all too soon the time was coming when we would be parted for much longer than we had ever been.

He now never mentioned Anna Maria to me unless I asked him about her. One would have thought from his behaviour that she was locked out of his mind for good, and consciously; indeed this may have been so. But judging by his reaction to any mention of her name I knew that in the characteristic Michaeljohn manner she had merely been driven underground, and that the sum total of her miscarried relationship with David sent out its influences like thieves in the night to raid the resources of his being.

But of Mary he spoke to me more and more and even asked advice of my father and mother. I do not suggest that these discussions represented the totality of the experience and knowledge of Mary in him. I should say they were no greater indication of the whole than the top of an iceberg above the water is indicative of the bulk underneath. And on the surface of their relationship David and Mary were almost entirely concerned with an open conflict that had broken out between the two and which was daily becoming more acute.

Mary had finally decided on educating David for the Church. She had always talked vaguely about this but she had not raised it as a matter of parental policy until immediately after our Black Sunday. It is an amazing example of the loyal tribute we pay to the duality which rules us by dividing us against ourselves, that Mary did not dare produce a decision already formed until she had found some plausible external circumstance to sponsor it. The incident of the golden sovereign at once set her off reasoning with Albert that only a life dedicated to the Church could save David from the complexities of this manifest waywardness of his nature. Albert, whose indifference to the Church increased daily towards his end, was hardly an enthusiastic supporter of the idea. Besides, the only thing that he really understood in David was the boy's desire to paint, so the most Mary could obtain from him was a weary and disillusioned neutrality.

But the moment he was dead and she assumed full charge of the family, her approach to the matter quickened. Her discussions with David, which started in a loving suggestion, quickly became an urgent plea, then a determined order, and finally an uncompromising ultimatum. Mary produced the most convincing arguments why David should do as she wished. All her charm, her intelligence, the immense prestige she had in her family and our world, her reputation for goodness and unselfishness, were deeply committed in this battle with her son. The knowledge that she herself had unwaveringly practised what she now preached lent an aggressive ardour to her convictions in the matter. The choice before him quickly became, in her mind, a choice between absolute good and unqualified evil. She found instant proof of the sinister content of his motives in the fact that ultimately his argument amounted to no more than that he wanted to paint, had always wanted to paint, was happy painting, while he never had any desire to enter the Church and was filled with a bleak and wintry despair by his experience of organised religion in our community.

Words like "want" and "desire" alone were enough to fan the flame of Mary's resolution into a leaping fire. No one could question the burning sincerity of her stand, but what interests me to-day is not her sincerity but the extent to which her attitude was rounded and complete. Which of two relevant aspects of reality, (and I say "which" because clearly they were not joined), had the greater weight in the attitude she adopted: the one she consciously proposed or the one of which she was totally unaware? To what extent did David have any individual rights in the argument? How far were his peculiar and unique needs honoured? What validity was granted to his nature, so different and distinct from the others?

To the first of these questions I would answer that the unfulfilled and rejected Mary decided the matter. I am certain that David, merely by "wanting" to do something for no other reason than that he loved doing it, at once turned himself into a fresh battleground for the ancient campaign in Mary. In his person she fought again the fight between herself, her family, and the community when she had had to choose between Albert and Pierre. How could she let David have his way without repudiating her choice? How let him win without defeating what she had become? She did not know that though we can cheat and defeat ourselves we cannot cheat and defeat life.

To this day I marvel that David managed in the next few years to hold out day after day against Mary's determined onslaught. I wonder if he would have been capable of standing firm, considering so much that was fearful and obscure within himself, were it not that he was able to escape to us for the long vacations. On arrival he was usually a tense, nervous, exhausted person. He would regard my father and mother with a searching, wary, and stricken look as if he fully expected them to have changed in his absence. But as a rule one night was enough to reassure him, and to set all the happy associations of his childhood with us in motion in his mind and heart like the white sails of a ship being shaken out on the metalled edges of the doldrums before the first blue ripple of the South Atlantic trades. Being loved purely for himself had the most healing effect on his spirits, and were it not for the thunder storms of summer, and the steep, angled memories of Anna Maria and Mary always so close to the surface of his mind, one would not have thought he had a problem or care in the world. It was only as the day of his return to Fort White drew near that one saw disquiet creep over him like the shadow of a hail cloud over a field of ripening corn.

87

"Aunt Fraser, do you think Mary hates me?" he asked my mother suddenly one night before his return home.

My mother had just done his packing for him, and we were all four sitting by the fire with its light and warmth like a da Vinci halo about us.

"Of course she does nothing of the kind," my mother answered with such instant and emphatic conviction that I knew at once that the thought must have often been debated in her own mind. From the way in which my father looked at her over his pipe, I was certain that he, too, had been deeply concerned in the question.

"Then why must she pick on me for the Church?" David said with rising agitation. "Why won't she let me be what I want? She doesn't mind what the others do."

"There's another explanation you would do well to remember, David," my mother said. "She may care more about what happens to you than to the others." Then as David looked up with quick amazement, she added: "No, I'm not saying it just on the spur of the moment; I've often thought of it." She turned to my father and asked if he did not agree with her.

He answered her indirectly in a typically country, masculine fashion.

"Don't think you have to worry about your mother's love for you, Davie," he said slowly: "I think you're taking a fence before you've come to it. You still have a couple of years before you have to make a choice. Why not just go on quietly as you are?"

My father's advice to David was as good and sound as advice could be, and it comforted and reassured him. But the situation needed something more than advice, and came to a head sooner than any of us expected.

When David came to us on the very next vacation at the end of the year, he brought the news that the issue could be postponed no longer. He had just written his final school examination. He had thought that he would automatically

88

go now to a university as his brothers had done. But the day before he left Mary had had a long talk to him—a talk which ended in a heated quarrel. She made it quite plain that, unless he undertook to enter a theological seminary on obtaining a university degree, she was not prepared to send him to a university. That, in her opinion, would be a sheer waste of money. Painting and music were all very well, but they had to be kept firmly in their place if they were not to lead one to the devil. He was over eighteen now and the time had come when he should put away childish things and childish desires, think less of what he liked to do and more of what he should and ought to do—less of selfish, egotistical things and more of his duty, of what he owed God, the community and his mother.

The word "mother" issued from her lips reluctantly, with an almost apologetic diffidence, and two tears gathered in the corners of her wide, grey eyes. Had she burst into tears it would not have been one tenth as effective. It was almost as if she knew with an infallible instinct what would affect the artist in the boy.

David was at once in a panic of agitation, of violent and confused feelings. Suddenly he felt mean and ugly inside himself. He might well have capitulated if Mary had not made the mistake of taking his hand and, putting the other arm round him, trying to draw him towards her. The spontaneous, involuntary, instinctive shrinking from her physical touch that had remained with David ever since Albert's death immediately caused him to hold back.

I remember so clearly, when David told me this, that a feeling of awe, a sense of the miraculousness of our physical bodies came over me. They contain a kind of living wisdom which expresses itself directly in instantaneous action. My own mind, to this day, finds itself humbled in the recollection of this scene between Mary and David.

In trying to draw David towards herself and hold him there as if he were indeed part of herself Mary, without knowing it, exposed the whole of her case. That gesture was spontaneous, complete and final. But it differed fundamentally from the long, eloquent and emotional appeal she had just made to David. His own body instantly recognised the gesture for what it was, and he was saved not by his mind, spirit, or his heart, all three of which were infinitely troubled, but by an involuntary and slight shrinking of his own flesh and blood from the touch of her hand.

As Mary felt this physical hesitation and withdrawal, her own arm withdrew itself quickly and dropped to her side. A cold, bleak anger fell upon her and she was gripped by an icy determination.

"I see," she said with a long automatic sigh: "I might as well be talking to a stone as to this ungrateful son of mine. You've always been awkward, and pigheaded, and tried to be different from the rest. But you'll have to learn that you can't be a law unto yourself unless you want to come to a bad end."

"You're being horribly unfair, Mother," David interrupted, distressed and angry at the same time. "I've never tried to be different, I've never tried to be anything. . . . I don't understand how and why you say these things to me."

David's interruption merely served to inflame Mary's anger. "No! You never know anything," she said in a keen and biting tone. "But how d'you explain that you never do or want to do what the rest of the family does? How d'you explain that? You're different from the rest. Everybody else is guided by their mother."

"I don't know, honestly, Mother," David answered meekly, rebuked and humbled by the picture Mary had drawn of the gulf between him and the rest of the family. "Am I so different? I've never tried to be. We're none of us alike and I didn't know I was more different from the others than they are from me. If I am, I can't help it. It just happened to . . ."

David was not allowed to finish his sentence. Mary looked for a second as if she might really lose all control over herself. With a strange, ventriloquist's voice that seemed to come not from her lips but from a point deep inside herself, she said:

"It just happened! I know of something else that just happened to you too. What about my golden sovereign? There are far too many of these 'just happeneds' to you and if I'm not careful there'll be more. . . . I'd be neglecting my duty as a mother if I indulged you further. You either give me your promise to go into the Church—or you must go out into the world and earn your own living."

Mary looked at him as if expecting an immediate answer, her eyes bright with a concentrated and determined intent. She stood with her back to a window of the drawing-room which gave on to the veranda and the garden, at this moment washed and luminous with light and purring with a summery contentment like a lion cub in the sun.

Desperately David looked past her. He felt quite incapable of meeting that look of infinite and fathomless concentration. He behaved as if some instinct warned him that this were a supernatural moment in which one glance of his mother's, taken squarely in the centre of his own wide-open and defenceless eyes, would turn him to stone.

All he knew was that he had no real understanding of what was happening between them. His own clouded heart was putting questions at such a pace that he would need a lifetime to think out their true answers. Yet the response to the question which Mary was forcing on him now depended on these very answers. Why above all, it pressed bitterly on him, was she trying to pin him down to one moment on a Sunday in her bedroom, just as a collector might try to pin to the dead boards of a glass case a butterfly with wings still a-flutter and fresh with the colours of the bow of God's first great covenant with man against the flood waters of earth and sky? Why anoint that particular moment king above all others? What an abuse of sovereignty.

"Royal sovereign." "Sovereignty." . . . He repeated the phrases to himself and then realised with grim, inarticulate humour that he was making puns out of the incident. Instantly the thought flashed through his mind that this whole scene between him and Mary, this painful and weirdly charged moment, was not what it appeared and pretended to be; it too was a kind of pun—but a pun in three, four, five, and as many other dimensions as there were to circumscribe the totality of being. Could it be that Mary really was not honest either with herself or him, and was merely using the ostensible moment and meaning of the occasion to serve some hidden value of her own, rooted in some other cherished time and place of which he was not aware?

The ground seemed to be opening in a widening crack at his very feet. He was convinced that he was somewhere deeply at fault for having dared to question, even for a second, the honesty and reality of the good, true and beautiful Mary.

He continued to stare, deep in thought, out of the window, oblivious of the impatience that was beginning to creep over Mary at his continued silence. But how little mere thinking helps a soul in trouble. What a wayside mongrel it can be, running the length of the threatened kingdom of our being, barking at one master-instinct after another, sniffing at the trees of our natural selves for the scent of a bitch it can tumble, or whining at the back-door of our first warm-lit emotion.

As David stood, bewildered and quite incapable of knowing what the situation demanded, a slight movement outside the window caught his eye and distracted his frantic thinking. From the grape-vine which covered the trellis above the veranda, a black spider, half-a-crown in size, was letting itself down, midnight hand over hoary fist, on a thread, delicate and silver with light. As it descended it swung itself round deliberately from side to side with a pendulum-like rhythm, peering from end to end about it, like some hunchbacked pirate looking for a firm mooring on which to fasten the silken hawsers of his craft.

Though there was a window of oval, shadowy glass between them, David watched it with such intense and apprehensive interest that he did not hear Mary say: "I'm waiting, David. Speak up! Can't you . . ."

She got no answer. Looking more closely into his eyes, she saw their preoccupied expression and said: "I don't believe you've been listening to a word I've been saying!"

David became aware of her again. He answered in abstracted tones: "I'm so sorry, Mother. I was thinking over what you said when I saw that spider coming down, and it sort of fascinated me. It looked so pretty with the light on it, like the light on black silk, and yet . . ."

That was the end of their talk. Mary had turned quickly as he spoke and seen the spider. She seemed to find it the last straw. Instantly her anger knew no bounds.

"My God! A spider!" she exclaimed with outraged amazement. "I pour out my heart to you and all you can do is to stand there gaping at spiders! It's too much. I'll reason with you no longer. You've got until the end of your holidays to decide." And with that she swept, like the tail-end of a gale, with an angry flail-like swish of her clothes, straight out of the room.

"It was bad luck that damned spider turning up just then," David told us. "For it really seemed to finish everything. She refused to talk to me again, and would hardly say good-bye. I really don't know what I've done to deserve such an unlucky coincidence."

David was right in a sense, of course, in calling the spider an unlucky coincidence. But was that really the whole of the story? I know so well that garden of the Michaeljohns'. At that time of the day and in that season it is full of pregnant and colourful incident. There are flamboyant acacias and purple jacarandas wherein golden orioles with bamboo-flute voices sing phoenix-like amid the fire and smoke of their blossom. Black sunbirds turn scarlet and blue and green as the dark are of their flight across the sunlight draws together the tasselled tips of two trembling tree-tops like the ends of a Macedonian bow. Green-gold honey-suckers flash long, delicate curved beaks like Saracen swords over purple and crystal grapes large and heavy with increase. Below a crimson vortex of roses, dove-toned carillons of lilies, fierce flutters of cannas, the aching bosoms of plump hydrangeas, rocketing agapanthus and shrieking strelitzia call down the prodigal blue of the sky as a garden of coral, swinging calmly at the centre of the tide, calls the storm-tossed Pacific above. The air from the beat of translucent wings of bees and insects bound with officious ostentation on the lawful occasions of their summer, hisses with the faint contented effervescence of champagne. The shadows themselves lie close and secure among the trees like a rich wine from which the sunlight rises and bursts out in golden bubbles over the purple surface. Why then, I am forced to ask myself, if coincidence were all, why with all this to choose from, did those observant eyes of David, so in love with sunlight and colour, remain fixed on this one dark and questing spider? Did we but know the answer to that question we might have the key, I believe, to the riddle of the final rise in temperature of Mary's anger.

"But tell me, David, what precisely did Mary mean by 'or you must go into the world and earn your living'?" My father, peasant-like, went straight for the practical heart of the matter.

David answered as if apologising for an obvious omission. "I've never discussed it with her fully. There seemed no need to, anyway not yet. But I believe she has plans, if I refuse the Church, to article me to a chartered accountant."

"A chartered accountant!" My mother could not restrain exclamation of her surprise.

David nodded. "Yes. She believes that if I won't go into the Church, accountancy would be the best possible training for me. She thinks I don't know how to plan, reckon, calculate and all that kind of thing. She . . ." David hesitated slightly, while a quick flush flared up in his face but nevertheless he held on with an effort. "She thinks I don't know the value and meaning of money. She thinks I'm not to be trusted with money. She says I am not realistic enough and that my imagination needs disciplining. She believes accountancy would give just the right sort of balance to a nature and character like mine. Oh! she has thought long and well about it, and I must say there's a lot in what she says. I know I'm putting it badly. But when you hear her you'll realise her reasons are excellent." His voice went flat and cold with discouragement.

"And what do you feel about the prospect yourself?" my mother asked quickly.

"I'd hate it." David said quietly.

"Is that the only reason?" my father asked, while my mother gave an impatient little tug at her knitting.

David turned to him, a flash of alarm in his eyes. "That's what Mary always asks me," he began apprehensively. Then seeing from the look in my father's face that he obviously meant something quite different, he added more confidently, "Yes, that's the only reason, except of course that I want to paint."

My father nodded his head with satisfaction. "That's precisely what I am trying to get at. You've got two reasons really, a negative and a positive one. I'm not saying you're right, but if a man has a positive as well as a negative answer to a situation, I assure you it is sufficiently uncommon to deserve careful consideration. The point is what d'you think you'll do when you return?"

David looked round at us with a helpless expression. My own heart beat faster on his behalf and far down in the garden I heard a summer gust of wind set the windmill pumping water with a desperate clanking.

"I don't know," he said at last miserably, and turning significantly to my mother asked earnestly: "Aunt Fraser, what can I do?"

Before she could reply, my father, seeing the anguish of uncertainty caused by his questions, rushed in. "I wouldn't worry about it for the moment. We'll think it over quietly and see what we can do to help. Meanwhile you have two months of holiday in front of you. Enjoy yourselves while you can."

And there the matter was left for the moment as far as we were concerned. But the moment they were alone, my father said to my mother, "Well, it's come at last. I can't understand Mary. Most parents would give anything to have their children know as clearly as David does what they want to do. But she regards it as a sort of crime. You must write to her."

"I know," my mother consented readily, trying to consider Mary's attitude in the light of her own clear heart. "I know. I must write, but the problem is, write what?"

Her letter, when it was written a week later, was compiled with infinite tact and with a sure intuition of the intangibilities of the situation. Without going into the details her letter amounted to an offer to send David to the university with me at their expense.

Mary was genuinely touched by the offer, but her refusal, gracious and reluctant as it appeared, was absolute. If she had to accept money and help from anyone, she wrote, there were no people from whom she would take it more willingly and gratefully than from us. But there was more than just a financial difficulty to overcome. If she had to entrust David's education to anyone there was no one to whom she would turn more confidently and gladly than to my mother. Nonetheless she was David's mother and while alive she had a very special responsibility for him of which she could not divest herself. David was at the most critical point of his life. Only she knew the dangers to which certain clearly marked weaknesses in his character might expose him. For instance, he was completely at the mercy of sensitive, lively and unusually imperious senses. He was gifted, more gifted than any of her children, but his very gifts pre-supposed a subservience to those senses. His gifts, Mary wrote, could be contained properly only in a dedication to God and not to personal and individual ends. She appealed to us to do everything possible to persuade David to go into the Church, where both he and his talents would be safe.

My father gave a muted whistle of amazement when they read Mary's letter.

"As David says, she has the most impressive reasons," he exclaimed, and added grimly, using as he always did when moved, the homely idiom of our district, "I'm afraid the boy's pearl barley is properly cooked and ready for him."

CHAPTER 8

DAVID was, of course, not surprised when on the last day of his stay my parents told him the result of their efforts to help him. The fact of their having tried for the moment weighed more heavily and happily with him than this final evidence of Mary's determination. He had never really expected anything else and said with amazing coolness and affectionate irony, "Your fence, Uncle Fraser, is right in front of me now! How am I to take it?" and he looked steadily at my father, his wide grey eyes, so like Mary's, warm with confidence and love.

My father, who had known for weeks that the question was inevitable, had given much uncomfortable thought to it. I think he would have given away half his possessions rather than have to advise David on such an issue. He drew a deep breath, looked very tense, and then began to put the sum of all his thinking into carefully weighed speech. I can still see him pushing out the words with careful and tender implacability over the edge of his experienced mind, like a bird pushing its fledglings out of its nest, while my mother looked on, all the feathers of her own warm spirit aquiver lest his meaning should not take wing but fall and die.

"I want you, David, to listen very carefully to what I am going to say, and please try hard to understand why I say it, for if you don't I'm afraid you might be hurt," he began carefully, and this approach, combined with the ominous suggestion that David might be hurt, filled me with the grimmest forebodings. My heart turned black in me, while he continued with immense earnestness: "I want you to realise that if Alex were in your predicament I would say exactly what I'm going to say now. I'm not going to advise you. I'm going to refuse to tell you what I think you should do."

I could hardly believe my ears. It seemed to me the lowest depths of meanness, such a betrayal of our confidence in my father that I was plunged in despair. For months, indeed for years, I had been telling David not to worry, as if the worst came to the worst, my parents would put it right for him; and now my father refused even to advise David.

I looked at my mother for some sign that she at any rate was not associating herself with him in this, but she seemed quite undismayed, even actually approving of his words, and looked encouragingly at him as he continued.

"It would be quite easy for me to tell you what I think. But I'm not going to do so because it would be very wrong of me. The question is one which ultimately only you can answer for yourself. You must consult with your own mind and heart for they alone can tell you both what you can and should do. You don't need someone else's advice. In fact if your instincts seem reluctant to give you a clear answer at the moment, it may mean that already too many people and things have interfered between you and them. Your mother has thrust a man's decision on you. You are young but not too young for it. You must plough your life with your own plough. My plough might appear better than yours and I might lend it you for a bit, but in the end you will have to use your own. It is what life has given you, and you must work your lands accordingly."

He paused and looked from one to the other of us. I turned my head away to hide the tears that were rushing to my eyes but David, with a clearer, more objective instinct than mine, was looking back at my father with nothing but expectant interest on his face.

"No, I am not going to tell you what to do," my father repeated again. He paused, and then added in a lighter tone and so rapid was the plunge forward of his thought from a negative to a positive state, from, as it were, the potential fearful flight from the edge of the nest to the kinetic beat of fulfilled wings among the tree-tops, that I turned my eyes towards him with warm amazement.

"But I'll tell you what I am going to do! Since Mary has conferred full manhood on you by forcing this choice I'm going to treat you as some one who has come of age. I and your aunt are going to do now what we always intended doing when you two came of age. I am going to behave as if this were your twenty-first birthday. Ever since you two were born your aunt and I have set aside, every year, £40— £20 for each of you—as a twenty-first birthday present. Well, here is your present up-to-date and here is Alec's! I am afraid you will have to wait another three years though before the present is up to schedule."

And with that he thrust a neat sheaf of new £20 notes into each of our hands, put his pipe in his mouth and started smoking again like someone who had been without tobacco for many days. But he had taken only a few puffs when David and I, shaken out of all our adolescent inhibitions by this unexpected and generous conclusion to his speech, and with an instinctive return to the spontaneity of our receding childhood, rushed at him and kissed my disconcerted father on the cheek.

My mother, knowing how deep emotion was running in all of us, at once created a diversion. Calling us, she took us to the linen room and gave David a large travelling rug of hand-woven wool. It had the same generic sort of brown colour, the charged and ambivalent darkness of David's pictures, except that a slender line of clearest and warmest gold ran through it cutting it into neat squares.

"I have long wanted to give you something for your journey between your two homes," she said, "and at last Alex and I thought of this. The wool is from his own sheep. He sheared them himself for the occasion. I had the wool spun and dyed and then woven by hand in the village. I hope you will never use it without being reminded instantly that here there is always a room ready and a bed warm for you."

To-day whenever I think back to these last moments with David at home, I am reminded how flat and inadequate are the mental patterns we draw in order to make events comprehensible to our conscious selves.

In particular there is the naïve image we have made of cause and effect. We see them arranged, inevitably, in an orderly, straight line of hereditary progression. First, not only in importance but also in time, there is the cause which fathers an effect which begets a cause which produces yet another effect and so on ad infinitum. Cause, we say, is always behind us pushing us forwards into its effect.

But to-day when I look back at this period it seems to me that for months we had all been feeling the effects of something which really had not yet happened to David: yet which nonetheless was real, already in being, and drawing us irresistibly nearer to it.

David now deeply stirred by my mother's words about the rug, put himself between her and me, took our hands, folding them tightly together in his, and, looking from one to the other of us with a face cleared like a spring morning of compromise and reserve, said with affectionate mockery, "So Alexander the Great is a liar after all?"

I remembered that, while watching me energetically shearing my few sheep, he had repeatedly asked me what had suddenly possessed me to undertake so hard a task.

I had answered evasively: "Oh, I'm doing it just for fun."

But from his seat at the entrance to the shearer's shed, where he was painting the whole scene, he had looked up over the edge of his canvas from time to time and said with gentle irony: "Is it true, that enormous lie?"

I had given a laughing affirmative and he had gone on with his painting, a secret amusement at odd moments flickering in a quick smile over his happily absorbed face like summer catspaws on a sunlit pond.

I could, of course, have told him all I knew, which was that I was combining with my mother to give him a rug, as a present; but how inadequate that would have been—one more shadowy silhouette of the rounded substance which was pulling us all towards its centre as a sinking ship attracts the flotsam and jetsam of the sea. I could not then have told him more because I was not aware of more. Yet all our actions at that time presupposed within us the knowledge of a journey and a recognition that already it was somewhere in being.

More significant still is the painting David did that day. That morning when I went into the shed with our black shearers to shear, he'd automatically placed himself at the entrance to paint.

It was a brilliant summer's day and as the sun climbed slowly higher the light lapped in hot, electric waves at the entrance to the shed. The shed itself was deep, wide, cool, and dark. There were eight of us altogether in the shed: seven black shearers and myself. The shorn sheep, when we stood them up on their four feet, shivered violently now that they had lost their thick coats. As we released them with a slap on quivering flanks, they blinked in their great centre-less eyes at the trembling light and stood there for a moment like wrinkled little old people in their underclothes. Then they stumbled over the final bar of shadow as if it were a log of African mahogany catching at their feet, and went out bleating again into the full fever of the day.

David sat with his back to the light and painted as if this melodrama of an African summer without did not exist. The shed was for him again the deep container of that tense, emotional half-darkness of the awakening spirit. The light that breaks in on it comes almost entirely from the glow of heavy coils of golden wool at the feet of the black shearers. I myself am invisible in the darkness at the back, though the sheep I am shearing contributes a sheen of deep-mined ore from a ruff of curling wool just parted like a mediæval collar above its breast. But elsewhere the light of the wool thrusts itself through the darkness like the waves of a moonless sea flashing into life at midnight against the fine carved bow of an urgent ship.

The centre of the picture is dominated by the biggest of our Basuto shearers. Stripped to the waist, the silk of sweat on a dark purple skin which fits beautifully supple and full rounded muscles like a surgeon's glove, he is bent over a sheep with an earnest but delicate intent. Such a flame of light leaps from the wool falling over his feet that his gravely bent head is lit and warmed by it as if by an altar fire. This light rises even to a great teak rafter above and renews the warm glow in the tackle of tightly braided manilla hemp which emerges from the far corners of the loft and holds the block of a pulley with a hook like a harpy's claw over the sheep-shearers. Then the two lines of rope, of marigold hair, vanish into the opposite corners of the shed like the trail of shooting stars.

The figure of the Basuto shearer is charged and heavy with antique significance, the wool at his feet is miraculous, and one looks fearfully at that hook as if it might, at any moment, descend obscenely to snatch away what seems sacred and holy.

The sense of profound excitement implicit in that impression is both in the colour and texture of the paint, and in the quick, unfaltering sweep of the brush with which the paint is applied. The vision itself seems infinitely privileged as if it pulls aside a curtain on the final dimension of awareness and lets light fall not on the drab shearing shed of the Frasers in Africa, but rather into some workshop of fate where fine-grained wool is shorn and spun into the delicate strands of life itself.

It is as if the past in this painted moment curves so far back on itself that it completes a circle with the rounding future.

As one looks at the picture one knows, instantly, how the vision of the golden fleece must have flared up in the dark before Jason's eyes; one can almost hear the keel of a long ship being run out swiftly over the grating pebbles to the sea. It is the vision of someone who, whether he knows it or not, has already commenced a hazardous enterprise, and whose heart and mind have already disappeared over the edge of the conscious horizon.

It is all clear to me now. Cause and effect are but subordinate aspects of a greater whole. In these last days I see all our actions drawn by this fine, spiked cause towards itself as the tip of a Gothic spire draws the whole intricate being and design of a Cathedral after it. Yet at the time my knowledge was so much less than the sum of my behaviour that when David repeated his ironic question: "Is it true, that enormous lie?" I replied firmly: "Of course it's true."

And there was the rub of it; already it was true, and alas! it was also a lie.

But our unknowing did not end there, and I tremble now to think what our actions would have been had not we all four loved one another. More was to follow which to-day shows how faint and precarious the light of our awareness was, what a tender and dewy glow-worm moving deep in the "great forest of the Lord" where only love, which has need neither of light nor knowledge, could keep us whole.

The night before David left us, I woke up to hear him moaning at my side. As usual we were sleeping outside and I sat up wondering what had happened and whether I should wake him. It was a moonless night and through the embroidered hole in the rough shawl of grape vines stretching over the veranda, I saw the jewelled stars flashing their ancient message at me with such a pointed urgency that the faint rustle of grape leaves stirring in the soft summer air was converted into a patter of starlight. Somewhere near the cattle kraals underneath the dark hill, a jackal gave three mournful barks and as it barked David moaned more desperately.

I put out a hand in the dark, shook his shoulder, and called out softly: "David, it's all right. Wake up. It's all right."

He woke up with a gasp, held my hand tightly and said, "Thank God, it's you, Alex. I've had such a bad dream."

As he spoke a jackal gave three more mournful yaps. He shuddered and said. "There were wolves in my dream too, but that's only a jackal."

We lay down again and tried to sleep but David was still

tossing about so restlessly that I asked: "Are you still worried by your dream?"

"No, not worried. I just can't get it out of my mind," he answered.

"Tell me," I said, and he told me.

He dreamed that something terrible was happening to Anna Maria. He didn't know what precisely but it was a matter of life and death and vital that he should go to her aid. Only it was after sunset: it was nightfall. Soldiers were already shutting the city gates and Anna Maria was outside. He ran desperately from one gate to the other, his legs getting heavier and heavier, only to find the great spiked iron doors shut and barred. The soldiers refused to let him out because they said, "We dare not open the gate for if we do they will come in." The "they" was not specified but he knew "they" were something awful. He came to the last gate of all, was met with the same stubborn refusal, and yet had not a minute to lose. He was in despair when he felt a discreet tug at his coat from behind. Turning round he saw a little, old, black man with a wrinkled face and white negroid hair on it and an able-seaman's cap on his head. He was, David said, "a slave of some kind but terribly experienced and knowledgable." This little old man took him to a side door let into the walls. David wondered why he had not seen it before. The old man let him out whispering "Steer south by south." Outside it was now black with night. David set off as fast as he could. Behind him he saw the city illuminated from within into a tremendous golden fortress, like vision of some yellow and tartared kremlin in Ivan the Terrible's mind, and far ahead the dark line of the wood he had to enter in order to find Anna Maria. He looked at the sky and his eyes quickly picked out the Southern Cross. "It was terrifically bright," he said, "and right over the wood, which was sacred." At once he made for it. At that moment from the east to the west of him he heard packs of wolves howling to one another and coming up fast towards him. He knew they had picked up his scent and were on his trail. With sickening heart he strained forward and then saw on the flank of the wood a deep-red flame leap up into the dark with such violence that sparks flew from it like a swarm of fireflies. The light of the fire revealed the soaring columns of the cathedral of wood. He knew he would be safe provided he reached the fire. But the wolves were getting nearer with incredible speed, led, he said, by a lean and hungry grey bitch with a lace bonnet on its head. . . . He made a final convulsive effort to get to the fire, when I woke him.

Having told me all this he fell peacefully asleep but the dream thereafter seemed to enter my system and for reasons I could not fathom kept me awake. Hard as I tried I could not dismiss it as just another nightmare. I lay awake for a long time and whenever the jackal barked, an icy, anonymous apprehension clutched at the sleeves of my mind.

In the morning the memory of the dream was back with David too and would not leave him alone until he had made a picture of it. That painting, for all the speed with which it was done and despite the fact that it was not related to any living scene but emerged solely from David's imagination, is taut with a nightmare reality found only in some of the pictures of Goya. "Beyond the Fortifications" is the title David gave it. Nothing could have been plainer. Reverting once more to an ancient technique one could say that the dream was prophetic. I myself prefer to regard it as stating something which had already happened although its outward shape and moment had still to come.

The next day David left for Fort White. We all three went with him on the long journey by cart and horses to the station. Though we had often done this in the past, we all four were as upset as if we were now parting for the first time.

The country was singularly empty of life. The heat of summer had battered most living plants and creatures into retreat and the sky, buzzing like a fly against the windows of its own over-heated light, seemed to give welcome only to white-breasted crows, the indefatigable scavengers of our desolate plains. I tried to play the game of our childhood and arrange the crows into a pattern of hopeful auguries for the future: but though I got plenty of solitary "ones" for sorrow, I searched in vain for the combination I sorely needed: "two for joy".

Those plains of ours on the other side of the dark blue hills, always have a resigned and gentle melancholy about them. They were once the bed and shores of a vast ocean. To this day the fossils of strange, deep sea fish are found in them, and they look as if no matter what we human beings have done, they can never forget the swelling waves and the white manes that flowed over them to pound at the shores and waterfronts of the forgotten races of our unremembered past. They are forever rediscovering their original vision in the blue of the sky and the great combers of cloud that thunder across them with the long hair of their arched necks and plumed heads a-dazzle with sunshine and lightning. The nostalgia of exile is implicit in the blue and unfaltering distances of these plains and I found no comfort in the scene. So empty was the day and so unimpeded our vision that we saw the smoke of David's train planted like a tree on the horizon two hours before it reached his station.

"I will see you in the winter," I said to him over and over again, trying to scramble out of the pool of our silence and then slipping helplessly down its steep banks again. "I'll see you in the winter. It's amazing how quickly the winter comes round."

He nodded his head emphatically and said, "Yes. It's amazing. Of course, we shall meet again then."

My father, never a talkative person, was really no more helpful. "Take care of yourself, my boy; make friends with yourself and hold on to yourself and good luck," was his farewell, and the only important contribution to our attempts at speech.

My mother did not seem to find it necessary even to try. She sat with her arm through David's and held his hand in a

manner which was her substitute for speech. I sat in front
with my father and whenever I looked back I could see the
silhouette of her and David, sitting side by side, silent and
motionless in the smoking dust at the edge of the road. Later
in the morning as the sun rose and caught us on the first level
vlakte, their shadow was immense and long and rode on
astronomic wheels to the rim of the farthest hills. But as the
sun rose higher the shadow contracted until by noon, when
we turned in at the station, it had vanished and was lost and
trampled into the hungry dust beneath our cart.

With the train's arrival a hysteria of whistles plunged us
into the final good-bye. "See you in June," from me, a silent
handshake from my father, and a warm kiss from my mother
who also said: "Don't forget to send us a telegram when you
arrive, and give our love to Mary."

So David left us. We stood on the side of the track and
watched the train out of sight. I could see David's handkerchief like a white tulip pinned to the dark flank of the train
long after his face had become undistinguishable from the
blues of distance. Then the engine rounded a bend at the foot
of a lone hill, moving slowly out of our sight like a royal
stallion at the head of a funeral cortège with a proud, black
plume of smoke at its head. Suddenly the station went very
quiet; the fitful air of a parched and sun-twisted noonday
tugged with dusty fingers at our heels. The abiding silence of
the immense plain broke over us with the hiss of a curving
wave, and far away I heard a lamb bleating for its ewe.

"You had better go and fetch the horses," my father said,
and I went. But so empty had the day become, and so devoid
of real and tangible meaning, that I would not have been surprised to find the station stables empty and the horses eaten
by the hungry nothingness about me.

CHAPTER 9

IT is a long journey from our part of the world to Fort White. It takes three nights by train with numerous changes on the way. We did not worry when on the third and fourth day we got no telegram from David announcing his arrival. Delays on such a long journey are not unusual. But when on the fifth day no word came we began to feel anxious, and on the seventh day we became so worried that my father sent me off to the post-office with a pre-paid telegram to Mary Michaeljohn.

But as I got to our front door, there was a loud knock and, opening it, I looked straight into the eyes of the black postal messenger whose face flashed into an astonished grin at so prompt a response to his summons. He had a telegram for us: "Cannot understand why David overstaying holiday. If not left already please see he returns home at once love Mary."

Our alarm, already alert, was instantly in full cry after our vanishing peace of mind. My mother went very white, sat down in the nearest chair and said: "I pray God nothing awful has happened to the boy. We should never have let him go. He should have been home four days ago. Oh, what shall we do?" She turned to my father.

"I don't know what can have happened," he said slowly, trying obviously to gauge the direction of some subtle wind of meaning beginning to stir in his wise spirit. "I don't know, but somehow I am pretty sure there's been no accident. If David is not at home, I wouldn't be surprised if it's not because he doesn't want to be."

My mother looked up in amazement.

"He's run away," she said with conviction, as if the thought had all along been her own. "How clever of you to see it, too.

You're right. He's run away from Mary. And by heaven, I don't blame him," she finished loyally.

"Yes, I wouldn't be surprised if he's bolted. But if so, why this secrecy, why not tell us? Unless he told you, Alex!" The look he gave me was not reproachful, merely full of puzzled concern.

I shook my head sadly and said, "I know nothing"; whereupon my mother's relief promptly vanished and she said despondently: "Then I don't believe he has done it after all."

"I'm not so sure. The Michaeljohns have all always had something unexplained and secret about them. And David, much as I love him, is not free of it. Besides, he may not have wished to embarrass us." My father, unshaken, continued searching for an explanation to match the intuitive stirring of his mind.

"No, Father, no . . . David would have told me," I said passionately, very near to tears for all my eighteen years. "He would never have gone off like this without telling me."

But as I spoke, unwished and uncalled for but none the less urgent for all that, the memory of David in the blue of a golden summer's morning suddenly thrusting his gun into the hands of a native hunter and taking to his heels out of fear of lightning from an unclouded sky, rushed in on me. My agitated thoughts ran round from one corner of my mind to another searching for comfort like white mice in a cage looking for escape.

My father, seeing my miserable despondency, instantly changed the subject.

"You'd better pack!" he said to my mother. "We'd better go to Mary at once or she will have the police after David. Alex, help me draft a telegram."

Together we composed the following for Mary: "David already gone all three leaving to-day to join you."

We arrived in Fort White none too soon. Mary, out of her mind with anxiety and fearing that only an accident could explain David's disappearance, was all for calling in the police.

Only our telegram, and the belief that we might be bringing her some reassuring explanation, caused her to postpone so drastic an action.

My father, however, on arrival had merely this unwavering conviction, this inexplicable hunch that David was safe and sound, with which to reassure her. But fortunately, soon after our arrival, a letter did come from David. It had no address but was stamped with the post-mark of the principal harbour of the country, another two days' and nights' train journey from Fort White.

"Mother," it began, with no "Dear" or "Dearest" before or after it, "I can't do what you want me to do, so I'm taking you at your word and 'going out into the world'. By the time you get this I shall be on my way to England. I'm afraid you will be very angry with me but please try and forgive me. I really can't help myself. I shall be all right and I beg you not to worry. I shall write as soon as I arrive. My love to you all."

The letter was signed "D", just that one letter, as if he were merely one in an alphabetical series and nothing more, not even the "loving son" with which before he had never failed to end his letters to Mary.

My mother was with Mary when she read David's note and she says her reaction was quite unexpected and very remarkable.

Instead of bursting into tears or getting angry, Mary put the letter quietly back into its envelope, placed it between the pages of her large black leather Bible and said with immense and fervent relief: "Thank God, he's not hurt. Thank heaven, he's all right."

"Of course she was relieved. She'd have been most un-natural if she hadn't been—after imagining David dead beside a railway track in the wilderness." My father's reply was just a little disdainful of so obvious an explanation.

"But I don't mean that at all," my mother said, "in fact, I have a distinct feeling that a part of Mary was pleased at David's defiance, and rather relieved that he hadn't come submissively home. I think he's not suffered at all in Mary's estimation by what he's done."

"Then why was he so secretive about it all? Why at least couldn't he tell us what was in his mind?" My father was back at the main source of his worry.

"Perhaps," I commented hopefully, "there's a letter waiting at home now, explaining it all."

But I was wrong. When we got back from Fort White that night and found no letter or even a telegram from David waiting for us, I was shocked and hurt in a manner which to this day I find hard to discuss.

At first I would not believe it. Late as it was I insisted on going to the post-office and opening our private box. When I found that empty, I went and knocked at the postmaster's door until he got out of bed and let me in. He was outraged and furious but the pain and unhappiness gave me such courage that I compelled this official, noted for his stubborn boorishness, to go through the mail that had just come in, and even stood over him to make sure that he looked thoroughly and proved to me finally that what he said was true and that there was no word for me from David. There was none, of course.

As day after day went by and no word came, the terrifying speed with which our rationed seconds normally run changed into the leaden pace of a nightmare moment. I became ill with hurt and anxiety. I could not speak about it even to my parents; for what nearly defeated me was the sense of ultimate separation. My many other separations from David seemed to have been no separations at all. The separation of physical distance even in our inexhaustible African geography, suddenly looked like a bold illusion of the eyes. Had David gone to the Pole itself it would have been easier to bear, provided he had not shut his heart on me like this and cut me out of the reach of his mind.

My own sense of suffering was so keen that I even felt a kinship and nearness to hurt and injured things.

I remember to this day the look of astonishment my mother gave me one afternoon when we were out riding and came by a little black boy of about five, crying by the roadside. I don't know why he was crying but expect it was because his mother, who was collecting fuel on this vacant vlakte, had moved some distance away from him. Although it was only autumn, already the coldest wind of our winter was blowing, a strong south-west breeze which sent the yellow sunlight of that fugitive afternoon shrinking and shivering to its home in the west, and this little fellow was quite naked except for a goat-skin strap which tied a discarded cotton tobacco bag, the lettering of the brand "Voor-trekker No. 1" still plainly visible on it, between his legs. His little, round, full belly was no longer black but ash-grey with dirt and dust, and the large pear-drop tears from his eyes, royal and bright in their own right in the dynasty of sorrow, ran down his cheeks and mixed freely with two thick trickles of dirt from his nose.

I pulled up my horse sharply, jumped off, took him in my arms, wiped his face clean with my handkerchief and comforted him until his amazed mother, who came running over the moment she saw us, took him from me. I don't think I had looked twice at a child of that age before, and if I had I could not have been moved to act in this manner. But now with David gone, his hurt seemed to be my hurt and the tears I dried were also my own.

The injuries of animals, of insects, of birds, and the smallest plant or flower affected me likewise. A wagtail with a broken leg curtseying to the day filled me with despair because I could not get at him to set that tiny spar of a limb that dangled at his side like the empty scabbard of a sword at the hip of a bobbing and bowing military martinet. There was a one-eyed kitten, maimed by a kick, which whenever a human being passed shut this permanently weeping eye, puckered its brows tightly together and drew its head back into its shoulders obviously expecting another kick. I could not rest until by constant attention and stroking of its head and body I had taught it to purr at the sound of my approaching foot-steps. Another time I saw a man flick a large purple and gold caterpillar off his sleeve. It fell in a water furrow where I could see it plainly, lying still with large, tragic, wide-open eyes staring upwards through the water at the blue sky above, little pearly bubbles of air coming out of its nose. Though I loathe caterpillars I fished it out at once and put it in a quiet place in the sun.

Then one morning—and perhaps this was the most cruel moment of all—I went out very early into the garden. The ground was still blue with memory of the night and only the hill tops and one far sail of cloud had caught the sun. I then discovered that a dog had come in the night and trampled all over our flower beds. In particular, it had damaged the last of our roses, a thick, swollen red bud, almost mature and racing the winter for its fulfilment. There it now was, sagging from a broken stem, a tender crimson tip staining the silver dew.

Slight as it was, my sorrow and sense of undeserved injury came to a point in that moment. It seemed to me as if nothing in life, animal, mineral or vegetable, was safe or excluded from this fatal circle of being hurt and hurting. The inevitable and inescapable logic of everything seemed to be one endless chain of hurt. To hurt and be hurt, there was no other way.

Oh, on that dew-silver morning, bent over the rose, I came near defeat. But mercifully the mood did not last for it was not complete and whole, and therefore was not true. I can think of no worse death than living an untruth truly, living the part as if it were the whole. And at that moment I was near it. What saved me was the image of David doing he knew not what. David making mud pies on Edward George in his baptismal lace, David in a mediumistic trance at his mother's window putting a golden sovereign in his breast pocket, and, above all, David running away from lightning in sunlight.

I remembered Mary's denial of her own love and her brave attempt to make of duty a substitute for love, giving to the rules and regulations of men what we owe only to the laws of God. I thought of Albert in his loveless exile from himself, condemned to work to the end of his days at the ramparts of his own prison. And I saw David between them, a slender lightning conductor rising to a dangerous sky.

At once I was comforted. Grief remained, but the hurt, gnawing sense of injury, that scavenger of condemned carcasses, that carrion love of the incomplete spirit forever sniffing the air of the world for the stink of decaying parts, fell away from me. Oh, the ecstasy of thinking no longer only of myself but of feeling my keen injury swinging back into its proper proportions in the wholeness of love.

Of course, David had no intention of shutting me out of his heart and mind. Of course, he had no intention of hurting me. Of course, he had not deliberately wounded me, my parents or himself. I do not pretend that I understand it at all clearly but it was enough that these childhood memories lit such a light in me that no script of David's soul was too small or secret for me to read thereby. And without this deep-drilled oil of unhappiness no such lamp could have been lit in me. I was almost grateful to it for my personal feelings withered quickly in a new fierce blaze of anxiety for the distant David, so unfree and so strangely invaded. When and where and how would David's reckoning come? Did he know that he was suffering? Was unhappiness the deep core of the secret itself? Would he learn, in time, that his silence was merely a tiny part of a silence and secrecy so profound that he was its victim? Would he learn, before it was too late, to inquire into the nature of his own consciousness which inspired such strange enmities?

As I asked myself these questions I knew how much I was to be envied. I had stepped out of my misery like the prodigal from his rags.

That night for the first time in months I spoke of David to my parents. What we said after so long a silence easily can be imagined and does not really matter. In so far as I have dwelt on my own feelings in the matter, I have done so only because this seeming violation of David's love for me gives a perfect illustration of the power of the secret Michaeljohn purpose, its system of submerged values, retarded fulfilments, Shylock reckoning and all its ancient and resourceful compulsions. For make no mistake about it—David loved me deeply, I knew that. He was incapable of doing to me what he had not done also to himself. If he was unconscious of having behaved cruelly to me that could only mean that he must also be unconscious of having done violence to himself.

So when I spoke again of David to my parents after such a long and difficult silence my mother bowed her head over the bowl of new emerald green peas, the first of an early season she was shelling, and for the first time that I can remember burst into tears on her own as well as my account. But happily they were tears of release and joy. My father then looked at me as if he had been specially sent to welcome me into the kingdom of maturity and quickly said: "I'm so glad you feel that about David, for I fear he may yet need your help. One can't ever run away from anything. Sooner or later everything catches up with you, panting for vengeance."

I knew instinctively he was right and yet felt he had forgotten one thing which seemed to me of the greatest importance.

"David wouldn't be the David we love, if he'd behaved differently," I replied. "One can't just pick out what one likes in people and reject the rest. That's using people not loving them."

"I know that only too well," my father assented in a deep, rumbling tone he used only when he felt in complete harmony with his family. "But it doesn't stop me from wishing it could have happened differently."

As he spoke I knew that I wished it too, and I shivered slightly for it seemed to me then that perhaps no matter how silently, secretly and cunningly one contrives one's escape, the parental pursuit travels with one in the spirit, the seas and the wind-blown spuming seconds to the shadowless ends of time.

When David did write many months later his letter confirmed how right I had been. He had had no idea of what he was going to do until the last moment. All through his journey back to Fort White an indefinable but deep and agonising uneasiness possessed him. The first two nights in the train he had hardly slept at all and on the afternoon of the third day he had fallen asleep only to wake up at nine that evening in the dark with a porter's "all change" ringing in his ears. The train was at the junction where he had to make his final change. As he heard that "all change", he knew that he could not face Mary and the old, old, quarrel again, and like someone walking in his sleep, without premeditation or forethought, shaking with strange inner excitement mingled with fear, he got instead into the first train for the coast. For the rest he wrote as if there was nothing to explain. No letter could have been more loving, grateful and appreciative of our rare relationship. It was crowded with detail and communicated to me only too keenly his own excitement over his new life. Already he had had some slight success as a painter in London. He had been asked to organise an exhibition and he asked me to choose forty of his best canvasses and drawings and send them to him as soon as possible. He wrote at length of his happiness in painting, and painting for the first time in his life in a community of painters. How wonderful, how absolutely miraculous, he wrote, that he was now, at last, thanks to my parents, free to do what he most wanted to do. My senses recorded the irony in his use of the word "free", and the poignancy of the realisation was deepened for me by the fact that I was reading this first letter of his in the spring— our spring and now his autumn. Even the seasons, it seemed, had turned against us.

PART III

The Crisis

CHAPTER 10

DAVID'S first exhibition in London was a great success. To his undisguised astonishment he sold all the African pictures and drawings that were for sale in the exhibition as well as a fair number of the paintings he had done since his arrival in England. His sponsors, who had hoped at the most for a certain "succès d'estime" from this first venture with the work of a completely unknown young man, were as gratified as they were astonished and immediately began making new plans. Pleased as David was with this practical justification of the lone instinct that had brought him to Europe, and in this vindication of our belief in his talent, what mattered most was the warm praise he got from painters he esteemed himself.

Published criticism, it is true, was confused. The exhibition was held at a time when the critical approach to art was determinedly and exclusively intellectual. The language critics used in describing the function, purpose and accomplishments of painting, had become so identified with rootless processes of the mind and intellect, so divorced from the natural and instinctive, that the critical reviews of exhibitions sent me by David read like complicated metaphysical tracts. But they were not unkind to him.

And some of the painters whose work David himself esteemed were by no means confused in their praise. They were genuinely impressed and told him so in warm, generous and simple terms.

Then there was also the Frenchman who wrote to David out of the blue. His name was well-known in the world of painting, for in his youth he had known Manet and Renoir, had befriended the young Picasso and now in his old age was a close friend of Matisse:

"Monsieur," he wrote, "I do not expect you know my name and I must ask you to forgive me if I say that until I saw your exhibition to-day I had no idea even that you existed. But I am compelled to take this liberty of writing to you by force of the emotion caused in me by your exhibition and the great happiness given me by seeing your pictures for the first time. I am an old man now and not since my early youth have I been so uplifted by an exhibition. Please do not think me patronising if I say that you have a very great talent, a very profound gift for painting, which is all the more reason why I feel bound to raise my aged voice before the confused clamour of blind and misleading although well-deserved praise explodes around your ears.

"Monsieur, I feel compelled to remind you of the grave and onerous obligations a gift like yours imposes. Oh! I do trust, Monsieur, that you will not regard it lightly. I have seen nearly three generations of painters come and go but none to whom paint has been so native, so much their own aboriginal idiom, as with you. You think, you feel, you wake and sleep in paint, and I hope you will not overlook the significance of such unanimity. All my life I have seen people painting with tired unsleeping eyes propped open by brittle theories of bright, determined minds. But you, Monsieur, so it seemed to me to-day, by some miracle were born free of mental despotism, and may well in time bring back to painting the sleep and the dreams it sorely needs. Therefore, I repeat, Monsieur, a gift like yours is a solemn responsibility. It is not yours so much as a great and difficult trust confided to you on behalf of life.

"Above all, Monsieur, I pray you, do not neglect the sane and wise and healing discipline of self-portraiture. It is an ancient practice that has long fallen in disrepute but if I may advise you, I would recommend that in your inevitable moments of confusion and doubt, you sit down quietly and look into yourself with those far-seeing, undogmatic eyes of yours and paint yourself as truly as you painted these African

animals, these black hunters and sheep-shearers, whose darkness reverberates with the tread of the ultimate sun like the
sound of a horn in the silence of the great woods, these
Southern interiors sullen with sunlight and these London
roof-tops gay with soot and rust even in their autumnal mist
and fog. If that is too much to ask of yourself, go to some
friend whom you respect and trust and ask him to do a portrait of you and borrow his eyes to read the magnetic compass within yourself. Whatever happens do not neglect what
is the natural and only sure way for a person like yourself of
increasing his knowledge of himself. For believe me, Monsieur, if you dedicate yourself truly to your natural calling, all
the self-knowledge in the world will not come amiss.

"Once more I beg of you your forgiveness for presuming
to talk to you so intimately. I thank you for the happiness you
have given me, and ask you please to accept my most distinguished salutations and to be assured of my most elevated
esteem."

David sent me this letter obviously extremely pleased with
it, as he had every right to be. But I must confess that I read
it over and over again with mixed feelings. It was a strange
letter. David had clearly accepted it at its face value, as a
manifest salute of praise and encouragement. But to me the
substance of praise and encouragement had point only in this
grave warning that tolled like a cathedral bell throughout the
letter. I could not shake off the impression that a sense of
urgency and warning had been the real inspiration of the
writer's letter.

I was in a difficulty. I knew David's African work well, of
course, but apart from one solitary painting of a grave-yard
in Chelsea, which he had sent me recently, I knew his London
work only from black and white photographs. From them I
noticed with reassurance that David characteristically had
started to paint the world that was about him. His reaction
as an artist was still immediate and needed no special scene
or condition to make it active. This evidence suggested

that his flight to Europe had not jerked him out of his true centre.

From these photographs I could read the detail of his life in London intimately. There were pictures of his bed-sitting room, of his landlady's cat asleep on a green leather chair in a watery beam of sunlight striking through a lace-curtained window; of red-brick and slate-tiled roof-tops, and fuming chimney pots burning mistily in the embankment air swollen with a tearful and nostalgic sunlight; of tranquil Chelsea lanes and houses which wore their front doors with a brilliant splash of colour like regimental neckties. There was too the picture of an unattended black cart-horse with shabby, travel-stained white feathers trailing behind un-shod hooves and massive head bowed in heavy despondence, standing at a fork in the roads close to a stone-tiled hostelry, from which a black metal sign with a most startling red heart on it flew like a heraldic banner at a lowering sky packed with heaving cloud and agitated by violent wind.

Was it this last painting, perhaps, that had first set-off that good and wise old Frenchman's alarm? I could not tell. And many months later David sent me the photograph of a portrait that pushed all speculation on the Frenchman's behalf far into the background by the interest it aroused. It was the portrait of a woman and David's first attempt at painting Helena Moystouan-Roswell.

The portrait showed her full-length, standing by an Adams fire-place with an elegant gilt mirror of the first Empire over it. She wore a long, simple gold and white gown, falling in heavy folds from a narrow, flat waist to the floor and though the dress is painted for its volume and colour and not its detail, one suspects its design to be young for the wearer. The head is turned side-ways from the painter, so that only the fine lines of the neck and the left tip of the nose and a well shaped head are shown. Thick sisal hair falls straight like rain to the shoulders where it receives a severe and abrupt Galahad cut. From the quicksilver mirror at the back the blue of the remaining three-quarters of the face stares mistily over its own clean, straight shoulder. The drawing of it is remote and its admission into the scheme of painting reluctant. Yet one has a distinct impression of a face perhaps too delicately boned, and features a little too finely drawn, even though the over-all effect is graceful and striking. The eyes in particular are big, wide, and come to a fine, almond point between high cheek-bones and a rather broad brow. Their colour is hazel-brown, but in the very centre of the pupils they hold a small, crystal star of glacier-green which does not altogether match the expression of resigned acceptance. The nose is longish, highish and slightly aquiline; the mouth long, rather than full, and the rounded chin is unexpectedly firm. One finger of the right hand is raised in the mirror and curved lightly against a cheek like a vague question mark and creates out of all proportion to its volume an atmosphere of interrogation in the whole of its mirrored surroundings.

I felt extremely uncomfortable looking at the portrait. I seemed to see a nature not insensitive, systematically refined, and the product of a long and carefully specialised descent, but also profoundly withdrawn, and strangely unfulfilled. It possessed, in fact, a quality of something unborn.

David himself seemed to have been unable to meet his subject face to face. A strange dream-like mist appeared to hang between the painter and his portrait, as though he and his subject had encountered one another in some November evening of the senses. Though it was plainly labelled Helena Moystouan-Roswell, she was for me in this portrait as I suspected she was to herself and David, essentially an anonymous and unidentified woman. And thus I continued to think of her.

The reactions of my father and mother to the portrait were characteristic and significant. My father said it looked to him as if David had painted it in his sleep and he wished David would come back and paint some more sheep-shearers, and the ploughed fields and the yellow waving corn of his native land. My mother gave a cry of astonishment and asked dramatically: "But don't you two see what I see? She has something of Mary about her."

She then fetched an old photograph of Mary taken two years before the birth of her first child. Though there were many obvious differences of detail, the woman in the portrait lacking Mary's animation, vitality and fullness, there was enough similarity for her to have been taken for a younger sister of David's mother.

AT his school in Africa David had made a real friend of the master who taught him English and French. From the start he had taken a close, sympathetic and most understanding interest in David's painting. The moment he heard of David's flight to England, which he openly applauded, he appealed for help on David's behalf to his eldest brother in London, who was not only a painter himself of severe and circumspect abstractions but also editor of *The Maelstrom*, a much discussed and controversial monthly on art. The brother had instantly responded, asked David round to his studio and at once took a great liking to him. It was this man who arranged David's first exhibition, which led to his meeting with Helena Moystouan-Roswell.

Helena at this time was already a woman thirty years old. She was the youngest child of a family of five—four girls and a boy who had been killed some years before in the course of an enigmatic prestige campaign on the North-West Frontier of India. The father too had been a soldier. Still Colonel of his county regiment, he had abandoned active soldiering only when he inherited, rather late in life, one of the oldest baronetcies in East Anglia, and the large lands that went with it. He was a person in whom an instinctive love of tradition had been narrowed down by his specialised training as a soldier into a fanatical attachment to the conventions, rituals, ceremonies and official aspects of life. He had developed quickly into a person of decided and intolerant views, whose emotions and feelings were in a continual state of violent agitation against the severe and arbitrary judgments he imposed on them.

Lady Moystouan-Roswell, herself a woman of character, breeding and what passed for practical good sense, had quickly learnt not to attempt the impossible with her husband. From the day of her marriage, which in any case was arranged by her parents and which she had welcomed more as a means of escape from a home of petrified Victorianism than as a way pioneered by her heart, she realised that she could never have a full, creative, individual relationship with her husband. Wisely or unwisely, but none the less irrevocably, she had from then on never attempted to achieve it, but devoted all her private energies and imagination to bringing up her daughters so that they would be spared a repetition of her own marital experience.

While her husband was actively soldiering, her self-assumed and secret purpose had not seemed difficult to achieve. His profession absorbed most of the aggressive ardour and blind energies of his spirit and she had a free hand and mind with her daughters. But when her husband's father died and he was forced to turn his attention to a vast and exacting landed estate, the baronet began to take an increasing and devastating interest in the life of his daughters. By the month and the year he became steadily more possessive about them.

He closed down their house in London on some plausible financial pretext and developed ambiguous heart trouble which occurred whenever one of his daughters was invited out. Though he himself never refused to participate in the most strenuous of ceremonials, though he presided annually over the formal parade of the colours of his regiment in the morning and the dinner to its officers at Claridges at night, rode to hounds from first to last of season, did his full round on the bench inflicting incredible sentences on petty pilferers, loafers and spirited young poachers, and invariably read the Sunday lessons in the village church, yet, once safely in his own home behind heavily curtained windows, he professed an illness which defied precise medical diagnosis but nonetheless necessitated and obtained such constant surveillance by dutiful daughters that they could never plan for a long absence from home.

Taking stock of herself one day after ten years on her husband's estate, Lady Moystouan-Roswell realised the trap her husband's nature had set for them all. It was already too late to help her two unmarried elder daughters. But for Helena, if she acted at once, it need not be too late. It was true, she was nearly thirty, but some life, some spark of rebellion still burned in her. Her mother concentrated all her forces on getting Helena out of her home. There were some terrible scenes with her husband. His heart attacks were most realistic. But when he did not die after his wife told him that Helena was going to London, Lady Moystouan-Roswell knew she had won.

Helena, who had always painted charmingly and sensitively in water colours, was sent off to Paris ostensibly to study art, under the protection of the wife of the ambassador, who was an old friend. A year later she was presented with a substantial income of her own and a studio flat on the borders of Chelsea in London.

For three years Helena had applied herself conscientiously to her painting at times not without a certain inspired and desperate talent. Her conscious imagination was rooted and had been formed for good or ill by the English countryside, its gentle and subtle contours, its unobtrusive flowers and sweet fugitive scents, the rich green of its grasses and the deep shade of its woods startled with snowdrop and warmed through with the purple of violet and bluebell, the starry glitter of its birdsong and everywhere the nearness and nostalgia of the sea. The winds, clouds and bare-stripped trees of winter moved her as much as the soft-rounded sunlight and fulness of increase in the summer of her native East Anglia. Her life there could have been complete if her father's war with himself had not devastated the scene and made her an outcast from it. London, really, was foreign soil to her, and it was pathetic to see how she tried to recreate her childhood vision in the pictures painted in these first years. Posies of ragged robin, birds-eye, cowslip, woodbine and buttercup, and carefully selected snatches of scene from the great parks and commons painted like faint and inadequate preludes to the vaster countryside beyond, abounded among her canvasses.

Her work had brought her few friendships, and certainly none of the kind her mother had envisaged, though Lady Moystouan-Roswell continued to pin her faith in the efficacy of art and the intellect as the spearhead of some new form of sex-appeal in women.

Not only was Helena living in foreign land but her confidence in herself and in her womanly fulfilment had been so discouraged that she approached new faces with the utmost diffidence. As a result most of the friendships she made in London were either with the old or the very young.

The one exception was the editor of *The Maelstrom*. He had met Helena one Sunday in the house of her sister at Windsor. He was sufficiently abstracted as a man for her not to take undue alarm at him, while he was not interested enough in the womanliness of women to be dismayed by her awkwardness. They soon formed a firm, even if clearly delimited, friendship.

A week before her thirty-first birthday he had telephoned and asked her if she would like to go with him to see an exhibition of the work of a new young painter. She had accepted gladly for such invitations were rare in her life. But before the afternoon was over she had come near quarrelling with her companion, and was amazed by the passionate sense of revolt he aroused in her.

It all started over David's African pictures. She was quite startled by the effect they had on her. Her companion took her straight to David's most recent work, done in England, saying that it was by far the best of the exhibition. She was interested and pleased with what she saw but not unduly moved or excited until they came to the African section.

"You will see from this how much he has already learnt after eighteen months of civilisation with us," her companion said in his best *Maelstrom* manner. "Already we've taught him to think a bit before rushing into paint, to pay more attention to the demands of significant form and the abstraction of fundamental pattern and design and to cherish some elementary regard for the mathematics of real light and colour. But here"—he took in a whole room of canvasses with a disdainful sweep of the hand—"here, though there is no denying an uprush of a certain crude power, it is all just a bit too naïve, too naturalistic, you know, to be really interesting."

Helena's instinct instantly was to disagree.

This vision of David's childhood, youth and earliest manhood, as revealed in these canvasses, set an unknown pulse beating in her. As if in a trance she looked at the triumphal harmonies he made out of white sunlight and sonorous midnight bodies, finding herself deeply stirred. She felt as if one of the massive black women in the canvasses, with large black eyes so serene and profound that they seemed to hold the secret of life itself and with full exposed breasts swollen and heavy with rich white milk, had taken her right back to the moment of her own lost beginnings. This emotion of the past was so vivid and real, and assailed her faint and unreal present with such force, that tears of regret and agonising, remorseful self-pity rushed to her eyes, and she quickly turned her head to hide what she was feeling. Fortunately a blind rage at the cultured superior emotionless and sexless voice at her side, came to her rescue.

They had moved on and were standing in front of one of the smaller canvasses in the exhibition: a Zulu boy sitting on a stone with his naked back full on to the picture but head three-quarters turned. It was a wonderful back. Not heavy, yet broad at the shoulders and narrow at the waist, driven with swift and vital urgency like the head of a steel-blue arrow straight and deep into the curve of supple thighs. The boy was making a long, slender haft of a spear for his approaching manhood and peeling the cinnamon bark off a straight, round stick of young Assegai wood, the freshly peeled end of which, a simmering, green, sea-foam white, passed over the top of one arm and continued up the smooth firm neck and over the solemn, gently lowered anticipatory head. "You see what I mean?" her companion said. "A photograph would have done nearly as well."

"I couldn't disagree with you more," Helena was stung into saying, blushing at her own courage. "A photograph would never have given you that feeling."

"Feeling, my dear young lady," he replied with an ironical lift of the shoulders. "What is feeling? Everything is a feeling until the reason and will give it shape."

She was unable to answer although disagreeing still the more violently. Nothing in the exhibition thrilled her as this picture did. Never before in real life, or in her fondest early morning imagining, had any wayward, gypsy shape stirred her as did this painting of a young, graceful and athletic black boy. Some tremendously significant statement of truth seemed to her implicit in every line and shade of pose. Had not life in its fullest and most natural sense been for her, too, dark and unattainable, standing somewhere outside the threshold of her quenched being with its face averted and its back inscrutably and irrevocably turned on her?

She turned round to her companion and crushed the closely reasoned argument of the afternoon in an uncompromising manner by announcing: "I am going to buy this picture."

Her unexpectedly resolute tone imposed silence on her companion. And after the purchase of the picture Helena never lost an opportunity of hinting to him that she would like to meet the painter of her picture. She knew him well enough to ask outright for an introduction but her one gesture of independence in buying the picture seemed to have exhausted her confidence and courage. As a result, nearly half a year went by before she achieved, by diffident hinting, what might well have been accomplished in a week by straightforward asking.

When at last she and David did meet it was winter again and she was standing by a Chelsea fireplace very much as she stood in David's first portrait.

David saw her first without realising who she was though some remote and confused memory was at once set rumbling within him. He felt he had seen her before, known her intimately. . . . So worried was he by this sensation that he went to his host and asked who she was. "Helena Moystouan-Roswell," he was told. "She wants to meet you. Just wait a second and I'll introduce you."

Characteristically David did not wait but went over instantly, introduced himself, and said warmly and with real gratitude: "I can't thank you enough for buying that picture of mine. It was very good and brave of you and helped me a lot."

She blushed with embarrassment and yet, with a courage no one except herself could appreciate, continued to meet his glance.

At last the flat, shy, automatic voice of her upbringing, forced an answer. "It's I who have to thank you. It's such a very lovely painting. Only . . ." she paused. Dared she say it? And if she dared, how would she say it?

David continued to look at her, waiting patiently for her to continue. He had no idea of the effect he was having on her.

His own manner was entirely unselfconscious and spontaneous, and as he looked at Helena, suddenly he flicked back the hair which had fallen over his forehead as he bent down to listen to her. The quick movement sent a thrill through her stifled being, as if she had suddenly stumbled out of a dark wood straight on to a sun-lit clearing and seen a young lion stretching himself after a good, long sleep. Yes! Oh yes! She had never seen a lovelier face and head. Yet the very beauty hurt her and gave rise to a painful and terrifying anxiety. In what way was he already committed to life? Surely in such a way that she could only be an intruder. In her anxiety she forgot to finish her sentence.

131

As David waited the feeling of something familiar in the woman before him persisted, but the explanation came no nearer. He noticed suddenly that she was older than he thought. Her hair, he felt, should have been gathered together round her head, instead of falling in that wild, questing, little girl way towards her neat, uncherished shoulders. A sudden pity rose up in him: and at the same time a feeling of intense, inexplicable and quite indefinable alarm.

"I suspect you've already had second thoughts about buying that picture," he said with a quick smile. "Would you like to change it?"

"Good heavens no!" She answered fiercely, forgetting her embarrassment. "I wouldn't part with it for anything in the world. Only I wondered if you'd not done a companion piece?"

"A companion piece?" He didn't know what she was getting at.

"Yes." She nodded vigorously, the straight, sisal hair a-flutter. "I feel that, to be complete, that painting needs a companion; the subject done face to face, the other way round. What sort of a face did he have? What sort of a person was he?"

David was immediately interested in the point of view. "I know what you mean, but I'm afraid you're wrong," he answered. "I thought of it too at the time. But that's the only way I could possibly paint it. The face wouldn't have interested you either. . . . It was a face that has no meaning in this conscious, pale-faced world of ours."

As he spoke his eyes became bright. She noticed that they widened and changed colour as if the very thoughts themselves possessed colour. No man had ever spoken to her like that before, giving his thought naked and unashamed. She had enough intuition and painter's intelligence to see at once what he meant and said so.

"I do see it—but what a pity it should be so. I would so like him to have a real, not just a technical, face."

"It is a pity—an immense pity." And the pity of it uttered in David's voice which always was the least cerebral voice I knew and came straight from the centre of himself, lived with her for many days after.

So ended their first meeting, but before she left she asked her host: "Is Mr. Michaeljohn married?"

"Good God, no! What a fantastic thought!" The man answered, startled as much by the question as by the "mister". "David's only a boy!"

She had gone home her head ringing with relief, wondering how they were to meet again. She was not kept wondering long for, as she woke the following morning, a voice within was saying to her: "Commission him to do your portrait."

CHAPTER 12

WHEN David got Helena's letter some days later asking him if he would paint her portrait, his immediate instinct was to say no. He had come away from their meeting with a confused, troubled, almost frightened feeling. On top of it all he had suddenly begun to sleep badly. On the very night after meeting Helena he had been woken by a terrifying dream centring round Mary. Though his mind shirked the unpleasant detail of the dream, an impression of terror stayed with him all night and shadowed him by day. For some days he had been unable to work but had wandered aimlessly and restlessly through the parks, streets and round the picture galleries.

Helena was offering him a hundred guineas to do her portrait—apologising for this being so little, but saying that she could make up for it by sitting where and whenever it was convenient to him. . . . But if he would like to make use of her own studio she would be very happy to put it at his disposal. . . . Perhaps he would come to tea one afternoon and see whether he thought it a good idea. . . . In any case, whether he accepted the offer of the studio or not, she hoped he would have time to do the portrait which she had promised her mother to have done as soon as she found a painter whose work she liked sufficiently. . . .

David certainly needed all the money he could get. It would take him a year or two before he was ready for another exhibition and though his last had been unusually successful, he had been unable, as an unknown artist, to ask big prices. In the circumstances a hundred guineas was a remarkably generous offer.

He re-considered Helena's letter. It seemed almost irresponsible to refuse the offer. After many vacillations David decided that his hesitations were ridiculous and wrote a letter of grateful acceptance to Helena.

He duly went to tea. And saw the studio which was so much better and more comfortable than his own attic. Helena was so sweet, grateful and surprisingly intelligent about painting, that David decided it would be not only foolish but even inconsiderate not to paint her on her own ground. Once again out in the streets on his way home he was troubled and confused, but he no longer had enough patience with his misgivings to try and analyse them.

A fortnight later he began painting the portrait I have already described. He had his first great shock within a few minutes of starting it. Usually he had the end clearly in sight before he set brush to canvas. But no sooner did he start to pose Helena than he realised with shattering dismay that he had neither clear conception nor instinct of what he wanted and should do in her portrait.

A black mist of sheer panic for a moment clouded his senses, but will and determination compelled him to go on.

After an hour of frantic experimentation David had to say to Helena: "I hope you won't mind but I'm not going to rush into the final design. . . . I am going to take my time."

"Oh please do," she said eagerly, and added quickly with a nervous, girlish laugh: "Please do take your time."

David answered quickly. "I'm afraid I shall need it—because I don't find you altogether an easy subject."

"Oh dear!" she remarked with sudden wariness. "I hope that doesn't mean you find me altogether too uninspiring?"

"Of course not!" David answered at once. "It's just that you're not obvious, and quite different from anyone I've ever painted before."

"Have you painted many women, Mr. Michaeljohn?" The question rose like a hawk in the air and hung on trembling wings between them.

"My name's David. I'm not respectable enough to be a 'mister'," he said with an effort at lightness, and then answered: "I've never painted a white woman before, but if you include the blacks, why then yes, many."

"Perhaps that accounts for the difficulty," she remarked, hiding her delight at the answer behind an appearance of casualness.

"Perhaps, but I don't think so. I believe it's because you've a very complex and unusual character."

"Oh, have I? How nice of you to say so and how interesting," she replied, and instinctively turned her head to look at her reflection in the mirror near her side, saying while she looked herself steadily up and down: "I've always thought of myself as a very ordinary commonplace person—one of millions. I do hope you are right and—" The pause was hardly perceptible: "My name's Helena."

Her movement towards the mirror was the first unselfconscious action that David had perceived in her. It was so charmingly and naturally done that a feeling of potential grace and beauty fell like sunlight from a leaf about her.

David was touched by it and as he watched this woman turning on her reflection in the mirror a wondering, questioning gaze, some feeling from the past came to him with an elusive astringent poignancy. The feeling was beyond recall and left only a luminous blur, as mist on the ground on a summer's morning is all that is left of the great majestic clouds that brought rain and vanished over the darkened horizon in the night. Yet the sensation that "he had been there before" was vivid and real.

"Just stay like that for a moment . . . I think I know now how I'd like to paint you!" he said quickly before she could move. "Thank you . . . That's perfect. . . . Yes, I know your name is Helena. . . . I knew it even long before I met you."

But having found the pose did not mean that David's difficulties were over. Others crowded in on him. He'd never before felt in such a muddle. By lunch time he'd made so little progress, and was feeling so tired, that he gave up the struggle for the day.

Helena asked him to stay for lunch and it was obvious from the meal that she had not been caught unprepared. It was a solid, well-cooked, old-fashioned lunch. Helena's ideas of how men should be entertained were derived entirely from her experience with her own father. While she and David waited on food, she pressed a glass of sherry on him. David, who never drank in the day and rarely at night refused, but thinking he perceived a trace of bewilderment if not dismay behind Helena's features, he quickly changed his mind, had one glass and because it was so good and made him feel less tired, he had another. At luncheon there was a remarkably fine, dry white wine and a first-class port with his coffee.

David had been living for nearly three years on his own and all the good food and wine, beautifully served in pleasant surroundings, had the most soothing effect on his bewildered spirit. A natural reaction set in. His tiredness vanished. A warm feeling possessed his stomach and sent a sense of well-being, of calm and security, singing through his nerves. He became quite light-hearted and talked to Helena as he had never talked to a woman before. He found her an eager and intelligent listener and when she did say anything herself it was surprisingly to the point, sometimes sharpened with a curious, kittenish wit but generally backed by unexpectedly solid and substantial yeoman sense.

As Helena noticed David becoming more at ease, her own confidence increased. Shyness and awkwardness left her. Her cheeks grew flushed, her eyes widened and were bright with unimagined light.

When late in the afternoon David left it was almost with regret. For it had been nice talking to a woman again. But walking to his bus he soon forgot Helena. Suddenly one memory after another of his dead father rushed into his mind. All the way home he thought of Albert with such intensity and concentration that he was both amazed and puzzled. He'd not spared Albert a conscious thought for many years and yet there was the memory of his father, vivid and alive, riding the bus and walking the streets of London with him.

David telephoned to Helena the next morning with the intention of saying that he did not feel well enough to work that day but before he got beyond the exchange of courtesies, Helena said: "I had a feeling somehow that you wouldn't like to work this morning but would prefer the afternoon. Do say I am right? I've arranged everything accordingly."

Feeling curiously powerless to say no he went along dutifully to her studio in the afternoon, reminding himself all the way home how considerately she was behaving.

Yet the morning's rest had not made work easier. He realised painting Helena's portrait was going to be the longest and most difficult task he had ever undertaken, and again warned her of it. The warning did not alarm her in the slightest and there were even indications, which David dismissed abruptly, that she was pleased by it. At the end of the day she'd suggested that they should go out and dine somewhere in town. As David agreed he realised, with the same bleak sense of powerlessness which went over him, that he could not say "no" to her.

He sat glumly in her sitting-room, sipping a glass of sherry, while she changed in the room next door. The room was so near that he could hear the urgent swish of silk as she hastened to be ready for him. And that too, he was convinced, he had experienced somewhere before. Somewhere in his deepest memories there was a swirl and swish and rustle of shining dresses like the sea spreading the lace of its cloaked and mantled edges over yellow sands.

He jumped up, helped himself to another sherry and in a gesture that was not his own tossed it into his mouth and drank it in one gulp. That is how Albert used to drink, he thought, and at the same time became vexed with himself for thinking of his father again.

Then Helena came out dressed in a marshmallow pink that was rather too young for her, but the lamplight softened the lines of her face and made her eyes brighter. By that time David was responding to his sherry and feeling better. He made her race down the stairs with him and laughing and breathless they fell into the first taxi they could find.

Over coffee and after good wine and dinner, which Helena insisted on paying for, she said, encouraged by their mutual cheerfulness:

"Would you very much mind if I asked you your age, David?"

"Not at all. I'll be twenty-two in June," he said airily.

She didn't answer at once, bravely trying to absorb unnoticed the shock of his answer. She had known of course that he was young but she'd never thought that he was only twenty-two. From the authority of his manner and the maturity of his thought and work she'd imagined that he was at least twenty-six, perhaps older.

"What's the matter, Helena?" David asked, alarmed at her silence, and by the change in her expression. So touched was she by the concern in his voice that she put her hand on his arm with the first purely impulsive movement between them, and said in a low, full and true voice: "Nothing—except that you're so young that I envied you. D'you know how old I am?"

Fear within her protested that this was going too far, but she dismissed it and repeated her question to David.

"I never think of people in terms of their age," he answered, glad that on the whole he could do so truthfully.

"Well I'm much, much older than you," she told him in a bantering tone, thinking if I really frighten him first the truth won't seem so much when it comes. "I'll be thirty-one in a few days."

"You don't look it," he answered. "And in any case thirty-one isn't old."

"You're wrong," she said seriously. "It matters terribly if you are a woman. In any case women are much older for their ages than men."

"Nonsense!" he told her, feeling oddly responsible even for

the difference in their ages and desperately trying to reassure her. "Nonsense!" he repeated, and yet felt his reassurance was not fair to either of them.

It was late when David saw Helena home in a taxi. He went with her to the door, said good-night, and excused himself, but as the taxi was about to move off he saw her still uncertain and fumbling.

He jumped out, went over and asked: "Is anything the matter, can I help?"

She looked up, her eyes shining with a light which in his youngness he did not understand, but which was signalling with a desperate, underworld courage: Please don't go; please don't leave me. Please come in and stay.

"I couldn't find my key, that's all," she said with a curious huskiness. "But now I've got it."

"Good! Good-night," he said.

"Good-night, David," she answered, but as the taxi drove away she was still standing in the half open door.

For David now the days had begun to drag. Suddenly everything had become different; even time had changed its meaning. There were moments when it seemed to him as if the hours were not merely slowed down but actually running backwards. One night he had a fantastic vision of a large grandfather clock not going tick-tock but tock-tick, and both hands going anti-clockwise till at last the days and the months, the Reckitts blue chart of the sky and the stars above the time face, all moved resolutely and deliberately in reverse.

But even that had not been a warning to him. Then thoughts of Albert and Mary, at all moments of the night and day seemed to dart like rabbits out of their burrows, flash briefly, disturbingly in the sunlight of his mind, take alarm and vanish down their tunnels again. He went about with a strange, preoccupied air and even his landlady, busy and over-worked, thought he looked very unhappy.

Often he thought he would go and say to Helena: "Look, I'm sorry . . . I just can't do your portrait. I don't know why but I am dreadfully tired. Let's put it off for a year and I'll try again." But he'd no sooner decided to do so, than panic seized him.

The most intense and quite indefinable anxieties about Helena overwhelmed him.

And he felt responsible for her. Nowadays he felt responsible for everything, everything seemed to weigh upon him, to depend upon him, and to call for more and more effort from him. He would get up in the mornings and decide that the portrait was off for the day. But, as he walked to telephone to tell Helena so, these irrational fears would take possession of him. Not since he had stood at the gate of the Michaeljohn home after Albert's death, waiting for Mary to come back from the village, had he known such fear and anxiety on another person's behalf. Inevitably of course he would put on his hat and coat and go to the studio as fast as he could, but no sooner had he been welcomed in warmly by a new and more serene Helena, than he would realise how ridiculous, absolutely fantastic and impossible his anxiety had been. The fear and the Helena in his mind were in a sense not of that world, nor of that time and place.

Feeling foolish, he would settle down grimly to batter and drive his unwilling, confused senses to complete the portrait. He had never known more exhausting work and longed eagerly for the luncheon break which was now taken for granted between them. Yet once he had taken his wine and food, the midnight and morning mood vanished and he became a reasonable cheerful person, happy in Helena's company. He could not make head or tail of himself and in the end stopped trying, and accepted the disturbing paradox as inevitable. Only one thing he could never get used to and that was his apparent powerlessness to say "No" to Helena. So self-reliant, resolute and knowing of his mind and wishes in the world of men, the effort of saying "No" to Helena cost him such a disproportionate expense of spirit and energy that it seldom seemed worth-while.

I know that when David told me this, it flashed through my mind that the effort of saying "No" to Mary in the final issue in Africa perhaps had been so great that it had exhausted all his capacity to refuse a woman. Or was there, after all, another explanation? In a way, as my father had instinctively divined, David had not said "No" to Mary in Africa. In fact, perhaps in not saying "No" to Helena he was saying "Yes" to Mary by proxy, and continuing to bend himself to an archaic will at a distance. If only this question had been available to David at the time, things might have been different and that fatal portrait never painted.

Yet if David found his days burdensome and heavy, for Helena they had grown wings. Time now bothered her only when David was not with her. Her being which hitherto had been—to borrow one of the more sinister platitudes of our time—working to rule, had suddenly become a busy factory. Overnight everything in the world about her had acquired meaning. Even the dark and unusually dreary winter was packed and charged for her with a beauty she had never known. So keen had her senses become that she believed at times she could almost hear the bulbs stirring in their pots in her studio, and see round the head of David bent over his canvas a glow, a continuous ethereal emanation of the warmth and light of the innermost fire of his being, like a trembling crown of delicate pentecostal flame on the golden-brown hair. When he left her in the evenings and the door shut behind him, she felt in separation as if her body had been wounded in the quick of its being. And at night lying in the dark she would see his face, indelibly photographed in her senses, shining so brightly that she was convinced she could, did she wish to interrupt the blessed vision, read a poem by its light.

One thing only still spoilt her days and troubled her nights; the difference in their ages. Often when she looked at him she would be attacked by the most acute sense of guilt. She had no right, she would tell herself, to feel as she did. It was terribly unfair to him. "One day he'll hate me for it," she would think in desperation. "I should protect him." And in those moods she would go down on her knees before going to bed at night and pray: "Dear God, please don't let me hurt him. Please don't make me possessive. Please let me do what is best for him."

But her reservations, her prayers, her resolution, did not last and quickly burned to cinders in the fierce fire of her longing to be with David.

Two days before Christmas, which she was to spend at her home in East Anglia, she and David walked slowly through the park before tea. She noticed that he was feeling depressed and when they came to the bridge over the bottom of the Serpentine he stopped, and leaned over the parapet, looking solemnly at the ice below. Although he had done so abruptly without saying a word, she too swung round, joined him, leant over and taking his arm, tentatively and almost furtively said:

"You're feeling depressed, David, aren't you?" And as she spoke she hoped that this mood might have something to do with her departure.

"Yes," he agreed. "Christmas always depresses me."

"Me too. It brings back the past. But is that all?"

"I think so . . . excepting that sometimes I feel oddly doomed in a queer kind of way."

"Oh, David, what a horrible feeling." She'd never heard him talk like this and was thoroughly alarmed. "D'you often feel like that?"

"No, not often. But sometimes lately I feel as if a strange kind of vengeance is peering over my shoulder. . . . I feel I must hurry because soon it will catch up with me."

He seemed to shiver as he spoke and as he turned to her his eyes were unusually large and serious, indeed so naked were they and so defenceless that she felt her own regard walk like an armed intruder into them.

She turned her head to hide the tears that rushed to her

eyes. I love him. I love him, she thought tragically. And he tells me he feels doomed. . . . Oh, God, what shall I do?

A cold wind stirred over the park, ruffled the feathers of the ducks, drakes and sea-gulls standing frozen on the bank of the Serpentine, and raised a faint, harp-like moan from the tree-tops.

"I feel like those birds somehow," David said, trying to laugh himself back into a sense of proportion, "out of my proper element."

"But, dear David, you mustn't feel like that," she said, trying to rally both his and her own spirits. "You're so young. Already you've done so much, and you've your whole life in front of you."

But he gave an unconvinced, impatient shrug of his shoulders. "I expect you're right . . . but it makes no difference. I feel particularly doomed to-day—p'raps it's only Christmas."

He stopped and looked at the sky. In the silence they heard the noise of the distant traffic going like a waterfall over the steep edge of the wintry silence. Towards the west the dark, purple clouds massed over the town and drew its smoke and mists like a veil over their faces. As he stared silently the dark sky seemed to crack abruptly. The crack widened and a red and almost legendary and mythological light, a strange Wagnerian note in colour poured swiftly through it.

"Tell me honestly, Helena, have you never had a similar feeling yourself? Surely it's not peculiar to me?" David returned again to the question that she wanted to forget.

Helena shook her head, kept her eyes averted, and answered in a low voice, "No . . ."

"Haven't you felt sometimes about places, and peoples, and things that you have been there and through it all before? For instance, haven't you felt there might be something pre-arranged about our meeting? I have . . . I don't feel it's entirely casual and unexpected but part of a—a plan . . ." He was going to say "plot" but censored that just in time.

144

His mood was her enemy. She felt surrounded in her heart by dark, cloaked and daggered figures—but she was damned if she'd compromise with them.

She threw back her head with a determined lift of the firm, rounded chin, and said clearly and loudly: "No, David! I've always felt it to be most unexpected . . . I never expected to meet someone like you. For me there's been something miraculous about it. For me it's a fairy tale."

"How very sweet of you to see it like that."

Although touched, his voice was unconvinced and unconvincing, and his eyes still on the clouds. Red and black, black and red, he thought. Even the clouds are riding the sky in the colours of doom.

He turned to look at her and forced another laugh. "I'm sorry to be so depressing. I think it's the day. Rather a sinister evening, isn't it? Look, it's cracking like a mirror in the flames." He pointed at the dying day. "I expect it was on a day like this that Clytemnæstra decided to do Agamemnon in, or that Hamlet ran his sword through the scarlet curtains to kill his sweetheart's father."

They stood silently. Yes, thought David bitterly, it sometimes seems to me that I can read Hamlet's mind better than my own. Everyone supposes that Hamlet's tragedy was that he had to avenge his father. But only the middle-classes in our middle-class age imagine that sons can love their fathers enough to want to avenge them. . . . Only security and safety-first merchants dare keep up appearances to such lengths before our proud and ancient aristocratic spirit. But no prince of royal blood would dream of such a thing. No, Hamlet's misfortune was not that his father was murdered but that his father had to be killed again in the person of his successor. "The old mole indeed burrowed too fast for him," he said aloud.

Helena realised the heavy mood was still upon him but though saddened by her inability to distract him she thought that perhaps if she went with his mood a little way she might then be able to lead it aside. "Talking of Agamemnon, d'you remember those lovely lines about the nightingales singing in the wood near the convent of the Sacred Heart?

> '*And sang within the bloody wood*
> *When Agamemnon cried aloud,*
> *And let their liquid siftings fall*
> *To stain the stiff dishonoured shroud.*'"

"Yes," he answered, "but what about the lines before?

> '*The host with someone indistinct*
> *Converses at the door apart.*'"

"I could paint life like that," he added gloomily, "as a host with his back to a bright, warm room, conversing with us in muttered, half-intelligible tones."

She'd never known him in such a heavy mood. Despair overcame her. She turned and said tonelessly, the spirit gone quite out of her: "I'm rather tired. Would you mind if we went home?"

CHAPTER 13

HELENA never liked returning to her parental home but this Christmas she hated it more than ever. David's parting mood followed her like her own shadow and would not leave her alone. On top of it the sense of vital, amputated separation from him was so keen that she felt it like violent physical pain.

Then she was terrified by the slowness of time. She never knew that seconds could be so long, and could contain so much of conscious separation. It was as if all that was left of life to her could run to waste in a single day. And even when she realised that in a week she would be seeing David again, what had she to hope for judging by the mood in which she had left him?

On Christmas Day, after church, she could bear it no longer and decided to telephone him. She was amazed as she lifted the receiver to find her hand trembling violently. And when David answered the telephone even her knees were shaking.

But she came away from the telephone with shining eyes. Obviously David had been pleased to hear her voice, extremely grateful to her for ringing, but said he'd been very worried about her, apologised for his mood, assuring her it had disappeared the very next day.

That night after dinner she talked to her mother about David. Lady Moystouan-Roswell listened to her daughter's long, detailed account of her love with effortless patience and mounting hope. The only interruptions she permitted herself were practical and untroubled by illusions of any kind. After the first stammering sentence, she asked point blank: "D'you love him?" and when Helena said quickly in her little girl voice: "Terribly, Mummy!" Lady Moystouan-Roswell settled herself deep into the couch by the fire, and listened

147

with rising satisfaction for nearly an hour before she asked: "Does he love you?"

"I don't know, Mummy, that's just it," Helena said distressed. "But I don't think so. I don't think he knows what it is to be in love with a woman."

"A pity." Lady Moystouan-Roswell said in a matter of fact tone. "But if he's fond of you, that's enough to go on with. Many successful marriages have been founded on less."

Her mother's words went through Helena like warmed wine on a cold night. But, she insisted, there was always this awful, yawning gulf of years between them, nothing could alter that. . . . She produced this greatest of all her difficulties with a fearful and protracted diffidence.

But to her amazement, even this constituted no great barrier in her mother's mind, which on this issue possessed the simplicity of great and instinctive genius. That was a pity too, Lady Moystouan-Roswell said, but no more. Helena would quickly find out that it didn't really matter what age men were. They were all really only children, rather naughty and dirty children, too. Accepting that fact made life with them both intelligible and bearable. Look at her father, for instance. The world was just an enlarged, better, and brighter nursery for him; even his daughters had to be roped in as nurses and governesses!

Helena protested vehemently at this and said that if she couldn't do better with David than that she'd rather not marry at all.

"You should see David, Mummy," she said. "He's such a lovely, trusting person and I don't want to hurt him."

"I'm suggesting you should marry him, not hurt him," her mother said severely. "Contrary to what people think nowadays the two things are not necessarily synonymous. From what you have told me of this young man's character London must be full of real dangers for such an inexperienced young man. And from what you say I think he must be very fond of you—perhaps fonder than you know. I'm convinced from his point of view that he'd do well, and be wise, to marry you. And didn't I hear you say he was a Colonial?"

"Oh, Mummy, please don't start thinking of David as a Colonial."

Helena's eyes flamed with such real rebellion and anger that Lady Moystouan-Roswell accepted her daughter's rebuke with good grace, as she kissed her fondly good-night.

"Nothing is ever perfect, my child. What we must all learn early is not to let the best make the good impossible, otherwise life itself would not go on. But I'd like to meet this . . . David. When the portrait is ready send for me and I'll come down and talk it over officially."

The portrait was finished towards the end of January. By that time David had worked at it so hard that he felt quite dead about it. It left a lifeless taste in his mouth, like a mouthful of sawdust on a thirsty day. But Helena professed to be tremendously pleased with it. Her mother was sent for at once and a meeting between the three of them, and the portrait, arranged. On the afternoon of January 31st they met for tea in Helena's studio.

Lady Moystouan-Roswell's first reaction to David was to admire the perceptive accuracy with which her daughter had described him to her. While with the skill of an old hand she simultaneously put David at his ease, and looked at the portrait with apparent rapture, she yet was making a swift preliminary appraisal of his qualities as if indeed he were Helena's special creation and owed his merit entirely to her affection.

In this appraisal there was a subtle suggestion of certain proprietary assumptions, a consciousness of permission to enter and view with the option to occupy, which did not altogether escape David. Though he did not know precisely how to interpret it he translated it into an immediate feeling of hostility. As a result he returned her looks with such directness that Lady Moystouan-Roswell within a few minutes qualified the impression Helena had given her of David by saying to herself: "He is much more independent than Helena realises." But she requalified this assessment again a few minutes later. Stealing a glance at David she noted that he was looking at her daughter with eyes that had momentarily gone over to the object of their regard, as if he was hypnotised. That had reassured her and sharpened her appetite for immediate action of some kind. When Helena left them to supervise the tea, after again thanking David charmingly for doing the portrait and again telling him how much she liked it and how happy she was to have such "a speaking and graceful likeness" she decided that the crucial moment had come.

Her large pale blue eyes suddenly went dark with feeling and her features assumed an expression of intense maternal concern, as she told him that Helena had always been her favourite daughter, her baby, and added: "Loving her as I do Mr. Michaeljohn, I must confess to you and I do know you'll understand and forgive me, when I say that I have watched, from a distance, your progress in this portrait with increasing anxiety."

"I do understand, Lady Moystouan-Roswell," David agreed heartily. "I don't mind telling you it's kept me awake at nights too. I thought I'd never finish it. It's not been easy."

"I am not sure that we mean the same thing," she answered after a moment's hesitation. "*I*'ve been anxious about my daughter, not her portrait."

"I'm afraid I don't follow you at all," David said frankly, watching her with extreme and puzzled wariness.

"I can see I must be more frank," she replied, the blue in her eyes suddenly becoming lighter. "I thought that as an artist you would have understood more readily. You have taken a long time, I understand a most unusually long time, painting my daughter's portrait, and in the process, I fear, you've made her very fond of you."

David went white with despair and blind rage at the unfairness, the unprovoked and sheer, horrible unfairness of her suggestion. He looked straight back at her and saw that though the face of the old lady in front of him was composed and serene, and the hair that fell abundantly over her neck and ears was white as innocence, yet her eyes had became a very light, a very determined and unresponsive noonday blue.

"You cannot be as obtuse as you appear," she answered. "You've made Helena fall in love with you. You see, Helena told me everything at Christmas. D'you understand me now, Mr. Michaeljohn, she told me everything."

"What on earth d'you mean by everything?" David asked blankly, not knowing what more of disaster could happen to him.

"I do not propose underlining anything to you, nor do I believe it is necessary," she said rather severely. Then softening her voice and putting her hand lightly on David's knee she went on: "Forgive me if I sound harsh. I don't mean to be. But I'm nearly out of my mind with anxiety over Helena. You've—No, it is no good protesting—" she gave his unwilling knee an almost playful tap. "You've made her so fond of you that should you not return her affections I don't know what she'll do. I warn you most solemnly that I could not be held responsible for her actions—"

Any further discussion was put to an end by Helena arriving to summon them for tea, and Lady Moystouan-Roswell was well content to leave it there. One look at David's face was enough to convince her of the overwhelming effect of her direct approach. Whatever defences—and to do her justice she had no idea how pitifully unarmed and inwardly divided the boy already was—whatever forces of resistance David had, she was certain they had been dispersed. Her instinct was to leave the field now to Helena before any effort could be made to regroup these forces. So half-way through tea she made an excuse, most convincingly staged, and then rose to leave David and Helena alone.

After kissing her mother "good-bye", Helena walked back from the front door, with her knees shaking as they had shaken on her way to telephone to David on Christmas Day. Her mother had not mentioned her conversation with David. With the instinctive cunning of the experienced and disillusioned old hand she gave Helena no hint that anything unusual had passed between them.

Her strength, Lady Moystouan-Roswell told herself, will be that she is innocent. She can even disown me and my actions if necessary. So all she permitted herself to say to Helena as she held her warmly in her arms was: "I like your David immensely. I am sorry I thought of him as a Colonial. It was very wrong of me."

However, Helena had known all through tea that something serious had happened to David and she suspected it was connected with her mother. The look that she had encountered for the first time that wind-tossed evening before Christmas in the park was again deeply engraved in his features. And now she was about to find out what had caused it. Her heart was heavy within her and fears with no name to them flew round her head like bats in dying sky.

David, sitting deep in unbelieving rebellion against all the world, raised his head slowly as the door opened and shut softly behind Helena. The eyes she looked into were so charged with tension that all idea she might have had of being tactful, quickly left her.

"What is it, David? What's happened?" she asked quickly and anxiously.

"Your mother," he said gruffly. "Didn't she tell you anything?"

"No... Nothing to explain this. All she said was that she liked you immensely. She was really terribly, terribly impressed with you and the portrait." Helena's voice brightened defensively.

"Told you nothing?" David could scarcely believe his own ears.

"No? Why?" Helena asked tonelessly.

David jumped up as if the rage exploding in him had blown him out of his chair. He started walking up and down the room in an infuriated manner and then, coming to a stop in front of her he said suddenly, all inhibitions forced from his mind: "Helena, I hate your mother!"

Suddenly it was so quiet that they could almost hear between them an urgent traffic of thought. She'll never speak to me again now, David thought, a new anxiety overpowering him. She'll ask me to leave, and never see me again.

He looked at Helena searchingly, almost pleadingly, as if asking for understanding of the enormity of emotion that had possessed him.

But it was as if the force of David's emotion had overflowed and broken into an unknown part of Helena's mind too, for she looked up at him and said in a frightened whisper: "I think I hate her too a bit, if she makes you feel like that."

"My God, Helena, you're amazing," David said almost laughing in a kind of hysterical reaction. "I think you're the most surprising person I've ever met."

"But I want to know what Mother said to you."

"All right, I'll tell you. . . . But what about a drink first? I feel quite done in."

Vaguely Helena led the way into the drawing-room. David helped himself to a stiff whisky, tossed it down with Albert's celebrated gesture, had another, turned to join Helena and then saw the couch on which he'd just been sitting with her mother. At once he felt angry again.

"What did you tell your mother at Christmas?" he asked peremptorily.

Helena went very pale. "I don't know what you mean precisely. I told her lots of things," she answered, in turn feeling herself threatened.

"Your mother says you told her 'everything'. What does she mean by 'everything'?" he asked again, angrily.

"I don't know what she means by 'everything'," Helena's voice became almost shrill. A feeling of utter hopelessness overcame her. It might as well come out. "I only told her that I loved you," she said, and putting her head down between her arms on the side of the couch she began to cry in silent and choking spasms.

"Oh, Helena, don't please, for God's sake, don't!"

Utterly miserable David went up to her and patted her shoulder, near tears himself. This was the end then, he thought, with desolate bitterness. Suddenly he felt terribly isolated, like a climber on some steep and frost-bitten peak, out of range of the ordinary senses, far from normal traffic and desire. Yet this was the moment—he felt it intuitively—with the night already flying up and whistling towards him like a fine-feathered arrow from the red-combed west, when he should have been making camp and preparing his defences against the dark, even though the site on which he found himself was not the well-favoured and wind-sheltered pitch he would have chosen. But Life itself seemed to have thrust the situation on him and so he would accept it, he told himself, not like a pig squealing at a butcher's knife, but quietly and with dignity. He would take up this burden as if he liked it and make such a virtue, such a bride out of this necessity that fate itself would feel rebuked and defeated. Somehow he'd always known without knowing that this was how it had to be. But he could go to his doom like a man on his way to meet a long-lost friend and together he and Helena could take on themselves such a snow-bound beauty that they would out-glitter the dark.

"Please don't cry, Helena," he said kneeling beside her and turning her gently towards him with great and tender compassion as for a fellow victim. "Please don't cry. It's so sweet of you to feel like this about me. . . . Now please listen."

So absorbed was she in her weeping that she dried her tears like a little girl with the sleeve of her coat and looked up at him with swollen, misty eyes. Again the gesture was so unpremeditated and so without self-consciousness of any kind that it stirred him deeply.

"Listen," he said, with grave and new tenderness, "I must be very honest with you. I've never loved a woman. I don't know what it is to be 'in love'. In an odd way I've never felt free in that part of myself. . . . You don't know how I have

154

longed to, but it's always been as if love, in the normal sense of the word, is forbidden me. I can't explain it even to myself for I've never understood it. Apart from my sister, my own mother and Alex's mother, you're the only woman I've ever really known."

"For God's sake, don't say you're very fond of me . . . I couldn't bear that." Helena made a gesture of passionate rebellion, the tears once more coming to her eyes.

"You're wrong, very wrong, to reject that," he said earnestly. "That is exactly what I am going to say. I am very fond of you, so fond that I want to give you, out of affection, what people normally can only give in love. If you can accept that—then here I am."

"No, no! David. It's not fair to you," she shook her tearful head vigorously. She longed to be able to say, If you can't love me, run as fast as you can. There's the door, go and in God's name, never to return. But her response to him was too powerful for her to be able to make more than a formal protest.

"Fairness doesn't enter into it," he replied, his mind serving her motion rather than his own. "It's my choice and wish."

She drank in his rejections of her protest like a person who is dying of thirst.

"Oh, David, is it really? If only you could see into my heart it has more than enough love for two, even enough to stand between you and your silly old doom."

At her words the dark tide flooded back into him. He stood up, his hand still on her shoulder, and saw his face in the mirror one half with an ancient, flickering unstable glow on it from the light of the wood fire; the other deep in the shadow. It looked like an antique mask of his face on the head of a stranger, some celebrated actor from a far but famous country.

He bent down abruptly and took her hands. Poor, poor Helena, he thought as he saw her tear-stained face. Then he pulled her to her feet. "Let's go and drink to ourselves," he said.

CHAPTER 14

DAVID didn't tell any of us, not even Mary, that he was going to marry Helena, or rather that Helena was going to marry him. He didn't even tell us when they were married. We none of us heard of it until nearly two years later, and might not have known then if a significant coincidence had not suddenly brought it to light.

The Prime Minister of our country, who had owed much in his youth to Albert's generosity and who also was an uncle of the man who was about to marry Anna Maria, had therefore another good cause for remembering and considering the Michaeljohns. So on his return to Fort White from an important Imperial mission to London, he immediately telephoned to Mary and said:

"I thought you'd be glad to know that David is very well and most highly thought of in London. . . . No. . . . I didn't see him but I met his father-in-law Sir Arthur Moystouan-Roswell. . . . Yes, amazing wasn't it? He gave me all the news. . . ."

Too proud to show the shock the news was to her, Mary thanked him gracefully and after a few more inquiries put the receiver down without a tremor. But inside the emotions stormed at her. What had she done to merit that this shattering event should be hidden from her? How like her ungrateful, wayward and mysterious son. Had he imagined she would take the first ship to England and try to stop his marriage if he told her of his intention? Supposing he had, what need to hide it from her once it had happened? It was such a gratuitous, such a pointless and yet such a vital and effective way of wounding her, that it seemed calculated and deliberate.

She sat down at once and wrote us a passionate letter composed of urgent requests for any news we had of David's marriage, a letter tempered ironically by a consciousness that David appeared to have chosen his in-laws well. This last consideration in the end went a long way to softening the blow for Mary.

We, of course, could not answer any of Mary's questions for she in fact was telling us the news. The only important difference in our situation was that I was not entirely surprised by the news. For two years I'd suspected that something vital had either happened to David or was about to happen to him though his letters, after that first brief description which accompanied the photograph of her portrait, never again mentioned Helena to me.

I had ordered photographs of all his exhibited work, and his pictures had been having the most indefinable but nonetheless real and intensely worrying effects on me.

A disturbing element had appeared in them like the line of an eclipse spreading across the face of the moon. I began to notice, creeping into David's new work, an element of subtle, complex, almost deliberate disorder. No matter how closely knit and solidly designed his pictures continued to be, they seemed to be built round something out of harmony with the ordered whole.

In particular, there was one picture of a room by the Mediterranean which haunted my days as well as nights. Although outside its windows there was a wild, leaping, passionate and beckoning sea, David deliberately and pointedly rejected and belittled it, concentrating all his resources on the sunlight imprisoned in bars on the wall within. This picture's uncomprehended meaning rang deeply in me. David told me years later that it was the first picture he painted after his marriage. He had wanted to call it "Sunlight Prison" but thought the title would hurt Helena and so left it nameless.

Inadequate as these intimations were, I was most grateful for them when the secret of David's marriage finally exploded. For thanks to them I was able to take the news calmly. I must make it clear that, as with David's flight to England, it was not the fact of the marriage that upset me and my parents. It was once again the secrecy of it that seemed so sinister. It was a vote of no-confidence in us. Besides, my instinct told me that the good, true, and real in life not only has no use for secrecy but shuns it like the devil. It is a subtle, diabolic and corrosive poison which, unless utterly rejected, ultimately eats its way into every cell of our being. And already the Michaeljohn secret at work in David showed that it had acquired an alarmingly wide field of action. It was no longer merely a strange, irrational fear of lightning in sunlight but what was for most people the vital experience of maturity—his life with a woman. My heart went cold at the enormity and the unendingness of it. As I thought of the first small manifestation of this secret, this sly invasion of David's nature, as I called it, witnessed by me during that first thunderstorm after Albert's death, I felt as if I had been watching for a long time the shadow of an eclipse slowly climbing up the silvery rim of the moon's face, and I wondered to myself how much of that lovely, gentle light would have to be devoured by the bedragoned darkness before the full rounded beauty appeared again.

A heart-rending wail went up from the assembled instincts of my being like the cry of despair from a tribe of primitive negroes in the heart of Africa who, when watching an eclipse of the sun, believe that it is being devoured by a fabulous monster never again to emerge. For remember I had no experience, not a shred of knowledge to tell me how David would come out of this ordeal. I had only the faint whisper of my love, like a breeze in the spring bringing news of rain which told me: stand fast. Whatever happens just go on loving David, for you are the keeper of the memory of what he was and is meant to be. As long as you keep that alive, come all the world and all fate against him, he will not die. I drew courage, thank God, from an intuition whispering love through the tumult, and sent my own heart and mind with that old aboriginal tracker on the faded, desert spoor of the David within me. Yet it was not easy. Worse things began to happen to David, and finally, from my point of view, the worst of all.

I have mentioned my disquiet over the trend in David's painting during the first two years of his marriage to Helena. It was nothing compared to the anxiety I now experienced. For nearly a year David hardly painted at all. I know there were people who thought the break would do him good. But I knew it was a bad sign. I could not remember a day when David had not been modelling, drawing, painting or shaping something, and it made me mad that his intellectual friends could not see that it was natural and effortless.

A year later he started again, but the shock I suffered when I saw what he was doing was very great. Yet the applause, the maelstrom of praise swirling round him was so loud that I could hardly hear my own murmur of dismay.

David was beginning to paint in a new way. The outside world seemed suddenly to have ceased to exist for him. His back was determinedly turned on life as we normally see and experience it. He who until now had loved the ceaseless traffic of light, colour, sound and smells, the world charged with meaning and beauty, suddenly rejected it all, and began to paint only a strange world within. I have said "a" and not "the" deliberately for had it been the whole of the world within I would not have been so worried. After all, the world within and the world without are equally valid although neither of them in isolation is ultimately adequate. It is possible for a nature to be dedicated to all of either without damage to its integrity. But David's new world was only a fragment, a carefully selected portion of the immense within.

The world he was painting was centred entirely in his head. It gave me the impression that his nature, feeling itself threatened from within, had withdrawn itself to where it felt strongest and would be most accessible to external support; but in the process it had abandoned all its defences to the enemy. In three years his painting had become the painting of a man in desperate retreat, of a person holding on to life not by instinctive love but merely by a conscious and determined effort of the will and the mind.

And the images that crowded into his pictures clearly showed it. They had no colour or solid, rounded shape to them, no muscle and bone, but were so cold, thin, unfelt and miasmic that they drifted like the ghosts of unborn and miscarried children across his canvasses. No human body had any honour with this new David. From the chin downwards the body had ceased to have meaning; arms, legs, hands and feet were perfunctorily added, and often the ribs and spine were shown through a wide-open chest, like the columns of a chapel in front of a deserted and crumbling altar.

But if the shapes in David's pictures lacked recognisable bodies, they were never short of heads. Two, three and even four heads on one thin neck and one brittle, mist-dissolving body were not uncommon. Many faces had two or three rows of eyes, one mouth and jaw in front and another in reserve, and one noble, high brow stacked upon another. This obsession with the head, as if a multiplicity of these could make up for the utter and total rejection of what was below, was so marked that I could find a parallel for it only in the remote and legendary past, and I realised sadly that David had not only rejected the world without but also the world of his own urgent time. He had ceased to be contemporary; had ceased to meet the demands proper to his age and its time context, and had gone archaic. I felt the only people who could welcome this David and his work with understanding and sympathy were those Greeks for whom the hydra-headed monster was a living reality.

The sense of danger and unrecognised distress that went with all these multi-headed designs was truly alarming. One saw those colourless phantom figures fleeing in flames through streets, pursued always by some nameless thing out of sight, or else standing on the edge of bridges with broken arches, one row of eyes focused one way, the other row another, staring down into dark, unrippled waters at dead and drowning female faces staring expressionlessly upwards. But where was that inner richness of colour and shape which Life welcomes into the heart of the our being? Oh, it was very sad and most bitter. Finally, I saw the portrait of a man with a most moving, sensitive, wide-eyed face, and a noble head slightly bowed with infinite resignation. The head was full-face and was unexpectedly real, although it was supported on the left and the right by its own profiles. The body was a phantom shape composed of the dispersing smoke of a burnt-out fire. Out of the corner of each of the beautiful, tragic eyes, a tear like a Pacific pearl with a sad, submarine stain on it, was falling. This painting was called "The Exile" and the moment I saw it, I understood.

I was looking at the new photography, the photography of the great and threatened world within. What David was doing was to copy with photographic and unerring exactitude his own state of mind and spirit. He was constructing an Admiralty chart of the troubled seas of his own being. It confirmed every fear I had. I looked at "The Exile" closely and saw that the features were David's. At last, he had done a portrait of himself, as that wise old Frenchman had so long ago suggested. But he had left it dangerously, perhaps fatally, late.

I was not astonished when, after completing this picture, David stopped painting altogether. I waited, hoping against hope that the flame would flare up again and the smoke and phantoms vanish, but "The Exile" appeared final. The years went by without David completing even a single painting or drawing. I prayed every night that Helena would understand, as I did, and be able to help.

But she had not had the upbringing and the life which made it possible for her to help him. For years she had been so driven against her own instincts that she was ignorant of their infinitely varied, complex and finely creative implications and could recognise them only in their most vehement and elemental form; and then only as proved and doughty antagonists. There was no friendship for herself within herself. The more David withdrew into himself the more jealously possessive she became and the more fiercely her being clamoured for what was being withheld, in spite of her constant resolutions and prayers to the contrary.

David had begun by being absolutely honest with Helena. He had told her plainly he could only go into marriage with her as a friend. At the time it had sounded so reasonable, even dignified, that he thought it would be almost easy. But he soon found that there were other sides to his nature that took a different view. His body, for instance, was most crudely, obstinately and blindly difficult on this issue. It did not like being touched or fondled by Helena. No matter how much David's mind and initial affection objected to this behaviour, his body continued to shrink from Helena. Time and again he was startled and dismayed by the violence with which this impermanent physical substance of his being rose into rebellion, and its refusal to be convinced and guided by his own unselfish motivations. The only time when it was more or less tolerant of physical contact with Helena was when it was soothed by drink.

Very early on, David had, as I mentioned, discovered "the civilising influence" that drink had on his relationship with Helena, and he was forced to continue the practice. But the discovery quickly turned into a two-edged weapon. The relationship in which he had offered himself to Helena could only, it seemed, be maintained as a drunken one. Longer and longer periods of the day became endurable only if supported by drink. Within a year or two the same longing invaded David's nights as well. He would wake up in terror and could not sleep until he had drunk a glass of neat spirits. Finally he could not get up at all in the morning until he had had a drink to help him out of bed, and slowly the corrosive circle drew itself tightly round night as well as day. From then on David, desperate in his effort at self-appeasement, was so continuously under the influence of drink that he was sober but sober only in one key, only in one moment sealed off from all other moments, as if the burning draughts rediscovered for him the secret of infinity which he'd once possessed in the first drops of milk sucked from Mary's breasts. Ah! Mary's tender breast, what great, what monstrous longing and batlike thirst was started and nourished thereby.

In the end David had come to deny even the conscious, reasoned integrity with which he had begun the relationship. When Helena, crying and desperately unhappy, said wildly: "It's no use, you don't love me, you don't love me. I wish I were dead. I could gladly kill myself," he no longer said "But Helena dear, I was honest with you from the start. That was never part of our bargain." Instead in great compassion he lied to her saying: "Don't cry, Helena dearest, don't cry for I have changed and truly love you." But she still wept at his side because her body knew that David had failed it, knew that David had merely discharged a conscious duty with will and determination.

For a time David's pretence made her happier but in the end it was doomed to fail before the keen vision of that wise and unillusioned knowledge which unconsciously we carry about within us. This pretence, when seen through, was the final depravity, the ultimate indignity for Helena's spirit. So her failure to rouse the complete, adult male in him, she now projected on to David, and daily blamed him with an increasingly bitter and revengeful spirit. She began, too, to despise the conception of man within her, to think with contempt of the male principle which is creation to the female, and to force its betrayal outwards on to David.

As a last resort, trying to put things right between them, Helena at great danger to herself bore David two sons. When that made no helpful difference to the anchored and dreadfully, drunkenly becalmed spirit of David but, on the contrary, added the dimensions of two fresh deeds of creation, the universe of two newly-begotten hearts to a world which already set them apart, Helena hated him. She dismissed him from her affections as her mother had dismissed her father, as another retarded and incurable problem child. With that dismissal all hope of increase between them vanished and the hand of death was upon their relationship.

From then on Helena began to take an accountant's view of life, to draw up balance sheets and try to compute what the advantage of such a marital relationship was to her. The balance, as is inevitable with such an approach, quickly translated its conclusions in terms of money. She found that she was supporting the entire family, and that David's allowance from Mary paid barely half his drink bill. When on top of that he seemed incapable of resuming his work, she lost all patience with him. With the full support of her family and encouragement of her friends, who all said David was behaving disgracefully and was an "out and out rotter", she closed down the studio in London—she had long since lost all interest in painting herself—retired to a small house and estate she had inherited from an aunt in Norfolk, and gave all her attention to her two sons, allowing David, like an unwelcome guest, to live in the top of the house. However, the habit of thinking of himself as necessary to Helena, the habit which she herself had encouraged for years, had become so deeply ingrained in David that it continued long after it had ceased to be valid. And it might have continued indefinitely had it not been for an afternoon in spring ten years after their marriage.

CHAPTER 15

FOR David the day began unusually badly. He woke up feeling extremely disturbed and the normal alcoholic remedies failed to cure his mood. He could hardly bear to look at Helena, the children, or Lady Moystouan-Roswell who was staying with them. One glance at the women playing with the two little boys, was enough to show him the far range of emotions and feelings he could not share with them. The look of tender possession in their faces when they were with the children was more than he felt he could endure. Then, to make matters worse, at eleven o'clock he had run out of drink, the drink ordered the day before not having come. When he commented on it to Helena she had treated his need with contempt, and revealed the gulf that now separated them by saying casually, "What does it matter if your brandy is an hour or two late?" By lunch time the drink had still not come and David was told on the telephone that the van with his supplies had broken down between the town and his home and could not reach him until four in the afternoon. The fateful shadow on his track was closing in on him at last.

Despondent, he refused food but took his gun and dog and walked off alone across the estate. It was a lovely, still, afternoon in the early spring. The air was filled to overflowing with a golden and tender sunlight which was slightly, delicately atremble with the hushed expectation and tense, purposeful tremor of an infinite beginning to be. The dark hedgerows were starry with primroses, the black, winter-sodden bark of trees lit with the light of tiny yellow-green buds, and the sombre corduroy of a great, curving fold of land in the west, its deep brown furrows running true and straight to the sun, was everywhere pierced and speared with keen, shrill new green.

As David walked he could feel the earth, all the ice and frost gone from it, giving beneath his feet with an exciting resiliency. He walked fast and far without knowing what was driving him.

In the biggest field on the estate, at a point farthest from home, the dog sent several rabbits scurrying out of the hedges with flashing white tails. Quite automatically, David raised his gun and shot three of them. Two were killed instantly, but the third was still alive. He went up to it, quickly picked it up in his hands and broke its neck with his fingers, the delicate column snapping like a twig. Then he stood there holding the warm little body in his two hands, its soft fur flickering lightly at his wrists like a warm noonday breeze.

In the copse nearby the birds were singing with a lovely, silver urgency. From a dark, tall ash growing in the centre of a long hedgerow, a cuckoo suddenly dropped a few lazy notes into the afternoon like smooth round pebbles dropped into a deep well. The contrast between the dead, small body which he had just killed, and all the multitudinous evidence of life reviving about him, clutched at his heart.

He dropped the dead rabbit and went and sat on a gate between two fields and stared at the day. For the first time he realised how beautiful it was, but, as he did so, a bleak and desperate sadness assailed him. With his mind he recognised the beauty of the scene about him, but he could no longer feel it. A sense of horror overcame him that he, of all men, should recognise beauty and yet not feel it. Only his own inner ugliness could explain it: only a mounting hideousness in himself could give the answer. A sense of his own death overwhelmed him.

With a great, angry bitterness he jumped from the gate, emptied his gun, bashed the barrels against the stone walls of the gate, smashed the stock and then went and threw it into the scrub. Near by he found a seat on a wall in the sun and sat for a long time silently and without moving reading the illuminated scroll of the evening with its oracular writing as if indeed it carried a personal admonition to himself.

The dog came over and whined at him impatiently, but he sent it away. . . . Where and how had he gone wrong? He could put the blame on no specific moment or event, but two images kept on dancing to the tumult of his mind. Helena and Mary, Mary and Helena. A great resentment against both boiled up in him, particularly against Helena. He felt—and the horror of the feeling completed his humiliation—that he could gladly murder her. Instantly he rebuked himself, finding in the feeling fresh evidence of his own ugliness and utter unworthiness.

It got colder. The sun went down, slowly withdrawing itself from the day like an anxious young mother who has just stolen into a room on slippered feet to see if her first-born is safely asleep. As it sank the copse drew all the birds from the sky towards its dark centre as a whirlpool in the sea draws all the flotsam from far around towards it. And then the birds, already assembled on the rim of the spinning vortex, sent up an immense, vibrating, shining hymn and hosannah of sheer contented homecoming and joyful thanksgiving soaring into the resounding sky like a fountain in some Imperial garden. But David heard in it all only an echo of the sad hysteria of his own spirit. He stood up, feeling outcast again, and walked slowly home, his dog at his heels.

As he neared the house the first of the stars were brushing the ricks and the roofs of the barns. The air was of a delicate and pure texture, the dark, impulsive line of the earth rising to meet it like a bowl ready to be filled with a deep draught of the night. The house itself was being battened down like a ship for a voyage into the night but though the lamps were lit the curtains were not yet drawn.

Suddenly with astonishing clarity he saw the two women in the bathroom with the children. The two boys were splashing about in the bath and the two women stood watching them with proud, proprietary and deeply contented faces. Indeed, so deep did that look of contentment go, that it seemed to David to sweep all individuality from the two faces. It was

167

not even a peculiarly human look, he thought, for he had seen something similar on the faces of lionesses playing with their cubs. Then the two women looked at each other with such a strange and intimate communion that the need for words was eliminated. They smiled at each other as if they were smiling at their own reflections, and then at the same moment their arms went out to lift the children out of the bath and begin drying them.

Try as he would, David could not feel any connection between himself and that scene. He knew, of course, that he was part of the machine which had created it, but he could not feel it in living emotion. He realised sadly that he was less married to Helena, emotionally and instinctively, than to the bitch which was rubbing its head against his trouser leg at the moment. He concluded sadly that his was an inhuman character, grievously at fault, and walked slowly into the house and up to his attic.

The stairs passed close by the bathroom and the children, recognising his step, called out to him, asking him to come in. He dared not refuse, yet doubted the wisdom of going in. As he opened the door, he felt the human atmosphere change. He hesitated and Helena said sharply: "Please make up your mind at once whether you are coming in or not. I don't want the children to catch pneumonia."

"Please come and play with us, Daddy," the two boys called at the same moment.

David shut the door behind him. The two women watched him.

"Hullo, you two," David said slowly, looking past the women and the jagged hostility in their eyes. "Enjoyed your baths? I'm sorry but I can't play with you to-night. I must have a bath myself."

He heard the sigh of relief forming in Lady Moystouan-Roswell's bosom. But the eldest boy turned his head away to hide the tears that rushed to his eyes. David took him by the arm, soft and pink from the warmth of the bath, and asked: "Why, old fellow, what's the matter? What's bitten you?"

"You never have time to play with us," the child answered and then turned to Helena and hid his face in her apron, crying convulsively.

"See what you've done?" Helena reproached him bitterly. "You'd better go before you do any more harm. And do have a bath—judging by the state of your boots you need one."

David bent down, patted the child's head and said: "Don't cry, little old fellow. I'll play with you all to-morrow evening."

"And me too," cried out the lively and unperturbed youngest. "Me too." He did an Indian dance with arms and feet as he spoke.

"Yes, you too," David replied with a sad smile, and without looking at Helena or her mother he went out of the room.

All desire to go and change his clothes had left him. He went downstairs into the study. Thank God, his drink had come. He drew up a chair by the fire and began drinking. But his mood of the afternoon refused to lift. Drink merely confirmed it. At dinner he sat silently in his chair and spoke only when he was spoken to, which fortunately was not often. The conversation of the two women divided like a stream on either side of a black rock, flowed round him and then joined forces again and flowed on smoothly. As soon as he could he went back to his study and resumed his drink.

I've become a killer, he thought, and by degrees I'm killing myself. "I'm bewitched," he cried out.

Bewitched! The word made him look up at the door over which hung a large witch bowl of deep blue Bristol glass. Impulsively picking up a stick from the corner, he went over and shattered it with a blow, the fragments of glass splattering down like hail all round him and raising a series of angry tinkles from the stone. Now let them come, let all the witches of hell in, he thought, regarding the fragments with a defiant satisfaction.

Then from the other end of the room, a startled gasp made him turn round. Helena was standing at the entrance in a woollen dressing-gown drawn tight round her person, her hair tied back tightly from her forehead and shoulders with a narrow black ribbon, her face white, peaked and angular.

He walked down on her, took her fiercely by the arm asking: "Who told you to come and interfere? What the devil are you doing here?"

She shrank back and turned away her head. David thought she was crying as she'd so often done in the past, and at once his anger went. Poor Helena, what a monster he was. He tried to take her in his arms and said: "Oh, my dear, forgive me. I'm in such a mess and so unhappy. . . . I don't mean to hurt you."

She loosened herself from his grip and said with an icy astonishment: "I'm not crying. . . . Now will you go to bed before you do any more damage and wake the children."

He looked at her in amazement. Far from crying, Helena's face was lit by a white flame of angry resentment and what in his first portrait of her had been small crystals of glacier green in the hazel of her eyes were now the whole of the pupils, hard, stony in themselves and turning him to stone.

The shock added to the vast sense of isolation already inflicted on him by the rest of the day was so unexpected that he went upstairs dazed with it. He crept into bed with half his clothes on like someone overtaken by the night on a great, empty plain, and desperate for company took his dog to bed with him.

In the morning, when he woke, for a long time he could not make out where he was. In his sleep he'd been on such a journey that all memory of the present had been forfeited. When at last he realised where he lay, an agonising anxiety like a pain went through him. He was in the wrong place. How could he be lying there holding on to a dog for warmth and affection, when life was dark with danger. Something dreadful was happening, he was sure, to Mary perhaps. . . .

How could he have left her all these years. He must get to her at once or it'd be too late. Pray God, he'd still be in time.

He jumped out of bed and for the first time in many years was up before the household. At breakfast, he told Helena that he must travel to South Africa in order to see Mary. . . . He'd not seen her for close on thirteen years. . . . She was getting old and if he didn't hurry she might die before he got there. . . . He had a hunch that already something was terribly wrong at home and that his help was needed. . . .

Helena listened to him with a sceptical look on her face. The question "And who's going to pay for this expensive voyage?" was on the tip of her tongue, but her mother's unexpected approval of the idea and a long and intense look from her obviously beseeching her to acquiesce, kept her silent. When in the end she nodded and asked: "Well, when d'you want to go?" David answered with obvious relief: "To-day. . . . This afternoon . . . I know there's no time to lose."

CHAPTER 16

O N the third Friday afternoon in June I rode into the
village to collect the week's mail, wondering whether I
would find one of David's rare letters waiting for me. It was
the beginning of the winter school vacation and on all the
roads which cut across the immense plain behind the hills I
could see the spurts of dust raised by vehicles on their way to
fetch the children home. They filled the air with a quick sense
of homecoming. I remembered that it was exactly thirteen
years since David and I had made with each other that
appointment which he had never kept. The recollection
always saddened me for while it lasted it shut me out from
the familiar and steadfast rhythm of human life which
each year repeated itself so loyally around me. But on this
Friday my sadness was most acute. My father and mother
were away on holiday to the coast. They were getting old
and beginning to feel the strain of our highveld winters.
Already for three weeks I had been alone and as ever, when I
was alone, the wound of David in me, this deep scar in my
side where life had made its amputation, smarted anew. And
then on top of it all Mary and Anna Maria, in search of quiet
and cold for Anna Maria's children after the fever and heat of
the summer in Fort White, had arrived on the Michaeljohn
estate and asked me over. Already I had been there three times
and these visits too had revived the past deeply in me.

We had asked one another for news of David and compared
what we knew, and I was amazed at the small pin-prick of
light that our combined knowledge made in the dark sheet of
thirteen years. Yet in a way, I felt I knew everything from the
image of him in my own heart. I could not accept the darkness and separation between us as final. I believed, against all
rational evidence, that if I but stood fast by this feeling that he

and I had had for each other, a day would come when he would be forced back to it. I felt sure that at some moment, life, held for so long at a distance, would come rushing in on him with a completely new set of circumstances. Then he would need me. Then in the storm that would come howling round his ears he would need to rediscover the firm, still centre which he'd once possessed in life, for no ordinary wind, I was convinced, could send that archaic moment which had becalmed David scudding like foam over the coiled end of the leaden horizons. So every year that passed might be bringing that moment closer and this belief was my only comfort.

I rode fast past the church grey with dust in the hostile, wintry scene. I went down the main street, full of dust-covered cars, buggies, wagons and horse carts, black servants and excited children in school blazers storing baggage into them, and dismounted at the post office.

The postmaster, who had never really forgiven me for that night thirteen and a half years before when I dragged him out of bed and made him search through all his mail for a letter from David, gave me a sour look and said: "You must wait a bit, cousin. The mail's just coming in and will take time to sort. We're shorthanded, you know."

As I came out on the veranda of the post office I saw that the mail car at the side entrance was being unloaded. The driver of the car waved his hand at me and called out warmly: "Hullo, cousin Alex, glad to see you again."

I returned his greeting and then I noticed for the first time the man with whom he'd been talking.

This man was standing with his back to me, and was, judging by his tweed coat, plus fours and cap, a stranger and an Englishman. Yet there was something about the way he held himself that was disturbingly familiar. Moreover I thought that as he heard my voice answering the driver's greeting, a startled nerve had jerked his shoulders, for he at once bent forward and asked the driver something. The driver nodded and immediately the stranger swung round with a quick, careless, twist of his body that seemed more familiar still, swept the cap off his head and came swiftly towards me. Of course, I recognised him at once. He was older, more haggard, and his eyes red with fatigue, but the quick smile that broke from him and illuminated his clouded face was authentically David.

Instantly I went deaf and dumb to the world about me. All the loyal and tried servants of my daily, practical self stood aside to let one among them who had been bereaved give uninterrupted welcome to this moment.

How often I had rehearsed this scene with myself and gone through every possible circumstance of its coming so that I should not be caught unprepared. The least mistake, I knew, would be fatal and I had schooled myself as much as is possible in advance, telling myself that I must never behave as if anything unusual had happened. The slightest suggestion of resentment, reproach, or curiosity must be utterly repressed, and nothing solicited or forced which the warmth of welcome and unchanged affection did not spontaneously bring alive.

Many a night on my own I had felt wise enough for a dozen such occasions, but as I walked out now on to my inner stage before the keyed-up audience of my whole being, I felt utterly unfitted for such a meeting. All I could do was to take David's hand shyly and tell him that I was very glad to see him.

But David I saw at once had not found my greeting strange or inadequate. A similar shyness and an evident preoccupation within him seemed to match the diffidence of my approach and almost to welcome it. I took heart from it at once and felt more confidence. I looked at him more objectively and was horrified by the change in him. He looked desperately unhappy, uncaring and uncared for, and he smelt strongly of drink. Beyond recognising me, he didn't seem to know where he was. He rushed through his enquiries after me and my parents as quickly as possible, registered only perfunctory disappointment at their absence, and at once went to the matter uppermost in his mind.

"And Mary?" he said, taking my arm with a tense, anxious grip: "Have you seen her recently? Where is she? Here in the village or on the farm? How is she?"

I answered all his questions calmly and steadily, refusing to let his own turbulence join forces with mine. "On the farm, David," I said, "with Anna Maria and the children. I saw them only the day before yesterday. They're all very well and would have been here to meet you, I'm sure, if they had known you were coming."

I watched him closely, speaking with an apparent unconcern. He was, I could see, labouring under an immense strain. If I'd ever looked a ghost in the eyes it was in this face in front of me, although the hand which held my sleeve was the real David. I longed to bring him home and wished fervently that my mother had been there to take him in her arms.

"I didn't send a wire. That was my fault," he said with the despondent readiness of someone who has come to find wrongdoing a strange necessity. "I didn't send a wire. I just came as fast as I could, but please tell me, is Mary really and truly all right?"

It was clear to me that this was exactly how David would behave under compulsion. I concentrated instead on removing the overt cause of his anxiety and once more assured him that Mary was perfectly well.

"All the same," he asserted firmly, looking wildly round him again, "I must get to her at once. You said you'd take me, didn't you?" he said, turning to the driver of the mail car, who nodded his head, and then added to me: "Excuse me a minute. I must just slip into the hotel and get some cigarettes. . . . Shan't be a minute."

He came back in a few minutes, smoking, the cigarette never leaving his mouth, and smelling more strongly of drink. I noticed his thick coat had several holes burnt into it by cigarette ash.

He took my hand warmly, saying: "Well, Alex, I'll come to see you later. I must get to Mary at once, or I'll never forgive myself."

I could not really see what Mary had done to merit this intense concern on her behalf, but it was obviously useless to try and change his mind.

I got on to my horse and for a long time rode in the dust which the wheels of his speeding car left behind it still hanging golden and translucent between me and the cold, setting sun. I shook my head sombrely over this new-old David, the haunted, stricken look in his defenceless face, his odd precipitation, and the strong smell of drink . . . and suddenly the memory of Albert was riding the veld with me. I saw him in the twilight hour as I had known him as a child, with a look just like David's on his face, rising suddenly without warning in the midst of his family and friends to make precipitate visits to the drink locker in his study and coming back with the same smell of drink about him. I was amazed that in thirteen years away from his home and family in a far, strange land David, who was so much Mary's child and who had so much of her original spirit and looks, could have become so like the dead, buried, unmourned and uncommemorated Albert. A cold shiver went through me at this evidence of the sinister influence of the dead in a living issue. I felt almost convinced that if I looked carefully between the ears of my horse at the road ahead, thereby acquiring supernormal vision as the old Hottentot servants of my childhood had always assured me I could, I would see the devil and Albert riding fast on phantom chargers in David's tracks. But disappointed as I felt by this banal meeting in a dusty street on a wintry day, one thought pealed out in my mind like a festival bell: "He's come back, he's come back at last."

Three days later, when my impatience was urging me to saddle a horse and ride over to the Michaeljohns' estate, David reappeared with all his baggage, announcing that he had come to spend the night with me and asking if I would take him to the station in the morning.

My amazement and dismay very nearly caught me out and I was hard put to it to pass off this request as that of a normal and responsible person. I succeeded, but not fast enough for David not to be aware of my disappointment. He said apologetically: "I would love to stay with you, little old fellow, but I must get back to Helena and the children."

I made no effort to reason with him for I could see no reason in it all. Viewed rationally, his behaviour was preposterous, not that of a mature person. But if he could prop it up with some illusion of reasoning, then good luck to him. I wasn't going to deprive him of anything by arguing against him.

I said, swallowing hard: "How nice of you to come, David, and of course I'll take you to the station."

"You always were the most understanding fellow in the world."

He put his hand on my shoulder and rewarded my restraint with a look of deep affection and such an expression of relief that I knew Mary and Anna Maria had made the mistake of arguing the point with him.

"Yes, I'd have loved to be able to stay with you," he went on. "But this time I must get back to Helena and the children. I left in a hurry and there are all sorts of loose ends to be seen to at home and they all worry so!"

All day long he stayed close to me and though a strange silence had fallen upon us, I could feel him moving closer to the vacant place in my heart. It was as if some wise instinct had come alive between us forbidding any but the safest and most obvious words until the feeling between us, quietly and unseen, had moved into its ancient position again. In moments of crisis, I myself have never greatly trusted words. But we could at least start from the beginning and use our ancient affection to beat down the mounting years; and then one day the right words would come.

All day David kept by my side except to disappear at

intervals and return smelling strongly of liquor. After tea there was a longer disappearance. He was absent for three hours.

It was becoming increasingly clear to me that time in our sense no longer existed for David. He had, as I'd seen in the last of his paintings, moved altogether out of our time context and been driven into one fixed moment of the past against which the urgent flow of the years beat in vain. When I thought how the whole of human existence is little more than a spark of recognition, the brief pause wherein birth and death halt their footsteps to shake one another by the hand before they resume again their respective journeys on into the unexplored dark, David's rejection of the whole for such an unexplained and unidentified fragment of it, became for me as awe-inspiring as it was frightening. And I must confess that even David himself looked quite overcome when I told him gently in answer to his protestations that he'd been away three hours.

He followed me silently into the drawing-room, sat down in a chair facing me by the fire and raised a pair of bewildered eyes to meet mine.

"I don't know what's come over me, Alex," he said. "I don't understand. I was thinking it over there just now when I was out. . . . Back in England I was convinced that Mary needed me urgently." His look became anxious again and he stopped and asked, putting his hand on my knee: "Does that sound silly to you?"

I said "No" quickly and firmly to reassure him.

"I was so convinced," he went on, "that when you told me the other day that she was well and happy I thought you must have become extraordinarily unobservant——"

I smiled at him. "I knew you didn't believe me."

"My God, you are a good and sweet person, Alex," he answered, putting his hand on my knee. "And you're right." His voice broke in a rather bitter self-deprecatory little laugh. "There's absolutely nothing wrong with Mary. I can't tell you how foolish and tricked I feel by it all. I really needn't have come."

"Except that you must both have been very pleased to see each other," I interrupted.

"I don't know about that." He shook his head slowly. "I was too shaken to feel much except bewildered and foolish. But I'm sure she was glad to see me—until she heard I was leaving again almost at once. . . . Besides she and Anna Maria were very absorbed with the children." His voice was low and bitter again and then slowly the truth came out. The shock had been even greater than I'd realised.

It was already dark when the mail car put him down at the Michaeljohn homestead. His anxiety was so great that he'd rushed up the steps at once, leaving the driver to cope with his baggage. The windows of the large drawing-room which gave straight on to the stoep were bright with light, the curtains undrawn, and as he came up the steps he looked straight into the room.

He could hardly believe his eyes. The big, elegant room looked like a nursery. A hip-bath had been put into it by the fire. Two children were in the bath and two women, one at each end, were bent over it, with enraptured expressions, again so deep, anonymous and impersonal that he'd had difficulty in deciding which was his mother and which his sister. The shock this sight gave him in his abnormal, tired and drink-frayed condition, was immense. For an instant, he thought that he was quite, quite mad, and that the whole of his journey to Africa was an illusion, a product of his disordered imagination. He feared that he had never left England at all and that he was still standing as he'd done on the evening before his departure on the terrace of Helena's garden looking into the bathroom of her home and watching his wife and mother bathing their two children. As he watched the two women from the stoep they, too, looked up at each other and were suddenly so united in their function as women that without an exchange of words, they knew just what to do. Two shoulders bent down and out of the bath came two pink, wriggling, kicking, little bodies, convulsed and contorted with physical protest like rainbow trout jerked suddenly out of their element. All I've done, David thought bitterly, is to leave home in a relative way and to come back the day before yesterday.

He put his hands to his head which was throbbing with drink, fatigue and anxiety, and then he heard in the silence on the stoep the unmistakably African noises of his childhood, the windmill in the garden yanking like a hurt puppy, the ewes in the kraal bleating with deep, umbilical voices and the young lambs answering with bright, silver tongues tinkling like nursery supper bells in the dark, and far away the lugubrious notes of a jackal, which all the dogs at the back of the homestead immediately answered with a defiant outburst of barking. David turned, saw the car and the driver undoing his luggage and knew, of course, that the journey was no illusion. He'd travelled seven thousand miles with his body but inside himself he'd come out at the same place from which he had started. And what was the use of travelling, what price Marco Polo, if at the end there was no Cathay?

He went in to announce his arrival, chastened and bitter, and became even more bitter when he saw how well, happy and unperturbed Mary looked.

"I don't know now what I'd expected to find," he told me. "I never gave it a thought. The call was so imperious that I never questioned its validity. You've no idea how worried I'd been about Mary—and then what do I find? A placid, beautiful, serene, secure old lady helping to bath her grandchildren."

He laughed cynically at himself, and then, for the first time, asked me to give him a drink.

"It was too ludicrous for words," David continued. "Mary welcomed me as if I were a child that had just come in time to be put in a bath myself. She wasn't the woman I'd had in mind. She was not the Mary I thought she was. And there was I, the would-be saver, hoaxed, foolish and more unemployed than ever."

His eyes were bright with distress and he looked beseechingly at me as if I could explain the riddle to him. But all I felt I could do was to ask, "Why unemployed?"

"For a long time now life has hardly seemed to me a whole time occupation. Saving the 'Mary' I had in mind might perhaps have made it so, but the living Mary needs no saving. And what is more," his voice quickened, "I'll tell you the final irony of it all. It's the would-be saver who needs saving! And who and what could save me?"

I made no effort to answer his question. Some questions you can't answer with words. All you can do is to tell the questioner to go and live the answer to his own question, as, blindly and unknowingly, thirteen years ago, I'd had to live the answer to the question of David in me. But what I could do was to deny the hurting irony.

"I don't find that ironical, David," I told him. "I think that's the natural way of discovering our own needs. We all frequently start by projecting our own need on to the people nearest to us. You remember the parable about the 'beam' and 'the mote'? I'd say that the mote we see in our neighbour's eye is the reflection of the beam in our own. I'd say that perhaps we wouldn't even know we had a beam were it not for its reflection in our neighbour's eyes."

I left it at that. I was not going to make his points for him. I felt that already his life had suffered enough from other people making his, as well as their own, points in it. I mustn't join in that destructive game.

David went on to emphasise how he'd been made to feel the prodigal child among them. He told me how Mary seemed incapable of thinking of him as an individual entitled to a separate life of his own.

"Women and children, children and women," David exploded, "there seems to be nothing else in the world. It drives me mad, Alex . . . wherever you go you find there's either a woman or a child, or both, setting a trap to get you back into the nursery . . . I couldn't stand it at Mary's, so I quit."

After the long silence which followed he asked suddenly,

almost as if speaking to himself: "Alex, d'you remember that awful dream I had, just before I left you last time?"

"Indeed I do," I answered. "I still have the painting you made of it."

"What!" he exclaimed amazed to remember that he'd ever painted his dream. So I interrupted him and went to fetch the picture.

He took it from me with touching reverence in both hands. The gesture reminded me of one of our black down-and-outs receiving the unexpected and unsolicited charity of a penny, or of a child reaching out for some nursery treasure which to the adult world is merely a ridiculous figure stuffed with straw but which to the child remains magic. He looked at it deeply and long. An expression of humble and selfless wonder came into his face. In that light, with the flames of ancient and unnamed African wood lapping at the shadows about us like the waters of a lake at a darkened shore, he suddenly looked incredibly young. I was moved in every part of me. This was true. This was the true look on the true face of the true David. This was how we were all meant to be. All the rest was a havoc of unreality.

And it was this unreality that was the danger. I could have accepted everything that had happened had I been convinced that it was all part of a deep-laid necessity of life and conformed to the fundamental demands of an ultimate pattern. There are people whose life insists on their own doom.

But this thing that had happened so cruelly to David had never appeared to me to possess such final necessity. It seemed to have come not from him, but rather to have been forced on him from without. It was an invasion of David's proper destiny; an infiltration from someone else's doom. And the proof of it was in that look of his as he stared down at the picture in his hands, for that look had been born of a moment in our lives when we were all free and uninvaded, when the moon looked down on Anna Maria's fire on the river bank without fear of any great or permanent eclipse.

"Did I really do this, Alex?" he asked with amazement, and without waiting for an answer went on: "You know I'd completely forgotten it. I've remembered every detail of the dream but I'd forgotten that I ever made a picture out of it. . . . It's odd, very odd, isn't it?"

He stood there for a few moments in easy contemplation of the oddness but inevitably swung back to our hurt, partial and unfulfilled selves. "But it's too late, Alex . . . I left this Kremlin too late." He put the picture down. "You've only to look at Anna Maria's face to see she's lost too. . . . It's awful how hard and determined she's become. And as for me, the grey old bitch with the lace bonnet on has got me before I could reach the fire, damn her."

The word "bitch" came from him like the explosion of a gun. The violence and ferocity of it shook both of us, but I refused to accept his despair.

"D'you remember, David?" I asked him as quietly as I could, "when you told me the dream you said there was a little wrinkled, black man in it, a slave of some kind, who was incredibly wise, who showed you the way out of your Kremlin?"

"Of course I do!" David said, joining in the recollection with interest. "I can see him now with white negroid stubble on his face, and a ridiculous able-seaman's hat on his head!"

I took a deep breath. "I don't believe he'd ever have let you out of the Kremlin if it really was too late—if it was all going to end in that old wolf catching you."

He looked at me as if he couldn't believe his ears, and then seeing I was really serious gave an embarrassed laugh and exclaimed: "Why, Alex, I really believe you mean it! But what a fantastic thing to say! Of all the many ridiculous things in the dream that little old man and his sailor's hat was the most ridiculous. And after all, it was only a bad dream!"

"Yes, David, it was only a dream and yet you still remember it after thirteen years. . . . It was so vivid that it made you paint this picture, and in some curious way meant so much to both of us that we are still arguing over the detail of it."

"That's true," he admitted at once. "But why make such a ludicrous old man so important? Why pick on the ridiculous in the dream and ignore the rest?"

Then the words broke out of me expressing the feelings that been living and growing inside me for thirteen years. "Because some instinct tells me that perhaps the truth we need is often concealed in what seems to us insignificant," I said quickly. "Perhaps what life intends to be great it first makes small, so small that it can be almost imperceptible. . . . P'raps that's where we all go wrong. We're too impressed by what is great, established in the world around us to notice that bulk and greatness have already lost the power of increase and are doomed to die. . . . I think it's the last and the least we notice and care for within ourselves which is often destined to be first and most" . . . I took a step towards him and put a hand on his arm. "Oh, David, don't you see the significance of the little man being black? Haven't you wondered why he's black? I have, often. . . . And the answer, when it came, gave me great confidence in that dream of yours. Listen: . . . What is least and most despised in the life around us? The black man, of course. . . . And who is the natural man in our unnatural society? The black man again. . . . And who is growing great with revolt on behalf of the unrecognised future? The black man. . . . If you ask yourself questions on those lines then surely you must see how truly and poignantly the image of a little black man, member of a natural, instinctive people, expresses all that is natural and truly unfulfilled within us. . . . Of course it's not too late."

For a moment I was afraid I'd said too much. But David, strangely moved, took my arm, saying: "Oh, Alex! I do hope you're right. . . . But what am I to do now?"

I am sure that had I said to David at that moment, "Stay with me here where you belong and where you're still loved and welcome," he would have stayed. I think his own unhappiness and desperation were so great, that part of him even was hoping that I would propose something of the kind. I

184

could almost see the look in his eyes beseeching me to make up his mind for him.

But I realised that this selected moment could be chosen only at the expense of what had been proved and tested in our extreme loneliness. By choosing it I could do to him what others had done—wrench him out of the proper context of his own individual life and twist him to a prejudiced and therefore secret and vengeful end. I was born to cultivate my own tranquil garden; he was destined for journey and adventure. My will and need would deal death to him all the more deadly for being dealt with love. Already he was nearly destroyed. He was only technically alive and a little more will and determination, both of his own and others, would complete the crime. If I said, "Stay, David," he would stay—and another murder would have been done. And out of both his and my unhappiness I had come to learn something of the way that sort of murder is committed. It's not done by bright and flashing steel, nor even an honest stab in the back, but by the slow and subtle poison of enticement from our true individual destinies. For it is not destiny that is fated or doomed, but our evasion and betrayal of it.

How could I, therefore, lift one finger to help David evade his commitments in England as he'd once evaded Mary in unexplained and precipitate flight? I knew it would be better for him to die physically in the effort of taking up his own proper burden than to be murdered by more evasion. I realised, sadly, that I could take him in only for the night, and then, in the morning, help him, unfit as he was for further travel, on his way.

I shook my head unhappily and said, "I don't know, David. Don't ask me. . . . Ask yourself. . . . All I beg you to do is to try and trust this sense of a journey that has come alive in you, even if it does seem to you to have done so on a foolish pretext —and listen to the small, despised, natural voices within yourself and here"—I hastily picked up the picture where he'd put it down and thrust it into his hands—"here, take this with you . . . I've looked after it for thirteen years. It's your turn now."

PART IV

The Voyage

CHAPTER 17

DAVID was leaning over the rail of the ship watching the southernmost headland of Africa sinking into the sea. There was a strange, storm-made twilight hanging over both solid land and heaving insubstantial sea, very much like the curious half-light of the pictures of his own earliest beginning. A cold south-west gale had long since wrapped the blue-black mountain tops in thick, swirling cloud. Every now and then the violent wind would tear the dense clouds apart from their darkest foundations with a gusty tug, and in doing so a deep booming groan fell from the skies which, joined to the noise of the creaking, plunging ship, its shrieking rigging, tense vibrating masts and funnels, filled the air with a loud, continuous and pitiful moaning. Every time a rent appeared in the clouds a shaft of cold, unforgiving winter light darted through it, stood for an instant like a Phoenician trident quivering in the dolphined backs of the amber waves as they raced after the ship with their yellow manes sombrely aflame, and then withdrew swiftly into the hand of the vanishing sun above. But in that brief moment by the light of this spear of trembling sun-steel David saw one great albatross after another take up an appointed position over the curling, moaning waters astern and begin to patrol the skies on methodical wings, confident and superb, subtle and secure in the mathematics of the storm. Every now and then a ray of light would fall quickly on the white belly of a bird leaning perilously from the tip of a quivering wing over the abyss of its own speed as it rounded some steep slope of mounting air to shoot straight down at the ship like a skier on an Alpine mountaintop darting for home in the hour of avalanche and blizzard. It would flash past the ship plunging its swift, sharp purpose like a sword into the chaos of wild water, confusion of shrieking wind and disordered air about the ship and, once level with the bows, great feathers of foam would rise again high into the air to join the direction of the storm in the twilight above like the last triumphant note in the finale of a symphony of defied and defeated fate. Once in a flash of low-level light the golden reflection of an albatross troubled and trembling, yet firm and unmistakable, burned deep in the swelling flank of an angry brown wave just as it tumbled down on the bows with a crash which shook the whole ship and left it dazed and limp with shock in a steep trough of the seas.

David found himself inexpressibly moved by this vast, ethereal bird its great wings stretched wide with longing towards the storm. It left such a vivid, compelling imprint of the speed of its purpose and flame of its being in the dark, raging and enigmatic South Atlantic waters. The image burned deeply in him too, as if it were the centre round which both he and the great storm of winter turned. There was something infinitely heroic about this winged being which took to the storm as if it were its home, and danger the sure foundation on which the long archway of its flight was built. For David it made the thought of his whole way of life even more unbearable than it already was, and he waited anxiously staring at the waves and darkening sky, as if for an urgent message as yet only partially deciphered.

Gradually it got darker and with darkness the noise and violence of sea and wind steadily increased. Land vanished and the little ring of light around the ship narrowed with distressing speed. At last it was a ring no longer but just a flash of phosphorescence, a jewelled dagger plunged deeply, secretly and without warning into the prancing Arabian back of the night. Sometimes a bar of light falling from a bolted and shuttered scuttle made pathetic effort to assert domesticity in the waste of the expanding storm before it was caught deftly in a claw of outstretched water and thrown back over a raised, ironical shoulder into absolute darkness. The long, slender masts swinging a bent aerial like a harp in the wind, the funnels with smoke wrapped about them tattered and torn like the crepe of last year's funeral, soon became invisible, and the riding lights appeared more and more fitfully, clutching at the white strands of gale for support, pale in the smoke of battered spray and reeling in a drunken loop from one end of the night to the other.

David, who had watched the land disappear with sombre satisfaction, now welcomed the fall of darkness with a warmth beyond his comprehension. As the storm and the night, rocked in one another's arms in the fever of their ancient pre-creative passion, drew their black noose tight around the ship, he began to feel curiously at one in himself. Standing alone it was as if the vessel were an intimate and unique instrument of his own destiny. For the first time the journey communicated something of reality to him. However deceived he had been in point of departure and destination, the heaving ship, the storm, the night and the struggle to make headway felt profoundly and uncompromisingly real. The journey, thank God, was true, possessing with a great and awesome simplicity a reality independent of his own complex and powerful self-deceptions. He didn't know where he was going but he felt that he was on his way.

A strange new consciousness invaded him—a sense that he was dreaming vividly of being awake in the midst of his deepest sleep. Suddenly he felt purified within himself, free of other people's faces, of smells and colours and above all of other people's voices. He felt profoundly grateful that the only sound about him was this mindless, ancient, prehuman music of the storm. One human voice he feared would be enough to wake him and then he and all would drown. For this dream of being awake suddenly was more urgent than the condition of actually being awake. He felt like an explorer who had at last walked into the true unknown and found that the treasure of discovery was the realisation that true awareness needs not only the fact, but also the dream of the fact: these are the two vital ends to the journey between. Then in the swelling rhythm of discovery he was conducted to the edge of the world, to the uttermost frontier of tangible, coherent thought, where the exhausted mind and spirit fall down aghast at the view of the purple, unhorizoned distances they still have to travel and where only the humble and contrite, the sore-rejected heart is left to take over the journey to the final pass in the mountains where life itself comes and goes. It was as if in this wild night of wind and water, of uncorrupted and incorruptible darkness he was presented with the first, the aboriginal vision of the universe, brought face to face with the basic material, the raw and irreducible elements of the pre-created world. It was as if his own being had been driven back so far in time that it had emerged in the moment just before Genesis, when the earth was void and without form and darkness upon the face of the deep, and the spirit of God was about to set out moving upon the face of the great waters. It was a moment in himself of sheer nothingness and of absolute darkness.

How long he would have remained there he did not know, but an Italian officer in oilskins and heavy sea-boots came staggering along the deck and ordered David below in peremptory broken English. David had booked his passage home in the first ship sailing from Africa: it had happened to be an Italian vessel.

David turned obediently to make a dash for the hand-rail along the deckhouse when the sight of another dark figure hanging on to a stanchion some yards away halted him. An exclamation of surprise fell from the overwrought officer, who immediately made his way across the steep and prancing deck towards the blob of deeper black.

David could not see what happened, for at that moment the vessel shipped a wave which broke over the bows, crashed down on the well-deck and dashed itself against the bridge where the full force of the wind caught it, carried its confused fragments in an instant over the funnels and brought a cataract of spray down on the deck where he was standing. The spray spattered like hail on the boards and completely shut the officer from David's view. Even the storm itself seemed to catch its breath over the force of the blow. A strange pocket of silence came down around the ship. The wind ceased tearing at the masts and rigging, a ghostlike sheet of light fluttered slowly in the darkness round the crow's-nest like the white flag of weary surrender, and all round David heard distinctly, like a brood of excited black mambas, the hissing of invisible waves speeding after the wind. The heart of the ship, somewhere down the shaft of the black, frantic funnels, fluttered like the breast of a frightened doe and then the bells in the engine room rang out with a quick, startled urgency. The ship began to rise slowly out of this deep slough of its despondency and to shake itself free of such an unfair burden of water.

In that very moment two dark shapes appeared at David's side and the officer shouted: "Please to go quickly now!" There was no denying the urgency in his voice, and David dashed for the companion way across a deck slanted like the fringe of a glacier. As they put their hands on the door, the ship climbed at last to the crest beyond the trough and at once the storm came down on it like a pack of wolves on an abandoned pony on some Siberian steppe.

"Please to help!" the officer yelled at David. He was pulling at the handle of the door and failing to budge it against the pressure of the wind. At the same time the ship started another downward plunge with alarming speed.

David immediately grasped the door handle and with an effort that took all his strength slowly pulled it open. The officer and his charge slipped through and David went tumbling after, for as he slid round the edge of the door the ship put its bows into another mountain of water with such force that it reared backwards like a frightened horse on its hind-legs and jerked David off his balance. Instinctively his hands stretched out towards the deck flying up to meet him and the door, free in the wind, crashed to with great violence, brushing him across the threshold.

David pulled himself to his feet by the railings at the head of the companion way, just in time to see the officer hustling some one through the doors of the saloon lounge. The full light of the saloon fell for an instant on both of them. It was so bright after his long stand in the dark, that David's eyes were dazzled, yet for a second, before the doors swung to on the pair of them, he had seen enough to identify the third person as a woman.

Just before she stepped out of the saloon, she looked round and saw David. For a moment he thought she was going to beckon to him. He was convinced she wanted to make some sign of acknowledgment. Then, as the ship plunged forward again, she seemed to change her mind and disappeared down a steep slope of the deck along the alley way.

On his way through the saloon David got his first internal evidence of the storm. Not a single other passenger was in it. All the heavy chairs and couches were screwed down to the floor, all the vases and flowers removed. Two palm trees in large earthenware pots standing at the foot of the companion way had been hurled right across the saloon and smashed against a table in the corner. The grand piano had been pitched from its dais into the centre of the saloon where it lay on a broken back, like a dead ostrich with its legs in the air.

At dinner he was alone at his table with his abiding preoccupation. Once he lifted his eyes just in time to see a fair head with long, fine-spun hair gathered at the nape of the neck, turned quickly away from him. David studied the profile. Where had he seen it before?

He continued to stare so closely that the very atmosphere seemed affected by the concentration of his gaze, for suddenly she raised her head as if someone had just called her name and looked straight into his eyes.

For a moment in which time and the day completely

changed their nature, they looked steadily at each other. The sense of recognition was too unpremeditated for either to take refuge in any of the several pretences convention prescribes for these occasions.

Yet one glance into those blue eyes filled him with the most profound and quite indescribable nostalgia. The expression on the face was curiously relaxed, possessing a quality of remote and cloistered comprehensiveness rather than precise and immediate concentration, yet it seemed the face of someone absorbed in a patient dream of her own, someone barely awake and still held in a timeless trance of her own creation. Slowly she raised a hand to the brooch over her heart and began to finger it in a strange abstracted way as if it were her anchor to the reality at the moment.

David turned quickly away, but as he did so he was conscious that like the first swallow of the year some indefinable reality had suddenly darted first in and then out of the shade of his senses, leaving them unexpectedly colder and emptier. For a wild moment he thought of going over and speaking to her, but she got up and left the saloon. His eyes followed her to the door and in the doorway he saw her, in the act of steadying herself, throw a quick glance towards his table.

When he got up to the lounge it was empty, and he went and sat in the bar listening to the ship's creaking, the hollow, hungry moaning of the gale, and from time to time the forked and pointed hiss of a wave lashing out full length like an angry serpent towards the head of the ship. Every now and then the storm drew the tumult of wave and wind and twanging ship into a curious condition of harmony and then a bar of poignant and harplike music, accompanied from somewhere beyond wind and cloud and foam by a chorus of seemingly super-human voices condemned to make of singing the undoing of their own flame-like desire, hung for a brief moment on the violent, disordered air. Whenever this happened it was most noticeable to David how the sound of the engines appeared to quicken in the beat of his own heart and the movement of the ship swiftly joined a greater and more urgent rhythm in the night, as if the vessel were in very truth manned by a crew which had neither plugged its own ears nor bound its captain to the mast but with imperative command and straining, eager senses pursued the enchanted voices of sirens unwinding their fatal epithalamium in this storm.

Listening to them as if in some compelled dream, David ordered and drank one drink after the other. He had no desire to talk and discouraged the friendly bar steward, who was obviously bored and lonely. He was back in the mood which had been almost his only mood ever since meeting Helena; and in the world of that mood there were no words that could accompany him. By midnight even the storm without raged only on the uttermost perimeter of his senses. It is true that once in the mirror behind the barman he thought he caught a glimpse of a figure standing in a calm quicksilver glow of its own, and watching him with questioning intent. But as he turned quickly, he knocked his glass over. By the time he'd retrieved it the doorway was empty. He walked across the lounge and out into the alleyway, but it too was empty with its floor swinging like a pendulum beneath his feet. He watched the empty creaking scene until his head too reeled in sympathy. Then he quickly returned to the bar again and was convinced that he must have imagined the reflection in the mirror.

But there was one other reflection which he knew was real and which stayed with him; and in this respect his mood now was different. He was no longer alone. A bird had followed him into his mood and at all sorts of odd moments the image of a great white bird in love with the storm burned in the dark glass of his memory. It seemed to come in and out of his mind with a will and a way of its own. Even in his cabin just before falling asleep there was the albatross steadily patrolling the wake of his swiftly receding mind.

In the morning he woke to find the ship much steadier. The light at his port-hole too was brighter and though the ship still plunged heavily its movement was more assured and controlled. He dressed quickly with an indefinable anxiety as if compelled to hurry in order not to miss something of transcending importance.

On the boat deck he saw that the sky was blown clear of clouds and the gale had dropped to a strong and steady wind astern. Great waves of the deepest blue, with snow-white heads gravely bowed, rolled with a profound solemn rhythm after the ship, overtaking it, one by one, with a co-ordinated regularity and then lifting it up high to the sky like a winner of some ocean Marathon, carrying it for some way on proud determined shoulders before again sliding it down a steep incline into the outstretched arms of an eager follower.

Surveying the scene from the crest of one of the greatest waves, David saw that there was neither land nor ship in sight. Far astern a dark line on the horizon marked the crossed frontier of the storm and between it and the ship followed the albatross patrol. Their presence on unperturbable wings, surveying the waves with such unfailing confidence, was the seal of normality on the scene. It restored to its proper proportions the memory of the great storm of the day before in a symmetry of a shining and spotless sky and South Atlantic water hastening from the pale Antarctic to relieve the sullen, disheartened seas between Capricorn and Cancer.

Nowhere, neither in sea, sky nor ship was there anything tangible to explain or justify the anxiety and expectation which had driven David so early from his bunk. Even the ship which, in the night, had assumed the role of an instrument of heroic and majestic destiny now, with every fresh glance, looked less victorious and more commonplace, a small, unimportant and mongrel adventurer sneaking back into calmer waters, rebuked and frightened by the company it had tried to keep in a South Atlantic storm.

Dissatisfied, and once again drearily disillusioned, David found a place on a bench in the sun. He watched the sailors tidying-up the ship after the storm. In their movements they rode the waves as easily as a Tartar does a horse or a Bedouin a camel.

David sat there for some hours until the sound of voices recalled him and he saw that some of his fellow passengers had now emerged, pale and hollow-eyed, and were gingerly walking the decks about him.

At breakfast his own table was still empty but the saloon was filling up rapidly. He looked at once at the Captain's table but did not see the fair head of the night before. He sat on and on at his table drinking more coffee than he needed, feeling curiously angry with this woman whom he had never met but whose face had thrust on his grey, fogbound senses the dazzle of such a startling and mysterious nostalgia.

He sat there in a bitter mixture of confused and apparently disjointed memories, until the bar opened. He then promptly had three stiff drinks. Feeling better he went down to his cabin, took out his Shakespeare and went back on deck to read *Macbeth*, another large brandy at his side. But half-way through the first act, he thought suddenly: "I'll punish this woman . . . I won't appear for lunch. . . . She'll miss me and perhaps she'll think I have fallen overboard. . . ."

Fantastic as the thought was, he remained up on deck during the whole of lunch-time, watching the decks empty of passengers and then ordering more brandy and chain-smoking with quick, anxious excitement.

At two in the afternoon the passengers began to reappear in greater numbers than before. It was warmer and calmer and soon they were stretched out in deck chairs in the sun all round him. He bore this burden of normality for as long as he could, hoping that a fair head in search of reassurance would soon join them. But after an hour he accepted another defeat and full of unexplained resentment went down to his cabin.

He lay in his bunk until nearly tea-time, staring at the ceiling, and then could bear it no longer. This hour he knew from long experience was an hour of dangerous self-reproach. What happened to him between three and four in the afternoons he could not understand but for all that it was vividly and grimly real. If he allowed himself to be caught off his guard, as he was to-day, a bleak sense of failure invaded him in that hour. The light of the sea dancing on the ceiling, the wind in the port-hole, the wash of the waves and the speed of the ship beating the air like the wings of a bird, filled him with overwhelming remorse and sadness, until there was not a flake of light that was not dark with anguish, nor sound of wind that was not bitter with reproach. Sometimes even when the external world was absolutely tranquil the mood would come to him from within of its own volition, from far down the long tunnel of the years like the sound of cock-crow in the dark hour before dawn, or in a remote, resilient echo of the vanishing voice of Mary calling for him with wonderful, unbelievable urgency in the Michaeljohn garden. At times it came to him with such startling and vibrant clarity that his head rang with it before the bleak, black, nothingness came rushing in and he knew he had failed again. But why always at this hour? Why this moment above all the many others in the day? In his search for an explanation he had even blamed the sun, felt it was a first intimation of the sun beginning to set in his own blood, the dying of his own little day in his heart. But nothing more precise than that had ever emerged out of the self-searching of years. He knew only that the feeling could not be borne for long alone; so in despair he fled back on deck.

The deck round his chair was now so crowded and noisy that he abandoned it and climbed to the boat deck from where he had watched the Cape of Storms sink into the night and the sea.

He put his chair close to the edge of the ship. On his right was a white life-boat glistening in the afternoon sun and beneath it he saw plainly the solemn, heavy swell of the sea, its blue dark with the hush of afternoon. Behind him the red oval funnels were scarlet against a spotless blue sky. All three of them were full of smoke, bubbling like black water out of a three-eyed fountain with a strange volcanic pulse. With the smoke came the sound of the engines steadily turning, and this at once reinvested the ship with a sense of clear and unwavering purpose.

Then decisively the bell on the bridge suddenly rang out the change of the afternoon's watch. Over David's head appeared a pair of immense white wings arched and tensely tapered at the tips, aiming a long, quivering grey-feathered body at the purple heart of the distance like an arrow posed and pointed in a legendary bow. A white-grey head with a yellow beak to it turned and looked calmly over the ship as if it had a duty to examine for itself this changing of the watch. Once past the bridge and over the forward well-deck it swept round and up in a sharp, sudden curve looping the loop into the invisible air astern. From the deck below came the sound of excited laughter of children, which laughter the next moment was quickly lost and swept away in the abiding sound of waves and wind.

David felt all the more depressed. The ship was putting up a brave show of being unconcerned but he was not deceived. The odds were heavily against them all. No matter how methodically and obstinately the crew and passengers repeated the normal pattern of humanity, it was clear to him that with the sky and wind and fathomless water against them they possessed only the slightest and most precarious of advantages. The human issue was only one of many issues and by no means the most important. They, as human beings, were held in the grip of far greater, far older and quite impersonal considerations.

He tried to read his *Macbeth* again but could not go on. He put the book down to light a cigarette and then he saw her again.

She was standing exactly where she had stood in the night of the storm, but now she had her back to the sea. She was dressed in navy slacks, with a red cotton handkerchief tied round her neck. She was hatless and the sunlight fell responsively on her fair head. She had her hands deep in her pockets, and was looking straight at him, and it seemed to him that they were both quite naturally continuing their first look where it had been interrupted the day before. He thought he had never seen a face that was so much part of his own individual sense of beauty.

Again his impulse was to jump out of his chair and go over and speak to her, but in the moment of his impulse a dark rush of resentment assailed him. She had betrayed him even before they'd met. Pointedly he picked up *Macbeth* and pretended to be deeply concerned in it.

Had he been looking up he would have noticed the expression of utter unbelief and then dismay on the girl's face as she watched him resume his reading. For a minute or two she had continued to look from him to the waves, but as he did not look up again, she at last thrust her hands deeper in her pockets and walked off slowly with rounded shoulders.

When David, unable to nourish resentment further, did at last look up from his book it was to find the space by the stanchion empty. He leapt up to find he was alone on this part of the ship. In the east the sky was darkening, the noise of wind and water was louder and the patrol of birds astern seemed smaller and their wings weighed down with the burden of another sunset on them. He felt angry with himself but even angrier with the woman. Again she had proved his point. She was not to be trusted, she couldn't even wait. Again he raged, but in the end even he was tired of his unreason and told himself sternly: It's all your fault anyway. . . . You cheat yourself and then blame it on others.

At dinner he saw her in her place at the Captain's table, and noticed with sorrow that he appeared to have ceased to exist for her. When she got up to leave, she never lifted her eyes to him but turned quickly and walked out of the saloon with a light, sure step. That was more than David could bear. He pushed his half-eaten food away from him and leapt up from the table to go after her.

The lounge was blue with smoke and full of people, and looked exactly like any lounge in any luxury hotel. To David, compelled by his own stormy anxieties, the snatches of conversation which came to him sounded trivial and of the most presumptuous banality. He passed quickly along the lounge and into the drawing-room. He looked in at the bar, quickly drank a brandy, and then went out on deck. It was ready for the ship's first dance. The yellow boards were white with French chalk, the sides covered by tarpaulins. The night was shut out and the triumph over environment was as complete now as the ship could make it. David walked round the deck several times, peering closely at all the little groups forming on it, but she was not among any of them. He gave up and decided to return to his favourite deck where he had been all afternoon.

As his head came up out of the companion way and over the edge of the deck the full weight of the night fell like a hood over him. Here there were no awnings and no artificial lights but a black sky full of very bright and clear stars. Then the night expanded into a wide shell of jet-black water and he felt like a diver whose foot has just been released from the grip of a giant clam on an ocean floor and who is slowly rising upwards to where day rolls like a highway of stars on the surface. He stepped clear of the kerb at the head of the ladder and was out on the deck.

The night was so clear that he saw the tip of a long black mast stirring round a bowl full of stars. The funnels were invisible, but the pulse of the engines in them and their great bubbles of black smoke were keenly alive and reassuringly near at hand. He went to his old place by the stanchion and looked out. The sea was much calmer. Already the water was fingering the phosphorescence in its lap like an ancient oriental jeweller counting his treasure at the end of a good day. And down there in the valley of the water, round each flickering point of fire in the dark, an immensely urgent deep-sea conversation was taking place, rising up tirelessly and irresistibly. When the band below suddenly struck up bravely and began to pour the heavy oil of a German dance tune on to this babble of water and wind and crackling night it sounded so ineffective and absurd that it almost brought a smile to David's face. He went back to his chair, stretched out his legs and looked up at the sky towards wave upon wave of darkness breaking into foam against reef upon reef of stars.

But he had hardly settled down in his chair when he heard voices. Somewhere in the dark near at hand people were talking. He listened with concentration and eagerness. There were three people talking, two men and a woman. The men did most of the talking and their voices were of no interest to him. It was the third, the woman's voice, that made his pulse beat faster. He had never heard it before and yet he knew it at once. It was low and yet so clear that it maintained its identity in the midst of all that busy prattle of sound around the deck. If the voice's own effortless and distinct outline tended to be blurred, it was by a delicate tremor from within. It was the voice of someone who stood not at the entrance of her being to welcome in the world but rather deep in the garden of herself, waiting to be fetched. It matched the expression he had seen on her face, and completed such a sphere of single-ness in his mind and senses that he was moved with profound gratitude that the known-unknown woman existed and was there sharing the same night and the starlight with him.

Then at once the full guilt of his behaviour in the afternoon returned to him. He felt like someone who had told a deliber-ate lie to a person who trusted him. But he had been more subtle than that. He'd equipped his lie with all the dimensions of truth. He'd used the truth to kill the truth: set one half to ambush and murder the other half. But at this point all the habitual defences of his negation brought up their grim reserves of ancient, unexplained hostility and tried again to bind him in their fantastic spell. And as usual they blamed their fantasy on him, made his own strength their sword. They might well have succeeded and killed yet another spon-

taneous upsurge in him, if an instinct of which he was unaware had not intervened and taken charge.

Just then he heard one of the men asking the woman in a
diffident, hesitant voice: "I wonder if you'd care to dance this
one with me?"

The woman did not respond at once and the pause, short as
it was, was long enough for David. He jumped out of his
chair. The instinct which possessed him told him also where
to find her. He turned sharp left and walked straight to her
old place by the life-boat stanchion.

The two men had their backs to him, she was leaning
against the rails, looking at her companions. He could see no
detail, but the white of her dress showed up with a strange
dream-like vividness. David bowed and said in a voice that
seemed to him to belong to someone else but which to the
others sounded remarkably confident and authoritative:

"Sorry I'm so late but I've been looking for you everywhere. This is our dance I believe?" And he held out his hand
to her.

At once, as if this were exactly what she was expecting, the
woman stood clear of the rail. She appeared quite unem-
barrassed by his unexpected eruption into her company and
said simply to the man who had just asked her to dance:
"I'm sorry, I'm engaged."

Then bending down and gathering the heavy folds of her
dress about her with one hand, she took David's outstretched
hand with the other and said: "Yes I'd love to dance."

As they walked away her hand in his was cool, light, yet
strangely alive. It was so confiding that he was more ashamed
than ever of having doubted her. Suddenly remembering his
emotions of the day, he realised how heavily the chances of
success must have been loaded against him and without warning he began to tremble. She felt the taut ripple of it in his
hand, stopped on the step and looked up. He stood, a black
blur against a branch of stars shaken violently with light and
electric sparkle like a flash of may blossom in a summery

gust. Her face with the light of the dance-floor from below, was twilit with anxiety.

"What's the matter?" she asked. "Aren't you well? Would you rather not dance?"

"Oh no, I'm all right," he reassured her quickly, and feeling instinctively that he must hasten before the banality of the glittering dance-deck extinguished those delicate illuminations that live only in silence and shine only in a darkness for which even remote starlight is too bright. "Oh no, everything's all right," he repeated. "Only before we go down there, I want you to forgive me . . . I don't know what possessed me . . . I'd been looking out for you all day."

"There's nothing to forgive." A tremendous warmth flushed through her voice as if an instinct which she had been sponsoring had suddenly been proved right. "I—I think I knew that you couldn't help yourself. . . . You—you're very unhappy, aren't you?"

"That doesn't make it any better—" He tried to continue but she interrupted him, saying gravely: "It makes all the difference. Everything's different when one's unhappy." Then in a lighter note and trying to convey a sense of the gaiety which she was beginning to feel, she added: "Listen! My favourite waltz. . . . Come on! Don't let's waste any of it."

The Italian band had by now abandoned the heavy, galloping German dance music and was playing instead one of those Viennese melodies which to this day are illuminated from within, like pearls by their own submarine glow, with nostalgia for that brief moment wherein the spirit of men stole out from underneath Gothic archway, Byzantine colonnade, spangled tent and pointed, trembling minaret to observe a new rhythm.

But for years now the desire to dance had died in David, and in any case civilised dancing, except waltzing, had never appealed to him. He had learnt to waltz from Mary herself. His mind was full of memories of all sorts of formal and in-

formal occasions when Mary had insisted on dancing most of
the waltzes with him. Those moments ran like a clear and full
stream through the living texture of his life. Sometimes as he
watched the strands of swollen currents in a river running
straight and clean before the speed of their own advance until
suddenly, without visible warning, they curled in on themselves and their forward impulse turning tightly together
round and round some mysterious, eddying core, round the
dark, invisible centre of some downward pull, some urgent
whispered temptation from the river bed, he would remember those times without number when he'd been swept out in
Mary's arms on a stream of music. And now, just for a second,
his spirit sickened at the immense, desert distance between two
ends of himself which this memory revealed to him. But
somehow, in spite of himself he was able to smile at the girl
and respond to her mood.

When the waltz had been brought dramatically to an end
with one sharp clash of the cymbals, there appeared to be
complete silence on the deck for a moment. The ship gave a
slight, cold shudder as it sank down from another deep swell,
and then the noise of the sea and the wind passed over the
vessel like a breeze through a loaded chestnut in early summer
darkness.

They passed the band and David stopped in front of the
leader. "I'd like to buy you all some wine," he said. "Anything you like."

The leader jumped to his feet. "Thank you, Signor. But
what would you like us to play for you next?"

The woman turned to look at David. His eyes were bright
as she had not seen them yet, but there were dark lines underneath the eyes and his features were tight and drawn when he
was not speaking. She knew instinctively that he was beyond
normal comprehension, a deadly tired person from whom
at any minute the excitement and inspiration would depart
and leave his spirit sagging. So she took his tiredness on herself saying: "D'you mind if we don't dance again to-night?

I'm rather tired," and then thanking the band leader again they began walking in silence back towards the upper deck. Before they reached it, the woman stopped short suddenly saying: "I think it's going to be cold up there. . . . I'll need a wrap."

"Can't I get it for you?" David asked politely but underneath the conventional response all sorts of instinctive apprehensions started up in him again at the mere suggestion of her leaving him.

"You wouldn't know where to find it—but I shan't be a minute."

She started off briskly, then looking back saw David in the half-light by the ladder, his shoulders suddenly bent, his hair ruffled by the wind, and he looked so abandoned and forlorn that she quickly turned back saying, "Why don't you come with me?"

They went along silently side by side. Once they were together the shadow in David vanished like shade of cloud over a hill and they were back in the mood of their dance. It was amazing to him how natural and reassuring it was to be with this woman.

There was hardly a soul about on the lower deck. Curtains were drawn in the purser's office and there was laughter and the tap of dominoes from within. A night watchman was just taking up position under the ship's clock and he gave them a perfunctory salute as they passed. The passengers who were not on deck dancing seemed to have gone early to bed as if still exhausted by the storm. Pair after pair of shoes stood outside the cabin doors for cleaning, but the restless, ironic flick of curtains swinging ceaselessly in and out of open doorways belied their impression of pedestrian stability. Above, the steel ceilings clotted with thick white paint and lashed with pipes and cables twisted together like the stuffed entrails of an elephant, gave the scene an impression of submerged unreality. The stark electric lights glared down bleakly unwanted and unemployed like street lamps late at night on the

walls of locked and shuttered houses and the surface of un-
walked streets. To David the whole scene suddenly felt late,
desperately late.

"Is your cabin here?" he asked her.

"Yes," she said, walking on, "right at the end of this alleyway. I'll show you."

"Once I looked for you here," he said, the memory of the
futility of his search getting between him and her gay tone.

She looked up clearly surprised, so he explained how he
thought he'd seen her face in the mirror of the bar on the
night of the storm and had jumped up only to find it vanished.
"It was all an illusion," he ended bitterly. "One of many."

"But it wasn't an illusion," she said quickly, in some distress. "You may have seen me in the mirror. I was in and out
of that doorway several times to take a look at you."

"To look at me?" It was his turn to be surprised.

"Yes," she said, smiling. "After all, you and I were the only
passengers about in the storm and I was rather frightened.
The ship creaked so, like a haunted house, and I hoped you'd
talk to me. Besides. . . ."

She stopped, for they had reached the door of her cabin
and she ducked abruptly through a restless curtain. David
heard the click of a switch and at once the brown regulation
curtains of a first-class cabin glowed like amber.

"Do come in. I shan't be a moment," she called out without
self-consciousness of any kind.

But he could not bring himself to step through the curtain.
So long as he had this woman by his side and could touch her,
he could believe in her. But the moment she was out of sight
something inside him intervened, forced a twisted, malignant
mask of unbelievable antiquity upon her open, confiding face
and set a tranced and fated chorus chanting in the wings of
his memory. He had only to take one step, brush aside the
curtain in order to see her in the clear, unillusioned light of her
cabin. But it was too much. Inarticulate, he shrank from the
prospect, curling up inside himself with reservations like a

snake pierced too deeply in its new skin by the very thorn that had served to remove the old.

There was a barely perceptible pause before he answered: "Thanks, but I'm just lighting a cigarette and I'd hate to fill your cabin with smoke."

"Well, I shan't be a moment," she called back in the same frank, even tone.

Immediately he regretted his reservations and felt shamed by his hesitation. The next moment, she rejoined him, a stole of fine black wool around her shoulders.

On their way back they walked through the bar and David was reminded that he had not had a drink for some time.

"Wouldn't you like a drink?" he asked her.

She nearly refused, but some instinct bade her steer as close a course to David as possible, so she replied: "Very well, I'll have whatever you're having. . . . Only couldn't we drink it up on deck?"

"Good idea," David agreed and walked over to the bar.

When David joined her with their drinks it was to find her deep in some comforting dream of her own, a warm, happy look on her face. Again that irretrievable memory of something familiar flashed far back in David's mind like a lighthouse on an unidentified headland below the horizon of the night.

"What are you thinking about?" he asked her, amazed equally by himself and her.

"I'll tell you on deck," she said, returning to the present with an effort.

The boat deck was deserted, the night darker than ever, and the sea more hushed and quiet than it had yet been. From the funnels the smoke flared and streamed out behind the ship like the mane of the horses of night themselves. The stars, now fully deployed, were well and urgently on the march to their own far hinterland of time. The air above the long, black masts of the ship seemed to reverberate with their vast and measured movement.

David and the woman pulled their chairs up to the rail in silence.

"You promised to tell me what you were thinking," David said at last.

Although she wished he hadn't reminded her, she made no effort to evade the question. "I was wondering why you drink so much," she said slowly. Immediately she'd spoken she felt David's dismay in the dark air between them so she went on more quickly: "But I was sure that whatever the reason was it must be a good one and absolutely right for you."

She stopped and David, not sure he was hearing correctly, asked: "And so?"

She made an expressive little gesture with her shoulders and answered: "And then I lost all interest in the matter . . . and now here we are." She leant forward. "Isn't it a wonderful night? I feel absolutely at home in it, don't you? As if it were made for us."

Her hands in her lap, folded together, glowed against the white of her dress in the dark like arum lilies.

Deeply moved by the unfailing manner in which each act of trust in her defeated the lack of trust in him, David put out his left arm, took her hands and held on to them tightly, saying: "I do feel at home. For the first time in years. I think you're the most understanding person in the world . . . you and Alexander the Great."

"Alexander the Great?"

He told her then something about me and the explanation made him realise how little they knew of each other. He stopped and began to laugh.

"Why are you laughing?" she asked, wishing he would laugh more often.

"Because," he replied, becoming serious at once, "I suddenly realised that when you asked me about Alex I was completely taken aback. I'd taken it for granted that you knew all about him. You see, I can't help feeling you know all about me too."

"I feel like that too," she said quickly. "So perhaps it's true . . . perhaps we do really know each other?"

"I am afraid it isn't possible and yet the same feeling keeps on coming over me in rushes. Somewhere at the far, far back of my mind there seems to be a memory of you trying to reach me. . . . And yet I damned well can't get at the feeling though I know it's there." His voice grew agitated as a sense of his own helplessness swept over him, but he became calmer almost at once, and continued gravely: "But I do feel as if I've always known you, knew you before I was born, in some odd way."

He stopped as she suddenly averted her face. Putting up his hand fearfully to her cheek, he felt tears upon it.

In an instant he was out of his chair and kneeling by her side. "I've hurt you again but I didn't mean to. You see, there's the devil of it. . . . I wouldn't hurt a hair on your head but I can't help it because of some hurt I did you before we met."

"Ssh . . ." She pushed him gently back towards his chair, and the tenderness in her voice reached him reassuringly through the darkness. "But, my dear, you've not hurt me, you could never hurt me . . . I wasn't crying, or if I was there are no tears in my heart. You've just said a very wonderful thing to me. . . . How could I be unhappy?"

Yes, how could she be? . . . Ever since she could remember she'd known that some day someone would say just that thing to her. She'd nursed that knowledge against all the experience of her world. In the midst of a life of deliberate planning she'd clung to the irrational knowledge that one day from a far country, from a wild and perilous shore in a snarling and foaming sea, someone whom she did not know and yet would know instantly would make his way to her through great danger, recognise her instantly, and brushing the banal crowd aside take her by the hand and say: "Come!" And at once she would leave whatever she was doing, however urgent, and go. She had held on to this blind knowledge until even she had begun to lose heart; and reason, affection and loyalty had forced a compromise upon her, a denial of her true faith: yet even then faith had not died. Through the paralysis of compromise this dream had stayed alive. If her life were to have all its full meaning and become open-eyed and truly alive, compromise had to be killed and the last ghost of it exorcised from her heart.

So, the moment she saw David she'd recognised him. He'd walked straight into this image burning in the darkness of her being like a soldier into armour made ready for him. Indeed he was so like what she'd expected all those years that she was not even surprised and was able to look him up and down like an old friend.

But the signs of danger were here. He was in great tribulation, some terrible and perilous exile. And everything that had happened seemed to confirm it. Her sense of his danger, of the peril stalking him yet, had made her stay on deck in the storm to watch him with mounting anxiety. But could she tell him that now? Could she tell him too of the exquisite sense of release from the ceaseless, night and day stresses and strains of doubt, and hunger for completion, which his words gave her, cutting her free from the bonds which tied her, naked and incomplete, to a rough and swaying tree of knowledge which was both partial and unfulfilled? Could he understand that her tears were tears of relief because the shackled vigil at last was over?

David sank back into his chair, still holding her hand in his, and said: "I'm glad you feel it's mysterious too. . . . I don't even know your name and I don't expect you know mine. And yet—"

She interrupted him quickly. "Perhaps we know each other better for not knowing these things. . . . Perhaps this is how we were always meant to be known to each other. . . . Don't let's try and improve on that just yet."

To-morrow, she told herself, when the day of our brittle knowledge returns, as we watch the sun rebuilding the high and shining ramparts of that prison of which the dark now makes us free, then we can exchange passports and give names and ages, occupations and addresses.

"All right," David agreed, carried away by the emotion that he felt flowing through her. "I'm only too glad to postpone telling you my history—"

He stopped suddenly realising that nothing could prevent the past from dwelling with them, from sitting with them there on deck, hooded and disguised in the dark. The past was active in him, indeed its pressure from within was sometimes more than he could endure. It was as if all the forms of life that had ever been at work in him came to a point, prodding him on, making him responsible for them, wanting him to be their justification. And he was at daggers drawn with the past, and so could only hurt all who touched him. Oh, to be free of it all—

He leant over and peered intently at her face, which was so close and still, like a white flower in a dark wood in the dewfall of evening. Her nearness was almost tangible. And then again his heart overflowed with remorse. He had happened on another ground for self-reproach. In the past he had lived his life as if it were his to do what he liked with, as if after his flight from Mary no one else could have a say in the matter. He'd given his life to Helena as if it was his alone to give away. But he knew now how wrong he'd been. His life belonged not only to him but also to its own unique and lightning coincidence. Whether they talked about it or not, the damaged past was there ready to receive this girl. Oh, the great and terrible distances, the deserts, jungles, turgid rivers, dry stony places and harsh, distended skies that exist within. This night stretching out above them had no greater reach, and the light that was bleached in his bones to-day could come from a star that was dead and exploded in the first idea of himself a million-million years back.

An immense longing came up in his heart, as the great white albatross had come before his eyes on the day of the storm, aimed like an arrow from the bow of its wings at the immense distances about them. He saw again those giant, purple shadows with seven-leagued boots moving in on him and this girl. "Oh, my God," he said, "I wish I had no history at all, and that this was the great exodus from nothing into Genesis."

"So do I," she said, taking his hand in both hers. "But I'm not going to start regretting things now."

They sat for awhile in a silence that was sound of the sea and throb of the ship until she said: "You're very quiet. Have I depressed you?"

"I've never been less depressed," David said in a dreamy voice, "since Alexander the Great and I used to sleep together at home out under the stars. I was wishing he could be here with us and listening to you. . . . You talk like him, you're terribly like him, in fact—only of course I wouldn't know how to introduce you to him, would I?"

She knew that he was smiling and at once responded: "I tell you what," she said gaily. "Let's christen ourselves! Let's give each other names that are a part of the meaning we have for each other. . . ."

"That'd be too difficult."

The game seemed too complex and exacting, and he tried to evade it.

"But you must have some idea of a name that suits me," she persisted.

"I can think of many." He gave in as gracefully as he could. "But mostly I think of you without a name. I just think of you as 'woman'. In fact, I don't feel I've ever met a real woman till I met you. I've only known women as functions, mothers, potential mothers, and so on."

And as he spoke he had a sudden vision of the first woman as she stepped out of a sleeping man's rib in a garden when the leaves were still dripping and trembling with light.

"Oh, you're playing up very well," she exclaimed. "You must have done this before. Go on!"

214

"I don't really know that I can." David frowned. "Not anyway until I've yanked this memory of you out of its prison, rescued you from the dark tower in myself and set you free. . . . But I know you'd have to have some ancient, legendary sort of name."

"I hope not 'Eve' . . . I couldn't bear that." She laughed with genuine amusement.

"No, not 'Eve' at all, nothing like that at all," he replied seriously. "Through Eve offence came into the world. But I don't know what I want to call you, really." He hesitated. "So you'd better try naming me."

She paused, playing for time. "A minute ago, I seemed to know it clearly but now it's gone . . . I was thinking of you too as a man—or rather as a boy about to become man," she said.

Then she had it as surely as if she were back in that mellow-blue day in Florence, smelling the pines and flickering cypresses and looking in amazement at the very image which night and day had stared back at her out of the clear mirror of her heart. She saw it again as Michaelangelo had compelled it breaking into life through intractable stone, naked and un-ashamed, and in a vision so whole that even death, weary of itself, must have joined in the creation.

"I've got it!" she said sitting up suddenly. "A boy first, and then the boy David—"

David gave such a start that she asked quickly: "What's the matter? Are you hurt because I called you a boy?"

"Good heavens, no!" Then he began to laugh in sheer, joyful amazement. "You're absolutely incredible, absolutely amazing, but please don't ask me why until to-morrow. . . . But just tell me this. Why 'David'?"

"Because," she said slowly, happy to hear him laugh once more, "because once I feel you herded sheep against lions and leopards, because once perhaps you made music on a harp so beautifully that a jealous king threw his spear at you and . . ." A note of seriousness drove the lightness out of her voice,

"Because at any moment now you may hear Goliath calling on the other side of the hill to be killed."

She stood up and let her hands rest lightly for a moment on his head. She was feeling wonderfully content but tired as if she'd lived the whole of her life in the past few hours. Suddenly she yawned unashamedly, and said: "I'm tired, David. Let's go to bed."

Reluctantly David stood up, took her arm, and led her away. But the fear of her leaving him haunted him. He would have liked to sit there all night, planning names and plotting intricate courses under the stars. But he knew it was late. The clock over the purser's office said one o'clock. There was scarcely a sound of the sea down below, only the faint creak of a ship on the high sea. The stillness and the emptiness of it all, together with the one clock presiding over them like some old judge in a court from which there is no appeal, was almost more than David could bear. He was very near to becoming bitter again and trotting out his hackneyed resentments at being condemned to return to the tight, split cell of himself. But when he looked at the sleepy, tired face at his side his bitterness vanished.

He stopped outside her cabin, took her hand and raised it to his lips and said: "Good-night, unknown woman. A long, true, and good night to you. I shall wrap the thought of what you've done to me like a blanket around me—"

She smiled a happy smile at him and said: "Good-night, David. . . . Good-night. . . ."

CHAPTER 18

DAVID woke very early. It was still dark inside his cabin
but the dawn already hung in the port-hole like an
orange in a Mediterranean orchard. He lay very still watching
it first in amazement and then with increasing excitement.
Far below the port-hole there was a friendly, companionable
swish of the sea and the silky rustle of the ship's speed through
the air. He knew something had happened in the night; he
knew that he and the world were no longer the same. For ten
years he'd gone to bed as he'd got up in the morning and got
up as he'd gone to bed. For ten years the seconds had been so
long, so packed with tired and dreary reluctance, that the day
stretched in front of him like a hot, dry desert of eternity and
he did not know how he was to get through it, except by
attending constantly to his unspeakable thirst. All the clocks
round him had ticked on busily, but his own moment in
time had refused to budge and had remained a stale lagoon
locked out of the swell and swing of the sea. Technically he
had lived ten years but in his heart he had lived so little that
there was no record of the years in his blood.

But in this night just behind him somewhere on some
pioneer perimeter of sleep on the other side of the broad white
highway of stars that hemmed in his view of the night there
had been a change, and it seemed that the meaning of that
change was about to reveal itself in the day opening out in
that lovely fruit of light, in that far eastern persimmon of gold
swinging with such a slow, steady rhythm deep among the
leaves of darkness at his window. And then suddenly in a
flash so violent and startling that it cracked like lightning in
his head, he understood.

With the importance of the discovery he went deathly quiet
like someone waiting breathless for the crack of thunder that

would surely follow on so keen a flash of lightning. He was not seeing the dawn as he'd seen other dawns during those long ten years. He was seeing it, but—and this was the wonder of it—he was also feeling it; and the bright warm feel of it in his blood was new. The dawn was no longer just swinging in the sky with cold, infinitely objective colours, a mocking and untouchable Indian beauty to a night-bound spirit. Instead it was an experience deep inside himself, glowing in the dark of himself like a Chinese lantern burning in a temple in the yellow-moon mountains to the incense of sandalwood and the drifting scent of mandarin blossom rising up through jet-jade portals from the smoking valley of the seven rivers below.

He shut his eyes and the light was still there. He opened them and the light outside and the light within instantly merged without overlap of shadow anywhere. Slowly he got out of his bunk and went on his knees beside it. He had no words, no understanding of what he was feeling, but it seemed that he could express it only on his knees in an attitude of long-discarded prayer beseeching without words that this small reclaimed fragment of his original self should be defended to the last from his invisible and unidentifiable enemies. He stayed like that for some time before he got up and slowly dressed.

Even so he was on deck before the sailors had finished washing it down, and he stepped over leaking hose pipes and wet planks to stand at the rail and watch an alert, open-eyed sun climb with direct determination quickly up into the sky. Almost at once it was warm. Clearly they were already farther north than he'd realised and in a different almost seasonless season. The last wrinkled memory of the storm seemed to have been wiped from the sea and it was no longer blue, but black, the light sparkling on it like sunlight on the crystallised fossil of vanished and forgotten ferns in deep-mined coal. The swell following behind from the Antarctic still kept up with the ship but no longer pitched it about, rather seemed to be helping it on its way in long, easy, strides. In the night the albatross patrol had shrunk to one lone scout, one hardy frontiersman, the last white hunter and slayer of great distances, who David liked to think was the bird that had first flown like an arrow into his imagination. He remembered the vanished birds, which had escorted the ship into the storm in such numbers that the shafts of light striking through the clouds were adorned with diadem and fern of beating wings and stood briefly in the sky like the mirage of a grove of royal palms swaying in the wind, or else collapsed into the turbulent gloom like brown Corinthian columns with shattered wing-frieze of fading feathers. His heart warmed to their lone survivor, and its presence there seemed to him a great and heroic achievement. In the calm precision of its wide loops round the ship, this cool, white bird seemed gently to mock the flying fish which were beginning to burst in stainless steel coats through the hoops of the waves like frantic sequined circus troupes into a ringed arena. Just for a moment they were a shining mystery in the full light of the sun, their wings trembling like tuning forks with the shock of some high-sea melodrama before they disappeared from sight, like a handful of shingle cast by a bored child into the water. At every minute from somewhere around the ship these flights of glittering fish were exploding, showing that this sea was strangely and thickly populated. Once midway between the ship and the horizon a vast school of plump dolphins went by—busy, bustling housewives putting bright silver stitches in the dark, open seam of the sea. Obviously, for the sea this was the beginning of a normal day, but to David it all looked new.

He stayed on deck until the ship's gong called him down for breakfast. As he walked into the saloon his eyes instinctively went to her table but she was not there. He'd hardly expected her after so late a night and yet he was disappointed. He lingered long over his food but she didn't come. He went on deck and tried to get on with *Macbeth*; but his mind would not stay on it. The Lady was dead, had walked to her death in his sleep and the multitudinous seas were not incarnadined. . . .

All morning he stayed on deck expecting to hear a low clear voice at his side, yet at lunch time, still alone, he went below and she had not appeared. Then he began to feel alarmed, to feel desperate need of confirmation of the night before. The hour of his cock-crow was approaching.

When he emerged from himself again some long time later, he found himself sitting on deck in the sun with an old sketch book open in front of him, and a cool presence was bending over him, saying in a voice straight out of the green shade of herself: "Hullo, David. What are you doing?"

He looked up directly into two blue eyes clear of fatigue. At once he rose from his chair, saying ridiculously: "Welcome, Honourable little blue one."

"Please help me with this—" She had a collapsed deck chair by the shoulder but her eyes were on his sketch book. "And then show me what you've been sketching."

She held the book carefully between the palms of her hands and looked at his sketch for a while in silence. She saw that it was not finished nor related to the scene about them. It looked to her rather as if it might be intended as an illustration for some heraldic theme, some incident in Malory's *Morte d'Arthur* or Spenser's *Faerie Queene*. It was beautifully, unerringly drawn; a suggestion, made with the quickest and most amazing economy in line. Unfinished as the sketch was, one derived from it immediately a feeling of tense, violent excitement, almost as if it had been exploded into being through powerful resistances in David's mind.

"What a lovely, exciting thing," she exclaimed enraptured. "What is it, really?"

"I don't know exactly," David began faintly embarrassed. "I was just sitting here feeling miserable and dreaming away when—"

He stopped short realising suddenly that the sketch was in

fact meant to be a dream, a dream that he himself had dreamed in the deep of the past night and which had only just reached him consciously. In his sleep he'd seen a clearing in the forest. The vision had excited him intensely because he'd recognised it as the other, the far part of the wood for which he had once been heading with a wolf-pack, led by a lean grey bitch with a lace-bonnet on its head, close on his heels. Again the wood was very dark but the clearing was full of light. In the midst of it stood the girl who was now beside him. She stood with gold sandalled feet in green grass and amid wild red, white and purple anemones. She had her arm round the neck of a unicorn, trying to soothe it, for it was getting more and more impatient. Amazed, he asked in his dream what she was doing there; and then, although he could not see them, he knew that everywhere the black aborigines who made their home in this sacred, enchanted wood had begun singing to the rapid beat of tom-toms in deep bass voices, voices that came from far down the living well of themselves and sent the leaves shaking as in a great wind:

> *"Tam-bam-bu . . . Tam-bam-bu.*
> *They have waited as long as they could*
> *For the boy called David*
> *Long overdue and lost in the wood.*
> *Tam-bam-bu! Tam-bam-bu!*
> *We are hunting and tracking him too."*

He came to, in bewildered amazement, with the dream completely recollected.

But why had it taken so long to reach him? Ah, there was the old, old rub again. There seemed to be no distance so great in the world without that was not repeated, paralleled and reciprocated within.

Oh, what a vast, loose, untidy constellation the nature of man was! What black gulfs and terrible wide open spaces were concealed from our view by our own flesh and blood which enclosed our spirits as a frail Bedouin tent with its small pinnacle of light shuts out the mystery and immensity of a Saharan night.

"I've just realised that after all I do know what this sketch is supposed to be," he told her, apologising for his silence. "It's supposed to be a dream I had in the night. Sounds silly, I'm afraid, but it's only a dream."

He put out his hand to take the sketch from her, but she said: "Not so fast, . . . I—I must look at it again. . . . Yes, I see now that it's enchantingly dreamlike. . . . Why did you say 'only a dream' in that despising tone?"

She looked intently at him, but he just shrugged his shoulders and said: "No idea."

She looked again at the sketch. "I'd give anything to have a lovely, exciting dream like this," she said, "but to you apparently it means very little. And then, on top of it, to be able to draw as you've done." She looked up quickly. "I begin to suspect, for all your sombre look, that you're a very lucky and rich young man."

"I thought so once too," he answered, staring at a dark ripple of wind as it fastened on to the glistening afternoon horizon. "But my luck left me a long time ago. D'you know this is the first sketch I've attempted in years?"

"So I was right then?" she said with keen interest. "You are 'David' after all—but with a paint brush and not a harp."

"Yes . . . you were more right than you knew last night," he said simply.

For a second she was puzzled. A puff of wind overtook the ship, spread out the smoke from the funnels in the blue air like a black cashmere shawl and dropped the stain of a chocolate shadow on them. Then suddenly a look of delighted surprise flashed over her face. "Don't tell me your name's really David," she said excitedly. "Oh, how extraordinary! I think it's a good omen, don't you? But what's the rest of it?"

David smiled as he answered: "Michaeljohn: David Alexander Michaeljohn."

She gave a little laugh of amazement. "It sounds like a roll call of history! But isn't it rather mean not to have a real surname among them? Three-quarters Christian and one quarter pagan too. . . . Is that quite as it should be?"

"It might have been once, but it's all 'Alexander' now."

The answer, for all his gay tone, felt suddenly too apt and seemed to throw another shadow over them, so she rushed in to deny it, saying with breathless speed: "That's the extremist in you speaking, David. I think it was a wise dispensation of names to have an archangel joining the extremes of David and Alexander to the John in you. I'd bank on the Michael!"

"But what about 'John'?" He looked at her deeply and long. The sea-wind tuning a light waltz between the boats caught his hair as it had done the night before and made him look so young and defenceless, so like a boy without his Jonathan sitting at the feet of the melancholy and jealous Saul awaiting the throw of a spear, that a tender pity went through her and it was all she could do not to take him in her arms and hold him in a fierce, protective movement to her heart. She was amazed that he could be all things to her in her new found emotions.

"Tell me," she went on, her voice very low, allowing the wind to blow away the unanswered end of his earlier question. "Tell me, if you're David, then who was it who threw his spear at you?"

"Nobody's ever thrown a spear at me, you ridiculous woman," David said, laughing to keep down the wild flame of emotion that her concern touched off in him. "No one, unless—" He hesitated. "And that's too silly—"

"Please go on," she pleaded.

"Well, I was going to say unless it was Albert," he conceded.

"Albert?"

"Yes, Albert," he answered. "Albert the Great, Albert the Once Good, Albert the King, my father."

His answer was quite light but she was convinced that,

for a second, a new note, a new depth of bitterness had been revealed in his voice. So she used her game to try and race him out of it, and asked: "But wasn't there ever a Goliath somewhere?"

He shook his head solemnly but didn't speak, watching her warily as if at any moment he might have to defend himself.

"Not anywhere?" she persisted with light, feigned irony.

"No, no Goliath," he assured her. "And yet, to be honest, I think perhaps I've seen his shadow sometimes between me and the sun."

As he spoke he looked unwillingly over his shoulder at the westering sun as if he fully expected the shadow of a giant with uplifted club to be darkening its face.

A shiver of apprehension went through the girl as she saw David's involuntary backward glance. "It might have been Goliath's shadow," he went on bitterly, "because this shadow that I mean is vast. It's ten years long. . . . I'd like you to know that once I knew of no shadow. From the time I was born I'd always wanted to paint, and so in spite of Mary. . . ."

"Mary?" she interrupted.

Dear God, why didn't he answer more quickly? Why was he so slow? What was he trying to hide from her? Had the name just slipped out and was he now regretting it?

But David, the rhythm of his bitterness broken, was now merely trying to recapture the tone of the game which had so suddenly ceased to be a game to him.

"How stupid of me." He smiled apologetically and then said with a suspicious absence of emotion, "Mary, the Queen —my mother, of course."

"Oh, I see, your mother. . . . I'm sorry, but you see I couldn't possibly know," she spoke dully, dazed with the shock of her own relief. "Please go on."

"There's not much more to tell," he told her. "I arrived in England and for the first time in my life did nothing but paint. There were people of discernment who said that I painted like someone who had his own unique vision and revelation of life. Oh, how I wish you could have known and seen me then." David gave her one of his sombre looks of longing, and then continued: "I had no doubts and fears then. I felt like someone in the centre of a strong current in a clear stream on an early summer morning, making for the open sea and my own authentic Newfoundland. And then something horrible happened. . . ." His expression became so unbelievably malign and bitter that even she was frightened as she watched him struggling with himself.

Then he made a tremendous violent gesture with both his hands on behalf of all the words that were not fast enough for his purpose, and said: "It doesn't really bear talking about . . . but the stream was no sea-stream at all, it . . . was not ocean but desert bound, so there came a day—about ten years ago— when it just dried up, or rather went underground, disappeared into the sand right at my feet. It was then that I saw the first shadow on the sun—it may well have been that then Goliath carved his name on its face. I know nothing except that I've felt unemployed by life ever since and that this silly sketch"—he took the book out of her lap, looking at it with a strange light in his eyes—"is the first thing I've tried to draw for years."

"And this sketch, David," she said taking the book from him and clasping it protectively, "shows that your hand hasn't lost its cunning." She paused and then went on soberly: "Listen to me, David, for at this moment I don't believe I can be wrong. . . . I've known all along that something horrible has been happening to you. But I don't believe the stream has dried up at all . . . I think it merely went underground as you said yourself; and that when you get to the other side, you'll rediscover it. And perhaps this," she held up the sketch book, "is the first sign."

"I wish Alex were here to listen to you," he remarked with apparent irrelevance, and then added without conviction: "Perhaps you're right. But life tastes like sawdust to me. I'd rather not live any longer, I'd rather—"

He stopped suddenly for his last remark seemed to have hurt her. She drew back as if mortally wounded and tears of final defeat shone darkly in her eyes. She made no effort to hide the hurt, but asked in a trembling and almost inaudible voice: "You feel that now? You feel it at this moment, here, now?"

And as she spoke he knew it was no longer true. So long as someone cared for him as this woman seemed to care, then it could no longer be true. The realisation leapt up in him like flame, like that Hindu temple of fire with Anna Maria's antique face beside it on the night by the river when the lion roared in our childhood.

"No," he said in as low a tone. "No . . . It's not true here and now. That was the past speaking in me. But tell me what am I to do? Can the salt get back its savour? Have you got the recipe?"

She turned towards him, looked him straight in the eyes and said in a voice ringing with passion: "I know exactly what you've got to do. You've got to fight, David. You've got to trust the courage that has made you hold on so long after life had lost its taste for you, and you've got to use that courage, David, use it! I'd leave Alexander alone drinking in his fading Babylonian glory, and go to the Archangel, borrow his flaming sword and with sword and sling and pebbles fight, David, fight!"

"Fight, yes." He shrugged his shoulders. ". . . But fight what?"

"The shadow, David," she answered at once. Then she hesitated, finally decided to flinch from nothing and asked: "Why did you say just now that the shadow was ten years long?"

How he wished, as never before, that he'd not got to answer that question. He saw now how cunningly all afternoon his mind had sailed his thought away from this rock. He was tempted to lie to her or at least to evade the question. But perhaps the defeat of this temptation was the first pre-requisite of a successful issue to the fight she was urging him to begin. He summoned all his courage and replied: "I said that because of my ten years with Helena." Even then he could not be more explicit, could not say "my ten years of marriage with Helena."

She sat very still. She should have known, had known in fact, that a Mary would have to be followed by a Helena, but childish hope had chased her knowledge away.

"And who is Helena?" she asked with great calm and stillness.

"The woman I'm married to." His tongue refused to form the word "wife".

"I see," she said, not seeing at all but trying very hard to be quiet and still, though a great cry was going up from deep inside her. "Oh, David," she went on brokenly. "Didn't you know—" She'd been going to say "didn't you know I was here?" but stopped short.

"I knew nothing," he said in great distress and earnestness. "Oh, my dear, forgive me. I told you last night that before we met I was doomed to hurt you. I can only say that I'm so little married to Helena that I was tempted to deny it just now. I've never loved her. I've never known what love . . ."

"Then why did you do it?" she demanded fiercely. "Why?"

"Why?" He repeated the question, asking it of himself for the first time, and was aghast with the answer when it came. "I regret to say for no good reason at all—except that I just could not say 'No.' I tried to but I just couldn't do it."

He recollected that awful paralysis which had mastered his decision from the moment he met Helena, but, lame as the explanation sounded to him, it seemed at once to make sense to the woman.

She asked more gently. "Why couldn't you say 'No?'"

"I don't know, really," he replied miserably. "Except that I didn't want to hurt someone who so obviously loved me."

"She loved you? I see. Then didn't she know that you

didn't love her? Or was that withheld too, for fear of hurting?" She spoke bitterly.

"No, I was quite honest. I told her from the start that I didn't think I'd ever be free to love a woman—but that I'd do my best to make her happy."

"And how old were you?"

"Twenty-one."

"And was she content with that?" Her eyes flashed with angry fire.

"Yes, she accepted it. . . . It seemed reasonable enough."

"Dear God! Reasonable!" An invisible sword flashed in her hand. "I tell you, David, it had all the reason of hell in it. At twenty-one, one shouldn't be reasonable. And yet she allowed it—knowing it all, she allowed you. . . . And you dare tell me she loved you!"

Her scorn was like a spear hurled at a harpy. There were so many women who dishonoured their sex, who made infamous the name of the litter-hungry female rat. It was the oldest form of murder in the world, and when would men learn to see it? When would men realise, too, that they make women desperate by coming to them crippled by their own bitter, internecine wars? That was the axis on which turned the great, slow, unforgiving wheel of vengeance, of matricide and patricide, and infanticide. She felt as bitter against the man whose failure fed David to Helena as against Helena for consuming him.

And then suddenly anger left her, and she rebuked the nature of her reasoning, saw on the other side of the black gulf of her anger the discarded sister of herself, a rejected, unorchestrated shadowy Helena brooding over her own lack of music, eating her heart out for longing of counterpoint. No, she was being less than fair to all of them.

"Oh, David," she cried in absolute despair. "I didn't reckon on your being committed to someone else."

"I know." His own distress was keen and great. "But I tried to warn you last night."

"And you still only know the half of it," she said almost to herself, and then suddenly held her left hand out to him. "Haven't you noticed this before?"

David took her hand in his. It was unbelievably hot for someone whose whole being had hitherto seemed so shaded and cool.

"Don't you see the ring on it?" she asked.

"It's a most unusual ring."

She began laughing in a rather unbalanced manner, then suddenly became very serious, and said: "I'm just trying to tell you that I'm married too."

For a moment he scarcely knew whether to believe her or not. "But that's not a wedding ring," he said uncertainly.

Even as he spoke he felt his confidence increasing. So there was some balance in circumstances after all, some equality even if it was only an equality of sacrifice and not achievement.

"D'you remember what you said to me last night?" he asked her urgently.

"I said so many things," she replied wearily.

"You said," he reminded her, "that you weren't going to start regretting the past. D'you regret it now?"

She remained silent and then said, rather humbly and brokenly: "I'm sorry, David. I'm dreadfully sorry and ashamed. But I'd been so certain you were free."

As she spoke he put his arm through hers and pulled her gently round.

"My dear, there's no wrong between us—no wrong between us that can't be put right." He turned and faced the sea. "Come, let's watch the sun go down together."

She fell in by his side and they walked slowly over to the far rail. Then she said softly, the old fugitive gaiety once again in her voice: "David, I believe we got the sex of the giant all wrong. . . . I'll make a bargain with you. . . . Kill me a giantess, and I'll deliver you a giant in a cage."

He pressed her arm to his side in a manner that made words

unnecessary, and then leant with her, arm in arm, over the ship's rail.

The sun was just touching the horizon, solemnly carrying down the fading light to lay on the bier of a dead, good day. Already David could hear the sea joining the murmur of the crimson swell in his blood breaking on the coral of bone round the beaches of his mind. The wind of the spirit too was moving sails all set and billowing, going with the ship towards the night. A broad stream of light flowed along the water towards the ship, as if down there in the dark sea was a great highway colonnaded with copper-beeches ablaze. Above the ship the sky was a deep, Sumatran green, turning in the east to a dark blue and right on the horizon to a husky and muscular black. But there was neither cloud nor wisp of sea-haze anywhere. Everywhere the murmur and rustle of wind and water was like the sound of a night breeze in yellow corn under a round harvest moon. Even the rigging and strands of the aerial were giving a friendly murmur, twanging on the air like musicians in some suspended moment between arrival of conductor and the silence of the full house of the night.

David stared out at the scene with growing excitement. Conditions were perfect, but would it happen? He prayed silently that it would, asked in every beat of his pulse that the day should not leave them without a sign. He'd spent so many sun-down hours watching for it that he'd even come to doubt that it ever happened, but an old sailor had once assured him it did. One had to be in the right place in the right ship, the old salt had said, in the right latitudes, in an evening without cloud or blemish, and one could see it.

"Watch the sun carefully," David told the girl, "and if we're lucky we may see a rare and wonderful thing."

"What wonderful thing?"

"I've never seen it myself so I won't try to describe it," he answered.

She asked no more but instead pressed closer into his

shoulder. He took his arm out of hers and put it round her and they stood watching the sun go down with excitement in their blood.

As they watched, the wind suddenly seemed to drop and the ocean round them became quiet and calm as if the whole Atlantic world was holding its breath at the deathbed of so much light. In that hushed moment the sun itself seemed to gather together the memory of all its days and make one last gesture of full, cumulative stature. It grew enormous, spilt over the rim of itself in a great curve of crimson fire, and then they saw the shadow of the swollen horizon impinging on it like the crest of a dark, Carpathian wood. The sun began to contract. It was the golden dome of the Sailor Sultan's mosque in the Great Gulf, became a pointed Moorish minaret, a jewelled arc in Alhambra and top of the tattooed Caliph's tomb. Then it shrunk down until it was a lotus about to close among the lilies in the pool of the sacred crocodile. Finally, and briefly, it was the tip of Apollo's spear thrust for hardening into the fire of the great blacksmith, night. All along the horizon from north and south light came speeding with flashing spurs to join in that fine, pointed, spiked moment of fire. Then the sun disappeared. For a second the sea caught its breath at so great a loss of light, the horizon went dark with anguish—and then it happened. From below the horizon, from the other side of the gulf a tremendous flash of bright, emerald green light shot up across the sky in the most solemn, urgent, majestic and defiant wave of farewell. It came right over the edge of the sea like a flight of burning arrows shot straight at the breast of the advancing night by an army marching not in defeat, but victoriously homewards.

For some minutes the man and woman stood silent, overawed, feeling unimportant in the presence of the miracle. Yet they felt infinitely privileged as if they had just been presented with the fundamental symbol of the master pattern wherein opposites lost themselves in some greater meaning. They'd seen a demonstration of loss which was not loss, together with the heroic thrust which keeps life whole and unending.

David felt strangely uplifted and stimulated. Suddenly he turned and said: "Tell me your name—not the name of the man who married you, but your own."

"Alis," she answered, "Alis Denysse."

He repeated it slowly, impressed by the fact that it sounded especially designed for her. "It's like the name of a very special flower, a rare lily, or iris, or the first flower of chivalry. "It's old, isn't it?"

"Yes, it's old," she confirmed.

He hesitated and then turned to her simply: "I tell you, Alis, I'm even jealous for your name."

CHAPTER 19

THOUGH she'd spoken bravely to David of an "exchange of giants", in the days that followed Alis Denysse came very near the end of her courage. When she told me her story many years later the emotion of that time was still present in her voice like a shadow on sunlit water. While she and David were together, pouring information about themselves into the breach of the years and tracing the expanding outline of the coincidence of their feeling, she felt secure and supremely confident. But at night, alone in her cabin, listening to the uncompromising thrust of the sea, the ship's gallant parry as it sank down to its knees in a deep trough of water and then came bravely up to its full height under the starry sky and lunged heroically forward again, the past came crowding in and she felt unspeakably weary. Doubts would stand by her bed like giants with upraised clubs. How could she hope to get by them? Lying very still, eyes wide open in the dark, she would listen to her own steady, regular breathing and think how like a ship her body was, rising and falling, and carried darkly forward on the sea of her blood before the wind of her spirit, a small and incompletely manned cockleshell of tender flesh inexorably contracted to circumnavigate the globe and the seven seas of its own being. How would it end?

A few days ago, she would have asked herself also, how can it begin? But at last the true beginning had begun. She couldn't be wrong on that. On that issue her lone faith could not fail. This at last was the final choice. Of course, she could refuse to choose, and sometimes that was all she felt capable of doing. Oh, how she wished that the choice had presented itself in a simpler way, neat and tidied, instead of being overgrown by tentacles and mysterious parasites from the past which were clinging to it, demanding to be identified, classified and cut away, before the real act of renewal could begin.

It was not that she lacked courage. I've never known a person who possessed so much. It had never even seemed to her that the ordinary problems of life demanded courage, for she took them in an easy stride. It was indeed one of her own unspoken criticisms of life (as her family conceived and presented it to her) that it was pitched so moderately, had such modest and adaptable aims, that not nearly enough courage was needed for their attainment. Almost the only courage recognised in that world was the courage that made one ride straight in the hunting field, or die without flinching in the service of one's country. Not that she despised courage of that kind. She had too much of it herself and valued it too highly to deride it. But to her it was too normal and commonplace a quality to be called courage. No, courage for her was something uniquely needed to keep one in perpetual search of those first dew-early intimations of the future, something that took one out into the wilds on the track of complex, fugitive and maddeningly untamed perceptions that had peered briefly round a corner of one's senses before scampering off wildly over the edge of that forbidding wasteland of conventional normality. Courage, she would have said, was rejection of the repetitive pattern; was obedience to the forward surge of life; was the burning spear thrust in the dark.

As a result, she had found herself from early childhood straying continually over the normal frontiers of conduct and behaviour. Her family had a keen sense of tradition and an unquestioning belief in the conventions of their time. But not for a single moment could she ever remember thinking of life as lived by her family and their kind as the whole answer, or as wise, useful, necessary or even right for her. In the midst of all the comfortable security of her home, she felt curiously doomed. It was outside in the uncertain and dangerous unknown that her true security seemed to belong. What seemed solid safety to her own people, appeared to her a brittle, card-box shelter in a gathering storm. What seemed madness and recklessness to them was sanity and safety to her. No wonder therefore that her conflict with normality and convention started early and went deep. Yet it was not the crippling conflict of an outcast like Albert Michaeljohn who had been born well outside his protective covering and was doomed to sink into oblivion locked fatally in the social embrace which he had wooed so desperately in order to save himself from drowning. Alis's conflict was the conflict of someone born at the centre of convention and fighting it freely from within, in her own idiom, with the purpose not of rejecting it, but of compelling it to follow anew the trail that lone adventure had once blazed.

It was a foregone conclusion that no one in her family could understand the mysterious spur that raised Alis's imagination to such scorn of her surroundings. Not even her father who was devoted to her pretended to understand her. For one thing he, Gervaise Denysse, a talented and devoted Admiral, was seldom at home. His wife had died young. She'd borne him five children in rapid succession and then suddenly, for no cause clearly discernible or satisfactory to the medical minds of the day, she'd died. Alis, her intuitive nose already on the track, had felt that, whatever jargon the doctors used, Mummy had died because she'd never lived. But she kept her interpretation to herself as her own bedside glimpse of a star by which to steer her imagination.

Within two years of his wife's death Gervaise Denysse married again. He married the childless widow of a brother officer and friend. She was a pretty, competent, conscientious but unimaginative woman. She took over the ancient Denysse home in Hampshire as someone taking over a business, determined to turn it to good account and show a handsome profit. In her husband's almost continual absence on service duty she ran the big and lovely estate that went with the house and supervised the children's education on the prescribed lines of the period with admirable if somewhat cool and over-objective efficiency.

She was scrupulously fair and on the whole got on well with all the children, except Alis. It was perhaps, to use the outworn conception of the time, the fault of both of them. The even, predictable temperament which attracted the other children to their stepmother repelled Alis. It gave her the shivers. It was too good to be true.

Her disquiet increased as she grew older and she began to notice that doing all the correct things and having all the correct answers did not prevent the most incorrect and un-approved things from happening within the family. It became noticeable too, and particularly to Alis's stepmother, who re-sented it deeply, that many of Alis's own unconventional, wilful and so-called selfish actions, spontaneously committed without counting risk or cost, seemed to find their own unique timing, and to fit occasion and means like a glove. To Lady Denysse it sometimes seemed most unfair that the head-strong, undisciplined Alis should be so lucky.

Yet hard and irritating as it all was, she might have forgiven Alis if it had not been for her husband. Alis and her father between them had achieved a most unusual relationship. It was founded really on Alis's uncanny understanding of her father. She was the pivot on which the relationship turned, she was the responsible partner and he relied on her. It was as if she alone had understood that this gallant and distinguished officer, this leader of men and captain of ships, had never really grown up and was at heart still a lone small boy, bullied by himself, his career and life, and in constant need of reassur-ance and simple, protective, unexacting affection. Alis not only understood it but in her immediate, unquestioning way lived her understanding. Her stepmother might be his wife, but Alis was mother to the unfulfilled child in him, and he turned all the more to Alis for feelings before and beyond resolute living. The situation in the end became intolerable both for Alis and her stepmother.

When Gervaise returned to his wife and children after the War, having for long years conducted himself with great bravery and distinction in the face of continuous danger of the worst kind, an inevitable reaction set in. He left the War, but the War had not done with him and now began sending in its invisible returns. Strange emotions and fantasies began to knock at the door of his mind for attention and resettlement. His wife had her brisk, unhelpful way of dealing with these moments. So inevitably it was to his daughter that Gervaise turned for understanding.

Alis felt passionately that only her father could decide how to live his own life. They none of them knew what he'd been enduring. She felt intuitively that there was equal and opposite compensation for everything done. What one took from life with one hand would be restored with the other in accordance with some law so definite that it ought to be better known. There could be no permanent denial of this balance at the heart of things. She knew also, though she was incapable of putting it into words, that one interfered with this balance at great peril. Every instinct warned her that all forms of interference must be dangerous. Daddy had to strike his balance and add up his invisible accounts, and so good luck to him. But the problem, surely, was too serious to be approached with anything but the most absolutely humble and unassuming devotion to truth.

She had no illusions about her stepmother. Lady Denysse, however loyal she was to the rules of her understanding, however keen a believer in the conventional code, had little awareness of the great and rugged laws to which they were subordinate. She was really little more than a determined, successful and graceful half-truth and would, Alis knew, defend herself to the bitter end against all the rest. Alis did not mind for herself, but she minded for her father. She could see that her stepmother would never be able to help in the only way that mattered, by accompanying him, with imagination and understanding, down into the mysterious deeps of his inner being.

So one day Lady Denysse spoke to her husband about Alis. Gervaise was not surprised. The general complaint, of course, he knew of old. He'd frequently been told that Alis was wilful, obstinate, difficult, undisciplined and restless. Recently the restlessness had been qualified by a more up-to-date and fashionable adjective "neurotic". But what was new in his wife's declaration was that she would no longer put up with Alis.

Gervaise decided at once what to do. His dead wife's eldest sister had always been very fond of Alis. Married but childless, she'd frequently hinted that she'd like to adopt Alis. Despite his own personal sacrifice Gervaise now wrote to her, asking her if she would take Alis and a governess, and giving her in great detail the true reasons for his request. A letter agreeing enthusiastically to his request came by return post from Florence. Within six weeks Alis said good-bye to her family and from then on did not see her home again until she was twenty-one, except for the long summer vacations once a year.

Her aunt was married to a man who'd just retired, a senior member of the Foreign Service. They lived in an attractive villa just outside Florence. It stood in the centre of its own ample grounds on a terrace overlooking the valley of the Arno. It had its own orchard, vineyard, olive trees, fine, delicately pointed, flickering tuscan cypresses and dusky pines, whose purple shadows were lightened with bright gleams and flashes of distant water.

When Alis first described the villa in Florence to me, at once I had the impression that I was listening to the description of an extremely cultured and civilised version of my own home. I thought I recognised beyond doubt another marriage like that of my own father and mother. When Alis told me in that low, serenely centred, self-encircled voice of hers: "It was wonderful, Alex, to see two people not so much in love but living a love of their own," I saw again the fugitive David's clouded face come through a doorway in my home and noticed how it cleared with envious wonder as he watched my father and mother silent and contented in their chairs in front of our fire. Remembering these old emotions and scenes, the sense of awe, of the miraculous and magical in the direction of life in general and David's in particular, returned to me. I thought I recognised there, in that villa in Florence, the lengthening of an inevitable female parallel to David's masculine track. I thought I saw two life-lines begin to converge until finally they met in a sense of the infinite during a storm on the full, high sea. I considered it all; and the correctness in detail and timing with which two lives set out from two points in two different hemispheres, with all the seasons and years between them, finally to meet in instant understanding, seemed to shatter finally the presumptions of much of our rational knowing and planning.

Alis quickly drew her own characteristic moral from her welcome in the Florentine villa. "I can't tell you," she said to me, "how grateful I was to my stepmother; if it hadn't been for her, I'd never have gone to my aunt and uncle in Florence. I learnt from her that it's as important to trust one's unhappiness as it is to trust one's happiness and good fortune."

Now, for the first time that she could remember, Alis was happy. She was an individual in her own right. A tremendous peace established itself in her and no one intruded harshly upon it. She learnt Italian eagerly as if it were the key to all this new emotion bubbling up so ceaselessly within. When she reached the age of twenty-one she realised that, though she'd not acquired any useful means of earning a living, she'd been happy. Almost without her knowing, the love of her aunt and uncle had turned her into a disciplined and emancipated version of her militant and rebellious childhood self. That was the wonder of it to her. Nothing had been imposed on her, yet she had developed a keen sense of direction, obedience, and dedication to the freedom and responsibility of being herself.

And what was this sense of direction? Alis would have been quite unable to answer the question at that time, would indeed have thought it presumptuous to attempt to do so. She was aware only that in given situations the important thing for her was the certainty that so long as she followed her intuition, as long as she stayed close to what was real and alive in her, she was living the answer. No matter what unexpected events were thrust on her, no matter how unprepared she was for circumstances, this sense of direction had never failed her. As yet no crisis had overwhelmed it.

But it was not for her alone to give the answer. Of that, too, she had the deepest conviction. The answer depended not only on her but also on someone else. Who that someone else was became clearer in the eventful tranquillity of the years at the villa, but the initial realisation itself went back to the earliest days of her childhood. She had in fact always known, so it seemed to her, that she was not just Alis Denysse, but she also had company within. There was someone else inside who, step for step, through all the subtle twists of time and space and fantastic turn and flight of night-thought and day-dream, matched her unerringly. There were days when she thought she saw its reflection dimly in the faces of friends of her own sex. But slowly and surely like a flower budding and coming to bloom, it became a boy. He started as little more than a rose-hazy intimation, a phosphorescent sea-image, a white anemone in the dark wood within, but as she took on her own individual outline so his image became clearer with a startling, electric definition. He acquired complete personality.

All through childhood she kept on catching a glimpse of him in a face here, a hint in a head there. But in time she discovered that what she had seen was a part only, and not the full rounded picture. Impatient as she was at moments of finding this boy within in the world without, yet she never doubted that he would come. He had her within him, as she had him, for warning and protection. She was the magic mirror on his wall. Slowly but surely he was making his way towards her, growing daily in his strength and courage.

In the Villa the image became more adult, conformed more to the terms of external realities but in essence and meaning it remained the same. It became not less but more compelling. He was much nearer—there could be no mistake. This was not a creation of her own fantasy, it was the ancient and authentic television of life itself casting the light of the coming event before her, the symbol of the pattern-to-be and the new meaning to be made alive. It was the old lamp shaming the new with richest gold. And as if to prove its nearness the boy within suddenly began to speak in a voice and with a mind and understanding which was of fundamental and transcending importance to Alis. When this happened there was nothing save a fast expiring sense of space and time between them. It was so keen, this sense of nearness, that sometimes at night before going to bed she would stand before the full length mirror set in dark-red wood on the door of the massive Florentine cupboard with its frieze of grapes, trumpeting cherubs and singing Seraphin, and stare at herself glowing like a flower on the edge of a pool in a fertile valley under the full harvest moon. She wanted to see herself in the mirror slim, erect and clear like a candle in flame, like a sword emerging from the waters of Avalon or a lone white iris along the pilgrim's way. She wanted to see herself ready for him.

Yet the moment did not come, neither there at the Villa nor anywhere else, and when she was barely twenty-one her life struck its first really barren and bewildering season and the bad cycle suddenly began. First her uncle died. Alis had not seen, nor did she think she ever wanted to see again, sorrow like her aunt's. When she was told the news she did not cry or complain. She went very pale and said quietly: "I have always known that this is how it would be," and then quickly turned her back. A great, white, frozen silence went over her like the age of ice over the heart of the Antarctic. In the days that followed she made the most gallant and moving attempts to talk to Alis as usual, was in fact uncommonly caring, considerate and delicately tender. But it was soon clear that life had lost both meaning and reason for her. Within six months she had summoned her household to her bed, informed them quietly that she was about to die and implored them with brave good grace not to mourn her because death was what she most wanted. In the early morning she died of a fever for which the Italian doctors had a long name but which, to Alis, was just the fever of her aunt's impatience to be gone.

So at twenty-one years old Alis found herself alone in Italy, the possessor of a villa and enough money to maintain it, but not enough to keep her and the servants as well. She herself was without trained vocation or profession, so when her father suggested that she should let the villa and come home for a while to reconsider her future at leisure, adding that he was to do a term at the Admiralty as Fourth Sea Lord and would be at home himself, the suggestion made good sense to her. She accepted it gratefully though without enthusiasm. Her annual visits to her father's home had not endeared her stepmother to her; and, fond as she was of her brothers and sisters, time had only increased her dismay over the paradox, apparently so fundamental in family life, which allows extreme affection between its individual members to exist side by side with the most complete lack of mutual understanding and shared interests.

Within a month of her return Alis bitterly regretted it. It was no good telling herself that she'd had no choice. The rare instinct by which she'd lived would not let her off and insisted she should have done anything rather than return to her stepmother's fold. All the old sense of menace, of being darkly threatened in her father's home, revived and surprised her because she'd forgotten it at the villa and assumed it dead. Her sense of direction began to waver and blur and she became deeply alarmed.

When Gervaise Denysse had first discussed Alis's return with his wife, she'd said at once in her modern woman-of-action voice: "Of course, she must come home, darling and . . ." She'd paused a moment and then added: "Of course she must come home and marry Simon."

Lady Denysse disliked Alis for a variety of reasons but mostly she disliked her simply because in a way that defied her powers of understanding she was afraid of Alis, and she was afraid because a firmly repressed and long-forgotten part of her both respected and even loved the girl. She was, however, quite incapable of disliking any member of her own sex to the point of not wanting to arrange and organise their weddings for them. She had tried hard to get Simon, who lived in the large house on the big estate next door, to marry her youngest step-daughter who was her favourite, but somehow the plan had not worked. As she feared, Simon, an old and affectionate friend of all the children, knew the girls almost too well to be romantic about them, except Alis. It irritated Lady Denysse to observe how naturally and inevitably Alis always somehow became an exception.

Simon from his earliest days had been closely attached to Alis. Although two years older, he had turned instinctively to her even as a young boy for moral support in the uncompromising and ancient order of children. From an early age she'd found herself, as it were, his patron. In the unexplored tumult of their first parties, picnics and dances, Simon would make for shelter in her own sure and fearless conduct. No one else had existed for him when she was about.

When Alis went to Italy Lady Denysse had hoped that Simon's interest would be transferred to one of the other girls. But Alis's absence, even if it made his heart beat more steadily, certainly did not turn it any colder. To Lady Denysse's annoyance Alis, by her prolonged absence and brief visits home, merely acquired a rarity value.

Alis knew none of the detail of all this. Lady Denysse kept her own secret counsels and knew only too well how to hold her subtle, mediæval hand. But Alis did not need to know the detail in order to be aware of what was happening in the minds of the people at home. She knew that some determined and powerful purpose was in being on her behalf and she didn't like it.

She was very fond of Simon. He was extremely nice looking in a young, slightly immature way. She knew of no one with a gentler, sweeter, kinder or more lovable disposition: no one with such a clear spirit of true play, no one more loyal and dependable in his affections. But much as she valued all these things they were not enough for her. Even now, back from Italy, she still found Simon not grown-up. It was as if he too, like her father, was and had always to be "child" to her. Whatever happens, her instinct warned her, you must never allow yourself to be married to Simon.

Characteristically Simon's other qualifications for eligibility, which meant so much to Lady Denysse, weighed lightly with Alis. To Lady Denysse the fact that he was an only son and that his father—old Sir John—owned one of the oldest and richest private banks in Britain—was of the utmost importance. Alis, particularly since her exile from her beloved villa, had often envied Simon and his family their great material good fortune but had never seriously considered it as an argument for marrying him. It was, however, as an argument for marriage that this aspect of Simon's life was more and more brutally thrust on her attentions by others as well as by the circumstances of her own life. She could not get round the fact that unless she had money of her own she could never return to the villa and might be condemned to live indefinitely in her father's home—an eventuality which she knew might utterly destroy her.

Her instincts urged her not to delay but to set about acquiring a career at once; however when she discussed it with her father, he became so upset at the thought of her working that she was forced to desist. The moment she desisted, he counter-attacked with the question: "Why don't you marry Simon?" and added: "It's silly to talk of earning your living when you'll be snapped up at any moment by a man."

"I am very fond of Simon, Daddy," Alis replied, dismayed, "but I don't love him."

Her father had looked at her sadly and said: "Love, my dear, ah yes, we all have our illusions about it when we're young. . . . But we'd be happier if we realised from the start that romantic love, as we imagine it, does not exist. You could go a long way and find no better than Simon. Besides he adores you . . . and he'll take good care of you when I am gone."

And so the argument had raged for eighteen months both without and within Alis. Lady Denysse wisely kept up an appearance of not being concerned. But at night in their bedroom she prompted Gervaise with great skill. It was a combination and a method formidable enough to defeat the most experienced adversary. At this time Alis had only one real weapon for use: the idea of marriage had never presented itself to her as a career. She saw it as the one free, supreme, equal and opposite relationship with her embattled Boy fighting his way desperately towards her; a relationship, an adventure of two free and coincident individuals. She had this hatred and this faith so deeply rooted in her that she might even so have found her own unconventional way out of her predicament if it had not been for the skill with which Gervaise and his wife used his and Alis's special affection for one another against her. Lady Gervaise for her part would not have been as skilful in plying Gervaise with convincing argument had she not believed that what she was doing was for Alis's own great and unmerited good. What went on in the Denysse home during those eighteen months was a demonstration of the terrible truth that there are no panders, procurers and pimps so cunning and irresistible as those parents who themselves have not experienced love.

After eighteen months Alis's courage for the first time failed her. She said "Yes" to Simon and as she said "Yes" she felt that she too had committed the great and final betrayal of life. From saying "Yes" to Simon she went straight back to her room and wept bitterly and long.

"You poor child!" David said with immense sympathy when she told him. "Wasn't there really any other way out?"

"No, David . . . you see, I too had my enemies," she said. Then, feeling it was vital that he should understand how she'd been tempted to make so false a move, she went on: "There were so many reasonable arguments inside me. They said you didn't exist: you were a romantic adolescent illusion. They hinted that you were dead. . . . You don't know how I hung on, but you were so long in coming that for a moment I believed it. . . . And a moment was all that was needed."

For a moment David made no reply, recognising only too plainly from his own clouded experience the technique of the deeper, not fully recognised meaning becoming impatient of delay and translating itself blindly into action without waiting any longer on conscious recognition and permission. Then he said slowly: "But don't blame yourself. It was all my fault really."

"Your fault? How could it be?" She was touched by his effort to console her but refused to accept it.

"Yes," he persisted. "You were right. I was dead. I'd been dead for ten years until you worked a miracle and started to bring me alive again. You see," he turned to her earnestly, "if I hadn't betrayed myself with Helena, you would never have married this Simon, I believe that. No, it was I who started the rot."

Alis remained silent, a complex of warm healing emotions flaring up in her as David spoke. Perhaps what he said was really true and this gave her a new insight into the mechanism of the past that had brought them so mysteriously to this strange point.

Then she heard David saying: "But I've interrupted your story. So you married Simon—and then?"

Yes, she married Simon but, very soon, she'd realised to the full what a cunning and labyrinthine trap had been set and shut on her.

All the reasons for marriage which had sounded so good,

true and valid, had been proved wrong and now trooped
out of her mind disinherited and disowned for the shame-
ful and plausible confidence trick that they'd played on her.

We've been betrayed! her heart cried out. But in those
moments of mindless, wordless sobbing the boy within her
lived again. She saw his sad but living face in the ancient
mirror of her tears, the silver thread appearing on the edge
of the darkened clearing as she had first seen it in the dawn of
her beginning, a glow-worm glimmer in the far hedge of the
twilight on the last tilled field inviting her to venture again.
The agony and relief of the rediscovery nearly broke her. She'd
been deceived and betrayed, but in herself she'd not been
wrong. He was real, he was not dead; he was on his way and
would set her free from this hideously pleasant, luxurious,
easy and affectionate unreality with Simon. He would understand and forgive the injustice she had inflicted upon herself
for he'd know how desperately she had tried to dedicate herself to him, had striven to come to him not as some common
coin interchangeable at any bank, but bright and warm from
the royal mint, the King's own stamp of authenticity upon
her. He would know that the slight young man beside her
really was only a child confided to her care, and she just
another confided to his. He would know the truth for all three
of them, and the truth would set her free.

As Alis told him this, David was so moved that he could
hardly trust himself to speak. He looked up at the sharp, blue
pinnacle of sky looming over the ship, and it was as if his
mind, perched like an eagle on the topmost crag of purple,
was looking down on the foaming, singing Atlantic gulf,
surveying converged time and space before them like a ship's
track without horizon or end.

"Please don't think that I don't understand," he exclaimed.
"Every second since I've met you I've resented bitterly that
I too should have to come into your life so travel-stained and
shop-soiled." He leant forward and took her hands. "But if
you could look into my heart at this moment you'd never be

troubled again, for there is that of you in me which can never tarnish nor fade away. You are in me a bright and perfect roundness, a moon of all four seasons so old and new that it is endlessly ageing and infinitely renewable. You are above reproach and beyond qualification—for that I give you my word." He dropped her hands. "But what of your husband?"

"My child," she answered slowly. "He's never really been anything else."

But as she spoke, the tenderness of a fair and delicate moment died completely.

"I'm sick of women and their children—particularly women and children your and Simon's way," he answered harshly. The world is over-peopled with child-mothers and boy-fathers and their infant children, he thought bitterly—children, children everywhere and not a grown-up mind and mature emotion in an adult body. Just children in grown-up bodies begetting beings whose adult causes their baby selves refuse to further. Life has begun to miss out a whole generation in its chain: the grown-up link between infant and child has vanished and a formless, stifling oblivion of wet baby-love, a damp mist of nursery emotion is taking the mature edge off the world, rusting through the all-weather steel in us.

Coming out of the hard focus of his thought he saw her looking at him with unbelieving surprise.

"Why, David," she exclaimed, "I believe I've made you angry!"

"Yes, very angry," he said curtly, gulping back the rest of his unaccustomed temper and hurrying after his own sense of reasoned proportion. "Sorry, but I couldn't help myself."

She smiled, and her voice recovered its banter. "Anger suits you. You should use it more often, but outwards not inwards. You absorb a lot of shock, don't you, which should really be tossed back."

But David refused to be drawn. "I want to talk about you,"

he said. "Not me. . . . So there you were with Simon. And what then?"

It had been a long "then" for her. Every day her life was invaded more and more by a sense of meaningless purposelessness.

Yet, when she fell asleep, in an exhaustion such as she had never known, like a ship's head plunging into an unfathomed hole in the sea, it was not Simon but the Boy who was near. It was as if she left Simon, like a fawn-child, asleep in the bracken on the perimeter of remote consciousness, while she hurried through the night to the far-off flicker of light and flame at the centre of herself. Across misty malarial plain of twilight awareness, hard by yellow fever-trees, down long starlit savannah of mind, wading through streams and fording rivers of blood in deep valleys among the scarlet mountains, over great coral sea of inmost being, guardian heart a-crying: "Hasten you poor, forlorn child of life, hasten, oh hasten!" she fled at last through the real jungle of herself, hearing on the black feathery rim behind her bay of night-hound, howl of wolf-pack and swollen and swelling cannibal drumming. Then with eager straining senses she burst through the tight ringed darkness into the firm centre by fire and rose-flare of herself. There, under the great protective arches and soaring Gothic columns which sustain the traveller's chapel of life-dedicated self, she threw herself down by the side of the tired Boy already asleep, wrapped in a silken sheet of ancient altar flame and dreaming confidently, bright spear at his side, of the way out. By night the forest about resounded with lion's roar and pre-historic victims screaming, the black mesozoic air sagged despondent with excess of vampire and weight of pterodactyl's wing. Close, oozing wood lane shook with mastodon's charge and sabre-tooth's rattle. The fringes of light grew blurred and black with crowding, anthropoidal shadow. On one great baroque branch the velvet panther lay, crampon claws deep in bleeding bark, keeping a hungry watch with emerald eyes upon the dark, while down below the angry hamadryad threw a phosphorescent hiss at slimy anaconda and clumsy boa the fallow deer constricting, filling to overflowing with sea-green serpents' spittle the carnivorous moon-orchid's cup. Over all the self-widowed spider, mate of midnight tarantula fatally pregnant, spun, with swollen belly trembling like plastic shake on cactus legs, the steel-silk web on whose strands the pearly stars were strung as bait to catch the retarded and shining new moon. But by the fire that never goes out and the light which has never known night, her half made whole with one boy and his spear, she found the sleep which knew no meaning and had no knowledge of fear.

Yet dragged out of such sleep, separated from such vision by the wealthy ease of her unadventurous day, Alis felt reduced to a feeble and destructive mockery of herself.

When she returned from her honeymoon everyone was shocked by her appearance. For the first time in her life she looked really ill. Simon seemed unchanged; perhaps confirmed and driven a little deeper into his abiding self, but essentially he was the same. Yet it was obvious to all that Alis had suffered a profound change. She looked like someone dazed by shock, a person in a strange, irreducible trance, which compelled her to be continually and restlessly on the move. Consultations with doctors on an exalted level now began.

"I know them well, the bloody clots," David exclaimed with considerable heat, as Alis told him this: "One might as well go to a Zulu witch-doctor—and perhaps that's all they are—witch-doctors, adding a new dimension to tattooing with their surgery."

Alis laughed. "I'd just enough sense not to let them start cutting me up," she said, "but I went on feeling dreadfully ill, except when I got away—so I just went away more and more."

For five years she was never long at home and slowly everyone had become very critical. Her father was most concerned of all, and openly puzzled and dismayed.

"I've always told you," Lady Denysse remarked emphatically, "that Alis is neurotic. This is the grown-up version of her behaviour before she went to Florence. Simon should put his foot down."

Alis could have borne her stepmother's disapproval indefinitely, but she was not indifferent to what her father and Simon felt. Her own mind, too, was determinedly and increasingly critical of her behaviour. Yet she couldn't escape from the fact that, try as she might, at home she became desperately ill and listless. Between two contradictory elements of herself, between the baker of Simon and the devil of the Boy as she'd almost come to see it, she was slowly but surely splitting in two. Her reason constantly upbraided her and called upon a greater and more determined exercise of will power and a consciously applied concentration and simplification of her life. At last, in desperation, an idea occurred to her. Perhaps, if she travelled far and long enough she would accumulate sufficient strength, courage, and joy to return to a life at home with Simon forever. And to make quite certain it would be "for ever", she'd make a pact with Simon and her father before she went. She'd tell them: "Allow me to go away, now, for four whole months—and then, when I come back, I'll settle down for good."

So she sailed for Africa. The inward pattern did not fail her; promptly it repeated itself. As David could see for himself there she was on her way back home, as well and as strong and as in love with life as she had ever been. But when she got back. . . . David's face darkened. It was the other side of the "but", the precipitous far-edge of the sentence that concerned them both.

CHAPTER 20

IN the days that followed Alis was obsessed by a vision of beauty such as she'd never known. She'd never in her life experienced anything so keen, true and centred. It was as if she were right in the heart of reality at the point where life and death meet, at the place where they are not only close but actually two aspects of the same whole, where they both stand nobly and heroically naked back to back, long shining gold hair against raven black head, holding the narrow pass in the mountains against the Tartar hordes attacking their great city's unending traffic. It was a sense of profound ambivalence, of opposites meeting, of all contradictions at peace. Whenever she looked at David she felt overwhelmingly grateful that one so beautiful to her should be alive and a male. At the same moment she suffered the most angry and bitter rebellion against the knowledge that one day he would have to die. She wanted him and this full moment in the warming sea to live for ever, to grow, expand and contain all, and it was the agony of its limitations, the fact of ultimate separation foresuffered nightly in isolation in their cabins, that sometimes made her cry out involuntarily.

Often as they hung together over the rail and saw a smoking rainbow blown by the wind of their speed out of white spray from the royal blue combers spiking themselves on the ship's bow, it seemed to Alis that life had borrowed this symbol of God's promise to man to hang there as the seal, also, of a covenant between her and David. But alone in her cabin, filled with the impersonal sound and cold objective night-wash of the sea on the grey, vibrating steel hull, her mind turned coward.

Only she knew how ill, listless, and disinclined she was for effort. Yet the last thing she wanted to do was to increase the clamour already in David.

She knew how close she was sometimes to doing this, but always at the last moment her intuition saved her. She rejected the temptation for the same reason that I had. She too knew without knowing that already the will, determination and desires of others invested in David were the cause and extent of the death in him. She knew that another intervention from the outside, even the most loving and tenderly protective one, might well be fatal. If ever he came to her he would have to come freely out of his own freed self. Only a complete and unforced coincidence of his male and her female being could save them. She could only pray that coincidence in the world without would come in time to rescue the coincidence they'd already experienced within. Yet, as she prayed, she feared greatly.

Yet one thing never failed to sustain her, the knowledge, daily more proved and certain, that David understood her as no human being had ever understood her. She felt at home in his mind and imagination. She felt him welcome her mind and attitude to life as a balance to his own, could feel him draw sustenance from them.

One night, sitting in their favourite corner in the dark by the shaking funnels, he told her how tragic it was that she should have had to find him in such an unprepared, unready mess. Because of it she'd had to train her own master, but from what he'd seen of life that seemed to be a world condition. Masters and their women were no longer ready-made. "This startled time of ours is too exacting," he went on. "We can only be made according to one another's measure. . . . We've all got to train one another in our parts. Life's made us the keepers of the authentic image, the original blue-prints of each other, and there's no escape from this charge. You, the woman, have to teach your male to be man; and the man his female to be woman. . . ." He turned to her. "Oh, my beloved," he pleaded, "help me to be my full self and I'll reward you with a life in which you need never submit to compromise."

After such moments, and there were many, she felt brave enough for any future, and even if they did not conquer her terror of physical separation from David, they held it in suspended balance.

And so from far south in the Atlantic they sailed steadily north, leaving the cool, temperate seas, the following Antarctic wind dying in the bubbling wake behind them. By day the air lost its own movement and blueness. The sun came up over the edge of the horizon with the speed and frenzy of a shrieking madman. It bounced like a red-hot cannon-ball straight up into the sky and at once it became hot. They longed for it to have done and to remove its raving, fanatical presence from the sky. By noon the blue of the day was white and drawn with heat, the horizon dim with sulphur haze and heat smoke. The sea removed its last faint wrinkles and turned a face of smooth and polished quicksilver mirror to the sky. All day the sun hurled quivering lance and javelin of light at it with such penetrating fierceness that their eyes and heads ached with the keenness. It was a world of glittering, sparkling, unbreathing and breathless sea-suspended life. There was no longer movement enough in the water to provide the flying fish with a wave high and firm enough from which to launch their frantic, starry gliders. They watched the fish sparkle abortively against the topmost layer of steel-grey water as they tried desperately to rise up into the air, but the unelastic, sun-embattled sea kept them firmly under. The only sign of deep sea life now was a black dorsal fin stalking the ship like a triangular sail.

"I know all about this," David told Alis, sweeping his hand round the shining horizon. "I, too, have been in a windless world. I, too, was once becalmed on a wide, wide sea alone with the soul of an ancient negro-mariner." And indeed so still it was that God himself had scarce seeméd there to be, he told himself. It was there that the signs of my Zodiac first mutinied against their captain: it was there that the crab got my goat, that the retrospective crustacean nipped my pretty

Billy in the Budd and Cancer got his claws on the hoof of Capricorn and started to drag him across the line of equatorial balance down to the northern bed of the ocean. He turned to her abruptly, saying, "And I'd still be there, for my internal combustion engine was completely stalled, if a grey-haired negro able-seaman hadn't directed me south for dry-docking and repairs."

"Do you usually talk to people like this?" she asked, half-laughing, her eyes shining and the sun weaving a harvest light in her hair. "It's peculiar, but it makes me very happy."

"Of course I don't," he said. "This is my first experience of the heraldry of love." Then he changed his tone and added simply: "It comes to me as my painting used to do, straight out of my head like a mediæval tapestry—and it makes me want to paint again. . . ."

All day the sea lay round them like burning oil. With relief they watched the sun's light go over the horizon like an engorged, silver-scaled python slipping to sleep in its hole in a dark wood. The night air was warm and soft and chain upon chain of yellow stars sagging wonderfully low, swollen and massive with light, hung over the ship like garlands of lamps in the garden of a summer palace. Often they would make of the night a home for their dazzled senses and sit with the ship's pulse vibrant beneath them, and a gold, metallic, clanking and clanging starlight against the masts and funnels above, until the dawn rang out like a bang on a Buddhist gong in some far Eastern temple. They would watch the impatient prancing light reveal the uncapped walls of steel of a new windless day.

But one morning enormous clouds lifted their grave, pearl-grey heads over the horizon. They stretched themselves slowly to their full height as if coming out of a deep sleep and stood shoulder to shoulder like a vast, soaring Himalayan range in front of David and Alis, whose eyes were now so charged and in love with meaning that every detail in the day's choice of ornament was profoundly significant to them.

255

That very night it was noticeably cooler, the stars were smaller and their light sharper. The dark world had already begun its true northerly task of discarding magnitude and flamboyance for penetration and precision. The following morning David drew Alis to the ship's side. "Look," he said, pointing to a dark ruff of shadow on the purple horizon ahead. "D'you see that?"

"What is it?"

"The wind," David said with a dramatic wave of his hand. "It's coming up fast! The world about us is on the march! It's the first winged messenger come to welcome you into your own true and native hemisphere." Then his tone changed. "But I could hate this wind and the news it brings. For this is a real north-north-west trade."

"That means our voyage is nearly over," she said slowly, holding his arm closer.

At noon next day they picked up the green Cape of Africa in a silver sea restored to a racing, heaving life, its white mane streaming as it leapt at that nose of stubborn land. Birds ready for quick, short, stormy distances appeared above them, the waves sparkled and rose sunwards with a dazzle of porpoises and distant bee-swarming flights of winged fish. By nightfall the Cape was sunk deep in the dark behind them and a mournful chorus of despairing land birds bewailed their headstrong passage out to sea before they wheeled round and went crying like rejected sirens to their clanging rocks in the pounding water. The next evening they saw the snow-capped volcanic cone of Teneriffe run up a cold red and scarlet sunset and wave it like a flag of farewell after them. The great mountain glowed for long like an olympian blacksmith's forge on the horizon, watching them over the edge of the darkness as once it had stared at Columbus on his way to discovery of a new world. At dawn they sailed down a narrow channel rolling steeply in the purple shadows racing between the emerald Madeiras, and then ran straight into a grey sea speeding south, streaming before the trades from the north under a greying sky relieved only in the east by the glow of destructive fire over the Rio de' Oro of Africa.

Five days later in the early morning Alis came out of her cabin after a short, sleepless night to hear the ship's bells ringing loudly and urgently in the engine room, with the order of "heave to" for the pilot. The voyage was nearly over. The community of wayward souls woven so tightly together in brief, bright, holiday pattern by the swift shuttle of their ocean journey was already being unravelled and torn apart. The sense of land ahead was brought up smartly on the shoulders of a spick and span pilot as he came up the ladder, and dealt death to the ship-made world. All round her Alis felt people preparing to turn their backs on each other, already plotting the kill of their deep-sea memories with aggressive, insurgent foreign days ahead. A sense of the death of tender things, of the dead and dying, littered the atmosphere everywhere for her. Cabin-trunks and tin boxes stood piled up on one another in the open landings by the purser's office like coffins wherein dead, good things were buried, wherein yesterdays, still warm, were nailed down. And presently the funeral procession of passengers would troop out with uncomprehended hysteria to make a graveside of the dock.

She surveyed the scene, almost faint with dismay, and then turned and went as fast as she could to David's cabin.

He was lying on his bed still fully dressed in the same clothes that he'd been wearing when she said good-night to him. He lay staring at the iron ceiling and did not hear her come in. The look on his face, so like the look on it the day when he'd first rejected her, raised terror in her heart.

"What's the matter?" she cried.

The look instantly vanished. "Thank God you've come. I've not slept all night," he said profoundly relieved. Then sitting up and making an effort to smile he exclaimed: "How nice of you to wear that dress again. Now I'll be able to leave you as I found you."

He looked at her and although she looked tired she seemed to David more beautiful than he'd ever seen her. "Thank God you've come," he said again. "I thought I was going mad without you."

He got up and stood beside her.

"Don't let's talk," she said, moving closer to him. "We know all there is to know about what we're feeling. Just let's stay as close as we can to each other." She was close to tears again.

David turned towards her. "I'll come to you the moment I've done what I've got to do," he said.

"Please don't be long—"

"Not an instant longer than is absolutely necessary."

"I do love you so," she answered, raising her head to look at him.

As she did so, she saw in the mirror over David's bed the embarrassed face of her cabin steward. Without shame or perturbation she asked quietly, "What is it, Giovanni?"

"Forgive me, Signorina," he said in Italian, embarrassment giving way to compassionate understanding, "but there are two gentlemen—I think one is your father, asking for you at your cabin. They are impatient to find you."

"Are we already alongside?" she asked.

"Si, Signorina," the man answered instinctively hating his role of messenger of landlocked evil. "Already the passengers are beginning to go ashore."

"I'll come at once."

The steward left the cabin. Down in the engine-room the bells rang a long, imperious peal-signal to the engineers that their watch for the moment was ended. On the bridge, a piercing whistle dismissed the deck crew. The boards above began to resound and throb with the tramp of heavy, hob-nailed feet.

Alis began to smooth her hair carefully with trembling hands. Oh, dear God, this is true, her heart cried out. Please keep this knowledge undimmed in me in the days to come. Please make of this moment, of this flame and light and wholeness, such a fire that no matter how black the night of our separation it will shine to guide us back to our right and lawful occasion in life.

It was as if David read her thoughts.

"Next time," he said, "there'll be no separation. We'll never, never be separated again." Never, he told himself fiercely, not even when the fires of this world are drawn and the dead cinders scattered on the great wind of time, even then we shall be not proud and angry dust but a glowing coal humbly and gratefully together, warm in some living and searching heart, going ahead in the dark, outer spaces this, our nearness, its true discovery expanding.

Suddenly Alis turned to him, the light of terror in her eyes. "Don't leave me, David," she said. "Don't leave me now. Come with me!"

He looked at her; then bent down and kissed her for the first time. But in his touch there seemed a doomed finality. Blindly she pulled herself from his arms and moved towards the corridor.

A loud voice stopped them. "Hallo, Alis!" it cried. It was a voice accustomed to command.

Alis let go David's hand and turned round. A tall man with a distinguished, rather red face, in a heavy tweed coat, marched briskly down on them, swept a tweed deer-stalker hat off his head and took Alis in his arms, while a slight, dark young man with a smooth, brown face and charming but anonymous expression came up quickly behind him.

Alis, coming out of greeting her father and Simon, looked round to introduce them to David, but the corridor behind her was empty.

"Oh, he's gone . . . and I so wanted him to meet you. . . ." she said, dazed and bewildered at the suddenness of David's going.

"Who?" It was her father asking the question.

"Someone called David . . . David Michaeljohn, and he's gone—I so wanted him to be here to meet you," she answered, and her voice sounded a long way from herself.

"I expect he knew," said Simon, who believed good of all the world and who'd seen David wheel abruptly and disappear quickly round a corner in the corridor, "that you'd want to be alone with us."

All through the official examination in the ship Alis looked desperately for David. But he appeared to have vanished for good.

I'm sure to see him in the Customs shed, she told herself, but when Simon came to tell her the car was ready to go and she'd still not seen David, she could endure it no longer. Curtly telling Simon to wait, and ignoring the puzzled look on his nice, gentle face, she ran quickly up the gangway and straight to David's cabin.

I can't go on with it, she told herself. I can't. I've tried it before and I can't . . . I'm alive and I belong to David. I'll find him, and tell him he can't leave me.

But David was not in his cabin. His steward was there and said: "You've just missed him, Signorina. He was summoned to the Captain's cabin only one minute ago. He looked unhappy—"

She ran down the corridor intending to go up to the Captain's deck and wait for him there, but at the end of the alley, outside the purser's office, her father was waiting for her.

"Oh, there you are again," he said. "I'm afraid we must hurry or we'll be late for your home-coming party in town." Taking her by the arm affectionately, he conducted her out of the ship and down the gangway. She could struggle no more and walked at his side like a condemned person.

A despondent, puzzled Simon was waiting for her at the foot of the gangway. His expression lifted as he saw her on her father's arm and he smiled. "Well caught, sir! I thought for an awful minute that she was off on another journey already!"

If only he knew, thought Alis wearily, I've travelled farther than I've ever travelled in life before and left them both for good. In fact, I'm not here even now.

CHAPTER 21

AS Simon stepped out from behind the Admiral to take Alis in his arms and kiss her, the clamour of a workshop of hell with shift refreshed broke out anew in David. He turned brusquely away and walked with dark, unseeing eyes swiftly to his cabin, where he lay down on his bunk looking at the ceiling with hands tightly clenched at his side. He felt for a moment like someone who had been climbing slowly out of a deep pit and had just laid his hand on the rim of the topmost surface to pull himself clear, when his hold was brutally loosened and he was hurled back again by the one person to whom he had looked for help and encouragement. In that moment he fell the whole distance of his dark, unfulfilled, imprisoned self, but once down there, back again in the deepest gulf, he heard clearly the words just spoken to him by Alis: "I do love you so, David."

It was then that he knew the difference. He was back in the bottom of the pit again and he still had to climb out—but he was no longer alone. Slowly the din in him subsided until he became quite quiet; and then, from a peak of snow-white silence far above him, he saw Alis's face and the terror of the distance between them, and heard her plea: "Please don't leave me, David—please stay with me."

The relief of feeling his thought leaping to share someone else's terror as if it were his own, brought tears stinging to his eyes, and with the tears, a strange, new confidence and faith in his unhappy plight. It was as if sharing her terror not only did not add to, but even halted, his own.

He could have gone on contemplating this discovery of the arithmetic of love which does the desired subtraction by means of the longed-for addition if his steward had not come in to present him with the Captain's compliments and a polite but urgent request for him to come to the Master's cabin.

Puzzled but compliant David made his way quickly up to the Captain's room immediately behind the bridge. There waiting for him was a tall, slight man of about fifty dressed in great good taste, and the owner of a long, sensitive and finely shrewd face. The man held out his hand to David the moment he saw him.

"I do hope you'll forgive me asking you to come here," he said, "but my business is urgent and most confidential and the Captain very kindly lent me his sitting-room. We haven't met but I know about you—I'm even the grateful owner of three of your early paintings. I am, or at least my partners and I are, solicitors to Sir Arthur Moystouan-Roswell."

"How d'you do," David said as he took the well-manicured hand held out to him, feeling completely at a loss.

A chair was put out for him by the table and they both sat down.

"I'm afraid I have some rather unpleasant business to transact with you and I hope you'll forgive me for being the instrument of a difficult duty which will no doubt be almost more distasteful to you than it is to me."

"Please carry on," David said, mystified.

"Well, then, Mr. Michaeljohn," the man exclaimed with relief, obviously reassured by David's calm detached tone and sober bearing, so different from what he had been led to expect. "It is obvious from this telegram that you did not receive any of the letters sent to you at the Cape?" He laid a telegram on the table in front of David.

David picked it up. It was his own radio-telegram sent to Helena from Cape Town asking her to send some money to the ship to meet him since Mary had failed to give him enough for his needs.

"That is very likely," he answered. "I left much sooner than I expected."

"Quite. So I gathered," the solicitor replied crisply, fixing

David with an eye for precise detail. "Well, Mr. Michaeljohn, I'm glad to say I've brought you your money. Here is a hundred pounds for you. But I regret to say that is the only pleasant part of my duty. Your wife has asked me," he paused, weighing his thought with great and expert care—"to say that she will not in any circumstances whatsoever consent to give you money again. She says that, in view of what has happened between you, she finds it dishonourable of you to expect to continue being kept by her."

"Dishonourable!" The exclamation broke involuntarily from David not so much because he felt it was undeserved but because he could not see what right Helena had to apply it to him. What honour has there ever been between us, he thought bitterly, save only the honour between thieves. I—thief, who stole her likeness to Mary and her rich worldly security to keep me, the eternal child, shirking my grown-up male adventure. She, cat-burglar of my best, my young inexperienced years, quickly exploiting the situation of my motherbound nature. . . . To cast it all off now with money must be the new twentieth century reckoning. I can pay her back her money, but who can restore me those bitter, wasted, sterile years?

"Dishonourable?" He repeated, again, a question this time clearly implied.

The civilised face before him consolidated its practised features for the next assault on its unpleasant duty. "Yes, dishonourable . . . I'm sorry, Mr. Michaeljohn, those were your wife's words and I was instructed by my clients to make a particular point of them with you." The solicitor spoke without personal heat or prejudice but his determination to discharge his brief to the letter was unmistakable.

"Did they wish you to tell me anything else of the same nature?" David asked, not having failed to notice the solicitor's use of "client" in the plural.

"I'm afraid there is worse to follow, Mr. Michaeljohn," the clear, refined, even, legal voice confirmed. "Your wife does not want you to return to her. She is at present gone with the children to stay with her father and mother and she insists that you must not make any effort to see her or communicate with her except through me or my firm. She wrote and explained all this to you herself in those letters that failed to reach you. If you had read those letters, or seen her as I have done recently, you would realise that her decision in the matter is irrevocable. And frankly, Mr. Michaeljohn, from the various depositions and affidavits with which I have been supplied not only by your wife and her admirable mother but also by your own servants and friends of the family, I must confess her decision appears entirely justified." The lawyer stopped as if in anticipation of an interruption by David but as David made no sign he went on to explain his mission at greater length.

Helena and her mother maintained that the marriage had come to a dangerous end. Helena had given the solicitor a highly coloured, but on the whole truthful, account of David's increased drinking since her marriage, his lack of interest in the children and obstinate refusal, as she put it, to pull his weight by continuing his painting. She'd borne it all with the greatest of patience and fortitude until recently it had become obvious not only that he would never change but also that the situation might rapidly become dangerous for her and the children. As illustration, she had given the solicitor a grossly exaggerated account of David's behaviour on the night before his departure. He'd left her in such a state, she averred, that she'd had a nervous break-down—the medical evidence was there, the solicitor said, as he tapped his leather brief case, reputable and irrefutable. She'd taken the children to an eminent psychologist who advised her that the sooner the children were removed from so unhappy a home the better, in fact, he foretold the most harmful effects on their development if this were not done at once. That had been decisive, and unless David gave Helena a solemn undertaking that he would not try to contact her or the children except through her solicitor during the period she needed for reconsidering the future, she would have no option but to go to the Courts at once and apply for a formal deed of separation. The solicitor said he would advise David strongly to consult a good lawyer of his own at once, to protect whatever rights he thought he had in the matter, but he had no doubt from the evidence in his possession that Helena would get her deed without difficulty at any moment she applied for it. Yet she was not anxious for scandal nor did she want to be unreasonable.

"You appear amused, Mr. Michaeljohn?" The solicitor sounded surprised as well as slightly irritated, as if he feared his well-reasoned plea was about to founder.

"No, not really," David assured him, and then before the solicitor could continue as he was obviously eager to do, he asked: "Tell me, would my wife agree to divorce me?"

The solicitor suppressed a glow of triumph which threatened the calm of his features, and camouflaged the eager, ready answer in long and quite unnecessary thought.

"Well, Mr. Michaeljohn," he answered at last, "I cannot commit my client, of course, without further consultation, but I will not attempt to disguise from you the fact that I, myself, think it would be the best solution for you all. I do believe Lady Moystouan-Roswell would agree with me and no doubt between us we could bring Miss Helena to see it that way too."

At once the pity which Helena had inspired in him when he first met her welled up, and with it came a tremendous and humbling realisation of his own share in the events which had brought such dishonour to both their natures.

"Well, in that case, please tell my wife and her mother," David said in a voice whose warm, resounding quality moved the solicitor in a manner which he would not have thought possible, "that I will do exactly as she wishes. I think what she has done is the best thing for all of us and I admire the courage that it must have taken to do so difficult a thing; and thank her for her initiative. I will give her evidence for divorce as soon as she wishes it. I know I must have been impossible to live with and I beg her to forgive me if she can for my unhappy rôle in her unhappiness. As for this money, I'm afraid I must borrow it for a day or two until I can obtain money from my own home."

"I assure you that is quite unnecessary," the solicitor interrupted almost fiercely. But David would have none of it. It seemed to him there would be some rough poetic justice in getting Mary to release, as she should long since have done, his share of the inheritance in Albert's rehabilitated estate in order to pay the charges and so redeem her fated likeness so long held in Helena's pawn.

"No!" he said, firmly to the solicitor, "I shall insist on refunding this within a day or two and what's more, if Helena will let me know what allowances she's made me in the past, I will repay those too with the suggestion that she uses the money for the children. All I would ask in return is permission to collect from our house my canvasses and painting material. I will let you have my new address as soon as I know it myself."

David stood up to go and was about to hold out his hand to the solicitor when something else occurred to him. "By the way, I once painted a young black boy with a beautiful back but an averted face. My wife bought the painting at my first exhibition and it was through it that we really met and married. . . . She was always asking me what the boy's face was like . . . it seemed terribly important to her, and I couldn't really answer then. I even said that perhaps he had no real face. . . . But will you tell her now, from me please, that I was very, very wrong." David turned and faced the solicitor. "When I can, I'll try to paint a full portrait of him and send it to her as a mark of the profound regret I feel for the great grief and sorrow I've caused her. . . . And thank you very much for meeting me and helping Helena repair the damage I've done."

David held out his hand to the solicitor, who appeared lifted far out of the legal content of his mission, and then quickly left the Captain's room. He walked across the now empty deck where he'd once stood in a storm, went smartly down the companion way, and past the purser's office, which was shut. He almost ran down the gangway and into the Customs shed. It too was empty except for his cabin steward and one bored Customs official standing with increasing impatience by David's baggage.

"Ah! Signor," his steward greeted him with relief. "It was such a pity, the Signorina came back into the ship to look for you."

"When?"

"You missed her by a minute, Signor. She looked for you everywhere and looked very unhappy not to find you."

"Thank you," said David, immensely happy that she should have come back for him. He pushed a large tip into the steward's hand and shook it warmly.

Within five minutes he was free to leave the Customs, free, as he put it to himself, to deal with the consequences of Helena within himself. If only I'd long since faced up to the consequences of the Mary within me instead of running away from them, as I did from her person, there'd have been no Helena and this mess in myself to-day to tackle, he told himself with impatient relief.

He gave one last look at the ship shouldering the grey-blue western sky with an unbelievably legendary and heroic air, its long black masts and red funnels white with the salt of storm-spray and ash of burnt-out, wind-driven sea distances, as if indeed it had just come from the outer seas of space.

And yet, he thought, as he stood there on the quay, despite all the evidence, I don't feel the voyage is nearly over. On the contrary perhaps, the real journey is just about to begin.

With that he turned, walked out of the shed into the station, and took his train to London.

PART V

The Discovery

CHAPTER 22

DAVID lay in bed in his room in a quiet hotel over looking a park. He was trying hard to get a system of priorities established in his mind of what was needed most to get himself right with life. His first instinct was immediately to seek Alis. The thought and feel of her in his senses was everywhere, in and around him like a sea underneath and about a ship. Her voice talked to him still; when he opened his eyes, and found her not there to complete this sense of her presence within him, it was almost more than he could endure.

Yet something held him back. Something warned him that unless he wanted merely to repeat the disastrous pattern of Helena and himself he must not approach her, at no matter what cost, until he'd come to terms with himself.

The argument within was seemingly unending.

Don't leave this room, something said to him in a clear, determined voice of its own, until you understand.

How do I begin to understand?

The reply at once surprised him. Stop drinking and smoking.

I can do that any time. He was disappointed at so obvious and tame a beginning. What about the real things?

Never mind about other things. Do as I say and see what happens, the voice commanded him.

I'll try, he told himself.

And now he was trying, and being humiliated every minute by the difficulty of it. It was so hard that time seemed to stand still. He'd never known the hours to go so slowly. He'd look at his watch, believing an hour to have passed, to find it was only a minute and a half. . . . He couldn't read, he couldn't even think of Alis. Everything was reduced and annihilated to one single thought. I must order a drink—or I'll die of thirst.

271

Yet he neither succumbed nor died of thirst.

If you're thirsty, his new voice asked him, why not drink water or tea?

So he drank water and tea until he could drink no more—but still the craving for drink was there unappeased.

You see, the voice remarked, you were being cheated all the time. Drink has nothing to do with thirst.

Then what had it got to do with? he asked, his confidence in the new voice strangely excited by this one, small discovery. Perhaps, after all, it had been wise to limit him to a single step at a time.

Find that answer for yourself, he was told.

Obediently he tried and at once the day seemed to begin to move, the watch on his wrist to tick faster. Yet he reached no answer and by night was so exhausted with the effort that he had a violent fever, and his hands shook so much that he had to hold his cup in both hands in order to drink from it.

To the management of the hotel he explained that he had malaria and would have to stay in bed for some time. He assured them that he needed no doctor and that they had no cause for alarm. That night he slept uneasily. The next day was a repetition of the first and even more exhausting if only because the conflict was more evenly fought. His second night was almost sleepless and he began his third day feeling terrified that he could not survive. But in the early morning the thought that Alis had never yet seen him as he really was helped him. She'd never known what he was like in the original, untainted pattern, and suddenly, desperately, he wanted her to see him with nothing fevered, artificial, unreal and unclean between them.

He got out of bed and went to have a bath. When he came back he shaved carefully, cut and cleaned his nails meticulously, and then crept back into bed almost instantly to fall asleep. When he woke it was to find with relief that the day which had seemed so ominous was nearly over and the twilight already standing gently in his room. The hand which he stretched out for a glass of water was much steadier. He drank his water and as he did so the voice within said with friendly amusement: Now d'you know? And the amazing thing was that, despite his quick pulse and high temperature, he did know.

Yes, he answered at once: I drank not for the taste or for the liquid but for the feeling it gave me. I drank for the glow it gave me in my stomach, for the fire it lit beneath my heart. I sought that glow and that fire because it was like the glow and fire lit by the first food, the first, sweet milk from Mary's breast in my virgin stomach. When Mary's firm soft breast was first denied me I was driven to a dream of substitute fire. I was the frustrated infant grown demonic in a man's physical stature, and with his grown-up power filled with thirst for his first secure living moment, thirst for his first deliverance from the long black road and perilous adventure of life brought out of the immense wilderness of the past, thirst for that deep stained-glass stillness at his mother's heart, thirst for that brief, cloistered moment between twilight ends of two great journeys; and so all the thirsts became one insatiable, all-compelling and all-consuming longing. Forever I wanted to stay at Mary's breast and when life pushed me out and on, frightened, I tried to double back. . . . And alas, alas, I found an ebb-tide to help me. I discovered a coward age to aid and abet me. I caught a bewildered and dark recessive moment of history in great peril, shirking its lawful consummation with the future standing veiled like an oriental bride on a dangerous, dawn-fired threshold. I was swept away in a black sea undertow of life imperilled, scuttling backwards like a crab to shelter of fabulous breast and nearby safety of womb. Mine was a coward soul wooing the dark negations of its day lit only by burning archaic thirst which no life before or after could ever satisfy. Between cloven hoof of goat and split claw of crab I looked on doom in a sea between the Capricorn and Cancer of my being.

The illumination within David as he finished addressing

273

himself was so intense that he instinctively shut his eyes as if the full sun had suddenly flashed into them. He felt as if he had really recaptured his first living moment as a separate being in life, had retracked a memory not of his spirit and mind so much as an experience basic in his inarticulate flesh and blood. He believed he knew at that moment exactly what the unbaptised baby experienced when first suckled at Mary's breast and at once it became possible to separate the original, the real experience from the super-imposed, the substitute one, which had had to insinuate itself into the graces of a real need like thirst before it could deceive him. Now, back at the beginning which, interpreted within the meaning of the law and act of life, he'd never really left, he could at last begin again. Now, for instance, he knew why he'd always been so irritated by Edward George, and knowing it suddenly discovered that he really felt a warm and lively affection for his gay, laughing baby brother. He knew now why he'd emptied mud pies on Edward George in his great baptismal robes; it had been his first act of war on all that came between him and Mary's breast. That was why Albert had been enraged by his misdeed, for his instincts had known David's secret vengeance. Ah! Albert, what light on him too there was in this moment! What a great example, what a royal pioneer had he been, too, of the self-same affliction of demonic thirst and baby rebellion against the forward surge of life. David now saw that his own flight to Europe was flight of Albert reversed, but flight it was and of the same, dark, tightly woven tribal pattern. His marriage with Helena was the alliance of a substitute Albert with a substitute Mary. Dear God, why hadn't he seen it before? His marriage was incestuous: incest the modern twentieth century way: ersatz incest; incest of one remove and second-hand, but nonetheless a felony compounded on the original classical transgression. No wonder he'd turned to drinking as substitute for the milk he could not get at Helena's breast. Hitherto he'd thought that he'd taken to drinking because it made it easier to sleep with Helena. But now he saw he could just as well say he slept with Helena in order to have a plausible excuse, the mother pre-requisite for his drinking.

All evening and all night he lay in bed very still, back in the earliest moments of his life, reconstructed and re-derived from the results they'd let loose in him. He scarcely moved, so that no awkward stirring of his grown-up self should drown these first faint whisperings now so charged with meaning and significant with light.

So concentrated and interested was he that the dawn stood in his window long before he'd finished. Instantly the sun was up he fell into a deep sleep and did not wake again until dark. It was as if night and day had changed rôles with him, investing sunlight with unconsciousness and night with the most conscious and creative awareness. At once his mind took up the trail where sleep had covered it in the morning. Weakened, however, by lack of food and by this sudden and violent change in his habits, and the immense questing surge of his mind, he grew feverish again.

But why didn't life protect me against such irrational fear, his heart demanded of his instinct in the midst of his rising fever. Surely this life which daily lives the answers to its darkest problems must have allowed for my cowardice too?

As if in answer to his question the door of his room opened and shut, and I appeared to be standing in the room with bags in both hands as if I had come to stay. In David's feverish condition the illusion was so convincing that it didn't occur to him to question its reality, and to this day he talks of it to me as something which happened not only in his mind but also in the concrete world.

He sat up in his bed to welcome me with a tremendous warmth of glad and grateful emotion, his fever playing strange full-moon music on his nerves like a rhapsodic gipsy on a guitar, and cried, a quality of a certain fantastic dream-fever poetry mingling in his speech: "Sweet fellow of my childhood days, in my dreams lovingly remembered . . . dear

275

Companion of my Bath, beloved astronomer Royal come to read my midnight sky, welcome—a long, warm, and a forever welcome to your observatory in my heart. . . . If I seem dismayed and hot tears blur the clarity of my welcome, forgive me, for I come through a fierce and lonely winter and your habitation has long been cold and I fear much neglected. . . . But did you not know my flesh was nomad, my blood Bedouin and I committed before birth to a terrible desert journey ere I could meet you honestly here? No matter: that is over now and what is done is done and I've eaten my fill of dusty dates and drunk enough of fire and water of the hot male sun. . . . Please be seated; uncover your great telescope and turn it on the dark, historic sky. . . . Please find me the run-away, unhitched satellites of time, so that I can bring them back to this helpless abandoned moment and make them wheel it forward from the dark ditch into its natural present. . . . Say, did you know I studied alchemy once? Yes I was a bright and expert alchemist once and incurred great infamy thereby. . . . One Sunday morning between the middle and the last bell, I found the universal formula. I turned the lead of my mother's love into gold. I held Mary's love, a coin of sovereign gold of pure and perfect roundness, in the palm of my hand, but alas! no one would believe me. Mary said it was the king my father's gold I'd stolen. She took me to him and he beat me cruelly for it. They stopped my time thereby. . . . Dickery dock this mouse ran up the clock, dickery dock the clock struck one . . . Twenty-two times one . . . and dickery dock, this mouse ran down the clock and turned the old pendulum's lock. . . . Wise astrologer, reader of pythoned oracle, what constellation would you bring under your focus thereby?"

"No constellation," I said, sitting down on his bed and taking his hot feverish hand in mine. "No constellation but allow me to draw your attention to the coal sack, the black hole, the entrance to hell of Nilotic Hottentot right in the centre of the Milky Way. You look there into a great gulf in the universe, a great pit in yourself. I think there you were first confused with fear and strangely divided, cruelly cut in two between Mary and the Albert in you. Consequently your Alchemy was divided. You confused gold without and discovery of gold within. There's a subtlety that escaped you both."

There was a long pause. David was now very quiet and did not speak for a really long time. He was not there in his bed at all. He was back in the crystal moment which had never been dissolved in him—the moment when he discovered that there were two of him.

That discovery had so frightened him that he'd refused to admit it but there were two for all that, and the newly discovered one was saying: Quick, look in that bag. That's where she keeps it. No, that other fellow won't see you: he's busy watching the pigeons because their wings beating in the air are, for him, sound of silk of Mary's clothes being pulled over her head in Albert's room. They are grim homing birds with news of Albert's twentieth century version of the Rape of the Pierre's Lucrece whose proxy you are. . . . You see, there it is right in the bag, your love, your treasure, your gold of Mary's heart. Quick, put it in your breast pocket and keep it there: yours safe forever.

"So I was a thief after all and Albert did right to beat me," David exclaimed bitterly to me. "I did try to steal his love, his royal treasure."

"Don't be too hard on yourself. You were at most only the half-willing receiver of stolen goods." I pacified him and put a cool hand on his forehead now burning and flushed with fever. "It wasn't theft at all, and neither Albert nor Mary was right to punish you but they couldn't help themselves. Provisionally I'd say this; it was no more than a noble and honourable confusion on your two parts. Others greater than you or me have fallen fatally into the same error through inability to arrive at its clarification."

David found himself back in Albert's study with the smell

of cigar smoke and cognac in the air. The physical pain of the beating and the voice of the ancient boy in him steering him through his ordeal was no problem to him. But the other voice, the voice in love with sovereign gold, was. As Albert beat him it cried passionately, Kill him, God! Strike him dead for this abuse of power, for this jealous injustice!

Dear God! how had he managed to hide it from himself all these years? When he was out of the study and crying under the gooseberry bushes the same voice had stopped him saying: It's a mistake to call on God for help because he's a father himself and has a Son who forgives everything. Let's whistle up the devil: there's a fellow of steel who never forgives an injury. Wait and I'll go and find him.

Then the voice was back almost at once: I've made the pact and fixed the price. The answer is this: Your wish is granted. Albert is already doomed. He hasn't long to live. You think Mary loves him now but it's not true. She has, I tell you, always loved her Pierre. She too is a hater of fathers. Although she won't admit it, she's never forgiven her father because he wouldn't let her marry Pierre. She loved only Pierre and in his absence loves you daily more, his growing substitute. Slowly she is poisoning Albert so that she can be free for you. No, you needn't be alarmed, the police will never know. This poison Mary uses is found in no chemist's book of dangerous drugs. It is unrecognised and irrecognisable in the world of science and reason. It's an imponderable pollen of a deadly night-shade. Every night when Albert is asleep, it enters his being to corrode his will and desire to live. It is a poison brewed from all the words, the delicate, tender, burning trivialities and petty endearments she's never used—but would so constantly have spoken if she'd truly loved him. Despise them not, these little sounds—they're as necessary to the human heart as golden bees to flowers, by taste of honey unmade, provoked to fly the traffic of love from cup to cup otherwise condemned to die narcissus-bound to one still reflection in their own deep scented pools. Make no mistake: Albert's tired rejected heart hungrily draws in the poison of this sweet neglect through his dreaming brain. If you but knew the detail of the secret which hides the explanation of your father's character from you, you would know how much he needed a sure and full unqualified love to heal the injuries of an unhappy birth and childhood. No, leave it all to Mary and that harsh will of denial planted in her by her father. And for this diabolic intelligence and expert advice, the fee is eminently reasonable and I'm sure to your liking. It's only this: in return, you're committed, once Albert is gone, never to love any other woman but your beautiful Mary.

So that was the way of it. How quickly the end then came. It seemed no distance between the pact in the garden underneath the gooseberry bushes and Albert's death in his last room with the windmill clanking in the garden and the jackals barking as if they were come to fetch him into the world of the dead. It was no distance at all to the moment in the garden with Anna Maria and me, and the church bell tolling out the brittle years of Albert's life and the second voice to which at that time he'd paid no attention was prompting him: Count them all. The annual blows life gave him were much heavier than the ones you suffered. Listen how well our bargain was kept.

He'd done what he was told but when the strokes of the bell had equalled the strokes of the cane, he'd wanted to stop the bell for it had seemed then that justice had been done and Albert had had enough. He'd stopped counting but the voice was angry and scolded him fiercely. He realised now that he'd never liked that voice and never wished to have anything to do with it. A cold shiver had gone over him and his daylight self had said: Look at that lovely face of Anna Maria: how wet it is with tears for Albert. Until you, too, can weep for him like that, all between you and him will never be over. He'd tried to cry but the other, the second fellow wouldn't let him. Then he'd been desperately frightened: and had continued to feel so.

His entire upbringing had made him assume that Albert
had gone to Heaven, was now living in a great home in the
sky with a God that knew everything from the fall of a
sparrow to the most secret pacts with the devil. This God
would surely know how Albert had died. He would know,
too, that David was accessory to the fact of a father's murder
and tell Albert so. Ah, there'd been good cause in a young
child's divided heart to look up at the sky with apprehension.
He knew now why all that spring he'd watched the coming
of the first storms with a heavy, oppressed spirit. It was not
strange at all any more. Now, in an instant, he understood that
moment of terror with me and our boys in the hut in the
storm, his vision of lightning from a blue sky. He'd thought
the lightning was a greater whip and the thunder the deeper
voice of Albert come to revenge his murder.

Oh! how great and crippling this confusion had been, how
corrosive the acids of an incomplete alchemy spreading outwards fast from initial error causing division. Yes: the division
had been terrible. The moment Albert was in his grave, the
voice in love with partial gold had said: You're free now to
love your Mary with all your heart. But all his heart would
not love Mary. True, he felt deeply concerned for her and
burdened down not only with his own but also with the
sense of her guilt. Whenever she left the house he was afraid
the police might arrest her. He stood for hours at the gate of
his home waiting anxiously for her return, saying that if only
she would come he would give her all his love. But when she
came back eager and touched by the anxious face of her
favourite son at the gate, he shrank away.

Yes, there had been something in him that refused her, the
something that made him paint with increasing application
and absorption. He did not know what instinct it was but he
remembered that even his evil voice said: Go ahead, it'll
appease your fear of Albert for he liked your painting, and
make you freer for Mary.

Free for Mary! What a cynic that voice was! As if he could

be ever free of the pair of them again. What with the necessity of appeasing the rage of Albert in him, warding off the tide of vengeance rising in his blood, and trying to love a beautiful Mary who'd committed murder for him, he was torn in two. A dark gap, becoming slowly wider, opened up in him. But, alas, there was neither King nor Queen to stand in defence of his royalty. Albert was dead in him; and Mary, because of her guilt, he could not enthrone.

"That was the meaning of that painting of mine," the words broke from him. "The throne room, two empty chairs and no royalty left in my land."

The ancient despair broke out in a heavy sweat and he looked at me out of bloodshot eyes and said: "It's no good, we can never go on from there, can we?"

"You can and shall," I said confidently. "You had royal allies—a royal uncle and aunt."

At once the tension went out of him and his calm returned. Yes, he'd had his Uncle and Aunt Fraser and me, almost a twin brother. We'd been his own, true people. With us he was loved and could love, with us he painted, followed his own creative trade, and was safe from Albert's vengeance and his and Mary's guilty greeds. No wonder Mary had been against his painting for it'd made him free of her, protected him against her. How lucky he'd been to have an alternative set of parents and as he admitted his good fortune, he stood breathless in the midst of his next great discovery.

He sat up and wagged his forefinger at me with playful accusation, saying: "You knew it all along, honest teller of lying truths. A wise and generous dispensation of life has given us all two sets of parents. First, I have Albert and Mary, my technical father and mother who beget me on behalf of life, who push me out in front of them in their own dark, un-lit image. But inside my heart I have a royal Aunt and Uncle, the lawful regents and wardens of life, who draw me towards them in my own unique and timeless self. My real father and mother are far, far in front of me. I carry their image struck deep in the currency of my heart. They are my true north. On them swings my one and only compass. They are my unique and true direction. I, Albert, Mary and Anna Maria, all of us, all are but children making the dark and difficult journey towards them, all children of one and the selfsame great, good, creative and living life. Poor Albert, and poor Mary, hurt and hurting fellow-children of life!"

There! David was out of it at last. He was free of complicity in imagined murder and guilt of murder. The crime, if crime there had been, was misdemeanour of helpless, frightened and unknowing children. The relief was immense. He was free, now, to weep—and first he wept for Albert. For days he lay so close to his tears that the slightest recollection of Albert's many favours and kindnesses in childhood would set them flowing again. Above all, David saw Albert come up tentatively behind him as he started to paint again after that Black Sunday, Albert with a sad contrite face, eyes red with drink and uncomprehended misery, handing him shyly a brand new and handsome box of paints, and he wanted to cry out for Albert to hear: "Father, and fellow-child of life, forgive me for my lack of understanding and one moment of dark unseeing hatred. Thank you for taking a doom upon yourself great enough for me to be warned and guided, and in this night sky of my heart, shine again old star, for out of this sorrow great love shall spring. I'll show them yet that blood feud of father and son is neither inevitable nor permanent. There is love and to spare for all in life even for so harsh a father and so prodigal a son."

And Mary? He did not weep for her but he remembered her goodness, her patient, protective and loving care of him, her great and graceful beauty. And the excess of her, the iron exaggeration of her, forever went from his heart. Goliath was dead and his giantess slain!

At this point David fell into a deep sleep illuminated through his fever like a dark tropical storm sky with a steaming rainbow. In his sleep he stood once more outside the door of

Albert's study. He raised his hand to turn the handle of the door and go inside but something held him back. A curious, taut electric sound, like the noise of a great country's traffic inside the telegraph wires on a highway, was coming out of the room—a noise suggesting constant and unending energy. He looked up and saw over the door a notice saying, "Power station: danger". The notice had a realistic skull instead of a full-stop after "danger". How right he was to hesitate and yet he knew that he must enter whatever the risk. As he stood there wondering how to set about it the old negro, slave of his other dream, appeared suddenly at his side and hung a new notice in place of the old, saying: "Throne room. Transformer." Then he was inside the study which he had once painted so vividly. The room was as before except that now it was filled with a golden light, a dazzling fire in the grate, and two resplendent figures in the chairs. At first he thought they were Mary and Albert, then my own father and mother, and he felt intensely happy to see them so close and confidingly there. But as he went nearer he saw that they were two truly royal figures, male and female, two mythological persons. He stopped short in awe for he saw now that they were deeply engaged. The man was writing with an albatross quill in a large book open on his knees. The woman was holding a golden ink well in one hand and with the other blotting each line the man wrote with a most caring solicitude. David looked at them sideways. He saw they were writing "The Progress of David the Painter". His contentment knew no bounds and he began to cry softly and quietly to himself out of a new happiness over his discovery that this ancient throne-room was after all not empty but transfigured.

He woke and the dream, such a good dream, stayed with him. He knew now that these royal persons were no illusions. What is more he realised that they'd always been there, that they'd figured over and over again in his dreams, appealing to him with the greatest and most quivering electrical urgency to stop confusing them with Albert and Mary. He was so excited at this discovery that his pulse raced at his temples and the blood flowed like Nile cataract and African waterfall in his ears.

Four of them, four square being squarely defended, he rejoiced: ah, I'm no longer Hamlet with his time out of joint. How wrong he had been to tell Helena that Hamlet's tragedy was that he'd had to kill his father twice over. Hamlet's tragedy—and David knew it keenly for it had been so nearly his own—was that the sense of a mother's guilt had stood between him and his Ophelia, depriving him of the vital onward surge of a man's love for his woman.

David saw it now. A man must go down into the gulf and walk a lonely path among the dark and terrible dangers of his archaic self, he must visit his land below sea-level, and he cannot come out again whole until he has found, separated and healed the ancient quarrel between the four parents of himself, delivered all four from destructive bondage and fatal confusion of themselves.

There was a long pause during which David would hardly allow himself to breathe. It was as if his fever had wings and he astride a Pegasus of his own, flying fast through the night in search of a face beyond the farthest perimeter of stars.

"Adventure began with a face," he said, speaking to himself with very soft, slow and retrospective music of a fevered fantasy. "A face first tempted me to leave Mary. At three in the afternoon Mary's voice was calling, calling me in the summer garden. Light of a rich southern African summer was about me like a sea and my heart was shaking out white sails, with oars all set like a ship in a shining roadstead, outward bound on a sea unknown to a port that is not yet—when there came that lovely voice of woman's love calling, calling me back to the tree with the yellow fruit in the centre of the garden. My hungry, eager senses strained to return, but already my heart was strangely bound and contracted to vision of the face of some new woman folded in a young-girl face like flower of the future tucked securely in a bud measured and cut for fitting increase on earth. I was firmly tied with original silk to the mast-head of this delicate vision. So I sailed away from the voice, though my misery was great, for music of that voice pursued me still and forever called me back in the ebb-tide of my blood from the other side of the Arc of Iris on the horizon of my first flood."

But great as the misery had been, he'd had strength to bear it so long as the vision of the new-found face went before.

Then horrifyingly, the face had become unfriendly and seemed to reject him. The horror of Anna Maria's rejection of him had been so great that for years he would not admit it. Time and time over he rejected rejection and pursued that face as if indeed it was his to follow, prizing it even above music of magic voice in an enchanted garden of summer. But in my home, on the evening of that Black Sunday, Anna Maria left him for good; the vision of the face faded, and the light died in him. He was alone with the voice still calling from behind the horizon. He was free of a beautiful exacting vision only to be chained and enslaved to a sound. He turned back to the voice; and as he turned the dying light went out and suddenly it became dark.

It was the darkness of Albert and Mary's own unfulfilled and disowned love which separated David from Anna Maria. It was the burden of Albert and Mary and generations of unlived selves, the burden of the love and need of man and woman for one another struggling to be made alive and constantly being denied, that set him and Anna Maria apart. How clear it was to him now: whatever the parents left of themselves unlived, the children had to live for them before they were free to take up their own proper and special burden for which they were born. How could Anna Maria, Albert's substitute Mary, loaded as she was with the burden of a father's unfulfilled love, be free to share the heart of a brother wherein a vigilant mother had already staked a gold prospector's claim and set her jealous mark? Poor Anna Maria and poor me, David thought, we were destined to become lightning conductors of demonic parental wrath: she of Mary's and I of Albert's. No wonder I was afraid of lightning once, for it scorched my earth at birth. But wait . . . give me time and I shall yet build a spire high enough to take the discharge for us both.

Now too he saw all the forms and images with which his mind had never ceased to provoke him to do battle so that he could resume his forward journey. Mary's unreality was the spider on which his eyes had become fixed that day at home when she got angry and he'd grown speechless. Her unlived self was the lizard, the crab pulling him backwards, the shark in his sea and wolf-bitch with lace-bonnet on, leading the pack on his heels in his dream. Why had his courage failed him after such accurate warning?

"Why, oh why, was I such a coward and why did I flee for so long?" he cried out to me at his side with a bitter return to hopelessness and dissatisfaction with himself.

"It's not true that you were a coward, you're too hard on yourself," I protested with force and energy. "We're not going to arrive at forgiveness of all injury of the past which must precede your own real and special beginning, unless you can forgive yourself. I suggest that it was not cowardice but just that the way wherein unreality was presented to you seemed so real that your courage was not convinced the occasion needed or justified your use of it."

He sat upright with surprise, but when I insisted on my point, he lay down to reconsider himself. Perhaps there was some truth in it. It had taken courage to abandon his first fort, to step out at nightfall from the strong Kremlin built by Albert and Mary in his east and, with a wolf-pack on his heels, to make for far-off fire in the wood, his only weapon still a sword of stars in the southern sky. And what gave him that kind of courage? Why, the thought of Anna Maria imperilled and endangered in that deep wood. Because of it, he had held on. In the midst of disaster and insatiable thirst of

Mary, in corrosive drinking with Helena, this knowledge
safe but undeciphered in starry symbolism had kept him on
the journey. Only a dream within a dream, a face by the fire
in the midst of him, had guided him in his sleep, a love-to-be
of a face-to-come like thread of Ariadne's gold wound between the trees of the labyrinthine wood. That gleam of
virgin gold had never failed. Through great creeper-entwined
trunks of trees, in dark air troubled with batswing and serpents' hiss there was always flame of fire on slimy, protozoic
waters. True, the wolf caught up with him, but the wolf had
been Mary no longer—it was Helena. Suddenly he felt intensely grateful to Helena. There was no illusion about the
warmth of that. Forgive me Helena, for making you a battleground not of my choosing. Without you I should never
have come out of this journey sane and whole. Without a
woman like you to go wrong with, I could never in life have
come to a woman to do right with. Tender, scarred field of
battle, fare you well and forgive me as I forgive you and the
more dangerous Mary in me.

So too, he was free of confusion of Helena, free and grateful to her. He was free already of them all, Helena, Albert,
Mary and Edward George, all except Anna Maria. There was
some slight confusion of sister still. Perhaps the vision of the
face had not failed him? Perhaps only he, in his lack of awareness, had been trapped into thinking so? For long David pon-
dered the question. Slowly he made his way through massive
Gothic trunks until, fording the last stream of his blood in a
high clearing on firm ground, he came out of the pure and unperturbed fire. And curled up there, fast asleep, was not a child
but a grown woman; the woman who'd shared the storm and
voyage at sea with him. As he bent down to look at her face
in amazement he heard nearby the excited whining and impatient hoof pounding of a milk-white unicorn. Then there
was confusion no longer for by the clear light of that fire he
saw in this new-found woman's face the likeness with which
Anna Maria had once been entrusted and which she had so

determinedly rejected. Instantly, anguish and painful memory of Anna Maria's rejection died, and her face became once again dear and beautiful in its own right.

At that moment happiness burnt like flame in him. Then all was very still. There was the sound only of the fever, of the immense and swift swoop of wings of understanding from star to star inside himself, like a wind going over the top of the great Michaeljohn garden. Ah, yes, that garden. . . . There it was, filled with yellow fruit and magic music far away to the east within walls of the golden Kremlin of his dream. He looked back at it without fear and as he looked the Michael within him placed one of his host with a flaming sword over its main gate. It was sealed, safe and guarded at last. "Pass by Alexander David," Michael the Militant ordered him, "and join me and John and be not dismayed. For what is exile even from such a garden when there is high heaven beyond?"

He was not dismayed for in this wood he was no longer alone but had found the woman he sought, his opposite about to be made equal. In a minute he would be free to bend down and say: Dear woman, let us wake one another with a kiss and with us a million, million years of life. All the life that has ever been sleeps here with you, waiting on our awakening to join it to its equal and opposite future. Beloved, we have slept long enough: help me to awake. He was about to take her in his arms when he thought, No, I must not be like the impatient unicorn in my dream. First I, too, must rest. I'm very tired. So he lay down quietly by the side of his discovery and at once fell asleep.

He slept all through that night and the next day, and did not wake until late the following evening. It was dark in his room, but whenever he shut his eyes and turned them inward it was to see the same fire burning bright inside him and his woman still asleep beside it. His fever was gone. His mind and head felt crystal clear and his awareness seemed to be moving and expanding rhythmically outwards around him like the ripples made by a stone cast on the surface of still, shining and very deep water. All around this circle of awareness there was still black, black darkness but no longer any confusion. He felt a happiness which was too great for him to attempt to put in words but which he wanted to paint as a world of yellow corn ripe for harvest without cease from sun to moonrise, wheat fulfilled, mother of bread drugged against injury of sickle, with black seeds of red poppy and a lark overhead starting a silver quarrel with the delayed day. Yes! The fever was gone. I, Alexander, was gone too from his bed, standing well back from the front of his mind in my original and natural perspective. There had been fever and microscope of fever but no exaggeration of meaning. The fire and the woman within were true.

There's the point, David thought—in the sleep wherein I turned archæologist and dug deep among the ruins of my own mind. I, man, discovered at last that aspect of my soul which was woman. Though male crew and masculine members truly man it, my ship of state, my royal barge is feminine. Therefore I shall take ship in the wide, open seas, and sail, at last, to my true continent and mainland. I shall kneel down humbly before this ancient and scarred foundation in the ruins of my own mind and on it help to rebuild a great city. Later I shall wake my dear, my sleeping Ariadne beauty and show her the city and say: We come not with black evening but red sails of morning. Enter at last your long denied home.

David's pulses quickened, and in the moment of deep excitement he again thought of me. Oh, Alex, Alex, Babylonian-bound old astrologer, find your largest glass and turn it on me quick, for here swift my heart grows wings and soars with me high above our white and slanted Everest. I find religion here; I find the experience before the dogma: the fact before the theory. I witness the advent of woman into heaven. Therefore I will cry to the Greeks in their mitres and scarlet Latin togas who still might assail a city rebuilt: Keep

your crest of marble columns in the mind of man, but leave
me the faithful intuitive heart, the corner-stone of humble
old Pythagoras who dedicated a life to far-off study of the
squares and their sums on the sides and base of the true and
right triangle. There was heaven in his geometry, equation
of awareness expanded and expanding in his mathematics,
for I witness his outward theorem duplicated and reciprocated inward. I saw the square on a heavenly hypotenuse
equal the sum of the squares on the sides of a sacred triangle.
I lived through the moment when the battle of the triangle
was won and the creation and consolidation of the square
begun. I saw the three points of the triangle, father, mother,
and son, joined by love, and learnt that if the angles were to
be rightly made for the true sum of the great square, then
love of father and mother for each other must be precise and
accurate if the sides and base are to be truly joined to apex of
child projected into the dark future; otherwise, fear comes in
and makes the angle acute. I know, for I have just learned
that my angle to Albert was too acute: and that with Mary
too wide. Worst of all there was lack of love at the base
itself.

I was a coward but I had right to fear, for this journey I was
contracted to perform without my seeking from birth to
death, from past to future, from world without to world
within on to world without end, is not possible without love.
He who tries to go down into the labyrinthine pit of himself,
to travel the swirling, misty netherlands below sea-level
through which the harsh road to heaven and wholeness runs,
is doomed to fail and never see the light where night joins day
unless he goes out of love in search of love.

Yes, thought David, lying on his back and watching the
sunlight break into the room, it is only the slender and
fragile thread of delicate gold of love which distorted being
cannot destroy. Given that, there is provision for all against
the deepest darkness within. There is imagery and the reflection of love in heaven-bound life, and there is fire un-

ending passed on from Prometheus direct. Only awareness, fully extended and humbly maintained, is needed to know that no moment is without love, and no night truly dark. There is provision for all in life.

In that love nourished and defended in the dream of woman asleep by the fire of my farthest inmost camp, I recovered my courage; and in awareness and light of fire, my wholeness. I recovered my courage, for love is charged with faith and is infinitely heroic. Others have praised its light, its flame, its warmth, its delicate and infinite understanding. I must praise its unfailing, heroic, golden continuity. It is the universal coming-to-a-point in unique and individual adventure, after coincidence and completion of male and female being. And for me, at that moment of revelation, it was as if a fine wind, coming over the snow white mountain tops down through the pass in the dark hills of the world, brought the sound of Roland's horn to my ears and Charlemagne my manhood turned. Yes, I stood at the place where the great tides of the world are made and I saw the ebb of a cowardly moment in history turned, and the full flood swollen to a white-maned urgency, charged with leaping light, hurled back at the darkened main. From far above my white and slanted Everest I saw the universe expanding at the rate which astronomers are still measuring. I saw a noble and starry insomnia put somnambulism to shame, and through long dark passes in the outer skies I saw Michael, my angel, throw in his glittering forces like cavalry into a gap in the defences of the enemies of the world. I saw the belted stars with their ensigned satellites, solicitous planets, nursing moons and their red-moccasined scouts with long, deer-slayer hair astreaming, and fleet-footed comets come pouring through the passes in the black mountains and quickly fan out into the dark plains beyond. Ah, what a moment of infinite understanding, restoring to a hurt soul its courage in the search of love and its own wholeness, was found therein.

I stayed long in that moment, thought David and I was

healed in it. I was even tempted to stay in it forever. I craved
to live where the golden symbols of life-to-be are coined, and
to hold them warm in the palm of my hand as they come out
of the mint with the King's own image newly struck upon
them. But I was told that the symbol of my own time within
has first to be fully understood and lived.

Then for a while I was even tempted to the rôle of prophet,
to go into the market places and speak and warn my fellow
men saying: "It is late! Take up again the individual adventure before it is too late and assert your own, your true, unique
and basic differences. Your love of life depends on your living
your differences and your wholeness in love. Without love
and wholeness there is no security. Walk out of your mind-
made Kremlins before life stands still in you as it does in bees
and ants which can repeat only themselves. Live your difference for love of the increasing wholeness it brings, and you
will have adventure such as the world has never seen. Have
done with loveless, substitute begetting. Live out your own
nature fully and do not pile on the generations to come, who
already have loads of their own heavy enough, the burden
you shirked of unravelling your secret nature and letting out
your imprisoned and unlived self."

Ah! I was sorely tempted to tarry. And I was sorely
tempted to prophesy. But I was allowed to do neither. Life
has had enough of half-way prophecies. Besides, I was born a
painter. I, David, was born a painter and humbly must continue with my painting as my only calling. I have a fire of my
own to tend. So I prepare to tend it, to pile it high and send
it leaping to heaven, praying only that its light should not
dazzle a lesser nor diminish a greater one.

But before I finally turned my back on tarrying and pro-
phecy I was allowed to attend a victory parade, as it were, of
all the life that has ever been. I saw all that has ever been come
streaming through the long lanes and corridors of my blood,
through their arch of admiralty, round the inner-square and
then straight down past my own white lighted Hall. Out of

the darkness that preceded Genesis and flood, it began with a glimmer and a worm of the unformed earth in love with the light to come. Yes! a worm with a lantern, a glow-worm with phosphorescent uniform, marched proudly at the head, and behind came great streams of being protozoic and pre-historic. Nothing was excluded and everything included, their small fires of being clearly lit, tended and well beloved. This, it was said, is the true, the noble heroic and unique crusade of the love of life. For look, among them not a brain but only matter tentatively and awkwardly assembled. Yet remark on their bearing and the trust with which they hurl themselves into the uncomprehended battle. Ah! tears of love and grati-tude burned in my eyes at so urgently moving and life-confiding a sight. To feel, at last, the burden that they carry for me in my own blood, to know at every second several of these reflected in white corpuscle and scarlet cell are dying unflinchingly in battle for my all, to know that giant lizard and lion as well as unicorn came after, and were hurled too into similar struggle and defence of the totality of all. I was allowed, too, to see the first man and registered the seismographic thrill of the marching column at the appearance of so skilled and complex a champion. I was allowed to speak to him and I touched his skin riddled with snake bite, his shoulder pierced by mastodon's spike, his skull deep-scarred with sabre-tooth's claw. And as reverently and tenderly I took his hand shaking with marshy malarial fever, I was moved to pity him by the evidence of such dread and unending war. But he would have none of it. He looked me fearless in the eye and in a voice that boomed like a drum in his stomach said: "Brother, it was worth it. Whatever they tell you, add this, it was worth it."

I spoke to a Bushman half-eaten by a lion in the Kalahari, his only vessel a brittle ostrich egg with red and black triangles painted neatly on it, now broken and sand scattered. He looked in my grey eyes with the brown eyes of a people at dusk, slanted to bridge a chasm behind the face of a dying member of a dying and vanishing race. He too, my dying nomad brother, said: "Add, add quick before I go, 'it was worth it'." I spoke to an aborigine in the bight of the great gulf. Tattooed with dung he said: "I vanish, but it was worth it." In New Guinea, I met a stone-age Papuan, his black skin sheened with green after centuries in the jungle between basin and fall of water and spurting volcano, and he too said: "Doubt it not, it was worth it." Everyone said, "Lovely gift of a life that we blindly trust burns with such loving fire in the dark that at any price, no matter how great, it is worth it."

Yes, they all agreed and utterly convinced me, so that I can never doubt again. I wept when the great procession came to an end, for one and all, great and small—I loved them all. Yes, even to the worm that brought up the rear, with shaded night light and a nurse's white, in its dress concealing a phial of the drug of the greater sleep made with a touch of the hand of God's great, good night. Yes, David, told himself, I love them all; I believe them; I am ready for battle; and to continue at their head the journey of them all to the end of the road in my blood. At last, purified and complete, I am ready to awaken and defend my love.

PART VI

The End of the Beginning

CHAPTER 23

THE day had lengthened into a week and more before David dared to leave his hotel bedroom. Long after his fever had gone, long after he felt the struggle within and against himself resolved and the crisis over, he continued to lie in his bed in a curious trance-like state. He felt utterly blinded and dazzled by light, by the completion and brilliance of the new vision of life and himself that had emerged out of this battle. He knew that vision unaccepted was sterile and that his next task now was to give it life in his own life. But he could not at once free himself of its blinding, shattering quality. Now even the thought of rings on people's fingers, bells on their toes, bangles on their wrists, lockets round their necks, crosses on churches, flags at their poles, circles in geometry books, rosaries, necklaces, nursery rhymes about ladies on white horses and three blind mice, all gave him infinite delight. Slowly, by taking into his mind his recollection of these and other of the dear trivialities and minor fantasies of ordinary life, and dwelling on them reverently, he seemed to come slowly back to his contemporary self lying there in bed. I've come from Everest, he warned himself. I'm snow-blind. I must not be impatient and yet I must hasten. Even so, when he did get up, feeling a little dizzy but remarkably fit and well, he found it was almost too soon. The very first day out he found himself standing trembling on the pavement in front of his hotel, with the sounds of a bus's brakes quickly applied screaming in his ears. He realised then that he'd walked out of his room, taken the lift and gone down and out into the street, his eyes fixed firmly on the vision of his dazzling discovery and not at all focused on the world without.

This'll never do, he told himself with an amused smile.

It's no good finding the way to heaven and then not knowing how to cross a street in London. That night, back in his room, he wrote to me, my father and mother, Anna Maria and Mary, letters which made us, moved out of our anchored selves, turn to one another, as if we too had been released from a kind of inner bondage.

The next morning, David woke slowly in a dreamlike vision of himself as a green and pleasant land under a summer sun. From one end of it to the other, it seemed to him, armed men such as he had seen at his round table were riding fast horses, with banners and flags flying and heraldic trumpets sounding to some central point. He felt as if his mobilisation call had come at last, and quickly jumped out of bed.

Immediately after breakfast he telephoned to Alis's house in London and got his first shock. The servant who answered said Alis was away in the country, and sounded surprised that David had not heard that she was very ill. The servant said he was sorry but his instructions were not to give her address to anyone because she was too ill to be disturbed; but if David cared to write he would see that the letters were forwarded.

Would he do that with a telegram too, David asked, and the servant promptly said he would. David went at once and telegraphed "Forgive silence stop have been very ill myself stop Alexander dead giantess slain stop David Michael John all three completely recovered and free but only just allowed out stop Please send address I will come at once."

He waited all day in a fever of impatience, not daring to leave his room in case the reply came but at nightfall gave up hope and telephoned the house again. The same servant assured him he had sent the telegram on, and there was nothing more he could do.

"Is your mistress on the telephone?" David asked.

"Yes, sir," the man answered. "But I'm afraid I can't give you the number. Both the master's and the Admiral's orders were very definite on this point."

The servant's oblique reference to the Admiral made it obvious to David that it was he the servant feared rather than Simon.

"Well, would you be good enough to telephone for me? Please ask if my telegram was received and request permission to give me your mistress's address?"

The man agreed to do this, asking David to ring back in an hour's time.

When David did telephone, the servant answered almost at once with a note of disappointment. "I'm so sorry, sir, Madam was too ill for a message to be taken to her, and I'm afraid I was ordered not to give you the telephone number. But Sir Gervaise asked me to say that he himself is writing to you."

There was nothing else David could do that night. He went to bed but did not sleep. Poor Alis. . . . How dreadfully selfish was his sort of illness. It seemed terrible that he should have had to be plunged in such a war within himself that his mind had not been free to think and care for her and all she was suffering. She'd told him, of course, of the illness which had afflicted her whenever she came home, and he comforted himself with the thought that this present illness was probably of the same nature and origin. But he could not, of course, be sure, and all night long, his imagination still tender from its own desperate encounter, he turned restlessly in his bed with anxiety and remorse.

Yet towards morning a certain calm returned to him, and much of his remorse left him in the realisation that his battle with himself had, after all, not been entirely selfish but as much on her behalf as his own. His total absorption in it had been absolutely necessary for victory. But a new sort of agitation came to disperse his precarious calm when post after post arrived and no letter arrived. He remembered again with apprehension the keen, distinguished and determined features of Gervaise as he'd seen him in the ship taking Alis into his arms with a confident, proprietary air. Surely he must know

by now how anxious I am, David thought, or can he be
doing this deliberately?

When the last post had come and gone with no letter,
David took his hat, gloves and stick, called for a taxi and
drove straight to Alis's London home. A servant in a black
coat and striped trousers opened the door, and the moment he
saw David a nervous expression appeared on his carefully
trained features.

"You were good enough to send a telegram for me yesterday," David said. "I came to thank you and ask you for some
other slight assistance."

But the man was most unwilling to impart any information. It was only after David had told him some of the story
and impressed him with the urgency of the situation that he
at last gave David Sir Gervaise Denysse's address in Hampshire.

David went home, his mind made up and course of action
clear. The next day he was up early, refreshed and ready for
a journey to the country. Before leaving, he handed in his
key at the hotel desk and received in return a letter with a
Hampshire mark addressed to him in a bold, sprawling hand.
He opened it and saw his telegram to Alis folded inside a
letter. The letter itself had no address, only the date and began
at once: "Dear Mr. Michaeljohn, I enclose your telegram to
my daughter which I do not propose delivering to her as I
don't think she is in a fit state to receive communications
from you. On her return she informed me and her husband
of your undesirable relationship with her during her voyage
home. I know too much of the exaggerated feelings that the
forced and false propinquity of a long voyage by sea often
produces in human beings to take your and my daughter's
feelings for one another very seriously and have no doubt
they'll soon evaporate. Her husband, I am glad to say, shares
my view. I would appeal to you now to leave my daughter
alone as she is most unwell and will have at any moment to
undergo a serious operation for which, if she is to come

through it successfully, she will need all her strength. I hope you are the sort of person upon whom an appeal of this kind will have effect. I may say that I know your father-in-law, Sir Arthur Moystouan-Roswell. It is, therefore, I hope, clear to you why I do not want you to have any futher correspondence with my daughter. I warn you that I myself have taken precautions accordingly and will not hesitate to retaliate with stern measures should you continue to try and get in touch again with her. G. Denysse, Vice-Admiral."

For some moments David contemplated the letter with intense dismay and then a great and growing anger possessed him. The past with Helena was dead and the dead could no longer affect him. A father's care for a daughter he could understand and respect, but what a monstrous male presumption there was in this letter which sought to order a grown woman's love. He walked quickly out of the hotel. "Taxi, taxi!" He called out in a loud, clear voice. "Waterloo—quick!"

In the train much of his anger left him. The situation was far too serious and urgent for anger. Besides, deep down, he felt pained, and consciously humiliated that this great vision he'd had and his love for Alis had now to be steered through so sordid and unsatisfactory a channel. At a moment when he would have given anything for an opportunity to be as delicate and gentle, as loving, complex, understanding and fastidious as he felt, he was being pushed inexorably to the opposite extremes. Yet he knew, regret it as he would, that this was the only way. It was moreover a matter of life and death as her illness clearly showed. In this task, he felt sure, he must not let his courage fail.

His plan, if plan it could be called, possessed an inspired simplicity. Come what may he was going to see and find Alis and never leave her again. Nothing could stop him, but he had no idea how he was going to do it.

After an hour and a half in the train he arrived at his destination. The porter knew the address at once and told

David he would have to get a car at the local garage, for the "Admiral's place" was about three miles out. David soon found the garage, hired a car for the day and in a few minutes was seated in an ancient Rolls-Royce.

It was a lovely early autumn day. The air already precise with cold was yet still infused with a sad and gentle valediction of vanishing summer in its light. The rolling Hampshire fields were bare and harvested of their heavy yield. Here and there the beeches and chestnuts had started to turn and some leaves had begun to fall. The land looked tired and in need of sleep. It depressed David for he himself felt full of a flaming sense of spring.

Soon his careful chauffeur was driving up a long drive in a large park-like field towards a big red brick house that seemed to have retained all the features and comforts of English architecture from Elizabeth to Victoria.

When the car stopped inside a porch between large sandstone columns, David got out quickly, ran up the steps and pulled the bell rope at the side of the half-open front door. It was so still that he heard the bell peal forlornly far back in the enormous house and as it pealed he heard also a Pekinese's adenoidal bark. Some doors opened and shut and a voice which he knew at once to be the Admiral's said: "That's all right, don't bother, Saunders! I'm just going out myself and I'll see who it is."

In a few seconds the door opened and Gervaise, wearing his favourite tweeds, his distinguished face redder than ever with the cool air, stood in front of David. He obviously had no idea who David was and looked at him with a certain courteous puzzlement.

"Is there anything I can do for you?" he asked in a crisp but not unfriendly tone.

"Yes, there is, sir," David said, looking him steadily in the eye. "My name is Michaeljohn and I've come to see Alis."

"Michaeljohn? David Michaeljohn?" the Admiral exclaimed, not fully believing, and obviously disconcerted by not seeing in front of him the dissolute monster imagination had made of David.

David nodded and the man's face hardened. "It's evident that you haven't got my letter or you wouldn't be here now," he said, his voice hard and determined, already committed to pre-conceived action.

"On the contrary," David answered promptly. "It's precisely because of your letter that I am here."

"In that case I've nothing more to say to you except that what I said in my letter is my considered and irrevocable decision in the matter," Gervaise affirmed with the glitter in his eye of an eagle about to plunge. "I must ask you therefore to leave at once!"

"I'm not leaving until I've seen Alis." David said in a tensely clear voice. There was no bluster in his tone or bearing, and again Gervaise's preconceptions were thrown into disorder. He'd often seen courage and determination, and himself possessed enough of both to realise that here was someone who was quite unafraid. But what was more disconcerting was the feeling that the prepossessing young man before him appeared to think he was in the right. As a result the Admiral became even angrier.

"I'm sorry. In that case you leave me no option but to have you thrown out as a trespasser on my grounds." He moved back into the door as if to shut it in David's face.

"I wouldn't do that," David said, following him and asking with apparent irrelevance: "D'you love your daughter?"

The question and movement outraged Gervaise. "I've no intention of discussing my feelings for my daughter or anything else with you. I advise you to leave at once or I'll have you thrown out," Gervaise said furiously, moving deeper into the doorway.

"I warn you," David repeated moving resolutely after Gervaise with a confidence which was most impressive and disconcerting, "that if you do, the consequences for you, Simon, Alis and us all may well be serious and not at all to your liking. And I warn you too that, in the end I shall win, because I love your daughter and I'm right. I shall win because you're wrong and you don't know how to love your daughter."

As David spoke with passionate directness, Gervaise became more and more uneasy and uncertain of himself. "You're mad," he wanted to say to David in his sternest voice of command, but the words would not come. Here was a situation that was quite new to him and his mind followed David's declamation from one enormity to the other in a tense silence. Finally a feeling of powerlessness overtook him, the fire and fascination went out of his eyes and such a sad, hopeless look appeared on his proud and gallant face that David instantly felt desperately sorry for him.

"You'd better come into my study," said Gervaise wearily as he stood aside to let David in. "We can anyway talk there without danger of being overheard."

Once there he offered David a chair by a fire of damp wood in a large open hearth, while he seated himself opposite, almost directly underneath two tremendous and impressively rhetorical paintings of the great naval actions off Cape St. Vincent and in Quiberon Bay.

Seeing the stricken Gervaise like that in his favourite chair in his own home made David feel sickeningly conscious of his determined intrusion but he steeled himself against it.

"Smoke? Drink?" Gervaise asked David, holding out a cigarette box. But even as he did so a sort of revulsion at what he was doing came over him. "I hope you realise how criminally indulgent I'm being," he asked grimly. "I should be kicking your bottom instead of offering you tobacco and drink." He spoke as bitterly against himself as against David.

At David's refusal of both his offers Gervaise's surprise was considerable, and again the discovery did not add to his self-assurance. He helped himself to a large gin from the tray on the table beside him.

"The sooner we get all this over the better," David

appealed while he watched Gervaise gulp down his gin. "Where is Alis and how is she, sir? Please tell me at once."

"She's here in this house," Gervaise said after a long pause with great, measured deliberation. "She's staying here with my son-in-law who goes up and down daily to Town, and she's far from well. In fact she's going to hospital to-morrow for an operation."

He paused but David made no comment.

"As you probably know," Gervaise explained more naturally, "the doctors have been puzzled by her condition for years. When she fell ill again so soon after her return they made a careful study and count of her blood, and there is no doubt that the composition of her blood is dangerously one-sided. So they're going to operate in the hope that it will restore the balance. Her voyage, I fear, did her no good."

"On the contrary the voyage did her a world of good," David interrupted quickly. "Surely you never saw Alis looking better than when she landed at Southampton?"

"She did look well," Gervaise admitted reluctantly. "But it didn't last long. It's always like that and frankly it can't go on."

"Nonsense!" David said loud enough to make Gervaise flush with irritation. "There's nothing wrong with Alis except the wrong of her marriage to Simon. Surely you're not so blind, sir, that you can't see that?"

"You're extremely presumptuous," Gervaise said irritably. "We've had the best specialists in Britain to see Alis, and there's no doubt that the count of her blood is dangerously unbalanced. . . . You may be a painter but you're not a doctor and your claim to pose as an authority in so serious a matter is quite ridiculous."

"On the contrary, I am an authority," David replied with impressive gravity. "I have the authority of one who's studied the disease from within, who has contracted, endured, suffered it in all its stages to near death." He spoke confidently and with emotion. He might know nothing about

305

cancer of the body but he knew all about cancer of the spirit. For him it was no idle coincidence that one of the chief physical scourges of this age should carry the name of the crab, the sub-marine animal walking backwards, the convenient symbol of cowardly and destructive recession. . . . He knew from his own bitter experience all about that sort of cancer, all about the retrospective spirit, the proliferation of the one loveless cell in body and spirit, unloved by its opposite, falling out of love with the whole, and then desperately making itself multiply at the expense of the rest and totality. For how can one half multiply on its own without multiplying and endlessly repeating only itself?

"Listen!" David leant forward earnestly. "Alis has told me everything about her life—and how her mother died. I am sorry if it hurts you but can't you see that Alis is on the way to repeating the same pattern? She's on her way out just as her mother was and I'm the only person who can stop it."

The truth of what he was saying seemed so clear to David that he finished on a note of undisguised hope. And for a moment too it was obvious that Gervaise was both startled and impressed. Then he shook his head and said wearily, straight out of his dismayed, hurt and baffled heart, "Sorry, for I do believe you're sincere, but you make no sense to me."

"Then it's no use talking further," David said, standing up. "So now, please, may I see Alis?"

Gervaise stood up too, but much more slowly, as if playing for time.

"Please," David repeated more urgently, feeling Gervaise's problem like a shriek of bats in the air between them. "Please, don't let's go all over it again. My mind's made up and nothing can stop me. I'll not leave until I've seen and spoken to Alis."

Gervaise looked David searchingly in the eyes and said: "Very well, I'll take you to her. She's in the library. I was just on my way to fetch the car to take her for a drive when you came. Come, I'll show you the way."

Slowly Gervaise led the way out into the corridor but half-way along said to David over his shoulder: "You know, you wouldn't have won this round if it weren't that any scandal'd kill my wife. I'm only too thankful she's out for the day."

David was touched by the tall, distinguished figure walking with such a vanquished and beaten air in front of him.

"Believe me, sir," he said gently, "I've no feeling of having won. I'll only feel that when Alis is happy and well again."

Gervaise stopped at a door. Not looking at David (for he'd been strangely and inexplicably moved by both the tone and content of what David had just said) he asked, almost in a whisper: "Would you like to go in by yourself or shall I announce you?"

"I'd be terribly glad if you felt you could announce me, sir," David answered.

With that Gervaise opened the door, calling out: "Alis, I've brought a friend to see you." Then, pushing David in front of him, he whispered: "I'll be in my study when you've finished," and closed the door softly behind David.

David stood alone inside a large room, with many books in it, and dark, perfunctory portraits in heavy oils on the walls opposite him. One double french window was wide open, and through it a precise splinter of autumn sunlight struck aslant into the room. An enormous fire was burning in an open hearth, and between the fire and the sun stood a couch with its back to David. As the rest of the room was empty he assumed Alis was lying on it but she herself made no sign that she'd either heard her father call or David come in. The only sound within the room was the flicker of the fire lapping at the cold like a warm sea at the ice of some other time and dimension. Outside someone at the back of the house was cutting wood and a clock chimed the quarter hour from a yellow spire over the hushed and shrinking fields. Then from behind the couch a voice which David barely recognised as Alis's, so low and despondent did it sound, said: "Who is it? D'you mind coming round here, please?"

David didn't answer but quickly walked over. Alis was lying fully dressed on the couch, wearing a fur coat with a black rug over her feet. Puzzled by the silence, as David came up to the couch, she turned her head and saw him. David saw her eyes widen with terrifying surprise and was just able to observe how dark was their blue, before she quickly shut her eyes with an expression of unhappy disbelief on her face. Obviously convinced that she'd dreamed the vision, she turned on her side and moaned like a child in a deep troubled sleep.

Softly David went up to her, knelt by her side, took her hand, raised it to his lips and kissed it, saying: "Alis, it's me, David. Forgive me please, for being so long."

At the sound of his voice and the touch of his hand she gasped, sat up violently, a frightened look on her pale really sick face, and stared at David. Reassured that he was no illusion of her over-strained senses, she lay down again, turned over and holding David's hand to her cheek, began crying without shame or restraint saying over and over again: "Oh, David, David, how could you leave me like that? Why didn't you write? Why didn't you answer my letters and telegrams?"

"I never received any," he answered, stunned. "Although I wired you my hotel address."

"But I wrote and wrote—" she sobbed.

"Perhaps this explains why I never heard," David answered, handing her his own returned telegram together with her father's letter. "You see, I've been ill too. But I came as soon as I could—once I'd found out where you were."

Alis struggled to sit up, but it was some moments before she could read the telegram and letter that he handed her. Then it seemed impossible that her father should have intercepted her letters.

"Oh, David, is this really true?" she said, letting the hand with the telegram fall to her side, while she raised her face to his and looked at him through wet eyes. He nodded his head,

keeping his eyes on hers and what she saw there utterly convinced her, for she said: "Of course it's true. I see that now
and I'm so glad that you're here at last—if only I weren't so
ill. You do know they're sending me to hospital to-morrow,
don't you?" she asked abruptly.

"You're not going into hospital to-morrow," he said with
a firmness of tone and assumption of overriding authority
that reassured her deeply, shattered as she felt.

She then went on to explain to him that her family had
done their best to understand her illness, but that their point
of view had been unvaryingly limited. They'd insisted that
there must be some physical reason for it. They'd ignored the
fact that night and day her mind and heart had been crying
out for David. They'd even told her she'd get over all that in
time. . . .

"D'you remember that evening on the ship when we
watched the sun go down?" she asked suddenly. "D'you
remember how for a second the whole horizon went dark
and dead and then, when it was utterly dead, from the other
side of death came that lovely, defiant flash of light that shot
up and outwards and halted the night? D'you remember?"

"Of course, my beloved, my faithful keeper of the royal
image, of course I remember," he said responding to her
manner with a great lift of his heart.

"Well," she continued with solemn seriousness, "I've been
just like that sun." She went on to tell him how, before they'd
met, she had felt both dead and dying. Even after they'd met,
there'd been a dreadful period when she'd gone on sinking
until she'd sunk utterly, died and been dead. At least that's
what she'd thought; but then she'd discovered that it was
only the Alis of all those unreal yesterdays who had died. The
real Alis had shot up alive like the South Atlantic ocean-flash
to meet old night with new day. She'd lived again. Dear God,
how miraculously she'd lived again. She who had gone down
a sun had come up a moon, a silvery, quivering new moon.
And she'd come up alive, with moon crescent stretched fine

and wide to catch its star, as she'd been that night when they tried to dance each other over the edge of the music in the ship on a far high sea. . . . She'd realised it all on her return to England. But then she'd been left alone, alone without word from David and with only her father and Simon for reassurance, alone with herself and her illness.

When she'd finished speaking, David, knowing only too well the weary tumult that must be in her, made no effort to say more. For a long, long time he sat by her in silence, respecting and observing her silence, and spoke to her only in the ancient proved, mindless way through the touch of his hands and fingers, and, so it seemed to him now, through their predetermined and freely chosen nearness. As he touched her hair, lit with the light of a harvest of life which neither rust nor sickle nor wintry frost could injure, he loved it not only for himself but also on behalf of a life greater than themselves. He touched it reverently for in its colour was a gleam of the miracle of their journey, as sure in its wrongness as its rightness, the journey which had carried them through dark mythology of stillborn space and archaic time from the opposite ends of the earth to meet at last in wholeness. Yes, far, far back, before the word in the beginning in the timeless seed of life, this gold of her hair was lovingly included. It was in yellow fruit of tree in the centre of the garden, and it was in the sky on the other side of the rainbow under which the shining Mary had once called and recalled him home in vain. Hardly had he heard Mary's voice when first he had seen this thread of gold, and followed it in the manner of a man walking in his sleep. It had been in his heart and before his eyes on the night the lion roared, and it had fallen over Klara's black hand like cataract of gold and full-spun moonlight. He'd found it in sovereign of gold in Mary's black Sunday bag and though judged, condemned and punished he'd retained his love for it. It had visited him again in Argonaut's sheen of the curling fleece of a great ram held between black knees in a shed holding shade like a rock in a snarling and yelping sea of African sunlight. Confusion had hurt and delayed but never finally arrested him. Gold in black and darkness rolled round gold within or without had been equally valid; but now it was about to be made valid in both and both in one. For this light which came from the flame of her hair was the imperishable light of the inmost fire wherein the fine wax of their candlemass bodies burnt. In it the meaning of fire was rounded and complete. By it, at last, he was outward bound the inward way. Neither his time nor hers were any longer separate and out of joint but set to the time of the universe within. Here they were man and woman with no archaic drag on eager future between them, but both synchronised and made immediate. Through this woman he'd come to know that frail candle-pillar body, and great starry universe, and black prairie of night sky are only weave and texture of spirit seen from without. This spirit of the inmost flame was but body and universe seen from within. Gladly henceforth would he feed his body to this fire of the spirit, for it alone gave his body meaning. No faster than time immediate demanded would flame of spirit burn humble and eager body, but sparingly, caringly asking life's mercy and trueness for every drop and calory of the rare, irreplaceable, honey-sweet golden wax consumed. Yes, with this woman by his side, he had a flaming rose, with golden petals unfolding to mark all four seasons, he had golden rose-light, a hallowed halo, a pentecostal circle of radiant essence of original flame, the farthermost corner of outmost season containing. Ah! he would clean brushes in flame and dip them deep in colour of its light, mix his palette with oil of essential wax and, drunk with the wine of dawn-red dew distilled in burning rose cup, paint the universe anew, thrusting darkness back and hurling a painter's awareness like a burning arrow at the night. Yes, drunk with dew of inevitable dawn, he, a chronic dawn-alcoholic, would paint his world and Alis's joined, as world infinitely renewable and endlessly renewing. He would paint the day at dawn forever a rose-fingered virgin and bride-to-be, at twilight always a woman sun-fulfilled and by night freely delivered and maidenhood urgently restoring. He would join the world within to the world without and so at last paint world without end. . . .

"But where are you, David?" he suddenly heard Alis's voice speaking to him with a touch of her old, mocking gaiety. "Where are you? I speak to you and you don't answer. Speak."

He looked at her. Her eyes were dry now and wide open, their blue coming out of the deep well of herself and evenly meeting the soft blue of the day outside. She was smiling too, saying "Speak, speak!"

"Why, you're laughing at me," he replied, surprise and joy almost too great in him.

"Yes," she said tenderly, "I'm laughing at you, as I used to do in the ship. But what were you thinking about? Tell me."

There was a moment's pause. Then David raised her hand and held it tightly against his cheek. "I was just thinking," he said slowly, emotion deep in him, "that you're coming away with me, now. I'm never, never going to leave you again. Never."

END